FRIENDS
OF THE
MUSEUM

FRIENDS
OF THE
MUSEUM

A Novel

HEATHER McGOWAN

WASHINGTON
SQUARE PRESS

ATRIA

New York Amsterdam/Antwerp London
Toronto Sydney/Melbourne New Delhi

WASHINGTON SQUARE PRESS

ATRIA

An Imprint of Simon & Schuster, LLC
1230 Avenue of the Americas
New York, NY 10020

First Washington Square Press/Atria Books hardcover edition April 2025

WASHINGTON SQUARE PRESS **/ ATRIA** BOOKS and colophon
are registered trademarks of Simon & Schuster, LLC

Simon & Schuster strongly believes in freedom of expression and stands against censorship in all its forms. For more information, visit BooksBelong.com.

For information about special discounts for bulk purchases, please contact Simon & Schuster Special Sales at 1-866-506-1949 or business@simonandschuster.com.

The Simon & Schuster Speakers Bureau can bring authors to your live event. For more information or to book an event, contact the Simon & Schuster Speakers Bureau at 1-866-248-3049 or visit our website at www.simonspeakers.com.

Interior design by Davina Mock-Maniscalco

Manufactured in the United States of America

1 3 5 7 9 10 8 6 4 2

Library of Congress Cataloging-in-Publication data is available.

ISBN 978-1-6680-3127-8
ISBN 978-1-6680-3129-2 (ebook)

The author wishes to thank the following institutions:
The American Academy in Berlin
The American Academy in Rome
Château de La Napoule
Virginia Center for the Creative Arts
Yaddo

CAST OF CHARACTERS

Diane Schwebe, Director of the Museum
    Dominic, her husband
    Chris Webb, her assistant

Henry Joles, General Counsel
    Annie, his ex-wife
    Audrey, his secretary
    Jack Corbeau, his best friend and a gallery owner

Shay Pallot, Chief Security Officer
    Malcolm, her nephew

Benjamin Rippen, Curator of Film
    Victor Robledo, a filmmaker
    Ruben Diaz, his superintendent
    Caroline Stuck, his ex-girlfriend
    Tom Reggio, his landlord

Nikolic Peša, Chef de Partie
    Jimmy, his brother

Katherine Tambling, Associate Curator of Costume
    Sammy, her mother

Clive Hauxwell, Head Curator of European Paintings
    Lucy, his best friend
    Jane, his sister

Iona Moore, Conservator of Objects
    David, her husband

Jakob Pastornicky, Chief Digital Officer

Kulap Stein, Head Curator Asian Art

Freda, an intern

Conrad Bellefont, Designer of the Gala

Kory Merizo, General Manager of Merchandising

Liam Stuck, a visual artist
    Clover DiNovi, his wife, an author

Abbas & Momo Khan, investors in a satellite museum

Tiz Sericko, trustee and former Director of the Museum

Kenichi Ichimonji, the Japanese Ambassador

Walter Wolfe, a collector of paintings

Julia Cohen, host of digital entertainment, *Vanity Fair*

Lucas Boone, a collector of armor

Fisk & Travis, federal agents, DHS

Zedekiah "Z" Willington, a donor

Marlon Tindall-Clark, a philanthropist
    Eleanor, his wife

Emerson Pitt, Executive Chef

Marjorie Wolfe, Chef de Cuisine

Anton Spitz, a fashion designer

Dario, an Italian professor

Ralph Kade, a trustee

Peter, Facilities Manager

FRIENDS
OF THE
MUSEUM

T his was last night, you understand, by all accounts an ordinary night, no different from a random evening last summer or some Thursday in April, and though they spoke on mundane topics—a new neighbor, an upcoming trip for work—there was a mysterious undercurrent to their conversation, as if everything Dominic said meant quite the opposite, and all Diane's comments had a double meaning.

They sat across the kitchen table from each other and spoke while eating grapes from a metal colander—red grapes, grape after grape—barely pausing between them as if grapes were suddenly essential to conversation. It was in the middle of all this grape eating that Diane decided she would tell Dominic what had happened three weeks ago, on Saturday afternoon.

You remember, Diane said, we'd decided to have a few people over for dinner. I set out around eleven to wander around specialty shops, picking up various items or reeling at the prices, thinking about these friends we hadn't seen in a while and wondering what they might especially like to eat. I'd heard about an exceptional florist way over on the East Side, which was how I came to be standing on First Avenue not far from the United Nations.

It was a crisp sunny day, the kind of beautiful day that people remark on after an atrocity occurs, as if the most difficult fact to grasp about a tragedy is that it can happen under a blue sky and white sun.

The florist was unremarkable, I decided to try another. There was still cheese to buy, several kinds, all the way back on Amsterdam. Also fish, if we were going to have fish, I wouldn't decide until I saw the selection, until I stared into those glassy eyes myself, checking for clarity. An unsettling enterprise, but the only reliable way to tell if fish is fresh.

Here's where it all got strange. When I came out of the flower shop and stood on the street, I couldn't remember what I was doing, why I was there, or which way to go. I had very deliberately set out with actual errands to accomplish, but now I couldn't decide which to tackle next, whether I should do something else entirely or, in fact, give it all up, cancel our dinner, and crawl into bed.

In front of me Forty-Third Street appeared insurmountable. It resembled a huge ascent. Denali or the Matterhorn. I stood at the base of it, holding a bag of chestnuts. I didn't need chestnuts, I don't even know what you do with chestnuts, I'd bought them solely for their color. Gripping this useless bag, I looked straight ahead of me, then right, then left. The only choice I didn't have was to walk east, since that would have landed me in the river. But each time I decided yes, I'll walk down the avenue and then west on a street in the thirties, I immediately decided that no, I would walk north for a while, but before I'd even finished that thought it seemed ridiculous and the better plan was to head straight up this daunting hill, which isn't a hill at all, of course, but completely flat.

I stood on the sidewalk, rooted there with my shopping bag, considering my options, at one point becoming distracted by an important-looking foreign delegation striding toward the UN. For several minutes I wondered what sort of destructive global action these men might be on their way to unleash, then I returned to this decision I had to make about how to travel west, which appeared to be the most critical decision I had ever faced. I was starting to panic that I might stand there for the rest of my life, holding a bag of chestnuts as my hair turned grey and tourists asked me where to buy water. Really, she told Dominic, my feet felt as if they were encased in concrete, my heart churned like the river behind me.

But as Diane stood there astonished and also not astonished, since this ambivalence was only one component of the piercing, restless uncertainty that had bothered her for a number of weeks, she happened to look up toward the crest of the hill where an office building on the corner stood mantled in beams of sunlight.

All of a sudden I felt at peace, she told Dominic. Our hot star calmed my turbulent heart, it settled my stomach, and there, while I basked in its light, the road ahead became clear.

Diane finished her story and looked across the table that she once found uninspired but now appreciated for its Swedish practicality. She gazed into the eyes of her husband and asked for his opinion. Well, said

Dominic, it sounds like the story of a lost person. He got up for a glass of water, turned to lean against the sink and proceeded to say more than she cared to hear.

Later, when Diane woke in the middle of the night, fresh from a dream about misplacing her passport, for she dreams about airports and travel almost exclusively, she lay next to Dominic as she had lain next to him for fifteen years. His expression as he slept was one of relief. And Diane thought back to their conversation in the kitchen, the details of which immediately began to distort, grow foggy, and fade.

At four-twenty-something in the morning, her mind darting from thought to thought, trying to remember exactly what was said as they ate grapes from a metal colander, her phone lit up.

Henry Joles.

Urgent, he said.

She was needed at the Museum.

5:30 a.m.

—Could he be faking?

—As the wife tells it, he's been up half the night with his head in the toilet. I'll try again around nine, he can hold a goddamn bucket if he needs to puke. I don't know who this wife thinks she is.

—Let's get started... Diane takes the armchair opposite... —We can wait on Kulap.

Henry scoots to the edge of the couch, the briefcase open on his lap, and with great trouble leans forward to hand Diane a piece of paper... —Printed from a digital file so the resolution's not great. Taken in 2002.

Staring down at the photocopy... —Where's my?

—Coffee, right here... Chris hands her a takeout cup.

—Thanks... immediately setting it down, hot!, and returning to the blurry photograph... —Tell me what I'm looking at, Henry.

—Dancing Shiva. *Our* Dancing Shiva.

It's a violent image. Diane has only ever seen Shiva in his current home down in Indian Subcontinent where the statue stands reverently bathed in a circle of soft light. In the photocopy Shiva lies tipped on his side in the back of a filthy van, surrounded by crumpled newspapers and encrusted with dirt, suggesting that the statue was not purchased from a private collector, not a deaccession from a museum, not stumbled upon in Pop-Pop's attic, but the statue was looted.

—There's more... Henry holds out another sheet of paper.

—Later... waving it off... —Start from the beginning. Is it only Kulap's department?

A nod, a sigh, a swift hoist of the belt, and then, with his usual disdain for chronology, Henry shoots off on a narrative that includes a number of detours and hesitations, introducing brief asides on the history of India, as well as the pros and cons of colonialism, laying down immaterial clauses as if he's building escape routes from an unsound structure.

—Guy named Dixit paid a French couple to pose as photographers putting together a book on antiquities in India and Pakistan... he continues... —These two run around rural temples snapping photos of icons and sending him the pictures. At which point, like he's browsing a catalogue for a pair of khakis, Dixit picks out his icons and a couple of local punks boost the statues. Guess they're not fucked about karma.

—Where did the pictures come from?

—Dixit's compound in Mumbai. IPS searched it, found a memory stick loaded with images of statues in their original locations, as well as objects in the process of being cleaned and boxed up. Not a whole lot of room for interpretation. Pictures got sent to Delhi, cops called in a couple of experts. One of them is a guy of mine, Greek national. He recognized our pieces.

—How many?

—Three small objects and Shiva. So far.

Four. Not great, but not terrible. She watches Chris stooped over the coffee table unpacking white paper bags, assembling a bagel tower on a paper plate... —Any idea where... turning to Henry... —Kulap picked up dirty pieces?

—From what I understand, Dixit slapped "Made in India" stickers on the bottoms of the statues, mixed them in with birdbaths and planters and labeled the whole shipment as lawn ornaments. With the help of a pal in customs, he shipped it through Hong Kong to a garden center in New Jersey. I assume they ran up a bunch of bogus documents, because the statues were sold through auction houses and legit dealers. I don't know which dealers sold us the stuff and I won't until Kulap gets his head out of the toilet and calls us back.

—Diane? Plain or sesame?

—Sesame.

Chris places the bagel on a plate and passes it to her, along with a plastic knife... —Lox spread?

—Maybe later, thank you... she watches him rip the top off a tub of cream cheese. He's wearing a T-shirt tight enough to highlight a rich assortment of muscles in his chest and shoulders.

—I have a dress shirt in my office.

—No worries... looking across to Henry slathering cream cheese...
—And we have this contained?

—We will. I mean, it's five thirty in the morning, so.

—You'll call State.

—When it's remotely possible Decker's in the office.

—But you left a message.

—Yes, Diane, I left a message, but really, we have plenty of time. DHS lost a bunch of cultural property guys in the last budget cuts, they're still playing catch-up. I'm not worried. It's happened before, hasn't it, and we're still standing.

—Yes, but right now, I mean, the timing's a little. It's hardly ideal. The current situation. I don't need another, you know, *challenge*, on my watch... Diane gets up and crosses to her desk, taking the uneaten bagel with her... —We need a solution in the works before the board gets wind of it.

—There are hundreds of photographs to sort through. It will take them days to track the stuff to us.

—But presumably more of our pieces could show up.

—Correct... Henry sets his takeout cup on the table and leans back... —In the meantime, we need to pull Shiva and the other objects my guy spotted... sighing, probing his sternum... —Who can oversee?

—I've emailed the entire Asian department... Chris glances up from his phone... —Nothing.

—Don't people go to the gym anymore?

—There is a tech downstairs right now... thumbing his screen... —Ferris Finotti. But he works in Oceania—

—Close enough. Grab him.

—Can we really ask—

—We can... Henry affirms... —Have him meet me in, uh—

—Rotmiller?

—Right, and what about Shay Pallot?

—Said she'd be here in... Chris checks the time... —Fifteen.

Diane freezes. Halting the dry bagel on its ascent from her plate to her mouth, trying to identify. What is it? Not the vague vertigo she's had for the past month, something else. A far-off rumble.

—Diane?

They're both staring at her, concerned, phones parked midair.

—Making a mental tally.

Henry's cell phone buzzes and he struggles up with an *oof* sound and moves to the window... —Freddie... murmuring, hazily backlit by the garden spotlights... —You got my email?

—Should you sit down? Diane?

—Who's Henry talking to at this hour?

—London. You look pale.

—No, I'm fine I need a... tugging at her shirt.

—Arriving before seven.

—What is?

—A new blouse. I noticed you were wearing yesterday's and I—

—Grabbed it, dressed in the dark.

—assumed it wasn't purposeful—

—Dom was still asleep.

—ordered you a new one.

—At five in the morning?

—Togz. Two hours guaranteed. Warehouse in Queens, I think.

—You dick... Henry, warmly into his phone... —You can fuck right off.

—Quick run-through?... Chris spins around, finds her coffee and hands it to her... —I've canceled everything I could.

Diane waves him on with the cardboard cup. A weather system is making havoc in her stomach. A result, perhaps, of eating grapes and only grapes for dinner. But she needs to keep her mind on the situation at hand instead of trying to recall exactly what took place last night at the kitchen table.

—At eight thirty we have...

—I'm listening.

—Digital. In case Jakob has something impressive we can bring to your five thirty.

—My hands are tied... Henry, louder.

—Fine, but, Chris, let's keep it short, twenty minutes at most.

—We parsed the contracts a thousand times.

—At ten... raising his voice, Chris shoots Henry a scathing look... —A meeting with Goldfarb and Hernandez.

—God no, kill that, tell them I, whatever, set it for next week.

—They're hoping for a decision about the brunnel.

—The brunnel is not happening. That is the decision. How many ways do I have to? We need to close shop on this, we're... she catches Henry's warning glower... —Oh please... turning to Chris... —As if you don't know everything.

—Sorry, what do I know?

—About the new wing.

—I know we ran out of money.

—We didn't run out of money.

—We didn't?

—No, we did, but... Diane sips her coffee, electing not to finish the sentence... —Reschedule the architects.

—Listen to me... Henry, into his phone, beginning to pace... —I've told you exactly where we've stood from the beginning.

—They're flying to Sydney tonight. Ten days.

—Then we'll do a call.

Chris bends his head to his phone, tapping the screen.

—Freddie, Freddie, calm down, this is all negotiable... Henry, for some reason still in her office... —I'm there next week. We'll go to Bocca, order that scrappy Barolo you like.

Taking a bite of dry bagel in the hopes of quelling her nervous stomach. As she chews, she can feel her jaw making a figure-eight motion that can only be described as bovine.

—Eleven thirty, Diane. Diane?

—I'm listening.

—Quick check-in with merchandising. Shouldn't take long. We've canceled a couple of times now, so. Noon is a tour with the Khan brothers.

—Tuesday. Abu Dhabi's Tuesday.

—It was, it was, but Momo hated Paris, there was a snubbing and they left early.

—Okay, well... tearing at the bread... —Drum up someone impressive to bring.

—Clive Hauxwell?

—God no, not today. And postpone our visit to Walter Wolfe. We'll go next week.

—Christ on a cross... Henry, call ended, throws his phone on the couch. Picks it up and glares at it.

—About the Khan brothers, Diane, I thought maybe a brief walk-through of some galleries?

—Fine. Keep it brief... she reaches for her coffee. The Khan brothers unsettle her with their exquisite tailoring and polite contempt.

—Back in July I agreed to a lunch with Ambassador Ichimonji... Chris starts tapping... —Let me change it to a coffee.

—No... Diane tilts her cup, staring into it... —Coffee's not enough. We need his Samurai show.

—Didn't he decide on D.C.?

—Unconfirmed.

Chris taps his phone... —Okay, so a super speedy but lavish VIP lunch and maybe a zip around B24? Everyone loves storage.

—Good, yes, that'll work... getting up from her chair... —But Chris, preemptively warn—

—Him, yes, how busy you are, the gala and so forth. Directly after, Sutton will prep you for your three o'clock with Lucas Boone.

—Boone doesn't care how much I know about armor. In fact, re-schedule Boone... finding herself by the window, looking down on the lit-up landscaping... —What is happening... tapping on the black glass... —With the Van Gogh maze? It was supposed to be ripped out last week.

—Tomorrow.

—Before the gala, I thought.

—No, after the gala.

—At this point it feels downright pathological. Are we living in *Grey Gardens*?

Henry says ha ha, not actually laughing, from where he sprawls on the couch holding his phone in one hand and jabbing at it with a finger.

—Sorry, Diane, could we go back? About Boone, he seems commit-ted, and I wonder if delaying your meeting could possibly—

—You're sure he's committed?

—Positive.

—Because if he wants groveling and—

—Not the case.

—Fine.

—So we'll keep Boone. Restaurants go dark at four o'clock, at four thirty Security begins moving visitors toward the exits. Museum doors close at five sharp. At five thirty we have Silicon Valley.

—That's Willington?... Henry looks up, curious, but not especially invested... —How much is he talking about?

—Twenty, twenty-five.

—Nice, help get you out of your jam.

—Oh, *my* jam. Thanks.

—So, uh... Chris coughs, his anxious cough, she knows all the coughs in his range... —Yesterday a small news item popped up. Seems like Willington is, or was, *was* invested in a firm currently under investigation—

—For what?... Henry, alert now and lawyerly.

—Violating child labor laws.

—Child? No. Sorry, but *child labor?* Kill the meeting, Diane, please. The optics.

—Wait... Chris, with a calming motion of his hand... —There's more—

—We cannot accept money from someone who exploits or or or even *facilitates* the exploitation of kids in Dongguan or Dhaka or—

—Mill Valley?

Henry flops back on the couch and stares at Chris.

—Swear to god. The company was using local sixth graders to code after school. Called it a computer club, only the kids went home at night clutching their hearts and tossing back Zoloft. Parents investigated. Feds got involved.

—The Feds, lovely. Day at the goddamn beach.

—Apparently Z was clueless. He's an ethical steward. According to his website.

—A billionaire with ethics, good one. Now I've heard it all. I'm finishing the lox spread.

—We'll keep the meeting... Diane returns to her coffee... —Hair and makeup is at six?

—Yes, arriving at six along with your dress. If you need the full hour and a half it won't give us much time with Willington, but his assistant was, well, kind of a B, to be frank. She wouldn't budge on the time. Five thirty was the earliest I could get.

—But Zedekiah—

—Z, he goes by Z now.

—Okay, but he's definitely coming to the gala?

—As far as I know.

—Then we'll manage.

—Trustees and special guests arrive at seven thirty... Chris reads his phone... —Doors proper open at eight. Which is when you, Anton Spitz, and the team from Noizy—

—Not Noizy.

—No?

She shakes her head.

—Okay, so then, eight p.m. you and Anton greet arriving guests. Security promises everyone out by two.

—And this morning? Party installers get here when?

—Seven-ish.

—Set a courtesy call to Conrad around nine.

Chris types rapidly into his phone.

—Needs we can assist with and so forth, likewise a call to Anton. Looking forward, blah, blah. Don't mention his dog.

—Don't mention his, okay, and the Ambassador? What about a formal toast this evening? Nudge him in the right direction.

Henry looks up from piling papers into his briefcase... —What do you need from Japan?

—Their Samurai show. Made a small fortune for the British and was headed to San Francisco before their water pipe disaster... that fluttery feeling in her abdomen again... —We're offering to host, begging really, but Ichimonji loves D.C. so—

—Or the Met. They gave him some kind of medal.

—Medal? What medal?

—I don't know, some honor they invented.

—God, they are legendary suck-ups, aren't they? Why didn't we think of a medal?

In his hand Chris holds his paper cup which he waggles as he talks. She doesn't hear a word, distracted by his cup. It's making her seasick.

Diane jumps up, starts for her private bathroom. Bad idea. She doubles back, walks quickly across the office and out the door, racing down the hallway so they won't hear.

5:47 a.m.

—What the hell?... Henry turns to Chris for a translation... —Why'd Diane sprint out of here?

But the kid stays glued to his phone, thumbing the surface with chilling speed.

—Think she's puking?

—What?... now he looks up.

—Diane. Her skin looked clammy... reviewing his empty plate, the mess of crumbs and schmear, Henry considers another half bagel... —Pregnant, maybe.

Chris now looks truly alarmed... —I mean, she probably needs more sleep or, anyway, isn't she too... searching for the word... —Advanced?

—Forty-four, forty-six? Not impossible.

—Mr. Joles, I'm pretty sure that's too old.

—Trust me, friend. Happened to my cousin at fifty. Thought she'd hit menopause. Fuck, was she surprised. Now she's sixty-five with a kid in high school.

Chris blinks several times.

—Sorry, is that, maybe—

—I should... Chris points to the door... —You'll wait here for Shay Pallot?

—I will.

—Need anything... gathering bagel bags, plates, and cups... —I'll be at my desk... Chris slips out the door.

And Henry drops back onto Diane's cushy sofa, settling into the grossly expensive linen or shantung or pongee or whatever. What he needs is an antimacassar. There's no hair oil anymore, there's no hair, but he remains one of the great moisturizers. Both wives remarked on it. His grandmother had them on every seat in the house. She also had false teeth that rattled in windstorms. Of which there were many. She retired to the south of France, home of the mistral.

He closes his eyes. Dirty sculptures will be a headache, but not much more. The right phone calls, some diplomatic arm-twisting, a few veiled threats, and one or two outright bribes. Henry used to live for this kind of thing. The thrill of war, the rush of high stakes. Not these days. He's without his old sense of purpose. Ambivalent now, evasive. Capricious. And Diane can tell. He's caught her sizing him up. A month ago she breached his office with a bottle of Blanton's. Her smile was ominous, the pours too heavy. So she's discovered my shenanigans and come to fire me, he thought. But the business was personal. A minute for the bourbon to hit, then: I love my husband but I dream of running away. Henry stared into his drink wishing for an ice cube. When had they agreed to this sort of conversation? He felt a priggish revulsion to her conspicuous pain. The longer Diane spoke, the greater Henry's desire for ice became, until his need was so overriding and intense he could barely understand a word she was saying. It was his usual response to a personal disclosure of any kind, a focus on the pettiest issue at hand.

Diane's computer screen turns black and the word *peregrinate* swims across the screen, followed by its definition. Next to the keyboard, three mechanical pencils lie in precise parallel lines. Henry watched her position them as Chris took her through her day. She's been strangely scrupulous lately, squaring stacks of imperceptibly uneven papers, raking her skirt with the blade of her hand.

—Mr. Joles?

He looks up. Shay Pallot. Sharp in her black jacket and red tie. Trousers sadistically tight at the hips. The uniform's crisp cut and faux-military details would have excited him once, the prospect of discipline and authority in a curvy woman. But Henry has no energy left for such things. And the hunger he once had for Black women, what they call exoticization, he understood years later. Not good.

—Ready to go?

—Let's do it... Henry gets to his feet, sucking in his gut and hitching his pants.

5:53 a.m.

Pesto was a mistake. It's an amateur move, even made with weeds. Nikolic yanks the blender jar off its base and tips it over the trash, watching the pureed goosefoot surge over yesterday's sticky rice and a used stick of deodorant.

More coffee. He fills the kettle, sparks the gas. Too many sleepless nights have made mincemeat of Niko's sanity. The internet's advice about insomnia is all lame shit about meditation and keeping the room dark. What kind of idiot tries to sleep in a bright room? For a while he tried popping Benadryl, but it took three espressos just to get dressed in the morning. And pot makes him miserable. Lately he's been getting out of bed the minute his eyes open, no matter the hour. Three, four, the sky still dark. Oh goody, he says, in a facetious inner voice he fucking hates, look at all this free time. He splashes cold water on his face. Charges into the kitchen like the cuckold in a bedroom farce. Starts banging around with tongs and sheet pans, pulling out bottles of Asian condiments. The relentless drive to develop a new dish could be mania, he thinks, or OCD, knowing nothing about either. Or, a sad attempt to matter. If Nikolic invents a dish so delicious that Emerson adds it to the menu, well, then, there's no telling.

By six Niko's eyes feel like clay marbles. The water in his body has been replaced by coffee. And to what end. Garbage cans of green slurry. Burns and broken bowls. The neighbors bitching about the smell of fried smelt.

Across the room, row after row of mason jars stand empty on the shelving unit. Before winter, he'll go find sumac, maitake, black walnuts, pawpaw. But not from Central Park. A bigger trip, upstate. If Niko can make it past Poughkeepsie.

5:55 a.m.

Diane stops in the hallway, pressing her forehead against the cold window, staring down at the lit-up rings of rotting sunflowers. It isn't the Mumbai issue that's turning her stomach. Even today, facing PR crises on two fronts, as well as potential termination at the hands of the board, she remains irrationally positive. Which means the reason for the nausea must lie in

—You okay?

her marriage... —Grand... she watches a cardinal take several hops, red feathers glossy in the spotlights.

—What are you doing?

—Looking out the window... she can hear Chris stabbing the elevator call button with his usual excess.

—Something about the maze?

—No, just like, looking.

—Perfect. I'm running down to meet Togz. Fifty-five minutes. Can you believe these guys?

She turns around... —Very impressive. And then we'll need to... suddenly exhausted... —What do we need to?

—Draft the announcement of Tindall-Clark's gift.

—Tindall-Clark, right.

The bing of the arriving elevator. The doors sweep open, Chris steps inside, raising his phone as the doors close.

But how predictable to blame your marriage. That nettlesome fritz, that whisper, the pressure in your head when you wake in the middle of the night, why should that count as confirmation? Everyone from time to time, while married and going about their business has thought, what if I were not married and going about an entirely different business?

5:57 a.m.

In early summer the train pulled into Beacon and Niko fell apart. He couldn't do it, couldn't go on. He'd wept, shaking, a child's fit. The passengers around him openly stared. Pathetically, he tried to hide his wet face, tucking his head into his armpit like a napping duck. The train continued toward Poughkeepsie and Niko continued to cry. After a few minutes he felt a tap on his arm and he withdrew his head, opened his eyes. Reaching across the aisle with an extraordinary wingspan was a soldier dressed head to toe in woodland camouflage, pants tucked into a pair of sand-colored boots. In his hand the man held out a small plastic packet of tissues. He nodded sharply at Niko to take it as if they were participating in an illicit exchange. It was likely, Niko thought as he blinked back his tears and accepted the Kleenex, that the soldier did not wish to be seen in possession of such a prissy item. As Nikolic wiped his face he kept thinking, I'll just use one more, as if the man might want half his tissues back. But he ended up using every one, trumpeting his nose, mopping up all the snot, shoving the balled-up tissues into his jacket pocket where he would no doubt run across them later and thoroughly disgust himself. The soldier never again looked his way, staring ruggedly at the seatback in front of him.

Niko got off at New Hamburg and took the next train back to Grand Central. Was he managing? It's unclear. But there are times, sitting on the subway, or rooting in a bodega freezer for the last pint of banana ice cream, when the voice inside his head screams, I AM FUCKING MANAGING.

6:00 a.m.

—Curator's out sick, so a tech from Oceania is helping out. The items are small, shouldn't take long to remove them, but as I said before, discretion is uh—

—Paramount?... placing her hand across the door's sensor, Shay waits for the lawyer to exit the elevator.

—Exactly. The word of the day.

—Nothing to worry about, I hope... together they set off down the dark hallway... —Nothing too... too what... —Unpleasant?

—No, no, the usual. A misunderstanding. Needs a few phone calls.

The last time she saw the lawyer he was dressed drably, all grey, but today his suit is blue, the silk poking from his blazer pocket is a brilliant fuchsia, and as he walks, flashes of purple sock burst out above his shoes. Larry? Percy? His last name is Joles, that she remembers. In stark contrast to his wardrobe, the man's skin is the color of custard.

—Assume you're handling... the lawyer appraising, as they pass, a gallery through its doorway... —Security this evening.

—I am, yes. Could hardly leave that to someone else.

—Not one of your managers?

He appears to be making conversation, and Shay smiles enigmatically. Most Security managers are holdovers from her predecessor, placed in their positions by nepotism, backstabbing, or calling in favors, and as a group, fairly useless. Also, almost impossible to fire.

—But you'll get a break at some point, not work straight through.

—Yes, of course... does Joles really think she has time for a break and what, to head home and take a nap? These people.

They all think she's old-school live and die for the place, but not anymore. If she ever was, that is. Was she? Way back when? But of course she can't remember. Not of course, because it's not all lost. Every so often, a few times a day, a memory will arrive that has nothing to do with anything, of Tasha, say, next to her on the school bus, finger dug into the yellowing foam that erupted from rips in the vinyl seats, glaring out the window, pissed about breakfast. Tasha was always pissed about breakfast. She wanted the kind white people ate on TV with pretty waffles and table settings. Or a memory of Ma on a Saturday afternoon, sitting at the kitchen table, shaking a bottle of nail polish, the metal ball inside clacking away. And if she can, Shay will open up her notebook, try to fix in place this snap from the past.

—Chris?

Didn't see the lawyer getting out his phone.

—Make sure the tech from Oceania brings appropriate packing material and whatnot... and Joles goes on, a list of instructions.

One day you'll read your journal like a book you've never seen. One day you won't know how your life was. You'll be greedy for the details. Not to mention the ending, Shay thought, all those loose ends tied up.

Through the galleries that contain Egypt. Floor-to-ceiling arched windows. Glass cases choked with clay heads. Minuscule profiles on the coins of Ptolemy III. A child's necklace in the shape of a snake.

The notebook was the doctor's suggestion. Shay saw him three months ago at his office uptown. He delivered the news in a clinical torrent, couldn't get through it fast enough. And what did it matter whether patient #4129 was or was not losing her mind? Shay was just twelve minutes between lunch and an epileptic. She hated the doctor's round eyes and rigid hairline, the rectangular smile that looked like a letter slot. It was too much geometry for one face. A notebook, he insinuated, would help when her memory began to flicker like an iffy bulb. When it's far from reliable, you'll read these notes and memories and it will help. Help what? Shay didn't ask. Carl picked up a pocket-sized diary from the drugstore and she started jotting down the memories that popped up over the course of a day. Moments that at the time were simply minutes. Unexceptional fragments you never noticed, unaware that one day your mind would start to falter and your memory would go about ignoring notable events like weddings and graduations, choosing instead to recall an ordinary summer day when you waited at a Midtown crosswalk staring at the sky with the sun on your face. Or the way your father looked walking down a flight of stairs.

A wheezing cough from the lawyer as they cross the statue court outside Greek & Roman, thumping his chest with a fist. Is it simply the early hour? Or something more serious?

—Mr. Joles? Doing okay?

He turns to her, astonished... —Yes, of course. Don't I seem okay?

—Oh, I thought. You seem a little unsteady... boldness seems called for before he pitches into one of the Athenian warriors defending the hallway.

—Actually... he presses his chest... —Is there somewhere to sit? Doubt the tech will be there yet.

—We have time.

She follows Joles into the smallest Roman gallery, where he heads for the folding chair Shay leaves out for Astrid and her bunions.

—I should call someone.

—No, no... his bulk overwhelms Astrid's chair in a chubby cascade.

—Get you a glass of water?

Joles shakes his head... —Minute to catch my... hands gripping his thighs, Joles hunches his shoulders and whooshes air noisily through his mouth.

—These used to be my galleries, Greek and Roman... Shay puts on her most soothing voice... —First summer I worked here.

—That was a while ago... whooshing again.

—Right before my junior year. I was studying economics out West. Came to New York for a summer to stay with my big sister... crossing to a glass case, it was the summer Tasha got tested. Two shelves of terracotta objects are picked out in tiny lights... —Grave goods were my favorite. Imagine spending all that time making one little vessel only to go and bury it. Combs and perfume and coins to pay the ferryman. I always thought, uh... crossing to a new vitrine, hands clasped behind her back, is he still watching her?... —There's so much personality in a small object, you get a real sense of the person behind it, a shot into his or her life, but of course they're long dead.

—Long, long.

—In my mind there's a sadness that comes from... why is she still talking... —How brief our lives are. And how, for most of us, our lives will go uh. Unremembered or.

—Unrecorded?

—Uh-huh... trying to gauge, is all this too much for an ill man so early in the morning.

—For me... the lawyer leans forward... —Do you have children? I mean, if I may ask?

As always, the question makes her stomach corkscrew with pain. Shay peers into a case where a small cat yawns... —Children?... she doesn't lift her head... —No. I wasn't. I wasn't able.

—Shouldn't have asked, I apologize.

—No need, Mr. Joles—

—Henry, please.

—My sister has a bunch of kids and we're close. In a lot of ways I have all the worry of children—

—But none of the pleasure?

—No, I have the pleasure.

—Sorry, I thought that was the second half of the phrase. Anyway, worry's the right word. I suppose I ask because. When I was younger I assumed that by having children, my life would be, that there would be a lineage. I would be a father, grandfather, great-grandfather. I wouldn't disappear. But of course—

—We all disappear.

—Yes. Only a few, Picasso and so forth.

—Otherwise... she points to a case... —There's this spoon.

—A person behind that spoon. Someone's mouth once on it.

Memory isn't the only casualty of Shay's illness. There are other dis-combobulations. This, for example. Idling in a darkish room, hands in pockets chatting about what, lineage, with no concern for security measures to be double-checked for this evening or any one of thirty pressing items to be crossed off her list. And how is she supposed to feel? Because she is locked out of feelings, or at least, locked out of describing them to herself. It's a failure of recognition, as her own mother now fails to recognize Shay, gazing at her with the distant expression of someone trying to place a familiar person in a new context, the mailman in line at the ATM or a sitcom grandpa popping up in a black-and-white movie, twenty years old and disturbingly handsome with full lips and an unlined face.

—Okay... Henry stands, a bit shakily to her mind... —Good as new.

—Sure?

—Yes, yes.

Shay leads the way out of the gallery and through the next, her mind back on Tasha and the kids, thinking, this lawyer could be the ideal candidate, the person she's been looking for to shepherd Malcolm. She glances back to make sure Joles is following, straightening her jacket with a quick downward yank as she wonders how to phrase it, or if the question is actually an improper one for the workplace, and all. When Shay reaches the arched doorway she turns to the lawyer, smiles encouragingly and together they.

Wait.

Shay stops, confused. In the hallway outside the Purdue gallery is a marble lion she's never seen before. The air goes dead, as it does just before you faint. She walks toward the statue and her ears start to burn. The lion, poised to pounce, is squashed and out of proportion, with a concave chest and dopey face, a pair of hyperthyroidic eyes.

Joles catches her expression... —You're unimpressed.

—Where... forcing herself to breathe... —Did it come from?

—Trustee. Tindall-Clark. Jerked us around forever and finally gave up half his collection. The less valuable half. If he approves of how we handle it, we'll get the rest. Ergo... Joles points... —Pride of place, bang in the middle of the goddamn hallway. Some fuckwit's going to knock into it and lose half his teeth.

—Interesting... Shay's leaning toward the lion, smelling it for whatever reason, then standing back... —The preservation is—

—Shit.

She looks up. Joles is staring at his phone.

—I have to... typing with a pudgy finger... —Oh, what the... shaking his head... —Sorry. I'm getting Chris to shoot you the relevant details so you can explain the situation to, I'm being summoned. There appears to be a... waving his phone.

—Of course.

—The tech's name is Ferris Finotti. Tell him to call me if he needs additional... Joles walks back the way they came, stabbing at his phone and shaking his head.

Before she continues on, Shay takes a look at the statue's label. *Greek, (Attica), ca 325 BCE. Marble.*

No. Maybe it was thirty years ago that she spent all those weeks in Greek & Roman and maybe two out of five times she can't pull up the name of her own husband but no. No, no, no. There's no doubt in Shay's mind that the lion is fake.

6:17 a.m.

—Doubt is a luxury you don't have, my friend. Hesitate, you lose the confidence of your crew. When that happens, pack up and go home. You're finished. So make a choice, any choice.

—Sorry, Victor, could we go back?

—First, please, tip your screen down. This angle gives you a double chin and skinny eyes.

—I may actually have a double chin.

—No, Benjamin, you don't. Next time we talk about lighting. This lamp next to you is not nice.

As he adjusts his laptop, Victor's hand reaches out of frame and returns holding a small espresso cup. Benjamin snaps off the lamp next to him, the one he spent twenty minutes arranging, tilting the shade microscopically back and forth until it threw off what he believed to be a flattering light, framing out the bare walls and broken blinds.

—Okay, better. Stop fiddling now.

—I wanted to ask, Victor, about your decision to shoot almost exclusively with either an eighteen or a twenty-five. As far as I can tell you never shot with long lenses.

Victor cocks his head. *Can anyone possibly be that stupid?* is how Benjamin first interpreted this look. He's learned to ignore it.

—Was that an aesthetic choice or because you had difficulty finding lenses or...

—Think about it, Benjamin.

—Right, yes. I mean, I have.

—It was a paranoid time. Everyone so suspicious and afraid. Come in close at this time of dislocation? No. Today, sure, I'll use long lenses, depending on perspective. Am I inside your head or here... Victor holds his palm in front of his face... —What's the point of view? Back then, no.

—But we never, in both *Maria's*, or, uh, *El Ultimo Baile de Maria* and *Panóptica*, in addition to the distance, we only ever see the protagonist over the shoulder of another person or through a doorway. Like, even though we never leave Maria and go entirely objective, at the same time we definitely feel detached from her. In your early films there's this like voyeur perspective. It's unsettling, the contradiction, I mean.

Victor laughs, a staccato fusillade... —Because when you have neighbors, friends, colleagues, everyone spying on each other, you become so... he searches for the word.

—Self-conscious?

—Yes, you begin to see yourself from the outside. You are sort of spying on yourself. Do you understand what I'm explaining?

—Sure, yeah.

—It's not only intimacy with other people that is missing but also with yourself.

—That's fucked-up.

Again, Victor laughs, hu-hu-hu-hu. It's still incredible to Benjamin that he's speaking to Victor Robledo, asking any question that comes to mind, sometimes even teasing him, well once, when Victor had his T-shirt on inside out. In grad school Professor Thackeray worshipped Robledo, spoke of him in terms reserved for Bresson, Kiarostami, and Oshima. A master of the quotidian, Thackeray called him in his introductory lecture, memorable for Ted Fuentes falling asleep and ripping a giant slumbering fart. A painter of the banal, a director who made the ordinary transcendent. Benjamin loved Robledo as he loved

Tarkovsky and Bergman, but there were greater loves. Wilder, Lubitsch, Capra, Hawks. Despite being acclaimed by cinephiles the world over, and regardless of Benjamin's exhaustive arguments, directors who set out to entertain were not respected by his peers. Too easy, was the criticism. Corny, sentimental. It was that type of program. The students might not have sat around smoking unfiltered Gitanes, tapping their ash into Badoit caps, but that's the way you'll remember them.

—Could you tell me, Victor, how you avoided the censors or went around them?

—Why? We were not successful. Forty years of practice and nothing. People get tired. Those early films of mine, they were never shown in Spain, not as I intended, until many years later. Our culture suffered, as so many cultures suffer, from the stupidity of their politicians. The self-appointed moral authorities.

—Yeah, we're lucky in that way.

—What, in America?... again that laugh, hu-hu-hu like the shelling of a machine gun... —You think there's no censorship in America?... Victor's eyebrows find this incredible... —Oh my god, Benjamin.

—I mean, you can't show explicit sex or male—

—What about censorship coming from a, uh, financial, what... he swivels away from his laptop, speaking rapid Spanish to someone offscreen. Sofia, probably. Victor listens, turns back... —Marketplace. Your films must be acceptable to the *marketplace*. Is that not a form of censorship?

—No, because a movie has to earn back its cost. That's just common sense.

—But Benjamin, a censor's first job is to convince you that censorship is common sense.

—Yeah, but the United States doesn't have public funding—

—Sure, so then it's fine not to cast Black actors because China does not like movies with Black people? No, you stand up, you say, China fuck you, this is what, two thousand and ten, get fucking used to it. You don't pretend there's no Black people in the United States. Capitalism is a form of censorship, Benjamin, open your eyes. But you know... Victor softens suddenly, as if realizing the person he's addressing is a lost cause... —This is why I'm poor, probably. What time is it there? You look tired... turning to profile... —Sofia! Come say hello.

Sofia appears next to Victor, chewing, squeezing onto his chair...
—Benjamin, how are you?... she waves some type of roll or pastry...
—Victor is right, you really look ill. Get some sun. How is your book
coming?

—Plodding along.

—Are you giving the other directors hell or only my husband?... but
Sofia's smiling at him affectionately, parentally.

—Definitely giving Victor the most hell.

This seems to delight them both.

—Benjamin, I'm honored.

—Don't stop. He deserves it... Sofia winks broadly, elbowing her
husband. How in love they are, the Robledos, after all these years.

They exchange pleasantries and close their laptops, ending the call.
And Benjamin switches the lamp back on. How is that light not flattering? But you have to defer to Victor Robledo on the subject of light. For
three decades Victor fought to make movies, living in an apartment
with no heat, scraping to get by. A flogging from Franco's thugs left him
deaf in one ear. Proving Benjamin was right to abandon his dream of
directing. He wasn't cut out for the cost of art. Sacrifice his hearing just
to make a movie? Never.

Benjamin heads for the bathroom. A hair elastic belonging to
Caroline remains looped around the doorknob. It's been there for
months.

6:26 a.m.

So you hear I've been having wild nights, Katherine writes, propped
up by a mountain of pillows, stationery laid out on a cookbook she's
never cracked, a gift from an ex whose ambitions for Katherine were not
her own. Sure, if lying on your belly eating crackers bought on special
counts as wild, then I'm really going nuts, Mimi, really raising hell. Why
do you listen to your daughter's delusions? At night I break open a pack
of Wheat Thins and eat my dinner staring down at the street.

Until about eighth grade Katherine was a committed correspondent
with multicolored inks and paper she bought from a place that sold it
by the pound. Cerise, Mint, a shocking shade of yellow. Sending chron-

icles of her nine-year-old life to girls from camp, a French pen pal, a neighbor she never much liked who moved to Boston. Nobody wants letters anymore. Except Mimi. At eighty-five, she has no patience for computers or information that shoots through the air.

Katherine picks up her pen and continues: I know Mom told you I shaved my head. Sammy will say I did it to upset her or because I always do the stupidest thing I can think of at the time I'm thinking it. But it's been crazy hot here, ninety on October 1st. I don't have A/C and my brain felt cooked. I walked six blocks to a barber shop, the kind with a linoleum floor and combs suspended in blue liquid. Old men waiting, paging through sun-faded porn. On the walk over I had enough time to snap out of it, change my mind. But it's the inaction and double-guessing I'm sick of. In my head I was going to emerge all Mia Farrow circa *Rosemary's Baby*. Too late I found out you need cheekbones for that. I don't come across as sexily boyish, like some wide-eyed gamine, more like I'm being prepped for my eleven thirty electroshock. I don't care. Guess who does? Sammy. She made a surprise visit and I think the sight of my shaved head along with my shoebox apartment gave your daughter the vapors. Oh, Katherine, she whispered, gripping a wooden ladder-back chair so hard I thought it would snap.

6:29 a.m.

—A better question is why in god's fuck are we wasting shrimp on employees?

—Henry.

—Well.

—Dr. Sericko paid for the spread... over by the window, Chris looks up from his phone, behind him the day begins to break... —He wanted a special treat for the staff, instead of like, hummus or whatever.

Diane unfastens the top button on her new blouse. It's too small, the shirt tugs her shoulder blades. She's flattered that Chris ordered an XS but obviously ashamed of feeling flattered.

—Why did Sericko even get a party?... Henry exhales noisily... —We threw the guy a huge bash when he stepped down as director, massive. Seven years later he needs another send-off? Most people, when they retire from the board, go quietly. Understand everyone's sick of them. But Sericko, the ego is fucking limitless. I mean good riddance, I'm happy to never—

—Can we focus, Henry, on the problem at hand? How bad is it?... swinging around in her chair... —Chris?

—Eleven.

—*Eleven.*

—And who, uh... Henry squints, trying to sight Chris against the lightening window... —Who prepared the food?

—Emerson Pitt.

—Get him on the phone.

—Tried. He's not picking up.

—What about Marjorie Wolfe?... Diane pulls a jumbo-sized bottle of warm seltzer out of her bag and unscrews the cap.

—Who the hell is Marjorie Wolfe?

—Pitt's second in command... taking the glass Chris offers... —She's terrifically organized, though possibly a smack addict.

—I believe those are eczema scars.

—In any case, put Marjorie in charge... she fills the glass.

—Chris, Chris, listen carefully... Henry throttles down his tie. Already he looks like a newscaster fifteen hours into a hostage crisis... —Were there any trustees at the party?

—None.

—VIPs? Donors?

—The party was staff only, select staff. A couple hundred.

—So, no one important got sick.

—Correct.

—You're sure?

—Unless Dr. Sericko invited his friends. I'll find out... Chris checks his phone... —Oh.

—What?

—An assistant from Textiles is in the hospital.

—Jesus... Henry, lumped up on her couch, wipes his face. It's far too early for aggravated face-rubbing.

—Please tell me the Globe wasn't involved... Diane tries for an air of calm... —Or the Events kitchen, for that matter.

—Food was prepared in the Globe and served in Café West.

—Good. Close West... she picks up a ballpoint pen to click... —Tell Shay Pallot.

—West?

—Yes.

—But the shrimp was—

—Globe stays open.

—Diane... Henry's head snaps up... —We have to shutter the Globe. It's a health hazard.

—No, this is... clicking the pen rapidly, pretending it's a detonator... —Not up for discussion. Close West.

—We have people in the hospital.

—One person, not people. Some hyperventilating neurotic who, listen to me, Peter and his crew will get in there, sterilize the kitchen, they'll, you know, Silkwood the place. Ichimonji is visiting and Abu Dhabi. How's it going to look to our investors—

—How's it going to look when we poison the Japanese Ambassador?

—Henry, really. Save the drama.

—Fine... meaning, of course, very much not fine... —Your call. We'll need a statement prepared just in case and Mario's out, so.

—Okay, well, he has a team, doesn't he? What about his second?

—Fishman.

—Fishman? His name's really—

—Sadly.

—And he's on the poisoned list?

—Jury duty.

With discernible effort Henry shifts his weight, getting to his feet as if he's climbing out of a tub... —Chris, let me know when you get Pitt on the phone... moving to the door... —We need to find out, did this start with him? Let's hope it was the vendor, so we have someone to sue.

—Henry?

But the door is in mid-swing and slams into the frame.

6:35 a.m.

The short stretch of hallway between his office and Diane's has dark grey carpeting and beet-colored walls. It's the sort of look you admire in a historical home seconds before colliding with an unexpected table. In this soft passage Henry was once convinced he'd become stuck in a birth canal. The feeling was unpleasant and he had the impression, when he came to, that he may have been screaming. Indisputably, he was palpating the wall for an exit. He was quite high, it bears mentioning.

He should take a right at the end of the hallway, try for a piss. But won't. Can't face defeat at the urinal. Annie, he's thinking. Annie, Annie, Annie. He's pushed aside the situation in Mumbai, the news that the Museum is responsible for poisoning its staff. The conversation with Shay Pallot got him thinking. We all disappear, she said, reminding him that in a matter of weeks he'll remain only in photographs and a collection of moldering VHS tapes. It's time to get started on his list.

Figure out the money.

Tell Annie what you saw fourteen years ago, the night of Jordan's book party.

6:37 a.m.

—What's going on?, get your ass here in twenty minutes is what's going on.

—Okay, so usually it takes at least forty... Nikolic struggles to open the window without dropping his phone... —And the way the C's been running—

—See you in twenty... the phone goes dead.

Nikolic tosses his cell on the couch and grabs a towel off the back of a kitchen chair. Marjorie sounded grim. Twenty minutes? Understood.

No time for a shower. He wets a washcloth, running it around his particulars.

The bathroom is the size of a sauna and has a similar heat index. The only window is painted shut, trapping the persistent smell of stagnant water. Never mind that the water pipe in the corner is scalding to the touch, or that the ceiling is mapped with piss-colored patches, Niko loves his bathroom. To a man with rampant emotions, the constraint is comforting.

He brushes his teeth, rumples his hair, takes a quick sniff of the shampoo he brought with him from Philadelphia.

In the bedroom he grabs a T-shirt from the bureau and looks for his inhaler. The doctor agreed to prescribe it despite clinical proof that Niko's struggle to breathe had nothing to do with asthma. Back then even a fairly dickish medical professional could muster some sympathy.

He finds the inhaler under the bed, throws it in his bag, pulls on his shoes, locks the door, and runs.

6:39 a.m.

Eating fancy beans, they talked about root canals, movies, how Trevor's cat was mowing its belly clean of fur. The party was for Jordan's second novel. The writer's healthy, some might say stratospheric, self-regard gave his friends license to snicker behind his back that, really, one book would have been enough. Even Jordan mocked his sultry author photo. They were old friends, closing in on fifty. What right did they have to be so calm? Time was speeding past. There was insufficient panic, Henry thought when he withdrew to the kitchen on the pretext of stirring.

At the end of the night Annie went down to help with taxis and walk Maude to the end of the block and back. Upstairs Henry puttered around the apartment, setting things right, stacking dishes. How content he was to putter and put things in order, but in a larger sense he remembers feeling deep happiness, a kind of awe that his wife had ever chosen him. The windows were open, the air was fragrant and evoked the approaching autumn, things not yet dead. He was very aware of his life, as you are in certain moments, smelling the change of season, recalling the scents of childhood. He walked over to the window, pulled there by these fragrant eddies, wiping his hands on a dish towel scribbled with some French crap, *pistou* or *incroyable*. On the street below Annie and her friend Millicent were standing together saying good night. Henry watched these old friends as he dried his hands and, perhaps because he was thinking of his boyhood, a time when stars in the suburbs were still visible at night, it took him a moment to understand what he was seeing. An embrace. Not an innocent hug, no. This was lustful, hungry. Were they in love? They clung to each other, his wife and Millicent, the dog at their feet innocently panting. Henry stepped back, shocked but also, instinctively, to give them privacy.

That was fourteen years ago. He's never told Annie what it was that ended their marriage.

6:43 a.m.

Edgy in Connecticut, Katherine writes, before rethinking, amending, turning ~~edgy~~ into an inky blob, and inserting above it the word *restless*.

Your daughter, she continues, fingertip now blue, takes the Saturday train down to Grand Central, but once she gets here she can't relax. Mom, I say, go visit Mimi. California will soothe you, I say, really. Think of the sun. But Sammy glares at me as if I'm up to no good. She paces my apartment, inspecting the bottoms of mugs and candlesticks as if it's suddenly critical to know where things are made. About a month ago she got super finicky about food. Now she's suspicious of raisins and won't order off a menu. Tearing at her cuticles, listing what's wrong with a two-party system. Remember how obsessed she was with our garden growing up? Four types of roses and the wisteria trellis? Well, it's gone to hell. It's all weeds, muddy humps, brambles and tangled vines. The grass is balding. Divots fill with rainwater that stays there, soupy and brown. What's with the malaria experiment? I asked last time I went up. What do you have against the neighbors? No response. Weirdly, the more she kills her own garden, the more Sammy insists I need houseplants. I've told her a thousand times I murder green things, I'm human arsenic to anything with roots. But every time I open the door, in she comes, tottering under a ficus. Can we call it faith, Mimi, this image my mother has of me as a nurturing force? I'll take it, I guess, even if it's wildly misplaced.

Katherine sets down her pen.

Time for a shower.

6:46 a.m.

With a decisive stab, Henry hits send on his email, spins around, leans back and hooks a leg up on his desk. He's left the closet door open and he can see the black garment bag holding tonight's tuxedo. When Annie picked out the suit she called it classic, which Henry understood to mean clothing he could hold on to for fifteen years.

After the divorce Annie never took up with a woman. She dated old friends and the city's elegant bachelors until a hotdog from Utah appeared on the scene with a barrel chest and one of those mustaches they still grow out West. It's likely the man knew how to listen, was more patient than Henry, better in bed. It took six short months for Bruce's spell to work its magic. He and Annie moved in together one rainy day in April. Bruce joined the tennis club, appearing on court in frayed Lacoste and a red Fila track jacket. Swatting at the ball, the gems in his Chaumet caught the overhead lights, sending out blinding strobes to the other courts. Bruce was loud with the score and thinning at the crown. There were more than a few questionable line calls.

One evening in the locker room, Henry turned to see Bruce standing in front of the mirror taking appalling delight in his naked body. Pummeling dry sheafs of pink flesh. Henry had been raised properly, to fear and dread the sight of one's own nudity. Quickly he finished dressing, averting his eyes from his successor's mighty briefs. These Annie had undoubtedly laundered herself. She always liked laundry. Henry returned home that night to his second wife and young children feeling that someday Annie should know the truth.

He crosses his office to shut the closet door. The days remaining grow fewer and fewer. Little time left to confess. The divorce was not my fault. I fell on my sword to spare you shame. My affair was a reaction. What a thing for a husband to witness, his wife in the arms of another woman.

6:49 a.m.

Today, Clive thought when he woke up, I will get something. Whether it comes from Walter Wolfe or Jack Corbeau, I will have it. He stared at the bedroom ceiling, vaguely aware of a buzzing sound. The man next to him had a name like a cowboy. Ryder. Colt. Jesse. Or maybe it was a verb. Phil. Cary. Chase. The buzzing was his phone. Clive went down the hall to the living room where he found it under the stranger's clothes. A pair of depressing jeans, a cardigan, and a henley so ugly it bordered on a hate crime.

He swipes the screen... —Hauxwell.

—Clive, it's Adam. I'm sick.

Up all night with food poisoning, apparently, but was so looking forward to this morning's exhibitions meeting, could he perhaps speak to Clive privately next week about his ideas for Fall 2015?

A few stern words about fluids and rest and Clive hangs up the phone, grabs the stranger's disgusting tat and returns to the doorway of his bedroom.

Adonis from Murray Hill is splayed naked on the duvet. Owner of an inexusably gorgeous ass. It's unfortunate how short-lived it is, the oblivion delivered by sex.

Clive came across the man last night in a cheese shop in the West Village. He didn't need cheese. He was wandering, getting some fresh city air. The cheesemonger pinned him in place with a lecture on Shropshire cheddar. There was a schoolboy incident on a trip to Shropshire once, an indistinct scrabbling in the back of the coach. Clive pursued this memory while the shopkeeper went on about maturity and affinage. Immature boys in grey shorts, ties half-noosed, limbs unpredictable. The outing was intended—no, it didn't come to him, he couldn't recall why Shropshire. When the bell on the shop door dinged Clive paid no attention. Until Dustin, Shane, or perhaps initials for a name, J.R., now naked on the bed before him, requested a sample of Danish blue. An interesting baritone, Clive thought, glancing over. He watched the fromagier place a piece of cheese on the man's tongue, murmuring as he did, *the body of Denmark*. The stranger had a silly haircut and a big dumb head but savored the cheese slowly with his eyes closed, which made Clive think, well, why not? Twenty minutes later they sat knee to knee in a bar down the street. Danish Blue was thirty two, originally from Newark. Liked dogs. He chased his Manhattans with a truly staggering amount of water, treating hydration as if it were a calling. Again and again he shuffled to the toilet in a pair of plastic clogs. A high forehead tricked Clive into assuming the man had an open mind, but he spoke coarsely about socialized medicine. To shut him up, Clive brought him home and fucked him.

Danish Blue stirs, rolls over. A large pale foot emerges from under the duvet.

—I'm jumping in the shower. Afraid I don't keep coffee in the house... dropping the man's clothes onto the bed... —Door locks behind you.

6:55 a.m.

—As I said, I called the place yesterday... Chris scrolls on his phone... —And here's two emails.

Side by side they wait for the funicular doors to open.

—The customer service is unbeliev, I'll leave another message.

Again Diane jabs OPEN, but the doors to the funicular remain firmly closed. The last time she felt so betrayed by an insentient object was the day Mr. Biddles fell into the river. She screamed as he sailed to his death, smile unvanquished, corduroy paw raised in farewell.

—So, resign ourselves to the elevator?

—We're famous for, we can't just, not with both Abu Dhabi and the Ambassador visiting. It looks shabby. What about?... she mimes prising the doors apart.

Chris gets up close to the carriage doors, determining if he can fit a finger between the rubber strips, muttering... —Need like a... eyes roaming the hallway... —Maybe... digging in his front pockets and pulling out a quarter.

The idea for an indoor funicular came to Diane on her return from a trip to the Pompidou. Muzzy from jetlag, she walked into the museum while consulting her phone or searching her purse for a breath mint, and was struck, in looking up, by the atmosphere of the

Great Hall. It was staid and forbidding. Impeccable, marbley, over-columned. In a word, off-putting. The smooth, sparkling surfaces felt like a frustrated bid for perfection, as if the Museum were a fussy mother wanting the best for her children but crushing them instead with her drive for excellence. A funicular, Diane proposed, would serve the executive suite of the fourth floor and lead diagonally down to the Great Hall. The track would be purposefully garish, a marvelous contrast to the white marble. Of course the tram would be functional. Private, but functional. And it would serve as some good nose-thumbing fun. A little fucking levity.

—No... Chris has given up on trying to wedge a coin between the doors and lever them open.

Everyone was against the funicular at first, Tiz and the board of directors, former curators, historians, most of the significant donors, but Diane prevailed and up it went. The newspapers hated it, as they hated everything the Museum did to change and everything it did to stay the same. But the public went crazy. Hoards visited solely to gawk. They appreciated the audacity, Diane thought. Plus, it felt very American to interrogate or even debase all that imperious marble by throwing up a piece of madcap engineering. Soon after the opening ceremony she won an award, *Accomplished*, or something, *Woman of the Year*. She can never remember the exact title and that one can't be right, accomplished, but she won a patronizing lozenge-shaped trophy that currently sits on a shelf in her office and which, last week, she noticed had at some point sustained a hairline fracture across its surface.

—No point in calling Peter, I imagine the problem's... Chris pushes the OPEN button several times, quickly, as if a different tempo might solve everything.

Even today when Diane walks through the hall and spots a family gazing up at the funicular, posing and taking pictures, she allows herself to get a little smug that she was right and they, the trustees, the board, and especially ex-director Tiz Sericko, were wrong. Regrettably, this smugness may have led Diane to ignore her colleagues' objections to her next idea, the construction of a dazzling new wing filled with a collection of modern and contemporary art. God, the fuss they put up. Why? the board asked, when at least five other city museums focus

on modern art more or less exclusively. But Diane insisted. Not simply
so the Museum could appear fresh and forward-thinking, but because
ninety percent of their benefactors collect contemporary art and, at
some point, would need a place to stick it.

—Should I call him, for the hell of it?

—Peter? No.

The expansion squandered funds, torpedoed goodwill, and threw
the Museum into a sucking mire of debt. The project was so ill-
conceived that if it doesn't get her fired it will be a goddamn miracle.

—Okay. Enough of this... turning away... —We need to strategize
my five thirty with Zedekiah—

—Z. Remember to call him Z.

—And I need another coffee. I lost the last one.

—You finished it.

—Did I?

They head back down the hallway toward her office.

—When did I finish it?

7:02 a.m.

Because Benjamin was wearing headphones while he transcribed
his interview with Victor Robledo he has no idea when the banging
started.

—I know, I know... unlocking the dead bolt... —I hear you.

—Yeah? You *know*? That right?... Ruben shoves the door open,
smacking Benjamin's foot. His eyes are puffy and his hair sticks up in
greasy peaks. Instead of his normal spiffy dress shirt he wears a Knicks
jersey with drooping armholes. Even so, Ruben maintains an air of authority, taking two steps into the apartment... —So you know that I
come all the way out here specially to find you since you don't answer
the phone, you try to pretend you're not home. You think I don't know
what you're up to? Think I don't hear you on the other side of the door
creeping around?

—End of the week, I promise.

—Your promises don't mean shit.

—I messed up, Ruben. I know that and I apologize.

—Why you doing this to me? Why you making me yell and call and, I have to find out how do you evict someone, look it up on the computer because in fifteen years I never had to evict nobody, why?

—I realize that and I—

—Had a guy once, kept cats, against the rules, but they were good cats, nice and clean, didn't smell. And maybe I liked seeing their little faces at the window when I came up the steps. Had another guy started a business out of his place on the third floor, had to shut it down, law don't allow it. Year ago a woman on four had some mental illness, used to knock on people's doors at two in the morning wearing nothing but a baby's bib. All these people got me the rent in time, you understand, week late, maybe. But the first time I rent to some rich kid—

—*Rich* kid?

—He's going to make me sweat and curse and turn into the bad guy who has to leave home without breakfast because, as I tell my wife, this asshole, and I called you an asshole, Benjamin, is not gonna pick up his phone, not gonna answer his door. I gotta go ambush him on his way to work like I'm some kind of I don't know what... index finger on one side of his mouth, thumb on the other, Ruben flattens his beard scruff... —Why you do this to me?

—I really didn't intend, Ruben. I'm sorry you had to leave without breakfast. I can, I mean, I have granola bars or maybe... turning to indicate the kitchen as if it holds endless resources instead of half a box of... —Cornflakes? Let me make you a coffee.

—Your girlfriend paid fine. Every month. Early. Never had to worry. Out of respect to her I gave you more time.

—She left.

—I know she left, Benjamin. I helped her find boxes. Give me something. Five hundred. Show you're serious.

—Please, a few more days. It's coming, I promise. I got a great job, new job. Uptown.

Ruben doesn't appear to hear that. He looks past Benjamin into the apartment. Nods at the far corner of the ceiling... —Not leaking no more?

—No, it hasn't been a problem since. Thank you.

—I report to people, you know. I got a boss, not just me out here.

—I've put you in a terrible position. I'm so sorry.

—Tomorrow. First thing.

—How's next week?

—Don't push me, Benjamin.

—You're right, you're right. Tomorrow it is.

Ruben presses his lips together, harassing the change in his front pocket. Benjamin has always mostly liked the super despite his compulsion of touching up flat-white walls with semi-gloss paint, leaving behind blotches and spots that flare in the sun.

—End of the day, I promise.

—What flavor?

—What flavor what?

—Granola bar you got.

—Oats and honey, I think?

—Fine. No walnuts or coconut in there, okay?

—No.

—Give me two. And half the rent by tomorrow. No more excuses, nothing.

—You got it.

Benjamin goes to the kitchen cabinet, finds the box and takes out the last two granola bars. Ruben is leaning against the doorframe, skimming the living room with a practiced eye as if he's calculating the manpower needed to drag the couch to the curb.

—Breakfast!... brandishing the cereal bars as if he's escorting a plane to its gate, skirting piled shoes and a puddle of bills, striding toward Ruben like a person accustomed to locating a thousand dollars overnight.

7:09 a.m.

Coffee in hand, towel around his waist, Clive is in the kitchen staring at the note Danish Blue left on the counter weighed down by a corkscrew. No words, just ten digits. The idea that Clive would ever telephone this person, the confidence of it! Swanning about in that lamentable henley, not at gunpoint, no one forced him. The man went to a shop and selected it. Deliberately! Sorted through piles of presumably acceptable shirts to land on that faux-faded red ribbed atrocity. Clive crumples the note, bins it. No, it was unforgivable.

Quick slug of coffee, he scrolls recent calls until he reaches Lucy's number. She'll be awake by now, wrapped in a towel, spackling on the makeup. A month ago she took it into her head she has acne scars. It's one of Lucy's hobbies, finding new things to hate about herself.

—What is it, Clive?

—Don't be angry... walking down the hall to the bedroom... —I'm calling to apologize.

—Six days later.

—I'm a cunt... in the mirror, proof of last night's vodka is etched into his face... —Forgive me.

—For what? Do you even know?

—I'm sorry for... massaging the alcohol out of his skin... —Embarrassing you in front of Juan DeSoulas?

—That was nothing but sabotage.

Lucy must be well into her second coffee. Her words dart out in little jabs.

—I had, a minute earlier, confessed I was dying to work for him. That's why we were there! Why did I bring you? I should've known.

—But the work, you know his work is dreadful. I was saving you—

—You're the one who, the *Times* gushed about him a week ago, the whole show is sold out, okay? Anyway, it doesn't matter who thinks what, I love what he does and Micky had talked me up... the sound of Lucy pacing... —Micky had made me out to be like the second coming. All I had to do was shake his hand and smile and then you go and.

—The man needs a healthier ego if a fucking stranger can dismantle him.

—For the last six days I've been trying to figure out why you would deliberately insult DeSoulas. Why wouldn't Clive want me to have this job? And then I realized that what you hated, the thing you had to stomp to death, wasn't the job thing at all. It was before Juan came up to us when we were standing in front of his orange-and-yellow painting—

—To be clear, the Agnes Martin rip-off?

—And I was telling you why I loved it and you were scowling and

rolling your eyes. At the time I thought, well that's Clive and contemporary art, but thinking about it later I realized that your face, it wasn't
your, god I hate this painting look, it was a sour reaction to my excitement. You couldn't take it. I was too happy. You felt left out or, I don't
know what, but you had to shit all over it. Because that's what you do.
You shit on joy.

—That's a little much.

—You're a joy-shitter.

—Killjoy.

—Don't correct my insults. I'll hang up.

—So I don't want you to be happy, that's the idea?... switching the
phone to speaker and placing it on the credenza that stores his sweaters.
The Paul McCobb credenza that's been seared several times by Lucy's
sloppy handling of her water glass.

—As long as I keep it to myself you don't mind.

—But I'm always doing things to cheer you up. Driving to that
gruesome flea market, carrying your silly pots and vases. Massachusetts.
I mean, if that's not love I don't know what is.

—You can't bear that I have an easier relationship with the world.

—What have you been reading?

—I'm going to Berlin.

—That's the title?

—Tonight. I have a ticket. I leave around six.

—Impossible... Clive picks up the phone, switching it off speaker,
holding it to his ear... —You can't afford a flight with six days' notice.

An awful silence.

—I see. When did you book the ticket?

—A while ago.

He can tell she's trying to be gentle, and it infuriates him.

—Terry's taking my apartment for a month.

—Who the fuck's Terry?

—You met at my, does it matter?

—For an entire month?

—I didn't buy a return.

Clive pictures slinging the phone against the wall. Or climbing
back in bed, curling into a tight fetal ball and not getting up for several weeks.

—So, maybe a month, maybe longer.

—How much longer?

—I don't know. For good?

—Don't be obscene... trying to override a rising sense of panic...

—For good, really.

—I need to leave New York.

—And this is because of some job? Because of Juan DeSoulas?

—I don't know. I looked around at the people I spend time with and I realize I sort of hate them all. Find ridiculous what they find important, loathe their kids, or at least, loathe feigning interest in their kids.

—Avoid parents. Problem solved.

—People on the street bug me. They walk in threes, they're too loud, their ambition is disgraceful. I hate their hair and the way they sneeze. They're not weird enough or weird in the wrong way. No, no... Lucy's voice changes, as if she's taking hold of herself... —It's more that I feel a complete lack of interest in my own thoughts. Why do I care if Obama's still smoking? At some point this week I came to understand that I deeply, deeply bore myself.

—And you're planning to, what, find some magical version of yourself in Germany, of all places?

—I thought I might learn the language.

—God, the clichés are just endless.

—Something has to change. I need a challenge.

—We all need a challenge, and we all hate our friends, and anyone who's lived in New York for more than five fucking minutes thinks about leaving. The reason we continue seeing our hateful friends and not shoving off and moving to, I don't know, Coxsackie, is because normal people, sensible people, understand that outside the confines of New York City, other people and other places are even worse.

—Don't shout.

—I'm not shouting... he stops shouting... —I'm being emphatic.

—What are you so angry about?

—Because I know exactly how this plays out. You, back in a month, unable to conjugate two verbs, lonely, dissolute, nursing a nasty infection you got from dancing on a rusty barge repurposed as a night club. And guess who'll do the mopping up? Dry your tears and make the right noises as you describe the bore you fell for, the loser ten years your junior who treated you like shit. All because one night you picked up some lowlife as a lark and, immune to all reason, proceeded to let him annihilate you. Just as you did here in New York.

Silence.

In a softer voice... —You're behaving like some student finding meaning in a pond.

—Well, I'm going, okay? I bought shoes I can walk in and treated myself to an inflatable pillow I'm extremely excited about. Think I care how I appear to you with my naivete and comfortable shoes? I mean, I do care but I'm going anyway. Tonight. Six forty-six.

Suddenly lightheaded, Clive goes to the bed, pulls the duvet straight with one hand, and sits down. He can hear Lucy breathing heavily, taxed by her little speech.

—Clive?

7:19 a.m.

After Ruben left with the last of the granola bars, Benjamin was shoving the empty box into the recycling bin when he noticed that underneath the words OATS AND HONEY was a tiny treacherous addendum. WITH TOASTED COCONUT. He'd been grossly misled. Instead of a helpful photo of palm trees or an actual coconut, the box showed only bundles of oat sheafs floating against a beige background. Benjamin raced to his computer, jack-hammered the words *ciconut alldrgy* into Google and clicked and scanned until he was sufficiently reassured that allergies to coconut only occasionally result in death.

It was no accident that Benjamin had only a vague command of the ingredients in his cereal bars. He'd made a conscious decision to stop caring about food when he returned to New York from film school. The policy was hatched on the trip back East, in the wilds of Pennsylvania. He was driving, one hand on the wheel, the other messing with the window because the U-Haul's air-conditioning had shorted out somewhere back in Ohio. "Borderline" was on the radio, a golden-oldies station, one of only two that came in relatively static-free. The sun was shining, Caroline still loved him, they were headed back to the city they adored. It was a wonderful time and, typically, a wonderful time was when Benjamin reviewed the past for confirmation of his repellent personality. As the van shuddered in the wake of passing semis it came to him that for the last two years he'd been grating, dogmatic, and absolute. No one in the film program had any doubt as to which directors Benjamin believed were geniuses and which he thought were overrated. And it was suddenly clear that this unyielding attitude was the reason nobody from school ever wanted to grab a beer or stop by for a can of ribs. A married couple came over from time to time but they clearly preferred Caroline and only tolerated Benjamin because the wife was desperate for a friend and thought the women in the program looked down on her for being pregnant. The revelation of his pig-headedness hit Benjamin as signs for Harrisburg flashed past and by the time he took the exit for crab fries, a solution was in the works. He would choose a couple of areas in which to be easygoing and opinion-free, thereby proving he was exactly as laid-back as the next person. First up: food. Anything that was placed before him, Benjamin decided, he would eat. *Happily.* Attitude was key. In a matter of months he ate aspic, raw beef, jackfruit duck and a dessert made from celery. He consumed cheese not legal in seventeen states. At a gas station in Trenton last year he ate an extremely suspect egg salad sandwich. This objectionable item was grabbed in a hurry by Caroline from one of those grab-and-go cases that offer rubbery chicken wraps and travel-sized hummus and are never entirely convincing as refrigeratory appliances. Benjamin could not refuse the sandwich, though the egg salad was almost certainly a week old and quite possibly salmonellic. He had committed to a flexibility around food, and he would exercise that flexibility with absolute rigidity. In the end he was only sick for a couple of days, and it was worth it to stick to his principles.

7:23 a.m.

—I know it sounds like I'm trying to change the subject, but I only found out yesterday. Then I fucked someone I found in a cheese shop.

—A broken hip, Clive, that's serious at your dad's age. And after fracturing his wrist this summer.

Clive takes the pillow from Danish Blue's side of the bed, brings it up to his face and smells it.

—You should fly back, help your poor sister.

Sniffing again. Quite a nice scent. He wonders how to milk sympathy without it looking obvious and immediately hates himself.

—He's in the hospital?

—Rehab unit... Clive drops the pillow, gets up and crosses to the closet.

—Hang up the phone this second and buy a ticket home... Lucy's voice takes on the strict tone he loves. She's never more caring than when she becomes bullying and strident... —What if it's serious?

—Here's how I look at it—

—I'll book the ticket.

—Wait.

—Where do you fly into?

—Hear me out... swiping hangers, searching for a shirt, the correct shirt... —My life these days is quite agreeable. I have friends—

—But we've already established that you don't. None you actually care about.

—Unlike you, Luce, I don't expect to like my friends... selecting a blue-and-white striped... —I've got a nice apartment, a number of men and a few women who occasionally throw me a charitable fuck. Job's not too hellish... gesturing with the hangered shirt... —Why risk all that by visiting my dad? I wouldn't be surprised if the old man's waited all this time to drop a bomb of some kind, that he's got a second family stashed in Luton or that Uncle Snook's really my father. Then I'll have to forge on with some disgusting bit of news I was better off never knowing... Clive can hear how he sounds but is powerless to stop.

—Are you trying to be funny? When did you get so, I mean, is this because of Joshua?

—Don't.

—Because everyone has one relationship—

—I'll hang up.

—I'm only saying.

—And I'm saying don't.

—Clive, go home.

—*Home?*

—Don't leave it all to Jane. Poor thing.

Clive goes to the window. The building opposite went up last summer. The apartments are astronomically priced with high ceilings and enormous windows. Inside, the residents slink around naked or in slipping-down towels. Rich people love foisting their nudity on innocent bystanders. Clive watches as a man with a furry chest juggles a coffee mug in one hand and under his arm a small squirming dog.

—Could a quick visit really be so awful?

The man sets down his mug, picks up a watering can and tries to simultaneously water a spiky dracaena and nuzzle his dog on the forehead. It's best not to multitask while naked, Clive has found, especially around sharp objects.

—Clive? I feel like I'm hearing a cry for help.

—But you're not... only minutes ago in the shower he had in fact screamed the word help.

—Look, I'm hanging up. I hope you'll go see your dad. Stop by Berlin afterward, that's where I'll be reinventing my life.

And Clive is left with the dead air of the ended call. At one point he thought about agreeing to visit his father if Lucy promised to stay. But he was afraid she might find the offer distasteful. And it was, probably. He doesn't feel qualified anymore to judge correct ways of being.

Yesterday, after Jane phoned with the news of their father's terrifying plunge (off the kerb and into the street, sending his shopping flying, exposing laxatives to the neighbors, his father the most private of men), before Clive tore into the night sampling cheddar and fucking strangers, he spooned up leftover pho while trying to edit an essay that was overdue by several weeks. As he added then deleted paragraph breaks he kept saying to himself, but Clive, your father. This is your father we're talking about. Again and again he tried to summon suitable feelings as he hit return. But nothing could shift the block of anthracite behind his ribs. Last night he wanted to feel the way he feels now. Despairing, hopeless, orphaned. It seems very wrong to feel worse about your friend heading off to Germany than your broken father withering away in some grotty National Health gulag. Beginning the slide toward his inevitable end. That seems like crossed wires. As if you've fucked up somewhere along the line.

7:30 a.m.

—I don't know how else to say it, Niko. Food poisoning.

Out by the loading dock, the morning too warm for October, Nikolic can feel his lips moving as he silently parrots Marjorie's words.

—Shrimp from Sericko's reception yesterday.

—From the reception?

—Yup, barfing up lungs, hospital, all of it... Marjorie digs in the front pocket of her chef's coat, drawing out a pack of cigarettes... —Spider and Celeste both called in sick.

—Both Spider and Celeste?

—You're not an idiot, Niko, are you? Because you're repeating everything I'm saying and it's really, the new dishwasher, the hot one, he's out too... holding a pack of Marlboros to her mouth, Marjorie extracts a cigarette with her teeth, shaking and sparking a plastic lighter while abstractedly offering the pack to Nikolic.

He shakes his head. A steady beeping sound comes from around the corner and the two of them watch a white cube truck appear and start backing down the driveway.

—Pay employees so little they can barely afford groceries, then set out a bunch of free food, the fuck you think's gonna happen?

—What about Emerson?... Nikolic asks, trying to keep things on track... —Did he get sick?

A second as Marjorie takes a deep drag... —Canned.

—They *fired* him?

—Wake up, Niko, people are in the hospital. Who else is gonna take the fall?

—Yeah, I guess, but christ, he's been here forever, I—

—Anyway, the director wants to... a violent inhale... —Keep the Globe open and close West, that means moving staff—

—West?

—from the café over to—

—Wait, why close West?

—To disinfect it?... gripping the cigarette between her teeth, Marjorie hoists her sagging chef pants and folds the waistband over and then over again.

—But the food was prepped in the Globe.

—Wake up, Nik. The Globe pulls in fistfuls of cash. Can't attack Saudi Arabia? Invade Iraq. Close enough kind of thing.

Niko smiles placidly.

—What?

—No, it's just. It sounds a little nuts.

—Not my decision... holding the cigarette aloft, Marjorie exhales a vicious stream of smoke... —Plus we've got a walk-in full of proteins that won't live past Friday.

—So we're not.

—Not what?

—Shouldn't we throw out—

—We're not throwing out shit... flinging the cigarette to the ground to mash it with her clog... —Let's go... she swipes her pass savagely through the slot on the keypad and pushes through the door.

—Marjorie... Nikolic clears his throat as he follows her into the building, hoping a sagacious sound might bring his boss to reason... —I don't want to, you know, step on any toes or whatnot, but if we get customers sick... letting the door fall closed behind him... —I mean, if the meat is contaminated—

—Try to keep up, Niko. With Emerson out you'll be running the Globe.

—Sorry, I'll be...?

—Get rid of the rabbit and do not, I repeat, do not take the mac and cheese off the menu or you'll have a full-blown riot on your hands. With West closed we'll need a café option, so prep a stack of baguettes, use the Taleggio but call it Brie. Price them around fifteen. From the café I can give you a chef, a commis, and two dishwashers. Stick the chef on prep, guy's slow as fuck. From the Globe we have you, Otto, Ryan, Raheem, plus the pastry girl, what's her—

—Vivian, her name's... struggling to keep abreast of Marjorie as she races through the bowels, down the concrete hallway, past a row of golf carts and around the corner... —But if I could—

—Thank god none of you were pitiful enough to stay for—

—But Marj, when you say *running*—

—It's a short day. Service ends at four... kicking a stray hazard cone out of the way.

—I don't understand, why wouldn't you—

—Because I have a little thing to manage called the mother-fucking gala.

—The gala? Isn't that Events?

—It was, Nikolic, it was. Until three months ago when Emerson lost his mind. Bitched about his name being associated with stuffed mushrooms. Head office threw him a bone, said he could oversee the department. *Oversee.* Meaning sign off on their menus. Like who has time to take crostini as a personal insult? But you know what a prince he can be. Could be... at the elevator bank she chooses up. The doors open, together they enter the elevator and Marjorie presses MEZZ...

—Anyway, last night the boys in Events polished off three platters of shrimp, now the whole team is laid out, and guess who has to step up? Meanwhile, I've got deliveries arriving all morning and a couple of ding-dongs from West to prepare two thousand nibbly bits. I told HR this is not gonna work, not unless you give me some guys from Central America, but they refuse to close Central America, offered to truck in temps instead, caterers from fucking Long Island or some shit.

As they ascend, Marjorie stares at her reflection in the stainless steel door, eyes yawing back and forth as she solves problems further down the pipeline.

Nikolic smiles, pressing his lips together in case the screaming inside his head finds its way out. For nearly a year Niko refused to give it a name, the dark presence he lives with almost constantly, the pressure in his throat and stomach and behind his eyes. Finally he admitted it. He is afraid. Always. Afraid of failure but also of success. Of living in the past and of moving on. Of solitude, of company, of being too friendly or too aloof or the minefield that lies between. Anxious he's eaten too much food from cans containing BPA. Terrified a rat will run over his foot, that his penis is hanging out of his pants, that he'll accidentally shoplift, get caught in crossfire, or mortally offend a co-worker. Almost every day he's worried he'll break down in tears at work. At night he's afraid a meth addict will climb in from the fire escape and either murder him or fail to murder him entirely, leaving Niko so messed up he'll have to write with his toes. He's afraid he won't wake up in the morning and afraid he will. Afraid of being this fat forever, of losing weight, of ever loving a woman again or never loving at all. And then the phobias arrived. Candles that smell like food, articulated buses, marshmallows, zoodles, child actors, a certain type of shoehorn.

—Hey... Marjorie is watching him... —I'm happy to ask Otto or M.J. You have seniority so I came to you first.

Shove the fear aside. Bury it, refuse it. You only get one shot. And as Nikolic repeats no, no, I'm good, I'm in, I'm your guy, the elevator doors open on the mezzanine.

7:41 a.m.

And that doesn't account for his chronic indecision, Benjamin thinks as he unbuttons the shirt he's just buttoned and returns to his closet.

Back in April, for example, he went to see a program of short films by young directors, who knows why, he was pushing himself to do new things after Caroline left. The show ended, taking with it several years of his life, and Benjamin bolted from the movie theater, diving into the cool spring air, delirious with relief. He took up a spot in front of posters advertising upcoming attractions. His apartment was empty, he was in no hurry to get back. From down the street came the thump of a basketball and the semeny stench of Callery pears. Benjamin memorized the posters, next month's films were all foreign. I should really move to Los Angeles and start making movies, he thought, since it's impossible to come up with anything worse than those five mind-numbing shorts. I could easily become the best of the worst filmmakers if I relocate to LA and move in the right circles.

It was a pleasant evening so instead of dipping immediately underground, Benjamin decided to stroll for a bit, east through the park and up to Union Square.

Spring was finally here. Giddy dogs sent up clumps of mud as they shot around the dog park. Green sprigs were starting to poke through. Winter had lasted ninety-three years. Everyone was beaten by the slog. Now people were venturing out, kicking up their heels, bolstered by the fresh air. And Benjamin moseyed among them, roused by his beloved city but at the same time captivated by the image of the successful director he could unquestionably become in Los Angeles. From visiting two years ago, he knew it was a place that could be fragrant and peaceful when you're not trying to merge. By this point Benjamin was thoroughly sold on the West Coast, nodding at people he passed like a candidate for mayor, greeting children and petting dogs as he debated which books he should pack and which he should sell. Five minutes later, before he'd reached the other side of the park, Benjamin knew he could never abandon New York, it was the world's best city. Turning up Broadway, he was once again in Los Angeles debating whether the Eastside or Westside was the best place to settle when factoring in expense, gridlock, and the restorative breeze that floats in from the ocean. In retrospect it was incredible that over the course of their five years together his dithering hadn't driven Caroline completely insane.

Hunched over the bathroom sink Benjamin scrubs at a lentil stain on his favorite shirt, trying to ignore the intense sexual memories associated with it. In the background Bryan Ferry sings, "These Foolish Things." Benjamin listened to the song on repeat the night Caro left. It will run through his head for the rest of the day, reminding him that at his core he'll always be a bit of a shit.

He presses the wet shirt with a towel. No one will love him again. Not with that ferocity. There is time, perhaps, to form a new, more winning personality before he becomes entirely repulsive. This is not unknown, turning grotesque in middle age, for the Rippens. He's seen it in his uncles, his father. The low paunch, set inscrutably low, as well as a kind of wet-lipped fatalism.

A cigarette that bears a lipstick's traces

Well, he's not going to let Ruben rattle him. It takes weeks to evict a tenant, even months, and by then Benjamin will have a paycheck.

Oh how the ghost of you clings

And he's not going to let Bryan Ferry get to him either, not right now. He has to remain upbeat, keep focused on his new job. A man severely in debt, stingy with his affections and coping with hair loss. I'm not, he thinks as he buttons his shirt, about to add bathing in sentiment to that list.

Out the door, locking it, down the stairs, into the bright air, Benjamin heads to the subway station, semi-bathing in sentiment. He fishes out his phone and quickly texts Caroline so he won't agonize about it for two hours. *Lunch?* He swipes through the turnstile, jogs down the subway steps and onto the platform where a rabbi, or a man dressed as a rabbi, this close to Halloween who can be sure, sits on a pickle bucket playing the cello.

7:49 a.m.

—That was Dominic... Chris, from her office doorway... —I said you'd call back. And Elaine Mensdorf left a voicemail last night around seven. Didn't sound urgent.

—Put her down for tomorrow.

—And Dominic?

—Yup, I heard, I'll call.

—Also, the website's down again.

—Again?

—Back up by noon they're saying.

Diane checks her phone for the time. Four hours. Ridiculous. The technicians will have to be replaced, perhaps the entire IT department. But Chris is speaking. She swivels... —Sorry?

—I was just saying, an idea I had, what if you met with the artists from 1072?

—Met with them? What for?

—Explain why we're killing *Made in New York*. Or not explain, but like—

—Lie?

—Like a lying explanation.

—Unnecessary.

—But Diane, from a PR perspective, the optics of—

—I hardly think disappointing a group of young artists is going to, why are you hovering? Come in.

—That's okay. I'm about to... Chris takes three noncommittal steps into her office... —All I'm saying is, you know, artists are sensitive. We selected the pieces, we promised a show—

—Not now, please.

—Messing with artists, Diane, it's a bad road.

—Fine, set a time for next week... having no intention of addressing the 1072 situation next week or ever... —Has Conrad arrived?

—Half an hour ago... Chris checks in with his phone... —He sounded pretty upbeat.

—What else?

—Nothing.

—Something, because you're doing, Chris, that thing with your mouth.

—Constance is reporting another twelve out with food poisoning.

—TWELVE?... sitting back, resisting the urge to compulsively straighten her desk... —But no one else in the hospital.

—No.

—Zero?

—Zero. Well, two. Barely any. Remember to call Dominic... Chris turns and slips out the door, closing it silently behind him.

Chris.

For a moment last summer Diane thought she was falling for him. They'd been working together for nearly three years. Diane had poached him from Publications where his talents, she thought, were being wasted. She hadn't given Chris a second thought as he helped manage the installation of the funicular, wrangling the board and massaging the press. He had a gift for handling people. Then came the night they were working late. An electric moment in her office over pad see ew when the lights were low and their eleven-year age difference melted away. Oil from the noodles glistened on Chris's lips; his cheekbones sliced the air. They couldn't look at each other. The silence crackled. It was a frightening moment. Rules about employee fraternization screamed in her head. The next morning Diane checked Dom's calendar and booked a romantic getaway. She brought home oysters and chocolate mousse, mixing up margaritas which you could always count on to get Dominic in the mood. Before long, any desire she had for Chris was safely in the past.

7:54 a.m.

Last night's Rioja was deadly. Iona Moore stands in her kitchen struggling with the child-safety cap on a bottle of Tylenol. Finally she pops it open and shakes out three pills. Here come some terrible people, she thought when David's new friends arrived. Evidently they were artists. Kent had a thick red face, a loose neck, and mean eyes. His restless wife sought her reflection in the silverware. The restaurant was too quiet. There were too many ampersands. The waiters wore long denim aprons and roamed around looking saintly and resentful. David trotted out his greatest hits and the couple laughed appreciatively, as if it were the price of dinner. Gail and Kent were not the type that usually gravitated to her husband, but there was a conspiratorial quality to their revelry, the three of them. No one paid attention to Iona, who was factored in as the audience.

David shouts for her from the bedroom. He prefers Iona to do the traveling, so he can talk while he pulls on his socks. But since his return, Iona's hearing has become less and less acute.

Seven months ago, while Iona was lying in bed with a fever, David called from Grand Central. He admitted his timing was poor, then said I'm not sure if I'm up to the whole kids and marriage thing after all. After all!

Iona didn't succeed in finding the remote while her husband spoke, in order to turn down the volume on the TV. Consequently, David's cheery valediction was interlaced with a documentary about the tree beetle.

—Water pressure's off again... tying his tie, narrowing his eyes at Iona as he passes... —You have grape jelly in your hair.

She does not, as some wives might, tell her husband to get fucked. No doubt life would be easier if she had the nerve to say it.

—Where... David is digging through the breadbox, batting away bags of dinner rolls and half-finished loaves... —No more bagels?

—Frozen.

The week he left was mild for late March. Once Iona recovered from the flu, she strolled over to Prospect Park to take a look at this nature people were always boasting about. The plan was to assess the general state of things, and maybe creatures without a poisonous agenda of their own would help with that assessment. Lying on the cold ground, Iona looked up through knobbly winter branches stretching to the sky like geriatric fingers. The earth smelled rich, ancient, and mysterious. She pressed her palm against the city grass, its striving futile growth, to feel the world's pulse, to get at history, the leavening spirit, a correspondence. Or whatever. The music of living. The rock and hiss of growing things, nature's furtive whisperings. She stared up at a squirrel's nest, wondering if it might drop onto her face.

David tosses a sleeve of frozen bagels onto the counter... —I'll get something from the cart at work.

—Bravo... no idea why she says this.

He disappears down the hallway. She hears him rustling at the coat rack and unlocking the front door before calling back... —Remember to clean your hair.

—I will... by which, of course, Iona means get fucked.

8:01 a.m.

Katherine nabbed one of the coveted end seats of the pitted wooden bench by arriving exactly as the previous train was pulling away, practically snapping a femur as she flew down the stairs and launched herself at the subway's closing doors, crushing the evening gown that lay folded over her arm. She'll have to spend lunch steaming it out.

No word yet from Giselle. On Gala Day she's usually texted Katherine fifteen times before breakfast, long directives with semicolons. Often signing her name at the bottom.

Katherine takes out her phone.

On my way in. Everything okay?

But the text fails to send. No service below ground.

8:02 a.m.

Three weeks after David called her from Grand Central, Iona walked into the lobby to find him standing in front of the mailbox pulling out flyers and coupons, postcards advertising pest control. As Iona watched, he licked a finger and started sorting through the envelopes. She swore he was humming. When she finally said, David? he glanced up casually as if he'd popped out for a quart of milk. Now, look, he said, adopting the measured expression of a reasonable man faced with a hysteric. He always underestimated her antipathy for drama.

—You could've been dead.

Is what she said. But there was no time for bitterness. David needed her to be happy. Because while he was away he'd had an epiphany.

Epiphany.

In the hall mirror Iona uses a wet cloth to clean the jelly from her hair, hearing David's voice from seven months ago telling her, *Iona*, explaining how it wasn't marriage fatigue, but an exploration. He needed to write plays again, as he did all those years ago, college, some of the happiest days of his life. Not to worry, he wasn't quitting his job. This was simply a new habit: set the alarm for five, carry a cup of black coffee and his laptop into the living room and drum up some dramatic literature. Instead of divorce, David opted for a world of make-believe.

College! Iona pulls back her hair. You work at an investment bank! If anyone's successfully hidden his dream of writing the great American play it's you.

Returning to the kitchen, she opens the cabinet above the toaster, gropes wildly around the hot sauces and takes down David's tequila. Pours herself a finger of añejo. A slosh of orange juice to prove it's a brunch order, not the sign of a budding alcoholic.

What took place over those missing three weeks? Sorority orgies? Shared heroin? Betting their savings on a rooster? She found nothing incriminating on the credit card statement and David remained uncommonly silent for a man who described any bowel movement that departed from the standard.

Iona swirls her glass, sips the tequila. It's not that she's opposed to a midlife revelation. She tried to keep an open mind and at least appear supportive. Never reminding David that she was once on track to becoming an artist herself. One of those annoying undergrads with a pencil in her bun, pestering professors as they tried to eat lunch. But after graduation Iona wised up. Recognized in the making of art instability. Insolvency, selfishness, misery. A job in conservation meant a regular paycheck. Health insurance.

She drains the glass.

Dinner last night ended with a protracted cheese course. Iona was bored but forging ahead, smiling and glancing at her bracelet as if it were a watch. She was busily sipping her wine and practicing her posture when suddenly she saw the scene with absolute clarity. Gail and Kent knew exactly where David had gone. What he'd gotten up to those missing three weeks. They were positioning her as the outsider. The drudge preventing David from some large expansive life.

At the first detectable pause David brought up his play, the difficulty of act breaks, Aristotle. Swigging wine, the importance of catharsis. All three adopted interested expressions. Held a chin in palm, met David's eyes soulfully. Even Kent, a certified narcissist. They refused to let their attention drift to the next table where a couple were discussing their son's addiction to eating hair. David yammered on about his plot, which Iona never managed to retain. Did it involve Russia? The play was a satire of some kind. His expression was open, alive. Passionate. The passion was just. Unrivaled.

8:09 a.m.

—I need a play, Chris, you there?

—Yup, you need a play.

—For Dom and me... Diane straightens the curly cord of the handset... —Off-Broadway, or off-off but nothing opaque or gross, nothing with body fluids or—

—Let me find...

—I need like a...

—A wonderful night out, a date night.

—Yes.

—An interaction with art.

—Exactly, thank you.

—You spoke to Dom?

—Not yet.

—Okay, but he did sound...

—Calling as soon as we hang up.

—Excellent. One other thing. I've just had an email from HR. Giselle Desplat is also out sick.

—That can't be right.

—Afraid so.

—Why would Giselle go to some staff reception?

—I'm told there was a special connection with Dr. Sericko.

Diane can feel the tension in her neck. Imagines the vertical muscles tightening into steel cables. One afternoon her former Pilates teacher studied Diane as she walked into his studio. "To banish stress," he said, "imagine exhaling through your anus." He had a West Indian accent and the way he pronounced *anus* was oddly arousing.

—Still there, Diane?

—Prep Katherine Tambling to handle Anton Spitz. At this point it really is simply a case of the most inordinate sucking up. Don't put it in those words.

—I can be honest. We knew each other at Harvard before she dropped out.

Because she's said it often Diane doesn't say, Or college. You can always say college. School, university, there are lots of ways.

—Hold on, I'm coming in.

Diane hangs up.

A soft knock on the door and Chris edges into the room.

—Stop creeping around. You make people nervous.

—We've just had a request—

—No. Whatever it is, no.

—from the digital director at *Vanity Fair*. They'd love a super short interview—

—What, today?

—Yes, but it's total fluff. Chit-chat about the exhibit, Anton's designs, New American blah blah, you'll have to fudge that you're wearing Lyle Kipsie. Change the subject if it comes up.

—Who's the reporter?

—Host, they're called hosts not, uh... Chris checks his phone...
—Julia Saban.

—You did a, you know, a background check?

—She's fairly well known. Interviews pop stars, socialites, designers. Visual artists, if they're attractive. Julia Saban is also the author... swiping... —Of a book called... scrolling... —*This Bitch.*

—I beg your pardon?

—*This Bitch.* It was a memoir, quite popular. Reappropriating, maybe, the term?

—Do we even have, I mean, when, really, Chris?

—Okay, I found fifteen minutes this afternoon, possibly twenty. Depending how quickly we ditch the Ambassador. We'd do it in Piquette, the crew sets up beforehand, you waltz in, done. In and out.

—And makeup or whatever?

—They'll have a P.A. standing by with powder and a hairbrush.

—Sounds rushed.

—Could it be useful publicity maybe, during this time?

—During what time?

A slow blink. Chris appears to gauge the wisdom of further explication.

—I swear if you say optics right now—

—I'm not saying anything... he goes to the door... —One last thing. The call with Shay Pallot.

—Not on Gala Day, dear god, not today.

—Okay, but it's been nearly a week since the vote. Feels like there's a real risk of her hearing the news from someone else... he turns to go... —Anyway, give it a think... Chris disappears and the door latches into place.

Leaning back in her chair Diane scans the bookcase. Tries to picture telling Shay.

8:14 a.m.

—Conrad Bellefont, the party planner or, uh, *gala designer*, Bellefont, B-E-L-L-E, has arrived along with about thirty that's three oh, workers to install the remainder of this evening's decor... Shay switches to autopilot, letting her mouth run one way while her mind goes another, replaying this morning's conversation with Henry Joles, general counsel. Sizing him up in her head, could this be the man for Malcolm?... —The ten of you will be working as security escorts for Bellefont's crew, as outlined by Dispatch... because Tasha has given up. Yes, Tash has fed and provided for her kids, but pushed them? Inspired them? Insisted on goals and progress? Not by half. Instead Auntie Shay's been right there with warnings and advice, tickets to exhibits and help with applications. Oh, Shay's made a downright nuisance of herself, barging in twenty-four/seven... —I would like to stress that *no one* on Conrad's crew goes anywhere without an escort, understand? Can I see some nods?... and Tasha's kids have mostly ignored her, gone their own way with jobs they're too good for, shiftless boyfriends, zero ambition and a vexing apathy they call chilling out. And that's fine for Tash's other kids but not Malcolm, saying as she thinks all this... —Yes, it's not ideal that the museum is remaining open during gala prep. I'm sure we've all thoroughly discussed the challenges it adds to our work. Workers carrying tools that could harm the artwork, a scissor-lift in the middle of the Great Hall... chilling out is not acceptable in the case of Malcolm, who was solving basic mathematics at the age of three and not many years later corrected his auntie's use of the word hyperbolic. So before Shay's mind turns to jelly she needs to find her nephew a mentor... —But I'm confident we can tackle these challenges with a smile and a positive attitude... someone to push Malc, steer him, guide him... —Spit out the gum, Blair, I can see your jaw moving... and that man is Henry Joles

—Can I ask?

Holding up a finger to cut off Donté, a kid who's always got a question... —Attitude is key. Some of you look downright depressed. Guests shouldn't be worrying over your emotional health... Shay turns to her vibrating phone, presses ACCEPT... —Keisha, what is it?

8:18 a.m.

—Got a gentleman here, says it's his first day, came in the wrong entrance.

Phone tucked between ear and shoulder, the security guard flips Benjamin's temporary pass over and over, giving it an unconvinced squint every second or third revolution.

—Yes, I do, Chief, right here, it says Benjamin Riplin.

—Rippen. It's Rippen, not Riplin.

The guard ignores him. Over her shoulder the moon is still visible, pale and half-hidden behind a fattening contrail. Unseasonably warm, is the prediction. He leans back to read the vinyl banner stretched across the Museum's facade: *One Hundred and Fifty Years of the Bohemian: Outsiders Looking In.* This actually hurts his neck, so he stops and faces the other direction where a bored-looking man in a green jumpsuit power-washes a marble bench, sending a fine mist into the air.

It was Professor Thackeray's idea that Benjamin should secure a steady job rather than move to Los Angeles and endure the suicidal hair tearing that goes hand in hand with trying to make movies. Benjamin had a gift for criticism, he said, and was better suited to a career in academia. Thackeray stated his opinion kindly and because they were drinking together, as friends might, Benjamin assumed a candor he may not have accorded the old man had they met in his university office with the musty carpet and the rising damp.

—Yes, Chief, I will... the guard sounds despondent.

Down the block two men, hairy in different ways, pile books onto a long folding table. Next to the coffee truck a caricature artist sets down a drawing pad to fight apart the legs of an easel. A dog trots past, head erect, owner bent over her phone.

Sipping his gimlet, Thackeray admitted he found Benjamin's thesis derivative. The film was supposed to be an homage, a winking joke, the way Godard played with gangster movies in *Breathless*. But Benjamin's effort didn't read as winking or playful, it read as amateurish, trite and imitative. It looked as if he didn't have a single idea of his own, which Benjamin wasn't entirely sure he did. The book of interviews was also Thackeray's idea. He should really send the old man a gift or a thank-you note. Thackeray had done so much for Benjamin, as he did for all his students. Besides being warm and quaintly boosterish, Thackeray spent hours writing recommendations and letters of introduction. Benjamin aspires to this sort of easy generosity. He sees himself, in distant years, as a source of wisdom for a younger generation. Gentle encouragement in a mohair cardigan. Tea and cookies, a small glass of sherry, though he is now actively mixing in the pedagogic classics, *Goodbye, Mr. Chips* or *The Browning Version* or

—Okay, Mr. Riplin.

He turns around.

The security guard holds out his pass, staring at a point in the distance above Benjamin's shoulder... —Go ahead.

—I hope I... taking the pass... —Didn't make things difficult for you.

—Tomorrow... she says, bored by his hopes... —Come in by the loading dock. Employee entrance. Find a map... the guard pushes open the heavy door and waves him in.

8:23 a.m.

Henry had already waited for the funicular well past the point of patience, tamping down his temper when the doors took their time sliding apart. Now he's inside the little carriage, and there's a sticky hesitation in its descent, as if the thing might suddenly stop halfway down, throw open its doors and jettison its occupant. Usually Henry waits for the elevator as a matter of principle. He'd fought against the funicular, which he'd found desperately unserious. The Globe was enough cutting-edge architecture for one Gothic Revival building, he felt. The point had been made. But Diane wanted a legacy.

Henry texts Chris to get the damn thing fixed. He'd prefer to skip some sort of public belly flop. It would be such a vulgar way to die.

8:24 a.m.

Benjamin pulls on his backpack as he walks into the Great Hall. The familiar round wooden information desk has disappeared. The floor where it usually stands is covered with a patchwork of brown kraft paper fixed to the marble with blue painter's tape. In the center of this khaki island, a large wire armature is in the process of being assembled by several identically furious men in black polo shirts.

Lights in the gift shop flicker on.

Through an arched doorway lies the sculpture court and, above it, the Globe. The bottom curve of the restaurant forms a terrifying glass roof over the Greek marbles. Benjamin has never spent more time in the sculpture court than the minute it takes to cross the room. His trust issues include structural engineers and architects. Sculpture's so facile, he used to say, hustling Caroline past the gods.

Before moving to Ohio they used to visit the Museum on rainy weekends when their cozy apartment became a suffocating prison. Caroline had studied the Dutch Masters and Benjamin liked the way she was around these paintings, faraway and unreachable, tugging at her hair, communing silently with Claesz or Ruisdael, her expression one of hopeful fraternity. That there were parts of Caro he still didn't know or couldn't grasp was appealing. Benjamin didn't have all of her, he couldn't. Their last visit came only about a month before they broke up. A photography show, was it Winogrand? He remembers buying an obscenely priced tostada from the café and spilling crema on his pants. On the subway back to Brooklyn they fought about color.

As Benjamin heads toward Human Resources, he stops to watch the funicular carriage gliding down the track.

8:27 a.m.

Henry has a flash of recognition. As if this kid in a cheap windbreaker is an apparition of himself at thirty, lurching around with a moony smile and an air of apology, impatient to be noticed and eager to be overlooked.

The young man disappears toward the bank of elevators.

If only his father had provided more guidance. Seymour's legacy was a spirit of confrontation, a practice Henry passed down to his older kids. Understandably, both fled to Los Angeles the minute they graduated high school. Until the diagnosis, things weren't much better with the second batch of kids. But now he's making a serious effort. Slapping together sandwiches, getting down on his arthritic knees to play with trains. Tripling the doting and affection. He wants to spoil Echo and Noah, while at the same time cram a lifetime of wisdom into the heads of two children not yet six. Coating the education with rigorous fun, like packing bread around a heartworm pill.

The funicular arrives at the docking station.

Candytown, for example. Henry had seen the place advertised on the subway as a candy-lover's utopian dream. It was not. It was a diabetic hellhole. A tribute to unrepentant greed. Room after room crowded with pint-sized autocrats. What overpowering force had sucked him into this frightful sugardome? Guilt, remorse, a fear of being forgotten.

The carriage doors stay shut. Henry presses OPEN several times with varying pressure.

Olive and the kids stood bunched on the threshold as toddlers galloped past screeching like polecats. Henry ignored his wife's stricken face, certain of his actions. He led Noah and Echo past stacks of cookies, a waterfall of chocolate and bins of sugared fish. A gang of depleted nannies banked against the walls spoke darkly into cell phones. As Henry shoved the family into an empty booth, a man with an accordion squeezed out a menacing hurdy-gurdy. Fun would be had! A giant rabbit wandered past handing out lollipops.

Finally the doors open and Henry climbs out of the funicular carriage, happy his many neuroses don't include claustrophobia. He heads to South Asian to check on the tech's progress.

Because Olive keeps a sugar-free home, the limitless dessert was eyed with suspicion. Noah bit his fingertips. Echo's saucer held a single vanilla wafer. Outraged by his daughter's temperance, her possibly genetic reluctance to throw caution to the wind, Henry leapt from the booth, plunging into a jungle of pudding and doughnuts. He spotted a waitress inexplicably got up as an Alpine miss and pointed to his family, ordering a round of gargantuan sundaes, pictures of which were plastered on the sides of every city bus. He returned to the table short of breath but triumphant, carrying four plates piled high with goodies. In the future his children would search for a loving memory of their father and by god he was here to provide it.

As Noah and Echo dived in, Henry noticed a dog outside the window leashed to a bike rack panting in the heat and thought about bringing the pup a bowl of sherbet. His empathy could not be contained. Olive placed her cool hand on top of his, which sweltered on the table like a piece of liver left in the sun. She remained ignorant of the reason for this crackpot behavior, his spending sprees and late-night cheese attacks, the erratic swings from self-pitying defeatism to loopy elation. Henry was pausing long enough to plot his next move but at his wife's touch he felt a rush of calm. He looked down at her hand then into her eyes, which were compassionate but questioning. Desperation coursed through his body and Henry understood he wasn't here for the children. What was he doing in this monument to unappeasable desire? He was dying. Nothing could save him, not even this.

A lump of chocolate hardened on Noah's forehead. Echo, her cheeks bulging, her eyes roving, appeared to be on the brink of nervous collapse. Without a word Henry passed his credit card to the waitress in the Swiss-laced bodice. He smiled at his beautiful young wife. He thought he would return to her someday, via Ouija, to apologize.

8:34 a.m.

The stagiare from West is a lifeless halfwit by the name of Caleigh. Nikolic has just finished explaining the granola prep to her when the curator from Costume shows up. She has a new unflattering haircut.

—Otto around?

—In the back... he turns back to Caleigh... —All clear?

Caleigh nods and Niko watches her walk away, nervous about the yawn she stifled during his drizzle demonstration.

—Yum... Katherine snitches a piece of sweet potato off a sheet pan and pops it in her mouth.

—That's raw.

—Got it, yup... spitting potato into her hand.

Niko points to a garbage can for her chewed food. Despite being hot, or semi-hot now, with her new military hair, there's a quality to Katherine that suggests impending calamity, as if the minute your back is turned some clumsy business is going to unfold that results in a shard of glass hurtling through the air to pierce your carotid artery.

—Don't know why I thought that'd be cooked.

—No worries. A lot going on... a sleeve across his brow, working hard, maybe you should leave.

But she's not here for Niko. And Katherine's lopsided smile means that Otto must be walking up behind him. Black, taciturn, handsome, unflappable. Otto dispenses warmth sparingly, at least to Nikolic who has gone over their interactions again and again for the possibility he has at one point said something racist.

—Katherine, what's up?

—Came to bug you.

—Nice... Otto sets down a tub of yellow onions... —Espresso?

—Please. Oh, you have a... Katherine strokes Otto's cheek. It's one of her games, finding reasons to touch him... —Can you make it a double?

—How's the hunt coming?... Otto steps around the corner to the Pavoni.

—That's on hold for a while... politely, to include Nikolic... —I was looking to buy a yurt out in California.

—What's a yurt?... testily chopping celery.

—Come on, man, you know what a yurt is.

—It's not a dumb question... Katherine worms around him to take her espresso from Otto... —A yurt is a, like, circular tent only it has a frame so it's, basically it's permanent.

—Only crazy people get them.

—Ha, ha, actually... she glances at Otto appreciatively... —That's probably true.

Nikolic feels them watching him hack off the end of a celery stalk.

—Anyway... Katherine takes a sip of espresso... —Turns out my mom won't let me take the dog. I thought she hated the dog but...

—You need a dog to live in a yurt?

—Alone in the desert? Yeah, I do. Though he's not exactly fierce.

—Doodle?

—Lab mix. Butt like a table. My dad found him in a junkyard... Katherine holds the little cup with her pinkie crooked... —I don't want to call out my mom as passive-aggressive, but she named him Beagle. Picture what that could do to a dog's self-esteem.

—Mom sounds like a piece of work... Otto wipes his cutting board.

—God, yeah. Read *Rosemary's Baby* when she was pregnant with me.

—Where the lady's growing a devil inside her?

—That's the one.

Listening to this conversation is like bearing witness to an experiment in normalcy. As if Niko's standing behind a two-way mirror holding a clipboard, ready to interrogate the accepted compact, the one where people are inclined to chat warmly to each other with full eye contact and darting touches. When it's not horrifying it's fascinating, this idea of human connection. What a gorgeous concept. Except when it's frightening and untenable, maddening and corrosive. After living in New York for nearly a year Nikolic has only one person he can truly call a friend. A full-kit wanker from Scottsdale he met during the optimistic three weeks he played pick-up soccer in McCarren Park. Once a month he and Tim meet in a Midtown sports bar to watch Man City and drink beer in silence, Tim quietly confident in his mortifying regalia. At some point during the second half Tim's scarf tassels will end up in the ranch and Niko will watch out of the corner of his eye as Tim tipsily rinses them in his water glass.

—Now she's got a problem with raisins... Katherine tells Otto...
—*Raisins*.

—I got a brother, when he was a kid, used to stick things up his nose... Otto slices a shallot with that annoying delicacy of his... —Pills, buttons, a little padlock. Had to be careful where you put shit. Went to the ER like eight times.

It was the reason Nikolic left Philadelphia. It got too hard, pretending to be normal.

—Okay, how about this, my sister... Katherine, laughing preemptively... —Used to be in a cult.

Look how good they are at being human! Jokes and back-and-forthing like two ordinary thirtyish young folks up on the modes and conventions and whatever from the internet, the secret language of those in the know, crafty with their slang and slippery humor.

—Can't compete with a cult... Otto grabs vinegar from the shelf above his station... —But my sister did start a lifestyle blog.

—Oh my god, I'm sorry for your loss.

—Right?

—You two should get a room.

Katherine and Otto turn to stare. Didn't mean to say it out loud. Nikolic pulls the side towel off his shoulder and uses it to clean his knife, leaning in to examine the blade. No one asked for Niko's anecdotes: his adolescent scrapes and dustups with the cops, a brief but rewarding relationship with LSD. Flooding the kitchen during Cuisines of the Americas. Working the line in a Philadelphia turn-and-burn. Niko could compete. If he chose to. But those stories no longer belong to him.

The silence grows uneasier and expands until it seems to blanket the entire kitchen. Nikolic sets down his knife and walks away, convinced the two of them are shaking their heads in pity or disbelief. He elbows past Armando, taking up too much space as always, and steps inside the walk-in. The arctic air feels cold enough to numb his shame. But it won't.

He could tell Katherine and Otto the story he recounts in the shower every morning. That would get their attention. Because the chokehold he placed on reliving the past, something he pictures as a metal vise squeezing his brain, is useless against his worst memory. It always finds its way, arriving every morning as Niko yanks the shower curtain closed and ducks to adjust the temperature. After expressing gratitude for the impulse that made him stop around noon and buy flowers for Sandrine, the sequence arrives. Short flashes: his broken shoelace, the dripping faucet, a takeout menu lying in the street, bird shit spattered on the windscreen. Back to Sandrine, walking in and seeing the lilies, her face breaking into a huge smile. It was not an uncomplicated smile, they were trying to stick to a budget. Annoyed but pleased, Sandrine stooped to the flowers, closing her eyes, smiling, inhaling. There she is, over and over, stooping, breathing. They were out of milk, a screen needed fixing. He leaned against the ancient stove, adoring the crown of her head, the zigzag of her part. Eminem came on the radio, a classic, *there's vomit on his sweater already* and Sandrine stretched across the table to turn up the volume, it was nearly ninety, overcast with a gentle breeze. Down the street, Boltkiss started up his motorcycle. A dog barked. Niko ate mortadella on a hotdog roll as he jogged to the car, sticking the sandwich in his mouth so he could use both hands to unlock the door. He lifted his face to the sun, drove to buy a shoelace, there was bird shit on the windscreen, he filled her car with gas, *never let it go*, honked at a bike, answered his cell phone when it rang, drove to the hospital, and watched her die.

If you want to swap stories, and all.

8:45 a.m.

—Patrick Stewart... Diane repeats.

—Exactly. Imagine that gorgeous voice coming through your headphones.

—But why Patrick Stewart?

—From *Star Trek*.

—I know who he is, Jakob, I'm not... staring at Jakob's hair, newly styled, with a horsey forelock he's bleached bone white... —I'm asking how it's different from one of my lectures.

—Well, it's Patrick Stewart... Chris says helpfully.

—Not only that, but Sir Patrick's commentary... pausing to swipe his hair, Jakob flashes a fingerless glove made of black netting... —Is from the perspective of the art.

Diane remains silent. It feels unsafe to reply to such a concept.

—As if the artwork is itself a character. Embodying say the, uh, psyche of a sculpture or—

—I don't think so... smiling kindly to soften the rejection... —Thank you, Jakob.

—Aren't you interested in what a mummy might say? As interpreted by one of the world's greatest living actors?

—Let's move on... Chris nods... —Hear what else you have.

Jakob picks up the stack of index cards on which he's written his ideas for tech integration in a looping illegible cursive. He has an affinity for props, Jakob, with his oddly tapered head and gratuitous *k* spelling, as well as a love of the dramatic gesture. With a flourish of black netting he drops Patrick Stewart into the wastepaper basket, reads the next card and wordlessly moves it to the bottom of his pile.

Chris coughs, looking pointedly at his watch which he appears to wear solely for this purpose.

—Okay, instead of Patrick Stewart in your headphones, what about two critics in a heated discussion—

—Heated, like, fighting?

—Dialoguing... Jakob stares at Chris, daring him.

—I don't know. Sounds negative.

—First, it's a conversation more than an argument, okay, Chris? Second, it demonstrates the passion people have for art and... Jakob stops, as if it's pointless to make his case to such provincials and spins the index card into the garbage.

If Zedekiah Willington walks away without handing over a fat check, Diane will be, in common parlance, completely fucked. But it would be imprudent to mention offhandedly that her job rests upon Digital coming up with a jaw-dropping idea. That kind of stress could be too much for Jakob who under muddy circumstances once shattered a three-hole punch.

—Here's a fun one.

—Great... she tries to look open to fun.

—Kids'll love this. You scan a QR code next to a painting and it triggers a hologram of the artist. Van Gogh putting the finishing touches to a haystack or—

—Sawing off his ear?

—No, Chris. I said it's for kids, didn't I? Forget Van Gogh, picture Caravaggio—

—Stabbing a guy?

—Oh my god, painting. Painters painting... Jakob's voice travels up an octave.

—Fascinating. One thought... in a placating tone... —Wondering how a hologram sheds light, figuratively—

—It's not about shedding light, Diane.

—No?... mildly.

—The app's designed for a generation that doesn't trust nondynamic images.

She glances at Chris. A canyon of despair opens in front of her.

Jakob rips the card in half and lets the pieces flutter into the trash can. While it's true that Diane has continually positioned herself as tech-friendly in order to draw a distinction between herself and her predecessor, she is, in fact, exactly as old-fashioned as Tiz Sericko in sharing the frumpish belief that visitors to the Museum should actually look at the art. During her first few weeks as director Diane even suggested outlawing photos altogether, but the curators rebelled. Guests who snap pictures move through a museum twice as fast as those who stop to look, and nobody wanted a logjam.

—Soundscapes.

—I'm listening... but privately she continues to question whether technology has to permeate every goddamn atom of today's culture or if anything can be left in peace.

—Okay, you're walking through the galleries, making your way toward a piece of Native American art... Jakob pantomimes a stroll, complete with swinging arms... —Let's say it's a totem sculpture, now through your headphones you're going to start hearing drums, chanting, the sound of—

—Genocide?

—Chris!... she whips around.

—Sorry, sorry. Not sure why I said that.

—Jakob, please continue.

—Uh... fingertips to his chest, Jakob shakes his head as if to clear the image... —A different example might be, for example, Afghan prayer mats. As a guest approaches, he or she might hear the call to prayer or—

—Okay!... boring her eyes into Chris, warning him... —We get the idea. A contextualized audio track. Certainly need to marinate on it a bit to really get a sense of, what else do you have for us?

Flipping through his index cards... —This one's actually my favorite... Jakob glances up with contrived cheer... —An app called *Soooth*. Three o's. Made for visitors who feel aggressed by our more, uh, difficult pieces of art.

—Difficult? We have difficult art?

—No... Chris, unequivocally... —We do not.

—I'm thinking about the expansion—

—It's on hold.

—No contemporary art?

—That's not to be repeated.

—On hold for how long?

—I said... Chris, evilly... —That's not to be repeated.

—It's okay, he heard. Jakob, please continue.

—What about some of our Asian sculpture? I would say, not only challenging, but antagonistic, even.

—I'm not going to touch, you know, Jakob, maybe don't repeat that. Leaving out the specifics, tell us what the thing does.

—Difficult or not, people, some people, get nervous when faced with art. They know they're supposed to feel something, but what? *Soooth* sends out the Solfeggio frequency for anxiety relief. 396 hertz.

—It's like a noise?

—A vibration, Diane.

She glances at Chris for help.

—Prefer humans? Choose a monologue. Very calming. Reminding you there's no right way to approach art.

—Jakob.

—The actress who recorded it for us happens to be a Zen practitioner. A voice like honey, her cadence—

—Stop, please.

—I don't believe this... Jakob drops his index cards onto Diane's desk from a height so they scatter in an irritatingly rehearsed waterfall... —I have to say... he stops, lips moving as if he's been advised to count to ten before speaking his mind... —I find your opposition to these ideas incredibly, I mean, tell me what you want. Really, tell me, I'm all ears.

—I feel like we'll know it when we see it... looking to Chris.

—We'll know it when we see it, Jakob.

—Okay, but in the meantime, I'm, whatever it's called, twisting in the wind—

—Pissing.

—What?

—Pissing in the wind.

—No, not pissing. Is it pissing?

—Yes. Twisting means something else.

—What about this?... Chris holds up the virtual reality headset Jakob placed on her desk when he arrived... —Does this work?

—Of course it works, Chris, I mean. Of course it does. That's a prototype for next year's Bosch show.

Diane takes the headset from Chris... —And Jakob, you're coming along this evening? To meet Silicon Valley?

—Yes. Five thirty. I really don't know what the point is since you don't seem to like anything I, no, around your head, the strap goes... Jakob reaches out, fastening it around her head, wafting a pleasant soapy scent... —This is a journey through *The Garden of Earthly Delights*. We've only finished mapping Paradise and Hell so it's still a work in—

—Too tight.

—progress... Jakob loosens the strap... —Great thing about VR of course is the additional revenue from headset rentals, how's that?

—Good, good. I really, I need glasses, Chris—

—You keep cancelling appointments.

—Paradise, Diane, or Hell?

—Hell, please.

—Anything?

—Loading Hell.

—Give it a sec.

—It's very dark... and then. Oh. My. God.

She's landed in the middle of Bosch's sooty hellscape. A place of smoking earth, pyres, cragged black towers sticking up like burned trees. Flames dart from a pit as Diane swoops down, stomach lurching with vertigo, dropping into the pit alongside a flock of naked bodies. Before she disappears completely, she's suddenly zooming up again, narrowly escaping a huge knife emerging from a pair of ears, chopping away. Under the blade she goes, crowded on all sides by green creatures, ladders and parodies of crucifixion. In spite of her aversion to technology, she has to admit this is truly astonishing. This she can show to Zedekiah Willington. This will prove the Museum is a living, adaptive organism.

—How is it?

—I can't believe it, Jakob. I mean, I am *immersed*.

In front of her is the figure that's half-tree, half-man, with boats for shoes. His hat is topped with a demented pink blob, a sort of bagpipes scrotum. The figure's torso is a tavern, white and jagged like an eggshell.

—Where are you?

—The tree man.

Her favorite detail of Bosch's painting is the expression of resignation on the tree-man's face as he turns to observe sharp branches shooting off his arm and harpooning his stomach. How human it is that from time to time, or maybe even always, we feel powerless to stop some private agony we've cooked up and with a kind of fascinated disengagement sit back and watch as we stab ourselves repeatedly in the abdomen.

—Look to your left, Diane.

—I've got the bird-man with a jug on his head eating a naked body.

—He poops them out through a hole in his chair... Jakob tells Chris.

Another man, hovering over a pit shitting coins and next to him, a dead woman, her face reflected in the ass of a demon. Incredible that the twenty-first century lets you nestle up to wretches like this, watching from the sidelines as they vomit and bleed... —It's so horrible, Jakob. It's perfect.

—Finally. Thank you for saying that. I appreciate it.

Diane twists her head to take in the view... —So many ladders.

—Feels like you're right there, don't you think?

—God, yes... in front of her a pig in a nun's habit nuzzles a naked man... —I one hundred percent believe I am touring Hell.

8:58 a.m.

The heat arrives in a whoosh, spreading across her chest and up her neck, prickling her skin with sweat. She ducks into her desk drawer for tissues. Presses a handful against her face. It won't last a minute. Inhale for a count of ten.

Still trying to forget the lion statue from this morning. No doubt it's forged. But she'll keep her mouth shut. The Museum must know the marble's a fake and installed it for a reason.

—Excuse me, Chief?

—Mm... bringing down the wad of tissues. Denis is standing in front of her desk. This kid. Not a manager but all swagger. Aching for a promotion... —What is it?

—I noticed on the monitor, light's out in that small gallery between, I don't know, it's camera fourteen. Want me to call Peter?

—No. Stay here. Switch your walkie to three.

—Yes, Chief... excited to be useful.

And Shay grabs a set of keys from her desk drawer, pushes back from the desk, steps around a box full of folders she's midway through refiling, goes out of her office, through the main room containing the banks of monitors, checking, yes, Denis is right, no lights in Drawings gallery 17A. She nods hello to Bogdan and Trey, and slips out the door.

9:00 a.m.

—Shay! Hey... ostentatiously raising the paper cup as she sees Shay coming out of HQ... —Just bringing you coffee. Stopped by the shitty café on my way in.

—Well, look at that, a giant one, huh?... Shay pulls the door to Security closed behind her.

—Yeah, needed a jolt this morning because... because I had tequila for breakfast... —Anyway, is it too big?... Iona hands over the massive mocha.

—No, no... Shay prises the lid off the cup to release some steam... —Amar, that kid's gonna burn us all to death. Thank you... with a toast of her cup she heads toward the stairwell.

Iona follows... —So, I thought you probably would've called me if you had any leads.

—Still no leads.

—I wish there were a way.

—There isn't... Shay pushes the crash bar and backs into the stairwell, holding the door open for Iona... —I can't cross-examine your intern, not without evidence.

—Yesterday we had this conference with senior staff, *senior* staff, and in the middle of the meeting the kid pulls out a tuna fish sandwich... following Shay up the stairs... —Tuna fish! At ten in the morning. Talk about hostile. I'm not suggesting it's proof of anything. Where are we going?

—Drawings... Shay opens the door on the second-floor hallway... —Bulb's out again. Happens every three weeks. Takes an hour to get Facilities up here... through a gallery of prints and around a corner... —Can you... Shay hands over her coffee, crosses to unlock a hidden door. She wrestles a stepladder out of the closet, a small cardboard box tucked under her arm.

—Every afternoon I take off my rings, I don't know, my hands swell, maybe my lunch is too salty... Iona ducks to avoid the ladder... —I love that Chinese place, is it MSG that swells, anyway, for the last nine years my rings are always right there on my workbench when I get back from the ladies'. Until, what, Monday?... following Shay with the stepladder balanced on her shoulder... —Coincidentally the intern started last month.

—Not like I can strip search him.

—Too late for that!... trying for a joke.

—Even if it wasn't... Shay turns into Drawings 17a... —You know how it is with interns. Kid's dad's gonna be some kind of bigshot.

Iona stops in the doorway. Drawings 17a is the smallest gallery in the museum and Iona's favorite. Used for special exhibits, the space is low-ceilinged and snugly dim to protect paper several centuries old. Often empty, it's a great place to avoid people or try to dodge your own destructive thoughts. Gaze at a couple of ancient objects. Take comfort in their endurance. Today the space is dimmer than usual. Above the display cabinets only one of the three recessed bulbs is working.

Shay switches off the lights and sets the box carefully on the wooden edge of the cabinet.

—How do I tell David I lost both my wedding and engagement rings? He'll assume it has some hidden meaning.

—Does it?

—Hwah... Iona, laughing not entirely authentically as she lifts her cup to her mouth... —Right?

Shay positions the stepladder under a light, takes the mocha from Iona, sips it, nods, hands back the cup. There's a finality to her actions, as if she's signing off on the topic of stolen rings.

Iona watches Shay take a bulb from the box and climb the ladder. They became friendly during Iona's brief flirtation with lunchtime Zumba. The employee gym on -2 was a grim affair. A rank airless room, an instructor who clearly fancied herself made for a more devoted group. But Shay was a marvel. Her commitment to mastering the reggaeton pump was inspiring to Iona who had stubborn ligaments, a semi-fused ankle and could never recall more than two steps of any combination. Watching this formidable woman stomping through a merengue routine reminded Iona of the time she walked in on her grandmother parked in front of a rotary fan eating a popsicle in her Sunday slip. It gladdened the heart to see someone so imposing or, in the case of her grandmother, fearsome and splenetic, relishing life's physical pleasures. Growing up without religion makes you vigilant for signs of the spiritual.

Iona sticks her tongue into the oval slot of the plastic lid. This hurts and she quickly stops.

From the top of the ladder, Shay glances down at her... —Your friend Tiz Sericko had his employee send-off last night. Thought you'd be there.

—Yeah, I mixed up the dates. I was so mad.

—Don't be. Bunch of folks went and got food poisoning... Shay comes down from the ladder with the bulb, takes her coffee from Iona, swigs it, and hands it back... —Shrimp, they're saying.

—The museum served bad shrimp?

—Looks like it... positioning the ladder under the second light.

—That's terrible. Poor Tiz... accidentally sipping Shay's mocha, nearly gagging from the sweetness.

With swift and capable hands, Shay's sliding the dead bulb into the box, taking out a new one, returning to the ladder. And staring up, a coffee cup in each hand, Iona is a child again, standing by with a wrench as her crooked father lies under a car and reports the workings of a combustion engine.

—You seen this new lion marble they got outside Purdue?

—New? Are you sure? I was up there a couple of days ago.

—Installed last night... climbing down from the ladder... —So I was told... Shay switches on the lights.

—But Ian Pickmeyer's in Italy. He gives the go-ahead on new, that's very weird.

—Big donor, insisted, I guess... taking her mocha from Iona, sipping it with evident delight and handing the cup back to slam the ladder closed.

—Do you know who? Which donor?

—No. Three names. Martin maybe... Shay sets the ladder against her shoulder, picks up the box of bulbs, and walks away.

Still toting their coffees Iona walks directly behind the older woman as if by literally following in Shay's footsteps she'll become more assertive. Direct. Sail through life unmoved by the opinions of others. But nothing seems to work. She's read the books. Put her thoughts in writing. Recognized that she needs to change. Diagnosed herself as mulish, regretful, tetchy. Also, resistant to change. In July, at the annual Goldman barbecue, one of David's new colleagues asked him if his wife was deaf.

She catches up to Shay who is speeding through Prints... —How do you get a person to confess?

—This intern of yours?

—Anyone.

—Depends... Shay returns the ladder to the hidden closet and shuts the door, propping the box of bulbs under her arm.

—Back in March, my husband disappeared for three weeks. Never told me what he did or where he went.

—Huh... accepting the enormous cup.

—How do I find out?

—Try asking?

Iona shakes her head. It's impossible to explain.

—Sounds like you're playing a game of chicken.

—Can I trap him into confessing? You must have advice, like interrogation techniques.

Shay looks at her with kind if not slightly worried eyes... —Let me think about it... opening the stairwell door... —Going this way?

—Uh-huh, you know, I was thinking last night, wondering whether you'd consider running those self-defense classes again, the ones you taught last fall.

—You feeling, what, uh, vulnerable?

—No, why, I mean I live in Brooklyn Heights, am I going to get attacked by a, like a, I mean, the neighborhood is full of kids but I enjoyed those classes, Shay, I really did... jogging down the stairs behind her, voice ringing in the hollow space... —I used to go home afterwards and practice hammer strikes. David put a pull-up bar in the pantry doorway for me but it all ended at Christmas. I, my will for it evaporated. I don't even know where the pull-up bar went... taking the weight of the stairwell door Shay holds open with her foot... —There's a confidence knowing that when you walk down a street you could just haul off and kick a guy if you wanted, like you'd know the best way to do it. Obviously I'm talking about a deserved kick... the door slams behind Iona as she follows Shay back toward Security... —I would never randomly kick someone, to be clear.

—Classes had to stop.

—Who said?... she watches Shay looking down the hallway toward the open door of the film department.

—Legal. Zumba is one thing but when employees are throwing each other across the room, that's another thing altogether. Liability.

9:11 a.m.

Benjamin closes the door on the hallway conversation about liability. Quietly, so as not to be seen making a comment about loud women. He drops his bag on the floor, sets his New Employee packet on the desk. Takes a look around.

His new office has hospital lighting, acoustic ceiling tiles and, in the far corner, a stained leather armchair that appears to have been picked up off the street. The air still holds the lingering skunk of his predecessor, Ward Bjarnsen, a seventy-year-old legend of cinema who retired after his cardiac event in June. Benjamin met him once, back in Columbus, when he came and gave a rather stock lecture on pre-code Hollywood. At the reception afterward, the old man chugged Pinot, interrupted nonstop and, as his lips grew chapped and stained, began to badger the women students, becoming an increasingly angry flirt.

The faint sound of music comes from down the hall. *A hip, hop, the hippie, the hippie.*

Small tumbleweeds of what look to be human hair coast across the office floor. Remain positive. Buy a scented candle. Figure out better lighting.

Benjamin opens the door to a large closet. On its floor, a sagging cardboard box holds a few old film schedules. He drags the box over to a bookcase that fills the back wall. Starts clearing the shelves, throwing away jars of paperclips, rippled magazines, and bent manila folders. In goes a broken stapler, a couple of chewed pencils, a stack of yellowed envelopes.

After a few minutes, Benjamin sits back to massage his jaw. This morning's energy shot was a mistake. He can't stop clenching his teeth and spasms of pain have started to radiate up to his eye sockets. The drink was an impulse buy when he stopped at a deli for water. So he could crush his first day. Stride the halls like an emancipating hero. Place the old guard on notice. But mostly he bought it because the liquid came in a tiny fire extinguisher and he's always been helpless in the face of an adorable object.

Benjamin stands up, shaking his head like a dog shaking off water. Reset. He jogs in place. Follows that with five air-squats and a few jumping jacks. Down to the floor. Cat cow cat cow. Back to work.

A drum-playing rabbit, a sweat-stained visor, old books. Half a row of DVDs loses its buttress and crashes to the floor. *Rain Man, Nashville, Hoosiers.* One has a bottle-blonde on the cover squeezed into a corset. At first he takes it for an unfamiliar Meg Ryan rom-com, failing to see the word *BETTINA!* spelled out in throttling red lipstick. *America's Hottest Slut!* the description almost certainly over-promises.

—Ward, you devil... Benjamin tosses the DVD into the box, chucking a dead plant on top and scattering dry dirt over Bettina's bosom, trying not to glance at the armchair's dark stains with renewed disgust.

Poor old man. There's better porn. Dig a little.

From down the hall, *I go by the code of doctor of the mix.* The last time he heard the song was like seven years ago.

9:14 a.m.

You see, I'm six foot one and I'm tons of fun

The phone was ringing when she returned to her office from coffee with Otto. This is how the conversation went.

—Katherine?

—Yes, Christopher.

—It's Chris now.

—Right, sorry, of course. Chris.

—I'm sorry to report that Giselle Desplat has food poisoning and will not be coming in today.

The news was so startling that Katherine decided to remain silent in case her hearing or ability to process information was malfunctioning. Although it was exactly like the kid she knew in college to act bizarrely formal and provide her with the surname of the person she's worked with every day for the last six years.

—Diane is asking where that leaves us vis-à-vis tonight. Is there any extra help you might need?

At which point Katherine came to, assuring Chris that no she didn't need help, that the work for the gala was mostly complete, all the exhibits in place, and that though Conrad will undoubtedly get pissy at some point because he believes the party is more important than the exhibition, that she Katherine stood ready to run interference between the party faction and the exhibition faction and did Christopher, Chris, that is, know that chances are Gryphon Vanderweghe won't even show his face today, not on Gala Day, that's how much he hates Conrad?

—I do know that, Katherine, obviously.

They spent little time together in college. Back when his name was Christopher, Chris was restless and defensive, lacked muscle tone and confidence and had the nervous habit of plucking at his shirt where it grazed his stomach. One weekend a group of them drove to his parents' summer house in Newport. It was too cold to swim so they lounged inside, dismissing the view. Most had wintered in places with better water. As freshmen they were obliged to discuss universal income, confessional poetry, network television. While the others laid siege to the liquor trolley, Katherine wandered upstairs for a snoop. A bathroom had a clawfoot tub and wallpaper printed with galloping horses. Soap dishes shaped like shells. The medicine cabinet held cough syrup and aspirin but no medication you could reasonably call fun. On her way downstairs Katherine glanced through an open door into the master bedroom. A California king was draped in ivory linen sheets that seemed overly romantic for an old married couple. Chintz curtains framed a view of the bay and a ceramic pitcher and basin stood on a side table as if indoor plumbing had yet to be invented. Hanging on the wall above a wingback chair was a painting of a dog, a German-haired pointer captured in a regal profile. There were no other pictures or paintings. No silver frames steepled on the bureau. The scene was mesmerizing. She stood there, spellbound, until Chris appeared, noiselessly, his marzipan skin flushed with anger. "This room is off-limits," he said, closing the door.

—And for God's sake don't mention his dog.

—Sorry, I didn't hear that last.

—Anton Spitz. Don't mention Maxie.

—No Maxie. I'm making a note.

—Diane has decided against speeches so we need you to lay it on thick. Everyone's there to celebrate Anton, that kind of thing. I take it you're wearing him?

—Nobody cares whether an associate curator of—

—You're *not* wearing Anton?

—Neither is Diane.

—That is, Katherine, that's a different matter.

—I don't wear clothes designed to be pretty.

—So it's what, a matter of principle?

—I ran it by Giselle a month ago, she was fine with it... Giselle in fact was anything but fine with it... —Are we good?

A noise that sounds like a sigh... —Diane, I know, has spoken to you about the author Clover DiNovi touring Costume—

—Yes, at, this... trying to pull up her calendar... —Afternoon at—

—Three o'clock.

—Three, I was about to say.

—Her book agent sits on our board of directors. He and his family have given the Museum a great deal of money.

—Got it. I will VIP the shit out of Clover DiNovi.

Silence.

—Chris, it's taken care of.

They signed off with goodbyes that were a touch frosty and hung up.

So hell yes she's going to work with the volume cranked. *Not a dime 'til I made it again Everybody go* Typing up an email to express her sympathies, slightly hurt that Giselle reported the news to Human Resources first. But Giselle's old-school like that. Girdled and immaculate. Beige foundation and chunky heels. Never cowed or tired or even slightly demoralized. It's difficult to picture Giselle lying in bed with the covers drawn to her chin. Or even with her shoes off.

Katherine's call goes straight to voicemail. She debates sending over soup or flowers but ends up sending a free online card. *Sorry You're Sick!* Three white kittens in tiny bathrobes.

Fuck.

Giselle's absence this evening means that instead of drinking irresponsibly, as planned, Katherine will be the one running interference and groveling at Anton's ostrich slip-ons.

She collapses into her desk chair. And returns to her letter.

I can hear you yelling to get back out there, stop lazing around eating half-priced crackers. But I can't, Mimi. Not until I figure out what I need to change. It's a good time to be alone, I thought the other night. My friends have vanished, married, or relocated upstate, to London or Los Angeles.

Turning up the music. *To the rhythm of the boogie, the beat*

And I've begun to enjoy solitude which I used to associate with punishment. Congrats, you're thinking, Katie's finally learned how to be alone, what can possibly be wrong with that? Well,

I don't mean to brag, I don't mean to boast

I'm pregnant.

9:22 a.m.

Like hot butter on your breakfast toast

Benjamin arrived late to the field of pornography, only coming to it three years ago, on a night in early October. Fall was a lovely time of year for Columbus. The leaves were magnificent: the reds rich and baroque, the yellows unnatural, almost fluorescent. He and Caroline had driven to one of those straw-strewn pumpkin patches that after Labor Day appear overnight in the Midwest. They browsed an impressive array of gourds, offered hay to a goat and gorged on cinnamon doughnuts, washing each one down with cups of hot cider. It was a scene from a romantic comedy and the two of them acted the part, holding hands and laughing at nothing. Diving in for a spontaneous kiss. At home they skipped dinner and Benjamin went to bed early, waking up an hour later with his bladder at the bursting point. Sloshing past the kitchen on the way to the bathroom he heard Caroline say, "A lot of men are afraid of sex," and knew she must be talking to Jill, her sad-sack friend back in New York. Jill thrashed from crisis to crisis and Caroline spent hours dissecting her latest catastrophic date or one-night stand, as well as trying to talk Jill out of sending flirty texts to men she actually loathed. "Is it the fault of feminism?" Caro asked. She was standing at the kitchen sink wearing a pair of headphones so she could use both hands to wash a pan. A pan she attacked with unnerving vigor. "Rough a woman up a little. Gimme some hair-yanking, filthy talk, a tiny spank now and then..." at this point Benjamin lost consciousness. Unseen in the doorway, he watched Caroline's pink gloves douse a cast-iron pan, his heart sinking along with it, everything sinking really, his organs liquifying. It was anyone's nightmare, hearing yourself described as a bumbling fornicator. So he was not a pioneer between the sheets. He did not cook up hot schemes. In college once a woman accused Benjamin of failing to strangle with any enthusiasm. "I can tell you're faking," she said, her eyes cold and mean. Evidently, only a colossal asshole balks at choking his girlfriend.

And so Benjamin turned to pornography.

It was not as easy as it sounds. He'd grown up with a mother who read Andrea Dworkin at the beach, dog-earing the pages and muttering *exactly* between applications of sunscreen. Before he was entirely sure what pornography was, Benjamin knew it subjugated and oppressed women. In college, guilt prevented him from dabbling much. Sure, he caught a little internet fuckery from time to time. His freshman year roommate enjoyed it openly. A biology major and rabid pervert, Talbot was also unexpectedly sensitive and never without a girlfriend or two. And maybe Benjamin should have called his old roommate for advice because the sites he landed on during his quest to become a better lover and hearty smacker offered scenarios that were banal, repetitive, overly gynecological and horribly lit. The flares and hotspots and sloppy framing drove him berserk, distracting him from the task at hand. None of the actors would commit to the narrative, delivering their lines in a bored monotone completely unlike how an actual teacher or handyman would speak. Even Tina Larson, whose performance in the eighth-grade production of *Our Town* was reviewed by her own mother as "stilted" and "wooden," was a young Garbo compared to the women in *Twelve Angry Virgins*. And Benjamin refused to go down the road of amateur porn, in case the FBI raided his apartment on a bad tip and revealed his search history to the local news before he could locate a lawyer and set things straight. So he settled for Amber and Bunny rolling around on a bed, licking and scissoring, from all evidence, giving each other pap smears. And he learned a few strategies. New ways to please and so forth.

It turned out to be exhilarating, life as a person who worked on himself. The evidence was in. Benjamin Rippen heard his girlfriend gripe about dull sex and got on the case. He set aside his own debilitating self-consciousness in order to slap her on the ass and name her a slut. Roughing her up. On occasion losing himself completely and screaming nonsense: *Schnell! Giddy-up! Harpoon time!*

Benjamin wipes his hands on his pants and rolls up his sleeves. Throws a dusty box of typewriter ribbon into the cardboard box.

Anyone could see he'd tried to make Caroline happy. How had he managed to fuck it all up? Will she give him another shot? Does he even want another shot? He wants to walk into the apartment as Caroline is pulling one of her cheesy dishes from the oven, sit at the table and look into her eyes as he eats, free from worries about dairy's assault on his sinuses or the dumplings starting to form at his waist. But at the same time he wants a brand-new person who hasn't memorized his flaws, who smells different and likes the same bands he does, because Caro's taste in music is UNKNOWN

Benjamin silences his phone. The calls never stop.

9:30 a.m.

—Please understand, I'm on your husband's side. I'm trying to protect him from what promises to be a legal nightmare... Henry pushes back his desk chair and props his foot on the open desk drawer... —He doesn't have to get up. Let him take the call in bed.

—It's a landline, Mr. Joles, and Kulap's finally asleep. He's been up all night, except for the hour he spent in a fetal position on the bathmat.

Henry has only met Kulap Stein a couple of times, when the curator has come upon him in the galleries that make up Indian Subcontinent. After lunch it's Henry's habit to walk among the massive Buddhas, digesting, kicking ideas around. Farting, but reverential.

—I'll ask him to return your call as soon as he wakes up.

—Promise I'll make it quick. Kulap can scuttle off to bed afterward. Silence.

—Mrs. Stein?

—It's Lauderbach.

—Sorry, Lauder—

—Fine. Since it doesn't appear as if you people are going to give up, I'll drag Kulap out of bed... the sound of the phone being set down, the wife moving away.

One Monday afternoon Henry was staring up at the downcast eyes of a sandstone Harihara when Kulap stopped on his way through the gallery and held out a bag of celery sticks. Henry took some celery and complimented Kulap on the sweater he was wearing. An argyle knit, the sweater had a fogeyish appeal but its colors were unusually vibrant and Kulap wore it with the conviction of a person in tune with the latest trends. They went on to speak of museum concerns, new stone heads, visitor attendance. An ivory Ganesh lent to San Francisco had been sent back damaged.

—Joles?

—Kulap, there you are. I'm sorry to hear you're feeling unwell. Any clue why I'm calling?

—I've been up all night with my head in the toilet, I barely know my own name.

—Then I'll get right to it. It's about our Dancing Shiva. About several objects in your department.

—Please, Henry, what's your point?

—Dancing Shiva. How did you acquire it?

A pause... —Dealer named Vauclain.

The name brings to mind a squirrelly little lip-licker in white tie. Meeting him at a fundraiser. Business cards swapped, a promise to put the guy in touch with Jack because Jack was looking to stock smaller pieces. Henry scrawls *Call Jack* on a Post-it.

—Was Shiva a recent acquisition? Any idea on the timeline?

—Last spring, April-ish. Listen, I need to get back, I need to—

—Your Shiva's dirty.

Silence.

Suddenly Henry recalls how enraged Kulap became the afternoon they spoke about the damaged Ganesh. He remembers Kulap pulling again and again at the collar of his shirt, all the while pacing and muttering imprecations against the registrar in San Francisco. Kulap had gotten very personal about it, wishing some sort of terrible, as well as chillingly specific, accident on the poor woman.

—Kulap? Still there?

—Yeah, I don't follow.

—Our sources are saying that Shiva was looted from a rural temple in... starting to search his papers then stopping... —Southern India, I don't have the exact—

—Impossible.

—There's proof, I'm afraid. Right now at least it looks to be undeniable.

—And you're saying, what, that Vauclain knew it was dirty?

—Again, that's what the evidence points to.

—Jesus, Henry, the guy's been around for twenty years. Donates a ton to the Asia Society. This can't be true.

—Sounds like you bought other pieces, not just Shiva.

Silence.

—Kulap?

—Sure.

—But you have paperwork? For all of them?

Assuming the number of fishy items in museum cases is fairly low, this is mostly protocol. A mild but firm interrogation to frighten Kulap into being more careful.

—Museum policy is very clear on provenance. We follow the UNESCO rules to the letter.

—Mr. Joles. Henry.

—You dug into Shiva's background.

Another silence.

—And can produce all relevant paperwork when called upon... Henry selects a letter opener from the cup on his desk and attends to the dirt under his fingernails.

—We have optical due diligence.

—*Opti-*, oh, for fuck's sake.

—Vauclain told me, I remember now, that Shiva's previous owner was a wealthy ship captain and—

—*Ship* captain?

—That's what he said.

—With, what, a peg leg and a parrot? A hook for a hand?

—Huh?

—Did you ever lay eyes on this salty dog?

—Not that I recall.

—Not that you, okay, Kulap, now we're getting somewhere. You suspected the stuff was not legit.

—Now hang on a minute. Six years ago when I took over, Diane said that building South Asian was her biggest priority. We're getting lapped by Philadelphia, she said and that's a direct quote, okay? I'll get the funds approved, she said. Which she did. There was a tacit agreement—

—Tacit? No, buddy. Don't put your money on tacit.

—We were deserted, Henry, abandoned—

—Nonetheless—

—Relegated to hallways! We're still on the wrong floor, okay, still shoved into a couple of galleries outside Egypt. Why are we squeezed in behind Africa when Japan has four huge spaces—

—No one told you to break the law.

Silence.

How had Henry once lived for this? The conniving and manipulation, the games. This could be the last fire Henry puts out but winning means nothing. Not anymore.

—Should I be calling my lawyer?

—Not yet. Stay with me.

—I may mention, when I do consult my lawyer, the crippling case of food poisoning I got at the hands of the Museum.

—Up to you... Henry pages through the contents of the Mumbai file... —What about the Durga idol? Remember where he came from?

—Vauclain.

—The Uma Parameshwari?

—Also Vauclain.

—And the large Sitting Buddha, the one from Cambodia?

—Sotheby's.

—But you have paperwork. It's not like these are handshake deals.

—I have dealer's warranties.

—Dealer's warranties, please. Don't fuck me, Kulap.

—They hold up.

—No, no they do not hold up. You know that, I know that, the village cretin with his turtle on a string knows that. You may as well run down to—

—Wait, Mr. Joles, I—

—the Justice Department and confess—

—HOLD ON.

From the other end of the phone comes a rustle and clunk, what sounds like footsteps growing fainter, followed by the faraway slam of a door.

9:39 a.m.

How did I get myself knocked up seeing as I barely leave the house? Good question. Katherine wipes the nib of her pen. She's writing at a furious speed, blotting as she goes, imagining her grandmother's face at the news of an unplanned pregnancy. It's true that I quit socializing. More than a year ago. No more bars or restaurants. Brunch with friends or dinner parties. I used to love dinner parties. Back when they were, like, actual parties: volatile, dark, fueled by rotgut vodka, bristling with drama, when the food was only useful as a place to ash your cigarette. But one day dinner parties became the place where interesting people went to die. Conversation became painfully respectable, less about murders, sex, and fascism and more about food. Cooking was discussed in a spirit of fanatic competition. One day I drew a line in the sand. No more of these Caucasian death spirals, I told myself. Then about six weeks ago Ruth called. Come on, Katie, she said. Socializing, exalted matters and politics, white wine, and so forth. If there's anything I hate it's exalted matters, but lately I've been experimenting with being agreeable. So I got all fancied up in a vintage number and a lot of enthusiastic eye shadow. I ripped the hair off my legs, shaped my brows, even dug out some perfume. Staring at my reflection, I resolved to have a wonderful attitude.

Ping of a text. Ignore it.

On the subway I oozed positivity and when I arrived, bear-hugged the hostess, a woman I had never met. The guests stood around holding drinks and caprese kebabs, miming that they'd like to shake but they'd run out of hands. I smiled and chuckled all over the place. I touched an arm here, a shoulder there. When we finally sat down for dinner I was so exhausted I could barely lift my fork. Around me, a discussion unfolded about kohlrabi, while I tried to decipher exactly what kohlrabi was and how I could be cheerful about it.

At the other end of the table the hostess commanded the room in a rainbow dress with accordion pleats. She was very bright, in both intelligence and wattage. She didn't claim my attention for long. She was flawless, there was no foothold for your gaze. Instead you swept over her as you might scan the crowd for a familiar face and failing to find one, move on. Next to her sat a man from Milan, her professor from grad

school. The man was portly, neckless, and dressed head to toe in Done-
gal tweed. He bore an uncanny resemblance to Toad of Toad Hall. From
what I could tell they had never slept together, but I figured she had
fantasized about it from time to time. Professore was likely aware of his
power over this former student but chose not to use it. We ate snails.
Everyone agreed how difficult they are to find.

Another ping.

Dinner ended. A homemade sorbet, mango, I think, had failed to
set. We retired, as they call it, to the living room, which meant crossing
the room to a couple of couches. Everyone fussed with dishes and bran-
dies and finding a place to sit. A book editor mentioned playing a game
and I slunk over to a nonworking fireplace. I felt a sense of kinship with
its uselessness as I plotted my exit, calculating how few minutes I could
stay without appearing unforgivably rude.

Another ping. This one she reads. Conrad, asking about moving
part of an exhibit. Quickly Katherine types back, *ha ha please don't!*

The Italian professor crossed the room to join me, asking about
Spokane, which I had lied about during the soup course. Standing at
the mantel, about three sentences into our conversation, I realized I was
attracted to this tweedy little man who confessed to being extremely
sensitive to changes in temperature. And it's true, his face flushed from
pink to white to red even as we stood there. He was also plagued by a
tic, a kind of nervous throat-clearing. I'm positive his suit was older
than he; it featured the perfect stitches of a different generation. "I find
you attractive," he said, as if sounding aloud an implausible fact. To
which I replied, "You must be married," going for the humor angle.
"No," he said. "No, I have never married." I saw then that I had over-
estimated his age, he was only forty-five or so, where I'd taken him for
sixty. The other guests had assumed positions of relaxation, balancing an
assortment of small glasses. They were an advertisement for the kind of
good city living that comes with a variety of digestifs and an abundance
of cushions. I decided then that I would bring this fortyish Italian home
and attempt to seduce him. I don't want to get reductive but I needed
something new. As often as I believed tomorrow would be different, tomorrow always ended up the twin of today. This explains, I thought,
after Professore left my apartment at three the next morning, the mysterious dreams I'd been having lately, of sky-diving naked and trekking

the African veldt. Visions of triangular rooms, butterscotch daisies, and six-legged cats.

Well, Mimi, as you can see, this longing for novelty has worked only too well. There's no question that pregnancy is new and unfamiliar. I'm thirty-five years old. What should I do? Phone calls from the Professore I ignore. There are two options available and only one of them will ensure that my upcoming days are different. Different, but frightening. There are a thousand reasons not to have a baby, not at this time, not in this way. A single woman full of contradictions.

When I imagine raising a child I'm forced to admit that children have never impressed me much. So why do I avoid making the appointment that would return my life to normal? Every morning I towel dry from the shower, dabbing not rubbing as I once read is best for the skin. I make my coffee, eat my banana with almond butter, drink two glasses of water mixed with apple cider vinegar, and type another reminder into my phone. But at the end of the day I still haven't made the call.

Despite the unseasonably warm weather, I've been wearing a beanie to cover my butchered hair. I have an irregular head, it turns out. Mia Farrow has a perfect head. I think it must be rare to have a head shaped as perfectly as Mia Farrow's.

I miss you, Mimi. Please call me. California has never felt so far away.

Lots of love,

Katherine.

She hits replay on the song, picks up her cell phone and scrolls through her outgoing calls, willing herself. Do it. Tap the number. Call.

But first, a quick trip to the shitty café. Another coffee. This time a latté.

9:48 a.m.

Finally Henry hears the sound of footsteps returning, the clatter of the receiver being picked up and its travel up to Kulap's ear.

—Listen, Henry, I took a quick second to consult—

—*Quick?* I would've hung up but... skimming the email he's composed... —I assumed I'd never get hold of you again.

—Consult with my wife and—

—Wife? What's this have to do with your wife?

—I keep it quiet, but Samantha works at the Garrett School, in charge of admissions... a pause to let the full weight of that sink in... —Seems your Noah is on the waitlist. Way down, toward the bottom. You got to line them up when they're still in utero, Henry. Little Noah's going to need a tsunami to wipe out the Upper East Side.

The topic Olive most likes to bring up once Henry has strapped on his sleep-mask and settled in for the night is the doomed future of their two young children. The likelihood of Noah and Echo getting into the right school, an Ivy-track school, is microscopic given that Henry has neglected to suck up to the right sort of people, having spent his life hating the right sort of people.

—When it comes to the waitlist Garrett trusts Samantha to use her own judgment. One word from me and Noah could be second or third in line.

This is what Henry needs, not a trip to some Sugarworld, but a real legacy.

—We could help each other out.

—I'm hanging up now... better to let Kulap believe he has no leverage... —Pull on your jammies. Another nap, maybe you'll recall running those background checks.

—And you keep Garrett in mind. Picture your kids in those cute uniforms. Straw boaters in the summer.

—I'll do that... Henry hangs up the phone, leans back, and stares at the row of framed lithographs installed about four inches too high on the wall opposite.

The Garrett School. Interesting.

Stabbing the intercom button... —Audrey, get me Mike Decker at the State Department.

As a child, Henry often failed to leave enough room on a piece of paper to fit the words of a title or whatever kind of important sentence requires one line and no more. He was forever having to curve words around the edge of the page and write perpendicularly, or reduce the size of his handwriting, printing his letters smaller and smaller as he nervously eyed the space he had left. The struggle to forecast the future has been a lifelong one. It would be exactly like Henry to make this looting issue disappear in order to let Kulap off the hook in order to get Noah admitted to Garrett all the while neglecting to see there's no way in hell he can afford to pay for private school.

9:52 a.m.

Oh, now, really? Really? *To the bang bang boogie* So the white girl in Costume is planning to play *rhythm of the boogie, the beat* on repeat all day? Let it throb through the whole downstairs hallway?

Put it out of your mind. Pulling the door shut to HQ, Shay walks down the hall to the stairwell and heads to the second floor. The past few months she's been struggling to recall words, events, occasionally even the name of her husband, but two lyrics into "Rapper's Delight" and she's instantly back in Oakland, sharing a converted garage that stunk of cabbage. Her roommate had discovered some Irish blood on his mother's side and was struggling to learn Gaelic from a secondhand dictionary and a box of flash cards, cooking up colcannon, manhandling soda bread and boxty.

Out the stairwell to the second-floor galleries, past the women's bathroom and two silver drinking fountains staggered in height, through to the long, arched gallery where the walls are lined with history paintings: white men clustered in groups, pointing with stiff arms. It's a small range that's indicated: the heavens, a landscape, each other, maps or matters that lie off-canvas. Their fingers are instructive, angry, commanding, inquisitive. Masterful pointing, all.

—Ready for the day, Macy?... why are her guards so gloomy, even before the doors have opened... —Doing alright?

—Yes, yes... the girl makes an effort to perk up.

—Good... and Shay keeps walking.

Fish pie was on the menu the night the phone rang with news from home. In the background the music thumped *Like a millionaire that has no money Like a rainy day that is not wet.* In the foreground: Divorce. Shay couldn't make sense of the word and she remembers her father trying to help her absorb it. His voice was low and kind as he sidetracked to describe the weather or a fence he was fixing, before re-turning again to this awful decision he and Ma had made. She would have to conceive of her parents as separate people, Shay thought, and never return to the house she loved. The pink-tiled bathroom that smelled of fried hair. The attic bedroom where her treasures were ar-ranged along the windowsill and where in third grade she lay in bed for hours staring at the ceiling after Holly Margolies told Shay her skin was the color of poo. As she listened to her father, Shay watched the air outside the garage turn yellow, as if she were in a movie signal-ing a shift in location to somewhere poor and hot.

The next day Shay signed up for a poetry group. It was solely to spite her parents who had no use for pursuits they deemed impracti-cal. In a room thick with patchouli a disciple spoke on T.S. Eliot, *He do the police in different voices*, as Shay tried not to cry and fought to stay upright on a beanbag.

Turning into the Harper Gallery of European Paintings. Up ahead, two young men wearing CREW T-shirts.

—Pardon me, gentlemen?

Slowly the men turn, gazing at Shay with the unruffled expressions of people accustomed to getting away with minor transgressions.

—If you're part of Conrad Bellefont's team, I believe your work is confined to the ground floor. I certainly shouldn't find you alone in a gallery ten minutes before the museum opens.

—But I wanted to show him... the twerp indicates his moon-faced pal... —That famous picture, the Monet—

—Where are your security escorts?

The men shrug and act dumb.

—Back downstairs, please.

—My bad, are we—

—Now.

She watches the men slouch toward the exit, walking as slowly as possible to remind Shay who really holds the power.

Remember that you once had a father. Measured out his life with ketchup packets. When she talked about poetry Dad looked at her with weary apprehension. Dead on his feet from working two jobs. They were at a place in Redondo Beach famous for its clams. He knew Shay loved food that came piled in a red plastic basket. What did her father think as he ate a french fry and stared at the ocean, sitting across the table from his obstinate child and her foolish quotes?

9:58 a.m.

—I don't, actually I can't, Diane, repeat what he said. I went all the way down to the shitty café on minus one to get his voice out of my head. I bought a cheddar bacon scone.

—A scone? Don't eat—

—Well, of course I didn't *eat* it. I'm saying I was that disoriented... Chris folds his arms and immediately unfolds them... —I mean, I've been on the receiving end of, you know, anger before, but this was like getting battery acid poured in my ear, it was like.

—But you told Clive... Diane selects a ballpoint from her gang of organized pens... —I'm happy to go on Monday.

—Mr. Wolfe isn't expected to make it past the weekend.

—I see... leaning back... —Poor Walter.

—Look, it's fine. I finessed it. I mean, I feel like I did. I told Clive we'd make it up to him.

—Sounds vague enough to get us in trouble.

They were friends once, good friends, she and Clive, the kind that get together for cocktails on Fridays after work when most of the staff is sick of the sight of each other and can't flee the place fast enough. Twice a month they'd meet downstairs, at the restaurant near Central America that served enormous martinis, stayed open late and was accessible by the street. Often Clive's boyfriend would stop by, a Kiwi he introduced by saying, you'll like Joshua better than me, everyone does, which Diane took as a joke but then did, decidedly, prefer him to Clive.

—What else? Anything? Anyone else out with shrimp?

—No news... Chris crosses her office, staring down at his phone... —Looks like Shiva's been removed and replaced... in the doorway, he turns... —Another coffee?

—No, thanks.

Diane waits for the door to close, pushes back her chair and goes to the bookcase.

The boyfriend was less handsome than she would have guessed, given Clive's intolerance for the substandard but he was an affectionate and decent man who always looked you dead in the eye and was almost unsettlingly interested in what you had to say which, after a goblet of gin, was often quite stupid. One day Joshua stopped coming by, she and Clive stopped meeting up for a drink, and there was that disastrous trip to Paris.

Hidden behind a vase, she finds the green leather hippo Clive presented her with on the flight home. He danced it up her arm, begging to be forgiven.

10:01 a.m.

Clive sits at the head of the conference table pretending to take notes. He should have postponed the exhibitions meeting. Two of the more intelligent members of European Paintings have been poisoned by museum shrimp. But the news of Lucy's flight to Germany was so disturbing Clive could only blindly follow his calendar, shuffling down the corridor to the room where Hannah, Barry, Sasha, and Shipley were waiting. These brainstorming sessions he usually relishes, the lively disorder that precedes the dull business of PowerPoint presentations. Today he's parodying interest. A show that takes place five years in the future may as well be fifty.

—What about hands and arms?... Barry reads from a leather-bound notebook... —Or something around the gesture?

—Sorry, aren't we trying to share the outlay?... Hannah's constant crucifixion of poor Barry is the result, Clive suspects, of a soured romance... —Because how does the *gesture* bring in other departments?

Barry looks to Shipley for help... —No bad ideas, isn't that the rule of brainstorming?

Shipley nods in a sort of circular fashion to show he's not picking sides.

—What about like, the Tudors?... Hannah offers... —Or Medicine?

—Visions of Hell?

Is what Clive had on the subway this morning, imagining life without Lucy, his co-conspirator of the last twenty years. Nightmares of a lonely future. Most of his old friends moved away, returned to London or, in the case of Archie, took ownership of a Spanish vineyard that in a matter of months siphoned his inheritance and vaporized his marriage.

—Objects of affection?

Yes, his friends and lovers, how quickly they forgot Clive. Archie returned to banking, poor sod, newly single and the wrong side of forty. Perversely, Lucy remained. Year after year, impervious to Clive's increasingly jaundiced take on the world. Over the last two decades they've sat knee to knee in the city's brasseries, watching the other grow old and inflexible, like neutral observers of a war overseas. Pastis, Lucky Strike, Odeon, Raoul's. Florent closed two years ago, the end of an era. He hadn't been since the towers came down.

Suddenly realizing the conference room has been silent for several minutes.

—All very interesting... tapping a mechanical pencil against his teeth... —Anyone else? Ship? Sasha?

—Self-portraits?

—Poverty? Clive, what about poverty?

—Talk about depressing... with a nasty sniff, Barry leans back.

—Poverty and Wealth, then... Hannah looks around the table for support... —Or just Wealth.

Someone laughs, high-pitched and bitter. And Clive is forced to admit that these sessions are never what he hopes for. Never wild, or even slightly off the rails. The curators in his department have been unsparingly schooled. Decades of academia have corrected the slightest bend toward the unorthodox. He has never met people more petrified of being unusual.

—Here's an idea... Shipley's voice has the timbre of Morgan Freeman, which makes everyone shut up and listen even when he's talking complete shit... —Miniatures. Portraits from Holbein, Simon Bening, Jean Clouet. Other departments could include—

—Hardly a *revolutionary*—

—Pardon me, Barry, *could include*, from Greece, Rome, Egypt: grave goods. Mexican jade figures, Tongan ivory heads.

—South Asia.

—Velasquez's midgets.

—No, no, not that. That's offensive, I never—

—Relax, I was kidding.

—Sasha... Clive points... —An idea. Now, please.

—I don't really—

—Anything.

—Ugly? Or The Ugly?

—Go on.

—Other departments: Am Dec, Africana—

—Oh my god... Hannah, alert to aggressions both micro and sizable... —Ugly according to whose aesthetic, if you don't mind?

—Otto Dix and let me think—

—From a Western perspective?... Hannah cases the room for an ally.

—SASHA... Morgan Freeman booms from the corner... —Are you talking about the subject matter being ugly or an absence of form?

—I don't really know, uh, maybe ugly behavior? Breughel? Satan, murderers? Bosch? Crones... Sasha glances at Hannah and hurries on... —Jan Van Eyck? Drunks and vomit.

—Because if it's an absence of form—

—Ship, that's not what he—

—Arcimboldo or some comic—

—Again, culturally, whose conception—

—WHAT ABOUT, new idea, keep it simple, Italy in the trecento? Solid, inoffensive.

—Stop. Please... Clive pushes away from the table... —Certainly not the tre-fucking-cento.

—QUATTRO?

—Sasha, stop by my office tomorrow afternoon. Anyone else?... a picture flashes in his mind of Lucy walking along a foreign street in a pair of horrible shoes... —Perhaps something with more reach than Italy in the trecento.

—CLIVE, YOU HEARD I also suggested quattro.

—Fuck the quattro, Shipley... biting the words... —Really fuck the quattro.

—That's rude, why—

—Listen to me. I'm begging you, all of you, pleading, astonish me. Please. Give me something to believe in. I need... Clive's voice trembles and he coughs to cover it... —I want a show, a great show. A show that will make a visitor drop to his fucking knees. I want people to walk out clutching their heads and seducing strangers. Divorcing their spouses. Quitting their jobs. Grabbing life by the cock.

Silence. No one dares look at him. Hannah bends to pick up a pen. Sasha scratches his nose for longer than it takes to scratch a nose.

—Okay... Clive stands... —Looks like we're done. Write up your ideas. Email me, et cetera.

Gathering his notebooks and catalogues, pushing back his chair. With Lucy in Berlin, Clive will be left without a translator. He'll be utterly adrift and make no sense to anyone. Walking out the door, he slams into the head of Security.

10:09 a.m.

—God, I do beg your pardon... European Paintings looking faintly sick, reaches out a hand to amend, wafting a cologne containing vetiver, a copper bangle edging out from under his shirt cuff.

—No harm done.

He squeezes her arm and Shay watches him set off, eyes glued to the floor as he hurries away.

Without a functioning memory you'll be less human, more of a meat stick. Shay continues along the hallway, swiping out of the back offices and into the first of the smaller Middle Eastern galleries.

Let's say you're studying photographs that irrefutably belong to a stranger's life but then you're corrected, no these are pictures from *your* life. A childhood spent in terrycloth shorts, a pair of ashy knees and a bike with streamers, a rained-out wedding on the California coast.

Outside the Bistoff gallery, hands clasped behind his back, a young guard bounces to a song in his head.

—Top button, Terrence, if you please... glancing back to check he's fumbling with his collar.

It's possible that forgetting makes for a happier life. Imagine never having to recall the look on your father's face that afternoon by the ocean or the hateful words you blurted out, to your sister and others, words you could never take back.

—Pardon me, Chief.

Shay stops. Tapestry Todd.

—Very sorry to bother, but, uh, do you have a second?

Whether Shay does or does not have a second is immaterial. She waits.

—Had a few complaints, recently, the last week or so, about your guards. Guests have spoken, written, actually, of being made to feel uncomfortable—

—*Uncomfortable?*

—Maybe that's the wrong word, the guards seem angry or

Shay's eyes glaze into the neutral expression she favors when tuning out friendly bigots. *Uncomfortable?* Almost half the Museum security guards are Black. And how many Black curators? Two. Both in Africana. So if these white snitches are going to criticize her staff, many of them not much more than kids, every single one of them doing their best, keeping alert while standing still, destroying their feet on the marble floors, well, she's not inclined to listen.

—So glad we had this talk.

Shay hasn't said a word. Tapestry Todd has perhaps assumed from her blank expression and the uniform she wears that Shay must agree with him, even *defer* to him, that Shay will effect some sort of change or whatever it is he's demanded when, in fact, she was too busy finding constellations in his freckles to listen to his lecture.

Once Todd's flat ass has disappeared through the arched doorway, Shay continues on her way.

It's not only the happy memories she's sorry to lose. You have to mourn it all. All the times you were trailed, monitored, eyed suspiciously. Your presence questioned. The night outside Buffalo Carl got pulled over for a broken taillight, the cop angry about more than a taillight, how you shook for an hour after. Those movies will vanish too. Scenes of condescension, yes, but also resilience, endurance. All of it erased, so in two or three years you're left smiling stupidly out the window at a bird. As if you weathered nothing. Getting out her notebook Shay scribbles, *it was no cakewalk.*

Through Purdue and into the hallway outside the larger of the Roman galleries. And here he is.

Tindall-Clark's ugly beast.

10:13 a.m.

Fuck advice, Katherine thinks, sipping Amar's broiling version of a latté, fully aware that CAFFEINE lies between SUSHI and PASTRAMI on the interminable list of pregnancy no-nos. But her own mother drank coffee every day for nine months and tossed back a Fuzzy Navel or two on holiday weekends and Katherine arrived with a fully formed head, so.

The door to the film department is open and the new hire stands in profile, arms folded, glaring at Ward's poster of *The Maltese Falcon* as if he's about to rip it off the wall.

She knocks on the doorframe... —Hi.

The man starts, puzzled, as if Bogart has spoken, then turns to face her... —Oh, hey.

Katherine freezes. His hair is calmed into place, his face thicker and somehow sadder. Benjamin Rippen.

He drops the hand he's started to stretch toward her. An expression of wounded confusion, as if he's the victim of an especially cruel prank.

—Katherine.

—I remember, of course, Katherine. Katherine Tambling, you see? How long had it lasted? Six months or so?

—You work here?

—Down the hall.

—Your hair... touching his own... —Used to be long.

—Yeah, it's new. Had a rocky night.

—Like Shirley MacLaine in, I mean, this is crazy, how are you?

—Great. So great... she feels like puking.

—You weren't working here when, you worked at the Brooklyn Museum when we... he stops, pushing at his jawbone.

—No, yeah, seven years ago.

—Right. Of course, why would you still be there? Not of course, but it stands to reason.

Stands to reason. She had been falling in love with him when he broke it off.

—Do you like this place? Working here?

She shrugs. Was Benjamin Rippen the first person she really loved? Katherine remembers him as a person of high ideals who bagged his own groceries and gave money to anyone who asked. Seven years ago his hair was thicker and stood up in clutches. You were encouraged to believe he had no time for combs.

—You look well.

—How's your family? Gabe, right? Badminton serve still pretty weak?

—We're not really in touch these days. What about your sister? Still in that cult?

—Yeah. Oh, actually, no. Still in India, but now she's in the west with an NGO focused on educating girls.

—Nice.

—Didn't you study foreign policy in college? I mean, I don't remember movies being your thing.

—Did I have a thing? I was two years out of undergrad.

—Sorry, I meant... she's insulted him, she didn't mean to... —You worked for that woman uptown, Ellen.

—Eleanor, and you're right, I did, but—

—Doing something with water.

—Right, in Senegal. We're still close. I mean, we aren't... scraping his lip with his teeth... —But we should be.

—So how did the whole movies thing start?

—Buddy of mine had a cousin at NYU needed help shooting his thesis. I went along for the free pizza but the whole time I was like hauling sandbags I was thinking, I could make a better movie than this hackneyed crap about the triumph of poverty, you know?

—Sure.

—So I applied to NYU, got my MFA, then moved out to Ohio for a doctorate so I'd have a plan B.

No, *they* were falling in love. Both, not just Katherine. He ended the relationship one afternoon in the rain. Day drinking in a booth so she couldn't make a scene. There was a small gas fire, a wet-wool stink. Outside, a storm. She cried hot whisky tears. The window next to them

was spattered with raindrops. A pathetic fallacy. Exactly like their relationship, she remembers thinking, a pathetic fucking fallacy.

Benjamin is watching her.

—A plan B, huh, cool, so it all worked out... smiling inanely...
—Did they tell you what happened to Ward? Keeled over mid-burrito.
He'll be back, though. Guy's like an ox. We arm-wrestled once.

—Ward retired.

—What?

—Really.

—Jeez, that's rough. So you're... then, understanding... —Are you
like *replacing* Ward? Tell me you're not running a whole department.

—Yeah, as far as I know, I'm it.

—I was here for like five years before I got promoted.

—They got me cheap I guess is the reason. Plus it's a new department, right? How much damage could I do? Hey Katherine.

Still makes her heart jump, him saying her name like that.

—I'm trying to get a better sense of the museum but the website's
down and, I don't know, you think you could show me around? Give
me the inside story.

—God, sorry, I... pointing in the general direction of her office...
—Fires to put out. Big day for us in Costume what with the gala and,
lots of, you know... turning, she bumps into the doorframe, pretends
she didn't, and walks quickly down the hall.

Once inside her office Katherine leans back against the door,
breathing hard as if she's outrun something.

They met at jury duty, the youngest by two decades. He showed up
wearing a tie, an FBI haircut and the sleeves of his shirt rolled halfway
up his forearm. The look suggested that Benjamin Rippen was prepped
for a crisis and would restore order with a calculator, three pieces of
string and a nearby fire extinguisher. She'd always been a sucker for a
capable man with a squint and a world-weary forearm. The court case
involved a small insurance company suing another for theft of proprietary code. It was nothing more than petty score settling but Benjamin
took the trial seriously, with sharpened pencils and reams of notes,
sighing and frowning and jotting. Sticking his fingers in his hair like
the hero in a Scandi drama about a missing girl.

The jurors were excused one morning before noon and all twelve trooped to the nearest bar where they commandeered the jukebox and got thoroughly trashed. Civic duty served, they were high on a sense of shared sacrifice. The foreman, a woman, allowed the hold-out not-guilty vote to smooch her in the corner and run his hand up and down her glossy stockings. Benjamin bought a round of good scotch, not the bottom shelf swill Katherine was used to.

At Thanksgiving she went home with him to North Carolina. Katherine had the sense she was invited in order to become his family's apologist so that back in New York Benjamin could shoot them down one by one without hating himself. Slinging practiced barbs, "we're four strangers who gather twice a year to discuss craft beer and the losing season." But a wistful fragility lay under his contempt. Katherine would lodge an appeal on behalf of his father, call his mother's negligence preoccupation, defend Gabe's lack of ambition. That weekend an aunt appeared who had a habit both of talking to herself and speaking at an abnormally low volume. No one knew when to ask Aunt Sadie to repeat herself and when to respect a moment of reflection. Turkey was served. The fog lifted, the sun came out. A tepid game of netless badminton took place in the driveway. Katherine managed to tamp down her competitive streak.

The clock above the door ticks. Loud. Slow. Insistent. Symbolic. Why is she sitting here? Seven years, a lifetime ago. And what friends remain? Yes, the concept of solitude has been appealing. Exile of a kind, romantic. Bergman, Bowles, Mann. A number of friends drifted away when her father unexpectedly upped and died. Her grief was taxing. Worse, it was boring. Katherine wasn't mourning appropriately, or at least, in the way they believed was best. The old Katie, the fun one, was taking too long to return. Her friends grew tired of the subject and disappeared, one by one. "This is what I need to do," they said, "for myself." For myself, I need to take care of myself, myself, myself. It was a time of myselfs.

Then there was Sojourner, a new friend from Archives. At a music festival they took molly, and at some point Katherine kissed Sojo's fiancé. How did it happen? A bonfire, blankets. A starless night. And that was the end of Sojourner. So you're going to sit here? Being yourself again? God, it gets old. The injuries, the injustice. Friends shed like. Well, something. Don't do this. Not at thirty-five.

Katherine stands and knocks back the rest of her coffee, now luke-warm. Pops an antihistamine. Slaps a nicotine patch on her biceps. A couple of shoulder rolls, one or two ujjayi breaths. Social Katherine. Fun-loving, come on. Not this isolated shit, happy girl.

She pulls her door closed and heads back down the hall to Benjamin.

10:24 a.m.

When Clive got to his office a piece of chocolate cake was parked in the middle of his desk, a plastic spork lying ready on the plate beside it. He was still thinking about his unhinged rant in the exhibitions meeting and it took a minute to make sense of the dessert. Half a candied cherry eyeballed him from a swamp of chocolate icing. Was Linda expecting him to choke down this menace huddled alone in his office like a bulimic cheerleader?

—Hey... the administrator who replaced Linda a month ago appears in the doorway.

Clive tears himself away from a staring match with the cherry...
—What's this, then?

—Tim's birthday.

—Dinkelman?

—Yeah. Don't ask how old he is, not to his face... and she's gone.

Clive pushes the paper plate to one side, sets down his mug of tea and notebook, and collapses into his desk chair, spinning it to take in the building across the street, its effortful scrollwork and cartouches. Give me something to believe in! Christ. How's he going to face them after a comment like that? Outside the window, a pigeon flutters and lands on the cement sill. Pecks stupidly at its feet several times then swivels its head to look at Clive.

What can I tell you, Bird? I'm losing my mind. In reply the pigeon does something disturbingly elastic with its little head.

Clive spins back to his desk and without knowing quite what he's doing, he grabs the plastic spork from the plate, prises off a chunk of cake, shoves it in his mouth. He chews and swallows, releasing a blast of sucrose that rears up and slams him in the back of the head. God, that's fucking fantastic. Gripping the edge of the desk he closes his eyes to surf a wave of serotonin. The icing tastes like pure butter. The chocolate is darker and more decadent than your usual store-bought platter of chemical sludge. He opens his eyes, suppressing the urge to pick up the plate and bury his face in cake. Instead, with great restraint, Clive picks off the cherry oculus and pops it in his mouth. To think some saint went home last night and baked embittered backstabber Timmy Dinkelman a birthday cake.

Clive types up a short email, presses send, and, while he waits, bins the cake, using the camera on his mobile to check his face, licking his finger to scrub chocolate off his nose.

—Excuse me... a soft sound at the door... —You asked for an intern?... a knock-kneed girl stands in the doorway with the defiant air of the chronically nervous.

Clive forces himself not to stare at her kneecaps, which are rotated so severely they nearly kiss... —And you are?

—I'm sorry?

—Your name?

—Oh, Freda.

—Freda, good... Clive smiles encouragingly. Physical flaws have thrilled him since a preteen scrimmage behind the pet shed with Giles Woodward and his shriveled arm... —How are you this morning, Freda?

—Fine... cautiously, as if it's a trick question.

—Excellent, I need you to track down a woman in Objects Conservation. Museum website's down and I'm afraid all I have is a physical description. She's about five-five, skinny legs, lips like Mick Jagger.

—You don't know her name?

—I do not. Text me when you've found it. Along with her cell phone number.

—But, like, how do I find out who she is?

Clive stares at Freda until she turns and silently slips out of the room. Perhaps richer for the knowledge that in order to get ahead as an intern it's best to take some fucking initiative.

And leaning back in his chair, he takes a sip of cold tea.

Sweaty Freda must be twenty-one or twenty-two, Clive's age when he first met Lucy with her wide-set porpoise eyes and mothy sweaters. How alive they were back then, racing around the city, painlessly metabolizing vats of alcohol. A wild time. The city's pace, the madness of its occupants, thrilled Clive. For years the fever persisted. But then Joshua moved back to Auckland, and the unthinkable happened. The city wasn't enough. Clive's enthusiasms guttered. One day he couldn't recall what wonder felt like. He was tired of New York and, thus, tired of life.

—Clive?

Stretching to reach the intercom... —Yup.

—Jack Corbeau on one.

—Thanks... pressing one... —Jack!

—I emailed saying three's no good, you never—

—Because it has to be three, Jack. Not four, not two, and not tomorrow.

—But I'm trying to tell—

—Fifteen minutes tops, promise. See you at three... tossing the receiver in the general direction of the phone's cradle.

Lucy's defection makes no sense. She was the one who never stopped marveling, never lost her love for New York. And she was wrong about Clive. He didn't resent her joy, quite the opposite. He fed off it. For Clive, the situation was ideal. He had the rewards of happiness without the work. All that fossicking about for a silver lining, no thank you. Technically, Clive thinks as he sips his tea, that makes him more of a parasite than a killjoy.

Clive puts down the cup, stands up and grabs his jacket, punching his arms through the sleeves as he goes out the door, narrowly avoiding an elbow to Dinkelman's windpipe... —Tim!... he turns to walk backwards down the corridor... —Happy birthday.

Tim paws his hair, grinning feebly... —Thanks, man. Appreciate it.

—And how old does this make you?

10:31 a.m.

—So I ask the foxy brunette—

—The fuck you doing here?

—brunette at the hostess stand where I can find Nikolic Peša and she tells me you're the *interim* Chef de Cuisine like she wants to make it real clear you're not the actual CDC. Interim. Cracked me up... Jimmy drinks from a take-out cup, his eyes landing on Niko's belly... —Damn.

—Don't.

—You're fat.

—I said don't.

—Why'd you get so fat?

—Why are you dressed like a Russian pimp?

—That's not nice. I'm going to this party tonight... Jimmy flicks dust from his dimpled suede jacket... —What's got you so steamed?

—Are you, hang on... noticing a customer walking toward them... —Follow me... Niko turns, winding his way through tables, punching open the swinging door into the kitchen, past the work stations, the grills and oven, into the back, next to the locker, what the hell *into* the locker room itself, all the while telling himself this can't be real, I'm hallucinating. He's an apparition.

But no, Jimmy's right behind him, muttering... —Oh, okay, the locker room. Planning to shank me or—

—Shut up... spinning around to face him... —Where the fuck's my money?

—Ah, the money, I do not possess, unfortunately.

—Think I'm an idiot? I see the write-ups you get. Lines outside the door. Last week you were on TV being quoted as some kind of expert.

—There have been unanticipated—

—Meanwhile my right hand is developing this like tremor—

—Well, why'd you give me the money in the first place?

—Because you asked for it.

—Don't be cranky when I haven't seen you in so long. You know, Mom's not well.

—What happened to Mom?

—No, no, nothing. I mean, she's griping and hobbling, nothing new. But look, the two of us, all we have is each other. Down the road they'll both be gone, then what? Forget about this money thing. Blood's thicker than water.

—That's about war, spilled blood, not family.

Jimmy drains his coffee, tipping back the cup... —Even better.

—No, that makes no, oh, never mind... Niko pulls out his inhaler and takes a deep drag.

—Got a garbage for this?

—By the way... grabbing Jimmy's take-out cup and pocketing his inhaler... —Thanks for Seattle.

—What Seattle?

—Don't... going to his locker, hurling the empty cup into it... —Don't what Seattle. Bracci's new place. He told me, ate here a couple of months ago, obviously as soon as he saw me he knew we were brothers and he says, kinda of thinking out loud, I wonder why James didn't recommend you for my new place. I asked him for names, Bracci says. So I'm forced to make up some shit on the spot like I'm fucking ecstatic to be in New York. You couldn't have done that for me, Jimmy? Not even that? Recommend me for a job?

—You weren't ready. You aren't ready. And it would've been my reputation if you fucked up in Seattle.

—Who says I'd have fucked up?

—Nobody. Nobody. It's possible you would have.

Nikolic crosses the room to an instructional poster for the Heimlich maneuver, fixing on the poster's design, an homage to Russian propaganda with graphic lettering and blocks of primary colors. Dotted across the text are little red hands and arrows. A fish skeleton in lighter shades, half-blue/half-yellow, curves across the background along with a wheel of sliced lemon. The lemon undoubtedly inserted as a context clue in case during the hullaballoo of a choking you fail to recognize a fish.

—Come on, Niko, don't take it the wrong way.

A few weeks ago a picture ripped from a magazine appeared next to the Heimlich guide, stuck to the wall with green tape. It showed a field of grass covered in dandelions and, in the middle of the field, a yellow lab getting humped by a goat. The way the dog gazed at the camera made Niko want to rip the picture down. But he didn't. Couldn't risk looking humorless.

The squeak of the locker room door makes him turn.

Jimmy is looking into the chaos of the kitchen... —Need some help?

—No.

—Two kids out there mangling lobsters.

—Absolutely not... from his locker Niko grabs a couple of side towels he stashed under his hoodie earlier this morning.

—I'll yes-chef you to death. No one has to know we're related.

—We're twins! Are they morons?

—I don't know, are they observant?

—Leave, please... slamming his locker closed.

—Buddy. Buddy, buddy.

Niko is focused on making sure his locker has actually latched, it has an aggravating tendency to bounce back open, so it comes as a shock when he glances up and gets a good look at his brother's face. Sickles under Jimmy's eyes are as dark as bruises. His lashes are short and even, as if they've been burned. And the expression on his face is one Niko's never seen before, the earnest entreaty of a dog being assaulted by a goat.

—Let me help out.

But Niko has already turned and walked away.

10:38 a.m.

No one asked the intern-thief to toggle anything, yet here he is in his tight-legged chinos, toggling the switches that control the blinds up near the ceiling. If you can afford to work for free in New York City, what could you possibly want with a diamond ring bought on sale fifteen years ago? Out of the corner of her eye, Iona watches the intern sit down and pull out a pen.

The day she met David, Iona had also had alcohol for breakfast. *Caffè corretti* with the groundskeepers in the café bar of the Villa Giulia. The men were clearly habituated to drinking grappa at ten in the morning since they did not, as Iona did, grow more animated and affectionate with every sip. The day was already warm and the doors to the Villa gardens stood open, admitting a delicious grassy breeze. Over the sound of tinny Italian pop excited birds called out.

She'd left the groundskeepers with double cheek-kisses and crossed to the bookshop, tipsy from the booze and electric with caffeine. And there he was, her future husband, browsing souvenir pencils in a pair of high-tops. Iona had picked out several books, too many, a couple of which were written in Italian, a language she could not read above a third-grade level. A queue had formed behind a Japanese student. They'd waited, Iona and her fate, one behind the other, clasping informative guides to the Etruscans. And somehow, how?, she and David began a conversation. It was about the piped Chopin, which was stuck on repeat. And then they were married and Iona was pregnant. Why did she even need a guide to the Etruscans? Because of a vague plan to visit Tarquinia, Vulci, get stuck into some necropoli? It was her summer of death. Those dank Cerveteri tombs decorated with birds and banquets. Who could resist the Etruscans with their black vases and right-to-left writing? A language without a Rosetta stone. They really knew how to die. Had Iona visited the gift shop ten minutes earlier or half an hour later, decided against the damn guide or never visited the Villa Giulia, she might have married a more hopeful man. A man who didn't begin every morning with the words I feel sick. Who didn't slope off into the night only to return three weeks later with a hunger for art he'd never voiced before.

A text pops up on her phone. Shay.

Meet me outside Purdue rn? Take 2 seconds

Iona checks the time, stands up, and stretches.

Over the years there have been flickering urges for other men. A grad student who repainted the living room after David botched the job. A bashful Swedish neighbor with hooded eyes. He had a suggestive way of staying the elevator door as Iona hustled up, dropping her keys and gloves. She never said anything, or even met his eye, locked inside her own reticence. Last year he moved to Taos.

—Iona, hold on... Dorothy sets down the phone she's holding and walks over.

—Can it wait? I'm meeting someone.

—It's actually really hard to tell.

—What is? Why are you looking at me like that?

—Lips like Mick Jagger but... Dorothy pokes Iona's thigh... —Could you call your legs skinny?

10:42 a.m.

—Are you kidding, what's the wedge?... Katherine walks backwards in front of him... —How could you not know about the wedge? Don't they get newspapers in Ohio? The architects wanted like a Guggenheim vibe and inserted this ramp over the west wing so it bisects the second floor. I used to hang out with a friend in payroll, but it would take my calves like a week to recover. Soutine... pointing... —Cézanne. All the furniture had to be specially designed. Desks have legs longer on one side than the other. And you can't use desk chairs that roll, obviously.

It's been years since Benjamin's thought about Katherine Tambling. He remembers her as a dreamy girl with chubby cheeks, a helix full of silver studs, and a potbelly she flaunted in tight tank tops and low-slung jeans. Now she's almost gaunt. Her ears are bare. The messy curls shaved into a buzzcut. He can feel himself searching for ways to impress her, an urge he's fighting since she'll instantly see through it.

—Now there's a rumor they're going to connect the uh, north, I think, side and south side of the top floor with some kind of tube. Daumier, Courbet. A brunnel they're calling it, because it's both bridge and tunnel, you're looking at me like I'm making this up, Benjamin, but I swear it's all true.

She was romantic but guarded. Willful, but open to experiment. On Saturdays they'd bike over to Queens or up to the Bronx where Katherine took too long petting the dogs they came across. Benjamin was forever idling under an awning or paging through a magazine while she checked in with the city's mutts. Her salads were daunting. A weaker man would have been thrown by the size of her salads. She laughed at the wrong things. Her dinner parties ended up with guests squeezed elbow-to-elbow, a table gridlocked with serving dishes and no place to set your drink because she had an irrational hatred of buffets. With cab drivers she was chummy, with shopkeepers, meddlesome. A distrust flowered in her of the things in life most people find beautiful. The Grand Canyon, long-haired cats, those final tremendous sentences of *The Great Gatsby.* Consensus unnerved her. And then there were the affects: fountain pens, music on vinyl, kitschy tumblers and hostess pajamas. Crossing the stems of her sevens. Benjamin brought her home for Thanksgiving where he paraded her around: his Connecticut trophy. Because she spoke with Katharine Hepburn's clenched-jaw delivery, he assumed she grew up in a house with white columns and a lawn like a putting green. But her childhood home was a split-level ranch. The driveway was cracked, the kitchen counters made of berry-stained Formica. Her mother was impossible. Only the garden was gratifying, full of roses and vines.

—Benjamin?

—Sorry, what were you saying?

—I said as an employee you can be sure that at least one person in HR has it out for you but realistically, it's more like two or three. If you're forced to deal with them for god's sake don't complain about anything and bring cookies. Fancy ones, not supermarket junk. The kind that come in a tin.

—Bring a tin.

—We get ten percent discount at the gift shop and forty percent at the staff cafeteria on the second floor which has been closed since March for something called restructuring. Modigliani, second-rate Picasso. Never, this is crucial, *never* eat anything from the shitty café, that's the one near us on minus one. Coffee's fine but zone out for a second and Amar's going to sneak in flavored syrup or whipped cream. Keep focused, you'll get something drinkable. On the other hand, you could literally die from eating a baked good, I'm not kidding... Katherine meanders through to the next gallery... —I swear I got nerve damage from a hazelnut scone.

They didn't have sex over Thanksgiving weekend. Benjamin couldn't manage in his childhood bedroom. Not with the Bone Thugz judging him from above the bureau and a chipped Snoopy nightlight stuck in the socket. Before dinner they horsed around at badminton. Katherine came in hot with a fighting spirit, diving wildly for the shuttlecock and trash-talking Gabe. Benjamin had set aside his dislike of mulled wine, his mother had a heavy hand with the nutmeg, and stood on the sidelines drinking gløgg. Watching Katherine with his family, he had a feeling that verged on love.

—What's wrong with your jaw?

—Nothing.

—You keep touching it.

—No, I don't.

—Well, Benjamin, I'm looking right at you, maybe you're not aware of it, but I promise you you are.

—I bought an energy drink on my way into work. I may have been grinding my teeth.

—An energy, are you nuts? Those things are like eighty percent toxic waste.

—It was an experiment.

—In what?

Benjamin rolls his eyes in agreement. Earlier this morning he couldn't get his eyes to focus or stop his knee from bouncing. His pulse leapt so violently he pinpointed the infirmary on a map he found in his new employee handbook, flipping the pages with shaking hands. Half an hour later he was woken by his own snore, drooling in the stained armchair Ward left behind.

He follows Katherine into the next gallery. She starts to say something, then stops.

—Mr. Bluestein?

Benjamin watches an ancient man perched on a bench take a million trembling years to turn and discover the source of the sound. When the man locates Katherine, he smiles... —Katie... and holds out his hand.

She takes it and sits beside him as he explains how he's here early today on account of a doctor's appointment this afternoon. He's been putting it off but it's true that he has begun to lose the feeling in his feet.

And Katherine is exactly as she was seven years ago when she was versed in the frustrations of her elderly neighbors, their pains and peeves and fights with City Hall. Familiar not only with their names, and the names of their children, but those of their cats and plants. Each neighbor had a liking for a special type of tea or vermouth or a card game played only in Michigan, and Katherine remembered them all. Katherine Tambling may have been moody and opaque, as well as bafflingly small-minded about buffets, but she was kind, even when no one was watching. Why did Benjamin break it off? Because she was hinting at moving in together or having a baby. He had the sense she wanted more but all he had was less.

Benjamin nods at the man politely as Katherine stands. He follows her out of the gallery and into the next.

—So when Mr. Blue was a kid, that painting... obliviously barging through a school group and out the other side... —Hung on a wall in his kitchen and every morning, he was an only child, he'd drink cocoa with Renoir's little girl, pretend she was his sister. The first time Bluestein saw it in the gallery he burst into tears. Right now the cousins don't have the proof they need to reclaim it but... Katherine stops in front of a seascape... —Anyway, how come you're not in touch with your family?

—What?

—Your family, you said before you weren't—

—Oh, okay, I wasn't prepared for, uh, well, my mom got sick. Then she got better and... he lets himself be distracted by a couple kissing... —I'm not sure what happened.

—You stopped talking? Completely?

—Pretty much.

It turns out you get extremely focused when you come that close to dying. After it was clear she would live, his mother stopped cleaning the house and made a big deal of refusing breakfast. She went back to school where she joined a philosophy club, whatever that is. Christmas, bottled water, the neighbor's new Toyota were now dangerous topics for family chit-chat. No observation escaped ridicule for its lack of depth. In the meantime, his father retired early and discovered wonder wherever he turned. He was the Ponce de León of sunlight reflected in a puddle or the way the dog's foot twitched in its dreams. Driving Benjamin to the train station one afternoon, his father nearly wiped out a church van as he swerved across three lanes of traffic to marvel at some ducklings gathered on the shoulder. The whole family had lost their minds and Benjamin had no choice but to hide out in New York.

Katherine has stopped in front of a still life. She's telling him where it was made or when or by whom. How it's important, or erroneously considered important. She's wearing a sweater that looks very soft. Once he could have reached out and touched her.

—Clive.

A man with black hair and a lanyard around his neck waves at her as he passes, speaking into his cell phone... —Giftshop at noon.

Katherine turns to watch, saying in a low voice... —Clive Hauxwell. Head of European Paintings... she raises her voice as the man disappears into the previous gallery... —He's always prowling around, picking up a coffee or on his way to Archives.

But Benjamin doesn't care. He'd much rather think about stroking her sweater.

10:56 a.m.

Iona Moore has agreed to lunch. She spoke in a surprisingly deep register. It struck Clive as a voice put on for strangers.

—Mr. Bluestein, good morning.

A dismissive nod. In his lap the old man holds a hat, its shape long gone. His fingers curl inward like turkey claws.

—Here early today.

Another get-fucked nod.

—Mind if I sit?

Bluestein shrugs. Sighs, it sounds like.

Clive sits on the bench next to the old man and together they regard his Renoir. The painting has always reminded Clive of a drunk and rainy night he spent locked out of a hotel in Torquemada. That scene was also cheap, blurry and disappointing. Old Bluestein continues to believe that the fate of the Renoir has something to do with Clive. If that were the case, he'd pay the man to take it away. But Bluestein remains unconvinced and over time the man's unwavering hatred has become a comfort. There's a purity to it you're forced to admire.

Renoir's little redhead has that tiresome moxie you find in certain girls in certain paintings. She sits in a crooked chair, a trug of flowers aslant on her lap. In the background, a dog's dinner of lilac and puce swirls around in a mucky tornado. Six russet noodles fall limply about the girl's shoulders, spilling onto a couple of lumps that context suggests are supposed to be breasts. Was Renoir hoping for a portrait of innocence with this chocolate box monstrosity? Virginal radiance? Clive has only ever found in it anguish, fury, suffocation. How could you possibly admire a painting so desperate to be liked?

—Brush strokes are extraordinary.

Bluestein presses his lips together as if there are a number of observations he'd like to express, none of them involving brush strokes.

—Always loved what Monet said, what was it, I don't paint a landscape or a figure, I paint an impression of an hour.

Again the old man sighs, drawing air through a pair of splendid nostrils that bring to mind the tapered arches of the Brooklyn Bridge.

—Impression of an hour... Clive repeats gravely... —Of course that's Monet, isn't it? Not Renoir here.

Bluestein remains silent as Renoir's redhead observes them from her land of muddled paint. Why is Lucy finding it so easy to leave? How will he manage without his human periscope?

As Clive stares at the painting, he begins to feel for the girl. The tilt of her head, the lifted chin. Brave under the circumstances. Her eyes beg for release from this prison of ugliness. The humanity in her gigantic peach forearms.

But Clive's been going about this all wrong. What a mistake it's been to think one lives life to the fullest by enjoying it. Seizing the day and so forth. Why not find the art in abject misery? Celebrate the ugly, as Sasha suggested. Why fight despair? Embrace it! Picture it as a form of beauty. Quit trying to reason with melancholy. Fuck psychology, fixing things. Maybe the rancor that throbs in his veins is the deepest commitment to life there is.

Next to him Mr. Bluestein coughs, a rusty sound.

Clive searches for something to say.

11:00 a.m.

—The feet are definitely irregular, I'll give you that... Iona focuses on the lion's paws, putting aside the strange phone call that arrived on her way to meet Shay. An invitation to lunch with the head of European Paintings, a man she's never met.

—What about his name?

—His name, uh...

—*Mane*, Iona, the lion.

—Mane, right, that's what I—

—There's no detail in his mane.

—There is an unusual lack of detail... Iona chooses her words carefully, keeping any opinion loose and hypothetical, as dictated by her field's code of ethics.

—Like a fat clown, like some kind of squished, like it was slammed in a car door, crunched up like that. Regal? With that expression?... Shay makes a face... —Now, I've been back and forth not knowing who to speak to or whether to speak at all. We both know I don't have what you'd call the education—

—But you worked in these galleries for—

—Yes I did and... Shay drops her voice as two elderly men shuffle past... —And it doesn't smell right.

It's thrilling to see Shay, usually so equable and self-possessed, riled up like this. And she has a point. There's a history of forgers finding a slab of ancient marble and squeezing a sculpture into the existing stone. Iona stoops to read the title card. *Donated by Marlon Tindall-Clark. 325 BCE.* Why would the Museum install a statue with Pickmeyer still in Catania? It makes no sense. It seems unlikely the department would run the protocol without him. The most obvious answer is that the Museum is aware the lion is fake but doesn't want to risk insulting this Marlon person. The hypocrisy makes her sick. She feels personally insulted.

—If the statue's fake it will have to come down... Iona stands, coughing to cover the creaking of her knees... —I should call Tiz Sericko, he specialized—

—No, no. Don't do that... Shay sounds alarmed... —The director would not approve of contacting Dr. Sericko behind her back.

—There's nothing wrong with a phone call. Imagine all those people tonight—

—No one looks at art during a party.

—Still, I might shoot Tiz a quick email.

—So long as you understand he'll use it to embarrass Diane Schwebe.

—I know there's this rumor Tiz got forced out for Diane, that he's got some kind of vendetta against her, but I'm telling you, Shay, he's not like that. Tiz Sericko is not a vindictive man. I've been to his house. With his wife. His wife was there, I mean. They were very gracious. She made mustard in a blender.

—If you tell Dr. Sericko you've got suspicions about this lion he's sure to go public, talk about the Museum's decline under Diane. I guarantee it.

—Okay but, Shay, all I'm saying is—

—Your decision, of course. I leave it to you.

Are they fighting? It sounds as if they are... —Wait! Where are you going?

Iona watches Shay start typing into her phone as she curves a wide path around one of the elderly men. The man is bending so far over a vitrine it appears possible he might not possess the elasticity to unbend.

11:04 a.m.

Shay presses send on her text and heads toward the stairs leading up to the mezzanine, overtaking a group of schoolchildren, annoyed that Iona Moore's idle debate about contacting the ex-director has forced Shay to report her suspicions about the lion. She had intended to wait, review the options.

—Mind your step please... a teacher trying to keep her students in line... —As we head toward Rome and, children, please... tripping, recovering... —These are ancient treasures, no touching.

Within a month of arriving at the Museum Diane had forced out Shay's incompetent predecessor and promoted Shay to Chief Security Officer. Because of this, Shay has always felt somewhat protective of the director. She shouldn't, of course, having actually earned the promotion years earlier. And she never liked Tiz Sericko who snuck around in a careless suit and at one point grew an irritating and disproportional beard. His fitful pauses, which many saw as judicious, even magnetic, Shay found bizarre and manipulative. He took too long to answer a question. The ensuing silence always made her question what she'd said. Exactly as it was meant to.

—Ethan... nodding to a recent hire: a foolish white kid with a foolish head of matted hair he foolishly calls dreadlocks. Also, an aversion to deodorant. The boy moves in billows of oniony body odor. Shay has spoken to him about hygiene. Clearly she was too subtle.

Her phone vibrates. A reply from Diane asking Shay to please stop by her office to discuss the matter ASAP. Shay rounds the wall of the restaurant, walking in tandem with a waiter on the other side of the glass until he disappears into the kitchen.

11:07 a.m.

Niko glances up as the waiter borrowed from West swings into the kitchen and squeezes past Jimmy, who is bringing an almost sarcastic level of scrutiny to his layering of granola and Greek yogurt.

It was a childhood of unrelenting gamesmanship. One in which Niko was rarely the victor. From the age of two Jimmy lied and sassed, cheated at soccer and short-changed the neighbors at the Kool-Aid stand. For a year when he was eight he wore a brigadier's hat and carried a corn cob pipe, captivated by a picture he'd come across of General MacArthur. In middle school he smoked pot. In high school he sold it. He was kicked out of college for stealing a horse. And somehow this guy emerged the hero.

And now he's staring at Niko.

—What?

—I'm ready to tell you why I'm here.

Instinctively Niko reaches for his inhaler.

—Put that away. Look at me.

—I have a kitchen to run.

—Oh my god, grow up... Jimmy smiles falsely at M.J. walking past with a prep tub. He waits until she's out of earshot... —So, about a week ago—

—I'm not listening.

—Yes you are. About a week ago I was interviewed by this guy from the local newspaper. They're doing a profile on me for the Sunday magazine. Big spread, lots of pictures. Thing is, Nik, I may have blown a few things out of proportion about our childhood. Nothing big but I need you to back me up. I have enemies: other chefs, ex-waiters. A busboy I called retarded. Lots of people would love to see me ruined.

—Back you up how?... Niko reaches for a tasting spoon... —What did you tell the guy?

—I may have... with a terrifying sniff... —I may have hinted that we grew up on the South Side. Under, like, reduced circumstances. I might have mentioned the projects, Cabrini-Green or something, I don't recall the details.

—You said we... Niko stops, the spoon halfway to his mouth because jesus god even his brother isn't that stupid... —You said what now?

—Don't yell. I get that it was ill-advised, okay, I get that. But who the hell's interested in another middle-class dipshit from Winnetka? No one. People want obstacles, struggle. The struggle's the story.

—Why are you fucking around with this stuff? Just make your stupid food.

—That attitude, Nikolic, is why you're still sweating the line, taking orders from some Emerson Pitt no one's ever heard of.

—Really? I thought it was because some asshole never paid back my wife's life insurance... ripping a ticket as it comes off the printer, yelling... —Three skillet, one kale!

—You need to shape how the public sees you.

Niko stares at the plates on the pass, mechanically grinding a storm of pepper over the side-salads.

—Be a good brother, Nik. The story goes online tonight. Back me up. If anyone calls, you know, corroborate my shit.

—I'm not going to lie because you think it's cooler to grow up poor.

—Well, now you're being silly. Of course it's cooler to grow up poor. Rags to riches, it's as old as time.

—Dad nearly died escaping Serbia, that's not good enough?

—No. Hate to tell you, Niko, but no, it's not. No one gives a shit about the Balkans.

—I'm not going to tell people we dodged bullets in Cabrini-Green when our biggest headache was like piano practice. I may be a hundred kinds of jackass, but I'm not that kind. Call the journalist, off the record. Tell him you misspoke. Maybe he'll feel sorry for you.

—It's so much worse than that.

Niko wipes the rim of a plate. Why does he insist on loving this person who so predictably and relentlessly brings chaos into his life? With great cheer and that unshakable certainty, dismantling any small thing Niko has built for himself.

—A while ago Kia and I were at a bar with her friends... Jimmy takes a sundae glass from the shelf overhead... —They were showing off, boasting, and, I don't know, I was drunk, I came up with some story about being electrocuted by a friar when I was cooking in a monastery. Get it, friar, fryer? Trust me, at the time it was hilarious... intent on measuring granola... —I told them I was taking a bath, and a cenobite dropped his clippers in the water.

—That's a, who the fuck's going to believe that?

—Believe me they bought it.

—No, they didn't.

Jimmy waves this away... —Anyway, when we got home, she was really pissed, Kia, because, you know, I'd fibbed before and she was sick of it. Harmless lies, nothing big.

—Like what?

—I told her father I used to have ALS.

—You... Niko stares at his brother... —What you do mean, used to?

—I get colorful when I drink.

—But it's fatal.

—Sure, you know that but—

—Everyone knows that, Jimmy. Everyone.

—Anyway, in the end I convinced her dad I was a medical miracle.

—Oh, okay, your win, then.

—Well, Kia didn't see it that way. After her father, and then the monastery thing, basically Kia threatened to leave if I told another whopper.

Niko rips the ticket off the printer, yells the order to the line then aims a gentle kick at Jimmy's shin... —Call the journalist. Clarify.

—I did, I did. Of course I called him, Nikolic, it was the first thing I did as soon as I had time to think but then I realized that a correction was going to sound worse, and I hung up without saying anything. Can you imagine? A parenthesis saying later Peša called to explain that when he said the projects he meant Winnetka, Illinois, and when he said his parents were on food stamps, he meant they taught community—

—*Food stamps?*

—college. And when he mentioned an older brother, he meant his identical twin.

—An older, why would you say I was older than you?

—Because, duh Nik, it's a better story. Young guy with no cooking experience opens a chicken restaurant, four months later he's a national celebrity. Meanwhile, his brother slogged through three years of culinary school, paid his dues, did everything right and never got off the line.

Nikolic stares at the slip of printed paper in his hands until it blurs into an abstract pattern of slashes and curves.

—Come on, back me up. Say, I don't know, that we lived in the projects for a while, like, yeah, we definitely lived in Winnetka, but maybe for a little while—

—Anyone with two minutes on their hands is going to find out the truth.

—Look, I'm helping you out, aren't I? Think I want to be here dicking around with mint sprigs? We're brothers, we're bonded.

—No, we're, that's actually the opposite—

—What about the twin thing? We can feel each other's pain, according to studies. You and I, we're in sync.

This so disturbs Nikolic he needs to take a second to walk over to Maria Jazmin and pretend to check the status of the smoked eel, controlling himself, steering his mind to other areas so as not to spend another second on the horrific idea that he shares any sort of bond with his brother. The power Jimmy had over him growing up. The hatred Niko felt seemed stronger than the casual antipathy most kids had for their siblings. He spent weeks refusing to speak. Locked in his room. Taking extra shifts at his after-school job. For years Niko avoided mirrors, that's how much he hated Jimmy's face.

11:18 a.m.

—For God's sake, Henry... Diane sits down, motioning Shay to a chair to which she shakes her head no... —Shay guarded those galleries for years and—

—Two summers.

—Okay, months then... smiling, responding to Shay's military bearing by squaring her shoulders... —It's still what, a thousand hours living among Greek and Roman statues so if Shay says she has doubts about Marlon's lion, of course I'm going to worry and, my coffee... swiveling to Chris who points to it on the bookshelf next to her... —Thank you, assume that further tests are probably—

—Also, Diane, I did happen to consult one of the organic conservators, a friend, for her opinion.

—Who was that?

Shay gives her one of the great blank looks of our time... —At this exact moment I'm at a loss for her name.

—Well, when you remember... Diane sips her coffee, refusing to think about the depressing conversation she has still to have with Shay.

—This conservator made it clear that while she couldn't go on the record, privately she saw inconsistencies.

—We have time to take it down, don't we?... pulling back his sleeve, Henry checks his watch.

—Yes, we have *time* to take it down, Henry, but we can't take it down.

Diane leans back in her chair. From the beginning Marlon Tindall-Clark made it clear that granting the Museum the second half of his collection was entirely incumbent on how the first half was treated. And while there's nothing particularly earth-shattering in the first half, given that the man built his collection around a lion theme, the remaining pieces include two Rubens, a Cranach, and a Rousseau.

They worked on Marlon for months, Diane and members of the board, to nail down the complete collection. Flew him to Rome on a piffling pretext. Coddled, flattered, truckled, and groveled. Laid on blindingly lit soft-food dinners. Golf lessons. A private tour around the vineyards of Sonoma. Sent a specialist to fix his humidor when he mentioned a problem with airflow. Presented him with a diving watch good to thirty fathoms despite the old man's challenges with breathing on dry land. All without a firm commitment. And while Tindall-Clark might have the jolly appearance of an uncle who once tickled you behind the kneecap he's actually spiteful and ruthless and last year tripped an intern for giving him sugar instead of Splenda. One whiff of inferior treatment and the old man will happily overnight the rest of his collection to London.

—Who the hell's going to know the lion's fake?

She and Chris turn as one to stare at Henry.

—What?

—Tiz, Henry. Tiz Sericko's going to know the lion's fake. That wily bastard, pardon my whatever, there's nothing he'd love more than to catch me displaying a fake as if it were some prize.

—Is it possible that Sericko was poisoned by his own shrimp and isn't coming?

—No... Chris, from the corner... —I called this morning. He's fine. Giving a lecture at Yale this afternoon but definitely attending.

—You told him about the shrimp?

—Of course not.

—Back up a second, how did the statue get past whatsit—

—Really, Henry, does it matter?

—Ian Pickmeyer.

—Pickmeyer, and get installed in the first place? We have protocol in place to avoid this kind of thing. Strict protocol.

—Because, *Henry*... not bothering to hide her impatience... —Marlon made a whole scene about his statue being on show this evening. I believe Eleanor is—

—Dying, yes, confirmed... Chris nods.

—So I called Ian, he's abroad, I said, can we fudge the usual process a little and wait to run the protocol until your return. Ian, I mean the connection was, I could hardly hear him, but as far as I could tell he gave me the go-ahead. Now, instead of pointing fingers, let's figure out a way to keep Tiz from publicly humiliating me. Who has an idea? Chris?

—Hire hookers. Distract Sericko with hot women.

Nobody looks at Chris.

—Ma'am, I think I will return to preparing—

—Yes, yes, of course. Thank you, Shay, for bringing us up to speed.

Diane had no idea she was still in the room. The three of them watch Shay walk across the office in her silent sensible shoes and slip out the door.

—Sericko will sniff out hookers in a second. Prostitutes aren't actresses... Henry speaks with impressive authority... —They lose focus and wander off.

—Then let's get actresses. Or what about an intern?

—You two are being... tugging at her tight blouse... —How is an intern any different from a prostitute?

—Well, free, for one.

—Here's an idea... Chris, with the jovial high spirits he puts on in a sticky situation... —When Dr. Sericko walks into the gala I *accidentally* spill a big glass of red wine on him. He'll have to run home and change. Possibly not to return.

—If we could perhaps think of something that doesn't smack of the Three Stooges I'd be eternally grateful, I really would.

—We should keep it lawful.

—Thank you, Henry. I'm glad that has to be stated.

—Quick reminder of our... Chris lights up his phone for the time... —Eleven thirty with Merchand—

—In a minute.

—Yup.

—It's not as if... Henry struggles up from the couch... —Sericko never straddled an ethical line when he was director.

—Really? I'd love to hear more at some point... Diane picks up the phone... —I'm telling Conrad to dim the lighting around Marlon's statue and move the bar to American. And don't you dare... pointing at Henry as he crosses the room... —Say anything about liability right now.

11:27 a.m.

—No, no, let them all trip around in the dark... and shrugging broadly, Henry closes the door behind him.

He really should mention liability and maybe he will, this evening, have the lights turned up outside Purdue but right now Henry has more items to cross off his list. He walks down the soft dark hallway thinking about Kim and Colin out in Los Angeles. They deserve a phone call. A letter outlining his regrets.

Henry moves past Audrey, her back to him as she swears softly at the printer, and into his office.

He was thirty-five when Colin was born, too old to be frightened by the reckless deluge of a child's love. And yet. All that waddling wide-eyed trust, what the hell was he to do with it? How was he to read, surrounded by scampering? Friday nights the family drove to Montauk where Henry proved himself an excellent father. Setting up bocce, stomping croquet wickets into the lawn. Spraying the hose for the kids to run through. Monopoly in front of the fire when the nights got chilly. But it was performative, most of it. He never lost himself entirely.

The acceptance of his flaws is electrifying. He's ready to stare down his remaining days open to emotion. Tolerant, grateful, unafraid.

Henry picks up his phone. Calls Colin. He'll be fighting traffic. The call goes to voicemail and Henry hangs up.

11:30 a.m.

Pushing through the fire door into the hallway of -1, Shay fights the feeling she had in Diane's office, the sinking dread as three faces turned to her wonderingly when she spoke. They had no idea she was still in the room. She had taken the trouble to warn Henry and Diane of a potential embarrassment for the Museum and was almost immediately brushed aside, discounted as irrelevant. Just another statue. And that familiar feeling bubbled to the surface. The one Shay routinely pushes away, buries, tries to ignore. The one you have to ignore, not all the time of course, sometimes you have to take to the streets, but much of the time, if you want any hope of a happy life.

The new curator of film is pulling the door to his office closed, checking it's locked and hurrying away, down the hall. Shay watches as he stops in the doorway of the Costume Center.

11:32 a.m.

When Katherine found the newspaper lying on a bench next to the women's bathrooms, folded and unread, all its sections still in place, she thought, what fun, I'll put my feet up for two minutes and page through the *Times*. It was something she used to do a decade ago in the café around the corner from her apartment. She always arrived after the paper had been pawed through forty times when the ink had turned to an unreadable smear and the spine was full of muffin crumbs. Two minutes, she told herself as she walked back to her office. A short break from phone calls and emails. And there, on the first page of the arts section, was the news.

—Hey... Benjamin is standing in the doorway, holding a yellow legal pad.

—How long have you been standing there?

—Only a minute... he walks across the room and flops into Giselle's white armchair... —Is that yoga?

—No... Katherine gets to her feet... —It's just lying on the floor.

—Mind if I ask you a couple of... Benjamin crosses his leg at the knee, turning a long yellow page... —Administrative questions? I need a new desk chair. Do I call HR or is there like an office for office supplies? Also, there's a smell, I can tell it's going to persist and a scented candle won't... glancing up from his notes... —Damn.

—What?

—You look ready to punch a wall.

—Yeah. I made a huge mistake. So, so stupid. I could kill myself.

—Okay. I mean, first of all, don't. What happened?

—I lost the Bastovic archive.

—What's a Bastovic?

—He's a designer. Griselda spent nearly a year—

—Griselda?

—My boss, Giselle. Spent a year trying to secure his papers for the Museum and finally, about two months ago, he gave us a verbal commitment. All I had to do was follow up... from her desk, Katherine picks up the strewn newspaper pages, flinging them in Benjamin's general direction... —Check it out. Ernest Bastovic. Donated his archives to the Met.

—So, you... batting away the *Times*... —Forgot to follow up?

—Okay you don't need to, there were distractions, okay? I was planning a move to California. My mother was, oh my god, who cares? The point is, Griselda's going to, I mean, now she'll definitely fire me and I can't lose my job, really I can't. What else do I have? No, Benjamin, I don't. I have nothing else. And my health insurance? Lose my insurance and I'm fucked. Before I had dental I cracked a molar and spent a year chewing with my left teeth.

—I see... Benjamin nods, serious... —Give me a second.

—A second for what?

—To hatch a plan... he stands, tossing the legal pad onto the armchair.

—What plan?

—For keeping your job.

—What are you, there's no plan, Benjamin... noticing that his sleeves are rolled up, exposing his forearms.

—How old is she, your boss?

—Eighty, seventy-five.

—Gaslight her.

—What? No.

—Stick her keys in the filing cabinet. Plant a slice of bologna in her desk. Mess with her computer. At this point you're setting the groundwork.

—This is, I don't know where to begin, for one, her computer's password protected.

—Perfect. She'll never suspect you.

Katherine laughs. It's kind of comforting, Benjamin's problem-solving, even if it's solely for her entertainment.

Would Griselda ever believe she forgot to tell Katherine about Bastovic? Katherine isn't yet forty and sometimes loses the word for scissors. On the other hand, only a few minutes ago she read a *Times* article about a ninety-four-year-old being awarded a monster prize for her work on DNA. Current work. Not a lifetime achievement award, but the old girl in the actual lab today and tomorrow churning out breakthrough discoveries.

Benjamin's ended up on the other side of the room next to Giselle's pristine desk... —This her?... he yanks at a drawer.

—She wears the key on a chain around her wrist.

He picks up Giselle's keyboard, flips it over, smiles... —Password... holding up the keyboard so Katherine can see the slip of paper taped underneath... —For consistency, you'll need to break into her apartment.

—Break into my boss's apartment?

—I mean, ideally.

Benjamin is flushed, decisive, ready for adventure. As if he's hungry for plots bigger than his life. Maybe this is why he stopped speaking to his family. Maybe it all got too small.

—You saw that movie *Amélie*?

—No. Feel-good movies make me feel terrible.

—Right, right... blinking, lost for a second, as if he's recalling a memory... —That's right. So... returning to the present... —*Amélie* is basically the French version of *Gaslight*, only instead of a sociopath trying to get his wife declared insane, a cute girl with big eyes runs around dishing up karmic payback... walking over to Giselle's lateral cabinet... —Like breaking and entering is fine if you speak French and wear your bangs super short... Benjamin pulls out a drawer and takes out a folder, opening it and closing it before sliding it back in place... —I think it's best to imagine you're Audrey Tatou, not Charles Boyer. It will make the whole thing feel whimsical rather than, you know, criminal.

Benjamin seems pretty fluent in this whole business of gaslighting. Maybe he's done it before, gaslighted someone, maybe even Katherine, over the course of their short relationship, made her feel crazy. Although, thinking back, almost every relationship has made her feel crazy in one way or another. All those bungled attempts at having feelings. Lying in each other's hair and eyelashes, pubes and sweat, all warmth and goo, quoting lyrics and feeling close but then getting up, making coffee or noodles, and starting to feel crazy out in the streets with different ideas about where to cross, or in a bodega disagreeing about snacks and whether it can be justified, spending all that money on a nut milk.

—I know what you're thinking.

—You do?

—You're thinking how can I inflict this on someone I've spent years working with and who, even if I call Griselda, I also genuinely respect. But it's not easy to get a job out there, Katherine, not for people like us, with no skills. And as you said, what about health insurance? Sure, it's not going to be pleasant hearing your boss worry she found the remote in the shower, I get that. But keep the bigger picture in mind. Think about your teeth.

Benjamin actually seems attached to this ludicrous idea, pacing around the place deep in thought. Any minute now he'll form a rectangle with his fingers and thumbs and sight her through it.

—Is it even possible, Katherine, to get a job without a letter of rec? Okay, I see the look on your face. But go down fighting, that's all I'm saying. Don't go down without a fight.

—Can you hang on a second?... fumbling in the desk drawer for her travel-sized mouthwash.

—You okay?

But she's out the door, springing down the hallway toward the ladies' room causing the Chief of Security to turn in alarm from the doorway of the stairwell.

11:42 a.m.

Why is the Costume girl galloping down the hallway, Shay thinks as the stairwell door closes behind her, and she turns to take the stairs two at a time, hauling herself by the metal banister with her right hand as she texts Astrid with the left, inadvertently all caps, ON MY WAY, yanking open the door, almost falling into Greek and Roman, bearing down on the goofy lion, ignoring the beast as she hustles by, past tourists listening to a lecture in Purdue, around a copyist sketching Adonis, toward the lost child.

11:43 a.m.

—Okay... Diane turns to Chris as the elevator starts its descent... —Merchandising. Let's keep this quick... fixing her hair with one hand, trying to sort of rake it into place... —Twenty minutes tops.

—But we have to be thorough. Kory leaves tomorrow for two weeks in Antigua.

—*Two weeks?*... fluttering her fingers to let a loose hair drift to the elevator floor... —Who the hell takes a two-week vacation in October?

—Could it be rehab?

—Really?... finding that now she's whispering... —Kory?

—I'm not saying it *is* rehab... Chris tells his phone... —But I'm not saying it isn't. I have another email from Dominic. I thought you—

—I did, I did. I mean, I didn't, but I will. Listen... the too-small blouse is driving her crazy, squeezing her shoulders... —The funicular, did you find out, can they send a guy?

—No. Repairs have to go through the original dealer and Quasholt won't return my calls. I've walked over and tested it a bunch this morning and two out of three times it's worked fine, so in terms of Abu Dhabi or the Ambassador, could it be worth the risk?

Diane shakes her head no as the elevator lands, rests a beat, and the doors open. She follows Chris off the elevator and into the hallway, imprinting in her mind the need to return Dom's call at the same time fearful of what could be coming, bending to retrieve litter, a screwed-up museum map, then on down the hallway, past the Egyptian galleries, her favorite security guard who always looks cheerful to be standing, through a pack of schoolchildren, their beleaguered teacher... —Kids, listen up, please, the funeral rites of Ramses Two... teacher's voice dying out as Diane follows Chris around the corner, through the Great Hall, giving a wide berth to four traffic cones marking out a scissor-lift as well as Conrad, craning his head, now bringing his gaze down to include the two of them in an icy glare, to which Diane smiles broadly, sending back the kind of sunny wave that's sure to madden him.

While Conrad took the news well that he was to dim the lighting around Tindall-Clark's lion and move the bar setup, he has doubtlessly added it to the long list of aspersions he's had to endure at the hands of the Museum. Conrad's mind is a Lascaux cave of unforgotten slights and offenses.

—There you are!... Kory, loitering outside the entrance to the gift shop... —I was beginning to think we were being rescheduled.

Diane ignores the dig, treats Kory to a conspiratorial wink, and edges past her into a cramped meeting room fitted with retina-blasting overhead lights.

Two twenty-somethings sit at the conference table, hands folded, waiting. She's met them before. Can't recall their names.

—Good morning.

—Morning... the young woman gives Diane the despairing furtive glance of a person being held against her will.

Two seats down, a frattish ex-lacrosse type tips back in his chair. His hair gives off an oily sheen as if he's actually oozing entitlement.

It's difficult to resist immediately hating these two, their insolent ambition and unearned collagen. Life unfurling before them like an infinite road. If these kids knew what it was like to have your life half-over, dented, dinged, and currently taking bullets.

—Okay... Chris, briskly pulling out the chair next to her... —Diane has a packed day so let's keep things moving.

—We're eager to begin... Kory remains standing... —Our shops have seen a forty percent increase in sales of women's jewelry. The charm bracelets especially have proven impossible to keep in stock. I sent you, Diane, our mentions in *Vogue Italia* and *Seventeen*—

—You did... hoping it doesn't sound like a question.

—We're adding new charms every month, two silver, two gold, ones just in are based on Roman grave goods.

—Wonderful... still queasy, Diane keeps her eyes off a pile of glazed donuts mounded in the center of the table like a glistening cairn.

—Now, statues. We're looking to add a couple for spring... Kory checks her notes... —Reproductions of our Adonis Crouching, the new Greek lion, and our footless Aphrodite.

—No lion.

—But last week you—

—No lion. The others, fine. What else?

—June had an idea for commissioning jellies and jams inspired by our still lifes that feature fruit. I have to say I thought it was a little—

—I like it.

—A little likable... Kory makes a note... —For kids we're doing action figures based on *Christ Appears to Mary*—

—Stay away from kids for now.

—Stay away from, okay. For adults we have coloring books based on designs by Rennie MacIntosh or William Morris, let me find you the... her words trickling nonsensically, Kory sorts through a pile of papers on the table next to her.

—Adults?... turning to Chris... —Adults color?

—For relaxing.

—Kory, don't worry about the, let's keep it moving.

Abandoning the search, Kory returns to her list... —Swiss chocolates, dark, white, and milk, shaped like sarcophagi.

—Sarcophagi.

—They're about three inches high and couldn't be cuter.

—But, like, candy coffins?

—I mean, they're hollow.

—That's a blessing.

Kory does something with her mouth... —Delicious and designed for adults.

—You mentioned.

—Next, we're thinking about a tea service—

—What's a tea service?

—You know, cups, sugar bowl—

—Oh, I thought it was a delivery thing.

—No. Based on the cups and saucers in Monet's *The Tea Set*.

—I like that idea. Love it. Good. How much?

—Pricing it now.

—Keep it under three hundred.

Kory makes a note... —A fun new thing that I've been pushing, Diane, is mousepads printed with designs from Islamic textiles—

—Mousepads?... this wretched blouse cutting into her armpits... —Do people still use mice?... looking at Chris for confirmation.

—No. No one likes mice... he scrolls through his phone, tapping, shaking his head at some message.

—What is it?... whispering, while smiling at Kory.

—Nothing.

—Diane, what about, if you don't like mousepads, we could use the designs for coasters or shawls, maybe—

—*Shawls?*

—Tea towels, maybe?... this from Despair in the corner who visibly brightens at the idea... —Or oven gloves?

—Any suggestions, Kory, for a guest under seventy?... trying to keep her tone light.

—Men's socks? Lamp shades?

—What about something experiential?

—Experiential... Kory, eyes darting with a rising panic.

—Why do visitors buy things from a gift shop in the first place?

—Souvenirs?

—Right, yes, as mementoes, repositories for an emotional event. People are looking to capture and archive their experience with us. Why not interrogate the received notion of what that repository might be?

—Interrogate?... Kory glances toward the door.

—Anyone?

Silence.

—What about... Kory offers a spiritless smile... —A very tasteful breakfast tray?

—A tray... trying to disguise the urge to poke out her own eyes, Diane turns to the frat boy... —What about you? What do you want to see in the gift shop?

—Porn?... Sigma Nu swallows and drops his head... —No, god, sorry... searching the notepad in front of him... —I've been brainstorming dorm-type merch. Posters, wash kits, you know, things a grandparent might—

—Porn?

—I apologize. That was inappropriate. I've been taking improv classes.

—Interesting.

Everyone swivels to stare at Diane.

—Obviously we wouldn't call it porn. Erotica or—

—Goodness... Kory, with an expression of forced amusement... —What are we talking about right now?

—Call it *Body Beautiful* or—

—I get what you're thinking but that sounds like an ad for liquid soap... Sigma leans back with folded arms.

—Not *erotica*, either. We don't want to give our seniors a coronary. Give me a sec... Chris studies the ceiling.

—Really, Diane, I think—

—Hang on... she points at Sigma Nu... —Your name again?

—Tyler.

—Tyler, go through European Paintings, sculpture, our ivories. There's great erotica in Asia. Jade figures, netsuke.

—Shunga?... a whisper from Despair in the corner. The girl turns scarlet.

—No, I think that's perhaps too explicit.

—There should be an organizing principle though, right?... Chris taps his phone against his chin... —I mean, it can't be all boobies.

—This is like a calendar or—

—Hang on a minute, Kory. Go on, Chris.

—Could be a bit lubricious if we run around taking a detail from this Grecian breast—

—Hmm.

—and that priapic fresco.

—Good point. Full pieces only.

—Passion?... Despair offers, with an apologetic throat-clearing... —Could be a title?

—I'll leave it to you and Tyler to flesh out the no pun intended idea and get back to me next week and yes, Kory, calendars and maybe a poster?... clicking her phone pointedly to check the time... —Nine panels on a poster-sized sheet?

—Perfect for the freshman virgin... Tyler, with a filthy cackle... —What about a pornish tea towel for a certain type of granny?

—I have that granny.

—So you like this idea... Kory fires daggers at Despair, daring her.

—No, I just have a grandmother who—

—Okay... Diane pushes back her chair... —Afraid we need to move along.

—We're done? Already?... Kory appears to be close to tears. Her long-awaited meeting derailed by youth.

—Chris tells me you're off to Antigua tomorrow.

Kory closes her eyes and nods. Black kohl lies on her eyelids in thick uneven stripes.

—Make sure to visit Jabberwock on the north side of the island.

—Island? No, Guate—

—Dominic and I got slammed by a freak wave while we were snorkeling, went to a local bar all scraped up and dosed to the gills on Vicodin and... recalling mid-sentence Chris's comment about rehab... —Anyway, the beaches are pretty... waving in the approximate direction of the youngsters, nearly colliding with Chris in the doorway, stepping back to follow him out of the gift shop and back into the Great Hall.

The trip to Antigua was a decade ago, a last-minute escape from an interminable February. In a concerted effort to appear effortlessly casual, Diane packed the sort of filmy dresses and creamy scarves recommended by fashion magazines for romantic winter jaunts. She floated from the hotel room on a gossamer cloud, but a powerful wind came off the ocean and she spent most of her time pulling diaphanous material out of her mouth. She and Dominic had athletic sex every morning and afterward ate almond croissants at a tiled table. The hotel Dom booked was offensively Eurocentric but it seemed pointless to take a stand when the pastries were as good as Pichard's. It was a gorgeous, memorable trip. They loved each other.

—Need to hustle here... Chris checks his phone... —We have less than an hour with Abu Dhabi and the brothers have expressed... glancing up, he veers abruptly... —Shit, there's Hauxwell, follow me.

Obediently Diane copies Chris as he takes a sharp right, dodges a couple of malingering docents, and sweeps past Shay Pallot stooping over, hands propped on her knees to better address a small Black child.

11:58 a.m.

—The only reasonable response is tears, you're right about that. Now look here... and drawing her hand from her pocket Shay reveals the Halloween candy she grabbed when Astrid's text came in... —A baby Kit-Kat, what do you think?

The child stops crying, slightly more interested. He's five, maybe six, and has clearly listened to warnings about strangers because he's refused to budge an inch. Declined to accompany Shay downstairs where lost children are brought to wait until a parent has the good sense to ask a security guard for help. Her heart breaks for this solemn little man in his red sweater vest. Tentatively he puts out a hand and accepts the candy. But he doesn't unwrap the Kit-Kat or even look at it, clenching the chocolate at his side.

—My name's Shay, I've told you that, I'll wait until you're ready to tell me yours.

The child stares at his shoe, then whispers... —Denzel.

—Denzel! Well now there's a very talented movie actor called Denzel, were you named for him?

The boy turns to her suspiciously... —Are you a policeman?

Shay feels a surge of misguided love. Stop it, he's nothing like William. Stop it right now, this child has eyes more almond-shaped, a pointier chin, hair faded at the sides. She squats next to the child so they are eye to eye... —Denzel, sir?

He gazes at her with wide eyes.

—May I take your hand?

Slowly and apprehensively, Denzel allows it.

—Would you like to see a whole bunch of teeny TVs while we wait for your mom?

The child is not unswayed by this promise. Shay stands, turning to guide Denzel, catching sight of European Paintings disappearing into the gift shop.

Noon

Kory and Liz, according to their all-caps name tags, spin around, startled, when Clive walks in. They nod politely and continue to viciously organize postcards.

—But she doesn't respect me, okay? Like, who goes to the Caribbean Antigua? Nobody. Tacky losers.

—But didn't Diane say *she* went?

This piece of logic appears to stump Kory who takes it out on Chardin, jamming his pears into the revolving wire rack.

Clive leans against a glass display case affecting interest in the imitation jade masks nested in black velvet and earrings got up to look Egyptian. Silver brooches studded with plastic scarabs lie bathed in tiny spotlights like the crown jewels.

Over by the postcards Kory and Liz continue chuntering away, voices rising and falling, scaling little hills of umbrage before reorienting to begin again.

Clive checks his phone for the time. She'll be late, of course. She's the late sort.

He first spotted the woman he now knows is Iona Moore last spring at an employee preview for the Mantegna show. She worked in Conservation, Clive found out, a fact he filed away for future use. She looked like the sort of woman he could bully for a favor. Standing before *Agony in the Garden*, luscious lips pursing and unpursing as if recollecting some private torment brought to mind by egrets and apostles. Her calves were long thin twigs, encased in woolen stockings so thick and lumpy it seemed impossible she hadn't crocheted the things herself. That hair! Clive thought, watching her stick a finger into the barbaric nest on top of her head and give it a scratch before moving on to *Judith and her Maidservant*. Why not cut it? Give it a style of some sort? Yet the sight of her made him wistful for the days of slipshod women. Back then, New York was tired and grimy, aggrieved and half-feral. Tube sock vendors used to set their wares against the rolling hills of black garbage bags. Rats openly frolicked. Downtown sidewalks were spread with blankets temptingly dotted with pilfered clocks or faded sweatshirts promoting Vassar or Prozac. There was a sort of grudging wartime spirit in the city back then, a collective respect that came from standing shoulder to shoulder in the same foxhole. It took grit to live here once. But Clive has had this thought before, only to realize the rats are still here, so is the foxhole. It's not some sepia version of New York City he pines for, but the hopeless young man the city brought to life.

On the subway he looks for comfort in the rush hour faces of paralegals, secretaries, shop assistants. Once these girls in cheap shoes would have been fuzzy with sleep, mussed and musky. Eyes pouched and smudged with last night's eyeliner. The air would have been thick with the funk of hot horses. And while it's true that today these same women are kempt and groomed, camera-ready with arched brows, sleek hair and corrected skin, if Clive closes his eyes he can still make out the tang of last night coasting through the carriage. The odor cuts through a floral river of shampoo and perfume, delivering him back to the days when night bled into morning. That was two decades ago, a time when he too spoke of tender things.

A few days after the Mantegna preview Clive came upon Iona Moore sitting on the steps outside the Museum. She was lounging at the base of a Corinthian pillar wearing a poncho that looked to be fabricated from an unlikely material, possum fur or recycled bottles. Everything about the woman was semi-hysterical and secondhand. Almost lichenous. Clive was returning from a midday tumble with a Bolivian he'd met online, a part-time underwear model with an exciting prosthetic. The lunch hour had proven pleasurably punishing. Clive had a conquistador spring to his step. And there she was, the utter disaster of Iona Moore slopped on the grand staircase like a spilled curry. Clive watched her remove a lock of hair from her mouth which she appeared to be consuming along with her sandwich. The sight of this madwoman was like a face full of cold water. Gone were the images of his Bolivian, glistening, naked and short a fibula.

A commotion by the door. At the center of this kerfuffle, Clive wagers, he will find Iona Moore. And, yes. Here she is. Flailing among the marked-down Impressionists.

12:06 p.m.

Who the hell sets a bucket of posters right by the entrance like some kind of booby trap? A runaway *Haystacks* wrapped in plastic gets stopped by his black shoe, European Paintings, crouching to help, picking up a rolling *Sunrise* and handing it to her so she can jam it back in the bucket. She's saying yes, yes, except no one's asked a question and Clive Hauxwell looks up at her from where he crouches, smiling. Even this close up he's extremely handsome. Iona's blushing, hating herself for blushing, then hating Hauxwell for causing the blushing. Why has she agreed to this terrifying lunch?

—I'm afraid I've just discovered West is closed... Clive leans into her as he stands.

Only his eyes are truly spectacular. Icy blue, like a husky's, humored and hypnotic. Eyebrows so black and thick they verge on comic. A long nose saves his face from prettiness.

—We could leave the museum, go out... replacing the last poster.

—Oh... Iona yanks her sweater down over her hips, wishing she'd worn something, anything, else... —I'm under a deadline. What about Central America?

—I can't bear the ceilings.

—There's always the shitty café.

—God no. Tell you what, we'll do the Globe, my treat. Don't refuse, I'm about to exact a favor... his hand grazes her lower back, making her shiver... —Stairs or elevator?

—Elevator... the glass stairs give her vertigo.

Clive propels her gently down the hallway. As they approach the elevator, the doors open and two middle-aged men burst out, racing to get at the art. Clive places his hand across the door gap, waiting for her, squinting, craquelure beginning around those husky eyes. Encircling his wrist is a copper rheumatism bracelet or perhaps the fashionable or ironic version of one. She tries to remember how to walk, entering the elevator cautiously, catching Hauxwell's scent as he turns to press MEZZ. There was a missed opportunity once, on the Grand Roué, with a boy who smelled of tobacco and oranges. He kept asking Iona if she understood the word *baiser* and she kept shaking her head, staring down at the lights of Paris, unsure if he was pressing for the noun or the verb. She was sixteen, it was her chance for a wild fling. A story she could relive when she was old and tired with a feeble neck. But she was too nervous and the revolutions gave her a sour stomach.

They get off the elevator and walk around the curved glass wall. The Globe is fairly empty except for the tables along the far wall where a column of solitary guests sit, one behind the other, all facing the same direction. Bent to their maps with a look of grim perseverance, as if the job of art appreciation is a taxing and somewhat burdensome one. A swinging door opens at the back of the room and a waiter sticks his head out, looks around the restaurant and retreats.

Iona follows Clive to the hostess stand where a sulky brunette examines her manicure with the predictable indifference of a woman too beautiful for work. She looks up as they approach. Spotting Clive, she quickly adapts her bored pout, putting on a sultry lip business, tossing her hair like a show pony.

—Hey, you... needlessly stretching out both words.

—Adrina, darling.

Darling?

—No mac and cheese today.

—You're joking.

Adrina bites her lip and shakes her head which while gorgeous is perhaps overly large... —Got an interim chef today, took it off the menu. Total hack.

Clive turns back to Iona... —I have an idea.

12:11 p.m.

How dare he ask me to lie. How fucking *dare* he? Obviously Nikolic loves his stupid brother and would hate to see Jimmy publicly skewered but Niko's setting aside biologically seated affection right now, savoring his fury as he scans the kitchen: Raheem prodding a raviolo, Otto spinning sizzle plates like he's dealing poker, Armando doing god knows what, shambling around with a stupid look on his face. No sign of. But here he comes. Wiping his nose with his forearm, intercepting Adrina as she slinks across the kitchen, throwing his arm around her shoulders. Together they start pawing through the mountain of prepared demi-baguettes stationed next to garde manger. Is he? Nuzzling? Adrina's hair? Monster. His brother's a monster.

—Adrina!

They both turn to look at him.

—It's sit-down service only.

They continue to stare.

—Just because we're offering a few café items doesn't make this a gas station mini-mart. No grabbing sandwiches willy-nilly. Where did you even find a to-go cup?... saying all this with an anger disproportionate to the crime on account of the festering rage they've interrupted. Also, desperately wishing he hadn't said willy-nilly.

Adrina grabs a sandwich and two bottles of Perrier and disappears through the swinging door with an infuriating lack of concern.

—Niko, Niko, listen to me. Listen to your brother. Lighten the fuck up, will you? What's with this energy? You're depressing your staff. Put on some music. It's like a morgue in here.

Spinning around to rip the ticket clacking up in front of him, Niko calls out... —ORDERING TWO EGG, ONE MORCILLA.

Jimmy watches as he checks an oxtail Otto's setting on the pass... —Don't take this wrong, Nik, but you gotta drop those pounds. All that weight's going to shatter your knees.

—Runner, please!

—There's a Zumba class on Thursdays. Saw a poster for it when I took the trash down.

—You need to leave or make yourself useful.

—You need to torch some calories... Jimmy flicks a side towel onto his shoulder and walks away.

It's true that after she died Niko gained weight. He couldn't stop cooking the type of French food that's designed to kill you. It was suicide by forcemeat and it was out of his control. At one point the fridge held three types of pâté and a duck terrine. Niko used to gaze down at the roll of chub trying to make a break for it over the waistband of his pants and think, Godspeed, my friend, would that I could flee, too. He reveled in his oily skin and aching joints, the stretchy pants he had to buy, his grotesque state. For many months, even a year, Niko found a kind of relief in disgusting himself.

12:15 p.m.

Visitors straggle into the entrance hall, dropping scarves and digging for credit cards, stumped by the scaffolding that's replaced the visitors' desk. They alight on the ticket kiosks with expressions of relief, sidling toward the first-floor galleries with hunted looks, ready to be fundamentally altered or briefly entertained or snapped next to Manet's *Suicide* grinning like a lunatic.

Iona has stopped trying to close in on Clive as she crosses the Great Hall. He has the loping stride of a retired athlete, and her bra doesn't have the kind of support that's good for jogging. She passes two women in navy CREW shirts kneeling on the floor, pulling fresh daisies out of cardboard boxes. Money must be tight. Usually they close the museum on Gala Day. For good reason, since the construction work doesn't seem entirely safe. Already Iona's seen several tourists trip over the traffic cones that surround the scissor-lift.

Clive spins around, notices he's lost her, and waits. She doesn't hurry.

—Alright?... in one enormous hand he holds a pot of yogurt and a ham baguette, in the other, a to-go cup. Two bottles of Perrier stick out of his jacket pockets.

—Fine, yes.

They continue on in silence. The curator makes her nervous with his expensive scent and sweater and general musculature. He's made it clear that he wants something from her and Iona orders herself to stop hoping it might be intercourse. She tries to bring to mind her husband's face, but his features remain slippery and refuse to take hold.

Once they reach the sculpture court Clive heads for a bench under a marble kouros. The sight of the naked warrior with his articulated biceps and six-pack does not help the drift of Iona's thoughts.

Clive places the cup on the floor next to his feet and unfolds a paper napkin... —Iona... holding out a bottle of Perrier.

—Are we allowed to eat here?

—Sit... Clive tips his head toward the spot next to him... —Please.

Iona scans the hall for a security guard. As a child she was reliably obedient, as the children of criminals often are. Mama was a force in red lipstick, swam the breaststroke with her head held high and was told more than once she had lovely manners for that part of Belgium. On Iona's fifteenth birthday, she reached into her backpack during a matinée of *Risky Business*, found she'd smuggled in a bag of potato chips and had a near-on nervous breakdown. To this day, she can't take music that's heavy on the synth.

—Iona, please.

There's nothing for it. She takes the bottle from him and sits down. The bench is too short to fit them both comfortably and Clive's thigh ends up pressed against hers. She unscrews the Perrier cap, takes a small sip. Already Clive has ripped the metal lid off her yogurt, licked it, crumpled it, put it somewhere, plunged a plastic spoon into her lemon chiffon and shoveled a large portion into his mouth.

—There's a nothing shop over on the East Side... he licks the spoon, her spoon... —Jack Corbeau gallery. Heard of it?

Iona shakes her head, riveted by the sight of him eating her lunch.

—No, you wouldn't, anyway, not important, point is they have a cassone I want. It contains an immaculate panel based on *The Decameron* I'm convinced is Sellaio. As for the condition of the chest itself, I'm waiting for you on that.

—Sellaio? In some shop?

—Corbeau assumes the chest is junk, one of those postwar jobs crafty Italians banged together for tourists. The seller's a twenty-year-old from Albany. Great-Grandad just popped off leaving him a couple of houses filled with dreck. The kid brought the cassone to Corbeau's shop along with two Tiffany lamps, some Victorian furniture, and a silver-plated dinner service. Corbeau shoved it in a corner. One look at the piece made my balls shiver.

Iona breathes through her nostrils, willing herself not to blush.

—And my balls are never wrong.

She nods as if she knows all about testicles working a second job.

—I'm not asking you to authenticate anything. Examine the material condition of the chest, give me your thoughts.

Iona looks down at the pot of yogurt in Clive's hand. The pressure of his thigh is thrilling. She can't tell if he's sitting normally or actively driving his leg into hers. Suddenly Iona stands, whips off her sweater, unzips her plaid skirt, and straddles him, pulling down her bra, mashing her breasts against his

—Afternoon.

—Sorry, what?

—See it with me this afternoon.

—Oh, I can't, not today.

—Two forty-five on the front steps.

—You're not listening, I—

—Think the chest itself is a pastiche, the panel removed and reinserted more than once... consulting his memory with a lip scrape of his teeth... —Possible regilding. You'll say it's fine to disassemble—

—I won't say anything because—

—Not on the record, of course, but you'll indicate that the condition of the chest makes it—

—But I would never advise—

—Stop, Iona. Debate this when you actually see the thing... Clive hands her the pot of yogurt, now half-empty, along with his licked spoon.

He's playing a game of some kind, eating her lunch, but it isn't clear to what end. She turns away. There's a light fixture on the other side of the sculpture court, a replica of a lamppost from a London street circa eighteen-something or other. It makes no sense in this space. Think clearly. Her stomach has started to grumble. She tries to recall what she ate for breakfast. Oh, yes, tequila.

—What do you say, Iona?... he raises an eyebrow... —Come with me.

Why does he keep saying her name? She stands, crossing to the recycling bin, ostensibly to toss the yogurt container but also in the hopes of getting ahold of herself. There's an urgency to Clive Hauxwell's request that isn't simply about a ticking clock. All that cocky yogurt-eating can't disguise an underswell of desperation. As Iona returns to the bench she sees that he's leaning forward, elbows on knees, staring dully at the baguette he's holding as if his will to continue has been entirely sapped.

She sits back down, staring up at the Globe, the great glass ball above their heads. It's beyond her how it defies gravity and holds all those people aloft, never smashing to the floor. She's always loved miracles of engineering, as well as picturing miracles of engineering buckling, and sending a bunch of people to a gruesome death.

Diane Schwebe stands on the mezzanine with two attractive Middle Eastern men, smiling broadly as she draws their attention to an interesting tidbit about the restaurant's design. The new lion is unquestionably fake. Does Schwebe care? Not likely. The director's chirpy affability feels like a personal attack.

—In any case, thanks for hearing me out.

—Wait... she's given twelve years of her life to this two-bit operation.

—Here you are... Clive picks up the cup of mint tea stationed by his foot... —Still hot... holding it out to her... —Maybe when you've—

—Marlon Tindall-Clark.

—Take the tea. What about him?

Accepting the cup... —You know who he is?

—Of course. I've got piles of his frightful lion paintings down in storage.

—He gave the Museum a marble. Label claims it's 325 BCE.

—Claims?

—Yeah, I'm not sure.

—You're... Clive looks at her with what feels like newfound respect or maybe he's trying not to laugh... —You're not *sure*?

—I'll go with you this afternoon. But in return I want a favor.

12:25 p.m.

Diane watches Hauxwell get up from the bench in the sculpture court where he's been sitting with his thighs spread, illicitly spooning up some sort of pudding. Before the trip to Paris she would have gone to Clive with doubts about her marriage. They would have met for a drink, hashed it out, taken twenty minutes in her office with their feet up on the coffee table. The conversations about her personal life never lasted long. Too boring. For her, not Clive.

—And the carpet pages... Chris is saying... —Called so for their resemblance to carpets from the eastern Mediterranean, of course... checking himself... —I'm not telling you anything you don't know.

The Khan brothers appear to review and permit the compliment.

—Let's move on to Egypt... ushering the men ahead of him, Chris continues his monologue, describing the range of pigments in the Lindisfarne Gospels as Abbas and Momo glance politely back at him while simultaneously trying to avoid pitching headfirst down the glass stairs.

Despite desperately needing to charm the brothers into investing a small fortune in a satellite museum, Diane's thoughts keep returning to Dominic. Descending the stairs, remembering that night three weeks ago, the warm sleepy air that came from Dom as he read. How she was overtaken by the most wonderful sense of peace.

—And then of course there's Billfrith's binding... Chris continues, eager to fill the silence, describing treasures not actually held by the Museum.

Often in the winter Dominic will work his way through a muscular text of contemporary philosophy, Russian literature, or radical economic theory while Diane lies next to him paging through a swimsuit catalogue or a fashion magazine. As Dom submits his brain to rigorous mental calisthenics, Diane skims articles on self-improvement, a subject to which she is equally drawn and repelled since she enjoys information but rarely wants to improve anything a magazine wants her to improve, like the quality of her skin or the size of her thighs.

—Our own examples of zoomorphic texts

It's not as if many, many things about Diane can't take improvement, they certainly can, it's more that she objects to the harassing tone of women's magazines, objects so fervently in fact that she refuses to pay for them, relying instead on raiding the apartment building's recycling room. She reads the magazines in bed. Page after page of hideous clothes, all modeled with an insouciant air and put together in the most stomach-lurching combinations. Mid-calf polyester socks with staggering high heels. Belted sweater vests. Diane pores over the photos. Reads every word. Really studies the thing. She treats *Vogue* as if it's an instruction manual on how to be a woman.

—Careful, Abbas, Momo... stumbling to take the lead, overtaking a group of Spanish teenagers as they head toward the mummies.

At the end of that strange day that Diane stood on First Avenue holding a bag of chestnuts, trying to work out which way was home, she lay in bed next to Dominic. He was not reading *War and Peace* and Diane was not skimming a manifesto hounding her to improve her revolting appearance. Instead they turned to face each other, sort of dribbling their hands together and laughing, remembering a drive across country, revisiting their oceans. Jones Beach when they were young. The Rockaways last year after reading an article in *New York* magazine. Walking the beaches of Truro, Malaga, Big Sur. Dominic pulled her closer and they sort of breathed each other in, as you do, and suddenly she wanted to cry. She had a flash it was all ending. That neither of them had the courage to face the truth. But just as quickly she laughed to herself, wondering why on earth she would have such a strange thought and wasn't it exactly like her to have the most destructive thought at the very moment she was happiest.

—Abbas, Momo... forcing an expression of tranquility... —Welcome to Egypt. I think you'll find our death shrouds exciting.

12:31 p.m.

—How can it possibly make a difference? Musical Instruments is always empty.

—Oh, okay, look at the expert... Liam leans against the doorjamb... —First day on the job and he's a goddamn expert.

—I said the café, didn't I?

—I don't want a fucking coffee, Benjamin. I want to talk in your office. Privately.

Even for Liam, the guy is in rough shape. His eyes look filthy, the whites used and dingy. His stubble is flaked with scaly patches and a T-shirt advertising motor oil looks as if it's been pulled from the laundry hamper more than once.

—Whatever, I don't care... Liam's face is set into a fist of irritation, but he always looks a little bearish, even when he's happy. At his wedding he appeared positively homicidal. It's a condition of his intensity.

—Good. Great... watching Liam pace over to an ornate harpsichord and stick out his finger... —Best not to, uh.

But Liam's already withdrawing his finger as if all he meant to do was point, stepping back to study the wall of centuries-old violins... —All this money spent on dead things.

—Why are you, I mean, is this about Caroline?

—She told me the details, Benjamin, of course she did, I'm her brother. We've always been close. She's not going to hold something back.

—What did she say? That breaking up was a mistake?

—Didn't you end it?

—Technically, I guess, but—

—Now you're regretting it, yeah, who would've guessed? Look, may I talk about why I'm here, Benjamin? May I do that? Because this is how it goes, it always becomes about your shit when I'm the one who trekked all the way up here in person to ask you a favor in person and as per usual my thoughts or ideas or questions get hijacked in order to workshop some Benjamin life problem.

—I don't hijack, okay, whatever, tell me why you're here.

Clasping his hands behind his back, Liam bends to examine a Chinese zither... —You going to this party tonight?

—Of course not. It's a fundraiser. How're they going to make money off staff?

—Don't get pissy, Benjamin, I'm only asking... pivoting to face him... —You know what the Museum did, right? They promised, Schwebe met with a bunch of us at 1072 and promised that the first show in the new wing would be a big *Made in New York* show. Contemporary art, not this shit, whatever this is, moldy *craftsmanship*, but like actual art, things being created now for the purpose of like fucking art. Promised she'd buy pieces for the permanent collection. Invest in the future, Schwebe said. Well now that's not happening because... Liam trails off.

Benjamin turns around. A man in a three-piece suit has entered the gallery with an inquiring smile, holding his granddaughter by the hand. The girl in polka-dotted overalls. Grandad, hair dyed a harsh shade of ebony, a violent contrast to the soft slack of his skin. Benjamin doesn't see the look Liam gives the pair but the man spins on his heel and hustles the child away with an alarmed backward glance.

—Because this place, I mean, I don't know if you know what kind of circus you joined, Benjamin, but this place fucked up its budget so bad they can't afford new art. Your museum's broke. Not enough cash for a second-rate Cattelan, nothing. Probably they're gonna drag some shit up from storage and sling it around the new wing like they were never intending to expand their limited vision. Keep putting this crap in boxes... pointing to a vitrine of wooden castanets... —Dust off their hands, job well done. I mean, does this make you think? Does it make you uncomfortable? Does this, what the fuck is this... squinting... —Tambourine stay with you for one second after you walk away?

Did Liam really imagine the Museum was going to acquire his work? Art that openly condemns the corporatization of art? Clearly Liam hasn't seen the ads for Patek Philippe in the men's room. Despite the overwhelming urge to roll his eyes, another part of Benjamin, the part he ditched when he quit public service for film school, admires the guy. Unlike almost everyone he knows, Liam still believes in things.

Liam straightens, squeezing his eyelashes, that bizarre habit of his, and waits for an answer.

—So the Museum ran out of money, what can you do about it?

—I can object, Benjamin, I can object. Tonight. At the gala.

—Object how?

He shrugs.

—Is it illegal?

—As an American it's within my rights to protest. That's a First Amendment right.

Ignoring Liam's command of the Constitution, Benjamin tries a different approach... —You said Schwebe came by 1072, won't she recognize you?

—She's never looked an artist in the face.

—So, what's the plan? Some kind of action?

—Correct. But I can't do it alone and this guy, Saul, who I thought was my best friend, won't even entertain the idea because he has a kid. Having kids, by the way, silences any fears you have about being complacent because, how can you? Gotta think of the kids. Like, right, it's your kids you're thinking of, you unrepentant pussy. I'm talking about a prank not a felony... Liam drops to a squat... —I need to eat, I feel weird... looking up at Benjamin like a child himself... —Can I count on you to get me in tonight?

—Look, buddy, I'm not Saul, okay? It's not the risk I'm afraid of, it's that I just got this job. Isn't there some other way to vent your anger?

—Don't patronize me, Benjamin. Of course I want to burn this place to the ground, of course I do. And that's exactly what I would do if I were quote unquote venting my anger. But I'm not. Listen to my voice, does this sound like the voice of a deranged person?

—Gentlemen.

They both start at the sound. A Black woman in a uniform. Benjamin noticed her this morning, disappearing into Security headquarters.

—Ma'am... Benjamin says... —Afternoon.

They watch the woman pass through the gallery. When she's gone Benjamin turns back to Liam.

—Great, just, that was Museum Security and you're talking—

—Relax, Benjamin. I could've been talking about anything.

—Look, I get that you're upset, okay? Yeah, it's fucked-up that Schwebe canceled your show. Of course you're annoyed. But maybe you can redirect, like, maybe there's a more productive—

—There's no art without rebellion.

—Okay but that's definitely not—

—She's still in love with you.

Benjamin stops. His heart beats faster and seemingly louder. He tries to look unconcerned... —What about the new guy?

—Darren? Please. He wears pointy shoes and apologizes for drinking lite beer. Caro needed a distraction is all.

—Don't say that, is that true? You think I have a chance?

—Why not? Neither of you is dead or married.

—But like a real chance?

—Want me to put in a good word? How you helped out her brother when her brother needed help?

—Liam, come on, I have a job.

—She told me you left her behind. That the two of you went upstate to some cabin for the weekend and you got all whatever and drove off and Caro spent four hundred dollars getting home. Who's going to forgive that, Benjamin? That's not a forgivable offense.

—Well it wasn't like that. Of course that would be unforgivable but that's not how it went. Is that what she said?

—You're going to need someone to convince Caroline you're worthy, is all I'm saying... Liam picks his bag up off the floor... —Okay, this is, I can see you don't have my back, Benjamin. Never mind. I should've known.

—Let me think it over, at least.

—Why?... swinging his bag onto his shoulder... —All you do is dither around until the circumstances change and your options disappear.

—I'm having lunch with Caro later, maybe I could—

—I don't have time for this. Clover will be up soon. Point me to the exit. I need to buy a loaf of multigrain and find a person with a spine.

12:40 p.m.

—You came all the way from Connecticut to bring me a chicken sandwich?

The knock on her door was Sammy holding an insulated lunch bag, her hair newly auburn. Without invitation, she pulled up a chair. Warily, they face each other across Katherine's desk.

—No, honey, not only to bring you a sandwich, but I can't come into the city without stopping to say hi even though I know you get mad and this... setting the bag on the desk... —Has a ripe tomato and homemade mayo.

—I don't get mad.

—And white meat.

Katherine finishes typing her email.

—You're busy is what I meant.

—Hold on a sec I have to text... to the intern, *are you staying on top of Conrad????*... —Sorry... placing her phone face down on the desk... —Stop staring at my arms, jesus.

—You put concealer on them?

—Mom... closing her eyes to demonstrate the summoning of infinite patience... —Why are you here? Is something wrong?

Sammy pops the clasp on her purse only to pinch it closed... —Did I tell you I applied for a programming workshop?

—You did not.

—Thought my age wouldn't matter, but even with ten open spots they rejected me. So I went back, okay, said this is discrimination, I'm sixty-two years old, there are people with two decades on me working, vital, swimming a mile in the community pool every morning and if you think I'm going to sit around drumming my fingers, draining my savings you are sorely mistaken. Anyway, they called security. Do you have a fridge for this sandwich?

—In a minute... moving the bag out of reach... —But Mom, stop this, please. Let me send you money. What about getting a smaller place?

—Well, I'm not going to move, Katherine, it's the family home. How am I going to sell the family home? What happens when Stacey gets back from Jaipur? You can't sleep on a pull-out with scoliosis.

—She's not coming home, Mom. Stacey's been back, what, twice, in the last decade?

—I mean when... Sammy opens her purse searching for something, for nothing... —When she comes back for good.

There's no point telling her mother that Stacey has chosen India. That she's never coming home. Her sister is not going to appear at Thanksgiving with her eye on the guest room. Go ahead and sell the house, Katherine wants to say. But she is not yet that cruel.

Ping of a text from the intern, *literally on top of him.*

—Sorry, I have to... waving the phone.

—Chicken's white meat only.

—Sounds good.

Sammy gazes around the office, lighting on pieces of furniture, stacks of books, the crumpled newspaper.

—Okay, Mom... brightly... —Thanks again for the sandwich but this is the worst day of the year for me so.

—Don't worry, I'm leaving... Sammy doesn't move... —Sorry, honey, I know it's bad timing, but—

—What?

—I need you to take Beagle.

—Take him? Like forever?

—Yes.

—In New York City? In a studio apartment?

—There are thousands of dog walkers here.

Back in July when Katherine was planning a move to California Sammy wouldn't hear of her taking Beagle. But now, some arbitrary force has convinced her mother to dump the dog. These days everything about Sammy is arbitrary. After letting the garden run riot she turned the tool shed into a pottery studio only without a potter's wheel or clay or anything that's actually required to form a coffee mug or fruit bowl. A teacup pig appeared on the scene, scaring Beagle half to death until it ate the living room rug and was quietly disappeared. Who knows when the green tattoo appeared above her mother's ankle and Katherine has yet to get a good look at it. Maybe it's an ellipsis.

—And Beagle hates Chip.

—Chip's the hairdresser?

—He's a friend, Katherine. Don't be rude.

—Naming his profession is rude? Are you sleeping with him?

—Don't, that's. Not your business but, no, I am not. He comes over. We have dinner, I cook and Beagle goes nuts. Snapping at Chip, baring his teeth.

—He's sticking up for Dad.

—I don't know what he's doing.

—Remember a couple of months after Dad died, we were watching home movies and the minute Beagle heard Dad's voice he came running? Remember? All excited.

With an expressive snap Sammy closes her handbag and stands... —There's homemade mayo in that sandwich... patting her hair... —And a studio apartment will work fine as long as you take him for walks. Wouldn't you like the company?

—I don't need the company.

—You're all alone.

—Thank you... Katherine pushes back her chair and stands.

—It's a statement of fact.

—Actually, Mom, I'm pregnant... an unintentional bomb, but forging on... —So maybe I won't be alone, maybe I'll be far from alone and—

—*Pregnant?*

—My place will be stuffed with bottles and baby gear and that special skinny diaper pail. Toys that roll around beeping and... Katherine sits down, suddenly exhausted.

Her mother doesn't so much sit as execute a kind of sinking collapse. Ten years ago Sammy played Blanche Dubois at the local playhouse. Critics praised her portrayal of gin-soaked fragility.

—It's true.

—Oh, Katherine.

—Well, don't say oh like that, don't—

—How could this happen?

—How? Well you stare up at your popcorn ceiling while some random guy—

—Random? A random guy, that's the father?

Katherine examines the stitching on the insulated lunch bag.

—Of course it is. Why are relationships impossible for you? I don't like to say it, Katie, but you drive men away. Can't you be more accommodating? At least in the beginning.

From the time Katherine turned fifteen, her mother's warned her to gussy up the darkness.

—Do you know how hard it is to be a single mom?

—I mean, I've seen the movies.

—Susie Lenz, remember her? She had a kid alone, ended up living in a tent when her parents died in that pile-up on the Merritt. I bumped into her outside the IGA last summer. Eighty degrees and she's wearing two sweaters and a soiled pashmina. Is that what you want? I gave her a box of thin mints. Money would be gauche, I thought. She was crying when I left.

—Yeah, because you gave her cookies instead of cash.

Sammy gives her bangs a testy swipe... —You never liked babies. Aunt Belinda gave you that darling doll for Christmas and I found it in the garbage after church covered in eggshells.

—I'm not going to stuff my baby in the trash.

—Not every woman has a maternal instinct. Look, I'm your mother, I love you. I'll support you no matter what, don't think I'm not here for you, of course I am. I'll babysit and hold the little one and love your baby. I shouldn't have to say that, I'm your mother, after all. But you're the one I thought, out of you and Stacey, you were the one, this job, doing what you always wanted.

—I'm not dying. I can still work.

—You don't know, Katherine. It doesn't all come down to cute shoes and a plucky outlook.

—Plenty of women are single mothers. Why are you losing your mind?

—Because you never think ahead. You never consider consequences. You live minute to minute and you always have.

—Who says I'm keeping the baby? Who says I haven't made an appointment?

—Have you?

—No.

—What are you waiting for?

—I don't know. I don't know, I don't know... ripping open the insulated lunch bag, the Velcro makes a violent sound that matches the sound in Katherine's brain. She takes out the sandwich and starts tearing off the plastic wrap.

Sammy watches her jam a piece of chicken back between the slices of bread... —What are you doing?

—I'm eating this white meat sandwich I've heard so much about... taking a giant bite... —Oh my god... muffled, tomato splats on the desk, Katherine picks it up and shoves it in her mouth... —What a perfectly ripe... chewing heartily, feeling the bread in her throat... —And, and—

—Katie.

—Incredible mayo. Mind-blowing. Homemade, you said? Who would have thought homemade could taste so good?

12:48 p.m.

Shay walks past the Costume department, down the hallway, and into HQ. The missing child has been safely dispatched to his mother who was harsh with her son, too harsh, in Shay's opinion, though she stayed silent. She watched them walk away, little Denzel's teeth covered in chocolate.

Settling the bolster in the small of her back, Shay rolls forward, types in her password, pulls up her email. Another request from the budget office asking Shay to asap provide an idea of how and when certain cuts can be made because, as she knows, the museum is requiring cost-saving measures in every department. Shay does not write back to say her security cameras are only sixty percent operational as it is, that uniforms in dire need of an upgrade are not being upgraded, preferring instead to ignore the email a second, no, a third time, while she tries to come up with some non-essential she can slash.

Mostly her mind is on Henry Joles. This morning's friendly conversation in Roman & Greek has been tarnished by the way he treated her in Diane's office. Turning to Shay with that confounded expression, as if a piece of furniture had spoken.

But she can't get sidetracked by hurt feelings.

Why shouldn't she benefit from her connections? Shay tries to conjure a feeling of entitlement. After thirty years, she deserves a favor.

12:50 p.m.

On his way to the restaurant Henry cuts through Madison Square Park. He walks past a row of office workers lined up on a bench, picking at salads in plastic shells. A guy eating a burger patty with his fingers.

The day smells good.

Henry never managed to travel on his looks or wit. Always relied on a practiced anecdote, a genial charm that was entirely forced. Never siezed a day. Or cracked how to relax. He lumbered along trying to tune out a persnickety interior monologue.

A tiny skeleton walks past, holding her mother's hand. The city won't let him die with any gravity. Yukking it up with its cardboard gravestones, inflatable Grim Reapers. Henry searches for consolation and finds a poodle tricked up like a mummy.

He could really go for a burger.

Not that he deserves consolation. He ditched God years ago. Wrote off the Almighty on a winter Sunday at Trenton Psychiatric, faced with his mother's blank eyes, her scentless hug. Gone was the familiar mix of L'Air du Temps and mop soap. Replaced by. Nothing. Not even the antiseptic stink of hospital lay on her skin. Her hair hung by her ears in two skinny strings like a child's drawing. They should never have brought me to that place. Henry was ten and God was dead. It would be hypocrisy to reach out now, he thinks, crossing the street and pushing into the restaurant, casting off thoughts of his loony ma.

—Hank!

In the sleek vestibule, Tiz Sericko, on his way out, with a forced grin.

—Great to see you, Hank.

—And you!... ignoring the Hank, one of Sericko's little games...
—Really great.

Enthusiastically they shake hands. Tiz has a tan and somehow more hair than a month ago. Henry started balding in his thirties, making him a tireless detective of hair plugs in other men. But Tiz doesn't show any of the telltale signs. How did he secure the hair of an Italian teenager?

—Weren't you headed to New Haven?

—Canceled. Campus protest. Not about me. Only wish I were that controversial.

—You're coming this evening then?

—Of course.

—Promises to be a whopping bore.

—Not for me. I love an occasion... Tiz shoots his cuffs... —I'll throw on a tux for Tommy's puppet show.

Having no idea who Tommy is, Henry smiles faintly, resenting the implication he should have a working knowledge of the Sericko family tree.

—Listen, Hank, I heard a couple of employees got sick at my party last night. Awful news. Not much of a thank-you.

—Nonsense, it was a wonderful send-off, bit of bad shrimp is all. We'll miss your insight and, uh, tenacity at the board meetings.

—Couldn't have been easy for Diane, having the old guard hanging around. Take the old cur out back, give him two behind the ear.

—Jesus, Tiz.

—There's my car. I'll see you this evening.

As Tiz walks away Henry takes out his phone and quickly texts Diane, his fingers clumsy at the tiny keys.

—Mr. Joles?

—Uh-huh... glancing up in time to see the hostess's irritated grimace.

—I have you by the window.

12:54 p.m.

—Sericko confirmed he's coming tonight... Diane clicks off her phone as she follows Chris around the corner and into the Great Hall... —Henry bumped into him at lunch.

Chris turns, walking backwards as he says... —Sorry, could we? I'm worried we're making the Ambassador wait... resuming a forward-facing direction with only a second to spare before barreling over an elderly woman.

—You want me to run?... trying not to laugh at Chris's sideways leap.

—No, but maybe like, stride, or something.

—How long... increasing her speed as they skirt Conrad's builders... —Before these pills of yours kick in?

Chris checks his phone... —Not much longer.

Minutes before the meeting with Abu Dhabi Chris took out a bottle and shook out two bills. *Pills*, pills. Medicine, he said, handing Diane a glass of water. Herbal, exceptional for nausea. Issued by a Norwegian acupuncturist. Because you're super pale. I didn't think you even liked shrimp. I don't, she said, I didn't eat any. Well, take them, you look weird and damp. And Diane complied, though she typically rejects the offer of random pills, even Scandinavian ones.

—Abu Dhabi went very well, don't you think?... Chris says as they start down the hallway.

—No... pressing the back of her hand to her cheek, hoping to cool it... —I did not.

The brothers were not due at the Museum until next week. There was inadequate time to prepare. They arrived wearing beautifully tailored linen shirts, the type of shirt that conveys easy wealth and activities that don't leave creases. Abbas had big useless muscles built by machine rather than actual labor, which you sensed might disgust and even frighten him. The men were cordial and curious but Diane was distracted, her mind on this evening's meeting with the donor, the situation in Mumbai, the possibility that Tindall-Clark's lion might be fake. That her marriage, too, might be fake. Chris kept up a breezy anecdote-filled monologue that trailed off whenever he checked his phone, leaving the group in leaden silence. In retrospect, the Muslim gentlemen were extremely polite given the avalanche of nudity they were forced to endure. From every side rushed a wave of pink and white mounds: statues, paintings, even an innocent-looking kylix upon closer look depicted several romping whores and a priapus. Not to mention Jesus. Everywhere you looked Jesus, Jesus, Jesus. At the conclusion of the tour Momo and Abbas could not verbally commit to funding a satellite museum.

So, no, on the whole the meeting did not go well. On the whole the meeting was a fucking farce crammed with tits and Jesus.

—Your Excellency!... because there he is, Ambassador Ichimonji.

12:57 p.m.

—They say head wounds are the worst, bleed the worst, I mean, and it's true because the blood wouldn't stop. We kept thinking it was done, applied ice, went about our night but then I'd be standing there, chatting away and drip, drip, drip, it would start up again. Red drops appearing on my hand where it held a drink. That's how nights were back then, remember? You'd find yourself in a stranger's apartment, no idea how you got there, bleeding. Or stuffed into some grotty bar arguing that, no, a lime is not an unripe lemon, besotted with a person you were sure never to see again because back then, without cell phones or email, there was no way of running him down. You'd wake the next morning with only a rough sense of the person, dark hair or green eyes, recalling some random fact, he was from St. Louis or played baseball in high school. I remember looking over, catching sight of her dancing and thinking, fucking hell, joy personified or what? Her face was lifted to the lights, the music so loud my ears rang for two days after. She was wearing a tight dress, green stockings, and a ghastly wig, it was Halloween, Lucy kept losing her stuffed dog. Men would grab it believing no one else had yet mimed sodomizing a Scottie. We'd met for the first time earlier that night. Can you hear me?

—Yeah, fine, but Clive, I'm standing in Waitrose.

—I was coming home from a job interview when I saw her. It was cloudy, I wore a cheap suit, there was no money at the time. A man twice Lucy's size was yelling, his face in hers, poking her shoulder. She was yelling back, of course, hitting him with the toy dog. When I come close, the man took off running. I ask if she's alright and she says she's on her way to a costume party, it was round about now, October tenth or so, not yet Halloween. Apparently the man thought she was real, a real prostitute, and Lucy kept explaining, showing him the toy dog until she lost patience and bashed him with it. The man wouldn't stop arguing, as if it wasn't up to Lucy whether or not she was for sale. I walked her to the party but when we arrived, we noticed children in the lobby waiting for the elevator, dressed as robots and miniature policemen. She couldn't go in, not if kids were invited, seeing how she was dressed. I said, didn't you wonder about the four o'clock start? That four was too early to come as a hooker? It was Irma la Douce she was dressed as—

—Irma...?

—The movie with Shirley MacLaine. That was her defense. So we went to a bar where she wouldn't be hassled and lined up some drinks. I have no idea what we talked about. We played darts. I remember she had no rational response to any line of conversation. Her eccentricity was not for effect. Much later, after clubbing and drugs and my head wound, when Lucy's feet began to blister, she invited me back, changed into tracksuit bottoms and rootled around in the freezer. It must have been three in the morning. The kitchen was a disgrace. For decor she had patches of fake fur stuck to the walls. The wig I thought she was wearing turned out to be her hair. I can't explain how I felt that night. I knew I would love her. Platonically, only, of course. I'd been living in New York for nearly a year. I thought it was solitude I was engaged in, but it was less romantic, loneliness, and as I waited for the food I felt an enormous surge of hope. Not for anything profound, you understand.

—Of course. A friend's all.

—It was Desert Storm. We defrosted meatballs and watched the war.

—Clive.

—I'm simply trying to understand.

—I know. Listen.

—Sorry, that's not why I phoned, I'm. Where are you?

—Ready-Meals. Holding a moussaka, to paint the full picture. Listen, that's unfortunate about Lucy.

—I didn't mean to, I don't know why I told you all that, how's Dad?

—Comfortable. I'm sorry about your friend leaving.

—Not to worry, she'll be back. Dad?

—Good and bad. Trying to skive off physical therapy.

—What have you told him?

—That you're in Durban.

—Nice. Curious why South Africa.

—It was the farthest place I could think of. He'd never want you to spend the money to visit. Hang on, someone's having a fight.

And Clive waited, trying to listen.

—Okay... Jane, breathlessly... —The man's not kept his promise about drinking. Got a can of cider in each hand. Girlfriend won't be calmed, thank you very much.

He felt a sudden ferocious wave of love for his sister... —I'm sorry, I can't, you know.

—No worries. No one expected you to.

—I'm going to try. See if I can book a flight.

—Are you?

—I mean.

—Because it's fine if you don't.

—I thought I might.

And on it went, the conversation, as his sister tried to reassure Clive that no one expected him to return, and Clive tried to persuade both Jane and himself that there was still hope. That he might dash to the airport later. That he isn't the person they all believe him to be, though he is, in fact, exactly that person.

Also exchanged, details about his father's condition, numbers of various sorts, the hope of regaining mobility, doctors and visitors, interlarded with vivid descriptions of other shoppers, their sorry choices, frozen haddock or Granny Smith, their ugly shoes and neglected babies. With Jane it always comes back to children, on account of the many attempts and her guttering fertility.

Then they hung up.

Clive walks through the second gallery of twentieth-century paintings, his terrible predictability hanging on him like a wet coat.

He detours around a school group and heads toward his favorite paintings. This is what he needs, the conflict of a still life. A forbidding timepiece and a hunk of bread. Bruised fruit flanking hacked-at cheese. The glorious reds of roses and peonies. Snuffed-out candles, worms and flies. A testament to life's fleeting beauty set against the promise of putrefaction, shit, mold, death.

1:05 p.m.

—Check out this treacherous bowl of carbs... Jack falls into the seat across from Henry, upending the breadbasket... —Oops. When was the last time... tossing assorted rolls and sticks... —We had lunch?... back into the basket, retaining a brioche he holds to the light as if it's a diamond he's inspecting for flaws... —Unless, wait... dropping the roll onto his plate... —Is this some kind of bad news lunch? Today's not the day. They're trying to kick my kid out of college after only six weeks... flapping his hand at a waiter across the room... —Who knows what she got up to a month and a half in, they're being very tight-lipped. Drugs, I suspect. If so, I'll feel vindicated. Obviously that's beside the point, but you know how suspicious I was. I told Ellen all the chem majors we knew in college spent their weekends cooking up LSD, but I couldn't convince the kid to try a low-risk field. Sociology, I said. Statistics.

It seems to escape Jack that both he and Henry put away enough drugs in college to maintain the vacation homes of a couple of Colombian crime families and that sophomore year in particular remains almost entirely lost to memory.

A waiter glides up silently as if by water. With impressive disdain, he hands them each an enormous menu. The restaurant has a fetish for size. Salad plates as big as hubcaps. Forks like garden tools. What the hell, they agree and order martinis.

—So you'll, what, drive up?

—First thing... Jack scans the menu... —Ellen's beside herself, of course.

At the trials of his goddaughter, Henry tears up. He unsnaps the humungous napkin by his plate and buries his face in it, coughing and wiping his eyes.

—What is it, allergies?

Henry nods. He got all sentimental walking through the park. The beauty of the dying leaves, that kind of drivel.

A small frightened woman scuttles up with their drinks and disappears. They clink glasses, gazing into each other's eyes, a courtesy Jack insists upon. Henry's phone shudders in his pocket as he sips his gin. He ignores it.

Jack sighs happily, setting down his glass. He's always loved alcohol.

—So I do have some news, bad news, I'm afraid.

—I knew it.

—Remember Vauclain, the dealer I recommended? Ever buy from him?

—Couple of things. Nice Buddha last year, minor objects. Why?

—He's a crook. Been looting temples for about a decade. Supplier got busted in Mumbai yesterday.

—You're kidding.

—Do you at least have the appearance of checking provenance?

—Of course not.

—Dump what's left. Get rid of it all.

—Okay, okay. Take it easy... Jack looks pointedly at the amount of gin remaining in Henry's glass... —What's going on? You live for this kind of scheming. Is it your pissing issue? You were depressed last time we met.

—Money trouble.

—What kind?

—The broke kind.

—You're not broke.

Henry picks up his glass and takes a big swallow. The alcohol feels cleansing... —When I met Olive she had an assumption of my portfolio I was uh loath to correct. My savings went to the wedding and a new kitchen. I sold art so she could do the European capitals in luxury. Then came the kids. The nursery furniture, each piece rang up four digits.

—But once you got married, I mean, couples, Henry, they share their problems.

—By the time I suggested we calm down, spending wise, she was pregnant again. I couldn't risk upsetting her. And once Echo was born, all kinds of expenses showed up.

—You chickened out.

—No kidding. Now I'm drowning in debt.

—You'll have to come clean.

—I've got the kids on the court four days a week. Down the line, maybe one of them turns pro. There's money in tennis.

—And where are you when this happens? Hiding in an offshore account?

Softened by the gin, Henry decides to dive in... —Okay, as it happens, I have some other news.

—Gentlemen!... the waiter appears beside them... —Have you decided?

Instead of a burger, Henry orders a healthy salad. Jack goes for rare steak. The waiter appears to endorse these selections, nodding his approval and moving away with studied caution so as not to decapitate anyone with the menus. As the waiter's leaving, Henry remembers it no longer matters what he eats. To hell with his health.

—You have other news?... Jack folds his hands in his lap expectantly.

—A few months ago I went to a doctor. I'd been feeling rundown for a while and no amount of vitamin C was helping.

—Oregano oil. The expensive stuff. Don't chintz.

—He diagnosed lung cancer and by the—

—Wait, what?

—By the time—

—Hold on. *Lung cancer?*

—they found the thing it had spread to my lymph nodes.

—You're trying to tell me you have cancer.

—That's right.

—Please. Look at you, you're practically glowing. I've known people with cancer. Visited them in the hospital. And you do not have cancer.

Henry sucks his gin. He could kill Jack right now for denying him his moment. Having kept the news quiet for three months and feeling pretty fancy about it, to tell the truth, pretty martyr-like as he went about his day sparing everyone's feelings, Henry was unprepared to be shot down the second he confessed. He assumed whomever he told would squeeze out a tear at the very least.

—You never even smoked. A few bong hits in college.

—Well, they did all the tests, Jack. There's a mass, huge. Inoperable. It's all snarled and woven and. Inoperable. They said with treatment, I could expect six months to a year. Without it, two to four months. I chose to go without.

—What do you mean, *chose*? You don't want to live?

—Not like that I don't. Wasting away on chemo when I have zero chance of surviving.

—I don't know, Henry. Doesn't feel like you're making a lot of sense here.

—About a month ago, remember I canceled on you? Couldn't get out of bed, assumed this was it, my time was up. I started debating how to tell Olive—

—You haven't told Olive?

—Not yet.

—She'll be devastated.

—Only by the bills.

—Henry.

—Anyway, lately I feel okay... quick sip... —Short of breath sometimes.

—I don't buy it. You look great.

—Sorry to drop it on you like this.

Jack picks up his drink, swigging it so forcefully a wave of gin sloshes down the front of his shirt... —I can't believe it... he stares down at his shirt, sounding genuinely heartbroken.

—Let's get back to the bigger problem. Olive's never worked. I mean, nothing lucrative. Magazine stuff, retail.

—So the hope is your six-year-old turns into Boris Becker.

—He hit a nasty little dropshot the other day.

—Henry.

—From the baseline.

—Wake up. Stop spending money and cut your expenses. What about Annie? You still paying alimony?

—No, but... Henry's had some gin and seen some pretty trees, he's ready to unburden himself.

—But what?

—I'm planning to confess.

—Confess what? Don't confess anything.

—Tell Annie what I saw the night of Jordan's book party. She and Millicent down on the street.

—No.

—But Jack—

—I forbid it.

—But I'll die and she'll never understand why I, you know, strayed.

—And who says she wants to? Annie's got a nice life, a rich husband, a good address. What does she need with some confession?

—It feels right.

—I understand it feels right but it's actually wrong. I've known you since you were a scurvy little freshman who couldn't find his way to the dining hall and if there's one person who, the minute he discovers he's dying, digs up something completely unrelated to worry about, it's you.

—I'm not *worried*, I'm—

—Oh please. That whole bit with the waitress was a while coming. Forget Millicent whatsit. Frankly, I'm surprised it took as long as it did for you to run around on Annie. Stop relitigating the past. This is no way to die. Have you thought about dropping acid? I hear it makes dying palatable.

—That's for people who can't come to terms with their ending. I've made peace with it.

—And you've told the kids? Kim and Colin, I mean.

—Not yet.

Jack tilts his head, lips pressed together, acting as if he's open-minded.

—They're having fun in LA. Kim's frightened me since she was fourteen. They'll feel pressured to rush back and spout a bunch of maudlin, look, I know exactly how they love me and exactly how they resent me.

—And what about the two of them? What if they need closure, or. Look, it's not kind to keep silent, Henry, it really isn't.

But he can't think about such things right now... —I might write a letter, explaining about the money.

—You set cash aside for the kids, stocks.

—Of course, but then the place in Montauk needed a new roof and the landscaping was a shock.

Again his phone vibrates, this time he pulls it out.

—Jesus, Henry, landscaping?

A text from Olive.

—What is it? Why are you reading your phone?

—Echo has a fever. Olive's planning to stay home tonight... his blood quickens... —Instead of coming to the gala.

—That's a shame. I mean, isn't it? Henry? Why are you smiling?

—I'll have an extra ticket. I could invite Annie.

—No... Jack smacks the table... —Do not. I'm warning you.

—I'm dying.

—Well, then be a fucking idiot by all means.

—She needs to hear what happened that night. I'm trying to die with a clean slate.

The waiter materializes holding two titanic white plates along his arm and a pepper mill the size of a grandfather clock. After setting down the food, he proceeds to bully them with pepper. Finally he accepts their rejection and withdraws. Henry's salad is a pile of oily greens draped with Italian meat.

—I have a list, okay, Jack.

—What kind? The kind that has you coming away the hero? Annie hasn't given you a second thought since the day you divorced. Walk away.

In response, Henry impales a friggitello. Jack stares at his food for a long minute before picking up his knife and attacking the steak in his usual dominant manner, intimidating the meat. On the other side of the room a harpist begins playing "Passacaglia." Henry watches her pluck the strings, transported by her own playing. Overdoing the swoony bit, in his opinion.

—I have a thought, if you'd care to hear it.

Setting down his fork, Henry leans back, crossing his arms like a petulant child. They both wait for Jack to finish chewing.

—It is my opinion... chasing his bite with water... —That there is something seriously wrong with you. I'm not talking about the cancer. Grow the fuck up. You're sixty-three years old. You don't get a pass because Mommy got tossed in the nuthouse and Daddy was a grouch. Sorry, but there it is.

And, really, it's excellent advice. Grow the fuck up. Always has been.

1:18 p.m.

During quiet time at Camp Pootatuck, Mary Grace Harlinsky used to sit on the bottom bunk and lay out her future to the rest of the cabin. A three-story house and a dark-haired husband. Two to four kids spaced eighteen months apart. A small dog, short-haired, black and brown. The detail was remarkable. Tiffany blue walls, curtains in white eyelet. The years passed and M.G. continued to spend her summers pounding grain alcohol and trailing bands on tour. Shedding jobs for oversleeping or teasing her boss. Her friends got tired of M.G.'s faith, the belief she had in a life beyond the zone of crap decisions. Everyone saw the way she danced. But one night, at a dinner to celebrate her thirty-second birthday, M.G. held up a glass of vinho verde and announced that all the gallivanting was over. Enough aimless shit. Time for a life filled with purpose. Hear hear, her friends murmured, clinking glasses and avoiding each other's eyes. But they were wrong to doubt. Nine months later M.G. was married to a snippy litigator she met in a hot tub, ready for the serenity she'd dreamed of since she was twelve. When Katherine visited her, deep in the suburbs of Philadelphia, M.G. showed off a freshly painted guest room, pointing out a sconce she'd fashioned from a cheese grater. They drank iced coffee sitting on a bench in the corner of the kitchen, a spot M.G. referred to as the breakfast nook more than once despite never having used a word like nook over the course of their long friendship. To Katherine, everything about the house was rooted in fear. Spotless bathrooms. Chairs covered in neurotic prints. The lawn was a weedless rebuke. She listened quietly as Mary Grace spent an hour comparing sugar substitutes. Six weeks later Katherine heard from a friend that M.G. had packed a bag, gassed up the car, and was heading for Albuquerque.

According to this friend, Mary Grace realized she'd gotten it all wrong when she had a miscarriage and felt only relief. A rope was tightening around her neck, she said. A baby meant forever being attached to a man she wasn't sure she actually liked. Given everything we know about M.G., said the friend, can you see her surrendering to eighteen years of dependability? Imagine Mary Grace packing school lunches, holding down a corporate job. I think she'd end up gazing out the kitchen window dreaming of the time the three of us drove to Mexico in that van with sticky brakes.

It turned out M.G. missed life in the zone of crap decisions.

She'd been duped by commercials for chocolate cereal and school supplies. By friends at brunch burping their babies over one shoulder telling her to hurry up and get a bun in that dusty oven because after thirty your fertility sputters to a halt like the dying engine of a motorboat. Also, by all kinds of people, prime ministers, actors, activists, pole dancers, announcing at every opportunity that being a parent has been his or her greatest accomplishment. Not negotiating peace in the Middle East but coaching JV basketball. You will never know x or y, they proclaim, until you have a child, reducing people without children to a bunch of shallow loveless assholes. Parenting is the way people of all types and nationalities connect and bond. *As a mom* is one of the great connective phrases. Chatting about the school run relaxes everyone. It's a way even movie stars can be relatable. I'm just a mom, Hollywood ladies shrug as they pad past their infinity pools, chaga smoothie in hand. I am just like you.

1:23 p.m.

When he reaches the kouros, the Japanese Ambassador circles the statue to end up facing Diane. With the naked warrior between them, she's unclear what exactly Ichimonji is appraising, whether his eyes are truly flicking from her to the statue's marble penis.

They met for the first time last year, at a museum show of Rinpa screens. Ichimonji struck her as a man raised by doting parents. Into the world he brought the lordly, assertive quality of having been fussed at, worried over, spoiled and adored. His surroundings he canvassed with a restive hunger, as if in constant search of what could benefit him or who could be of use. He had ranging enthusiasms and a passion for pop culture. The adhesive product that held back his hair broke its hold when he talked about Beyoncé. With his jacket unbuttoned and his hands louchely pocketed, it was obvious Ichimonji was far too fit for fifty-five. As with any straight man with a six-pack after forty, this proved he was a psychopath.

From the other side of the kouros, Ichimonji directs at Diane the sort of withering gaze that used to weaken her knees. But she's not interested in other men.

Is she?

Difficult to be certain. A few minutes ago Chris's acupuncture pills kicked in and she's begun to feel bizarrely hopeful. In retrospect, Chris was right, the meeting with Abu Dhabi did go well. She recalls Momo smiling a number of times and Abbas complimenting the color of the gallery walls, wondering if he should paint his office the same shade of green. Investment in a satellite museum is surely only a formality at this point. And the Ambassador. Minutes away from awarding her the Samurai show, Diane can feel it. Money will pour in. Her job secured. God, she loves these pills. Imagine tackling your day with such optimism.

Ichimonji coughs but she doesn't look up. The marble expanse between them shimmers, the stone itself has a yearning quality. Verdicts on her wayward youth, her father's tragic playfulness are tantalizingly within reach.

—If I could quickly text Henry Joles... Chris has his phone out and cocked... —Double-check that exposure-wise this idea of yours—

—Put that away.

He doesn't, gauging her seriousness.

In a low voice, Diane continues... —Listen, we're competing with Los Angeles, the Smithsonian, and the Met. You said the Met gave Ichimonji a medal. How do we compete without a medal? With an insidery look behind the scenes... She feels a touch dissociated from her words... —People love, do you have a cough drop or a? My throat is so dry.

—I have a... Chris fishes out a piece of gum from inside his jacket... —Might be a little stale.

—Thank you... unwrapping it... —The Samurai show brought in thousands of fresh visitors for the British. Publication sales shot through the roof... popping the gum into her mouth... —So let's not worry about the niceties of so-called safety.

Chris swivels his entire torso to look at her.

—Calm down, I didn't mean *niceties*. Safety first, obviously... gnashing the stale gum... —What I mean is, we need to take a risk, tiny one, before the board meets next month and my job goes under the guillotine, that's all I meant, let's roll the goddamn dice.

Ichimonji finishes his appraisal of the kouros and walks back to them... —So cold, sculpture, don't you find? Limited, didactic even...

cheerfully dismissing three thousand years of global treasures as he tucks his glasses into his breast pocket... —I prefer the warmth of paintings, the uncertainty, the carnality... flicking his gaze to Diane... —Barring one occasion. I was visiting a small museum in Le Marche and I bumped into a Venus, I think it was, almost literally bumped into it. I turned to look and was hit by what can only be called a wave of ecstasy... eyes boring into her... —Very intense. Perhaps the mesial groove of her buttocks sent me.

Diane presses the heel of her hand to her forehead. The blouse tugs at her shoulders.

—Sir... Chris, encouraging but noncommittal.

—Then again, I was divorcing at the time, so.

—Your Excellency.

—Please, Diane, I insist. Kenichi.

—Oh, okay. Kenichi. We have an exceptional treat in store... nodding to Chris... —Lead the way, please.

With an unhappy glare, Chris turns and they follow as he walks briskly down the hallway, around the corner, through two galleries of Turkish delights and up to a yellow DO NOT ENTER barricade. He speaks to a guard who stands aside, granting them access to an antechamber constructed from plastic sheets. Inside this tent is a table piled with spaghetti squash. Correction: yellow hardhats. Chris takes three hats and hands them out.

Smiling, Diane places the helmet on her head. The Norwegian pills have miraculously quashed the urge to vomit but the side effects appear to include hallucinations.

Chris pushes through an opening in the plastic sheets that cordon off the work site, holding the curtain aside so that she and Ichimonji can enter.

The potential for calamity here is not trivial. Several burly men scale ladders hoisting items that appear to be either sharp or wet. An enormous sheet of glass stands propped against one wall, a grid of scaffolding against the wall opposite. Broken rubble lies scattered across a drop cloth that is rippled and bunched in ankle-wrenching heaps and serves as a backdrop for half a hoagie surrendered almost formally in the middle of the room, like part of a still life. In a circle around the abandoned sandwich lie hardened hummocks of plaster or cement or glue or paint creating what appears to be a mandala. Clamp lamps hoisted on metal tripods provide pools of light that, while dramatic, look alarmingly inefficient. Henry would have a fit. A workman takes the time to send them a surly look before returning to his clattering work. Against a wall their shadows are enormous.

—Kenichi... too sing-songy. Diane drops her voice... —I wonder if you recall from your last visit how confining this space was?... turn down the Snow White... —This new area will feature a larger library and once the glass is installed the entire space will be filled with natural light. Nine computer terminals along here will give guests access to any work of art in our holdings if we walk down this side, gentlemen, excuse our interruption, along here, Ambassador, we're putting in study rooms where scholars can order from Archives works on paper not currently on display, have it brought to them by white-gloved associates... her words start to thicken and arrive more slowly, as if through a clogged pipe... —Now, uh, attaining... an effort to speak... —Attaining the status of scholar will mean undergoing a rigorous screening process and working under the eye of a camera since academics are, of course, notorious for stealing priceless documents.

—Really?... Ichimonji, with a boyish smile... —Say more.

But she can't. Forming words has become an impossible enterprise. She turns to Chris.

—In Ohio, a professor razored pages from a manuscript commissioned by Petrarch.

—Petrarch.

—Scholars are the worst... Chris, appearing to allude to a mysterious past... —They have so little, you see.

Ichimonji reflects on this observation as he turns to sight the scaffolding, at the top of which a workman crouches, hammering.

—More domes. You like circles here.

—If I may direct your attention, Ambassador, mind your step... Chris points... —We're opening up, this used to be a storeroom, we've taken the—

A bellow. Diane whips around, sees Kenichi clutching his shoulder, listing to one side like a drunk, and Chris, darting forward, saying Mr. Ichimonji, Your Excellency, sir. Two workmen rush from opposite sides of the room, all jangling toolbelts and galumphing work boots. Diane stands rooted to the spot. The pills are making everything difficult to process. Ichimonji, staggering; Chris, trying to help. Is that the lights flickering or her eyes fluttering?

—Ambassador... drawing herself up to say... —What on earth happened?

Ichimonji looks at the floor around him, stooping to pick up a metal box... —THIS THING... for tools? no, too small, raising it... —FELL ON ME.

1:33 p.m.

—And the red hair? You don't find it—

—What, Benjamin? Find it what?

—I don't know. So red.

Caroline is wearing a crisp white shirt and, over it, a fitted jacket. It's an authoritative look, as if she's here to fire him. Searching his face with what feels like years of disappointment in her eyes. Why did he never fail to pick women who wear their expressions so clearly? Sad-eyed and straightforward. Where had they come from, this lucid tribe? In the future Benjamin wants, not these women with their clarity and eloquence, their easy emotional GPS, but the impenetrable ones, the ones who bury it all, have nothing figured out. Women who come to a furious invisible boil because he can't read their minds.

He smiles enigmatically, hoping to imitate the appearance of a person uninvested in any particular outcome. Because Caroline isn't coming back. Nothing will tempt her. Not his superior hair color, not his height, because it's impossible that the ginger is taller than he, not his sense of humor, though he's been less and less funny of late. Benjamin has to admit it's a lost cause. After work he should go home, pick up spicy ramen from the place on Wythe and find someone else to fuck. Some girl will fuck him. Some girl somewhere. He is fuckable. In these United States. In the tri-state area, the five boroughs. Where are you, ye cuckoo damsels of the five boroughs?

—Are you listening?

That look again, a sadness that Benjamin remains exactly as he was when they first met, about fifteen years old, emotionally. Though he could be reading into it.

—Anyone would think I broke up with you. Let's remember who ended it.

—Because you wanted to, Caro, you all but said so.

—I all but, that's some real insight... poking her seaweed salad with a chopstick... —I never wanted, I thought maybe therapy, a trial separation, or. You gave up, Benjamin, not me.

The waiter appears, sets down a geta of gleaming sashimi. The guy has a serious attitude problem. If Benjamin were the type to send messages via tip, this jackass would get about seven percent but Benjamin is not that person. He is a dutiful twenty percent tipper even if the waiter curses at him, which happened once in a place uptown.

—Please don't have one of your server moments right now.

—First of all, that was one time, not some kind of, and second, she asked, do you know how the menu works? which is a—

—Polite—

—*Fatuous*—

—question and you have to answer—

—It was rhetorical terrorism, Caro. I took a stand. Someone has to.

—Stop. I'm toasting... she lifts the thimble of green tea in front of her... —Congratulations on your new job.

—The one you thought I had no hope of getting.

—The what?... bringing down her cup.

—You said or implied at least that I wasn't qualified—

—Oh my god, are you, this is a joke.

—That's what I remember.

—No... sounding almost angry... —I thought you should give LA a shot. All that time and money you spent. Why not go for a year or two? Thackeray said he'd call his friend at Summit.

—Thackeray said my movie was derivative.

—YOU said your movie was derivative, YOU said you didn't want to move three thousand miles across country only to fail.

Didn't Thackeray say Benjamin's future lay in academia? He tries to recall exactly what was said in the bar that night. He remembers rearranging the votives because a shadow was making Thackeray look demonic.

—I thought you were giving up too easily, throwing away your dream.

—Dream, please.

—Don't. Don't do that belittling thing. You chose the safe route, Benjamin. You have no one to blame but yourself.

—Blame? I have a job every film grad in the country, who the hell's blaming? I thought we were celebrating.

—We are, sorry I—

—I'm programming movies at a prestigious New York museum. You make it sound like I took a job in finance.

—No, Benjamin—

—Why are you bringing me down?

—I'm not, I, it pisses me off when you stick your doubts in the mouths of other people.

—Doubts? What doubts?

—And invent dialogue for the people who actually believe in you.

—I don't do that. When do I do that?

But she's watching one thumbnail scrape the polish off the other.

Benjamin stabs his chopstick into a block of agedofu, intent on proving that he's manly and emotionless and this personal inquest has in no way affected his appetite. But he can't bring himself to eat. He stares at the white blob between his chopsticks.

—Hey... Caroline takes his free hand... —Let's not fight.

—Are we fighting?

—You invent scenarios. There's a lot of little movies going on up there. We could see it as beautiful, right? But at least recognize the fiction.

—Professor Thackeray really did say, I mean, reading between the lines.

—Benjamin, between the lines is white space.

Suddenly nothing seems sadder than a bento box. A city full of lunch specials. Glutinous salad bars in Korean delis. Steaming trays full of red dye #6 and dubious pig parts. All the garbage. So much lunch garbage. Trash cans overflowing with Styrofoam. How can a person go on in the face of so much Styrofoam?

—Remember I'm rooting for you.

—Okay.

—I hope the job makes you happy.

He looks away, ignoring the subtext, not subtle enough to be called sub, that nothing can make Benjamin Rippen happy. For a blinding moment he hates Caroline for knowing him so well. The way she has of spelunking his soul.

—Come on... picking up her cup again... —We haven't toasted.

Why did he invite her to lunch? So she would know that Benjamin is no slouch, career-wise, whatever else is wrong with him.

—To your fabulous new job. I know you'll be the greatest curator in New York City.

Benjamin picks up his cup and obediently clinks. He's lost control of lunch. He can feel it getting away from him. He needs to overcome this shift, leave Caro with the impression that he's fine, that he doesn't spend too much time wondering if he's made an irremediable mistake. Take back lunch. Think about Katherine, she never made him feel lost or worthless. With Katherine, he always had the upper hand.

Caroline sets her elbows on the table, looks up at the plastic clock on the wall above the cash register and at the silent couple next to them, guidebook splayed on the table. From this angle she seems fifty, resigned to some fate.

—Caro?... he nearly said honey... —You okay?

—Yeah, just... prodding her teacup with one finger so it inches forward... —Thinking.

Her preoccupied fidgeting makes him want to cry. For five years he loved those chubby fingers. Part of him wants to ignore his pride, grab Caro's hand, press it to his lips, beg her to come back. They could race to the apartment, rip off their clothes, fall into bed. Afterward he could read her his interview with Victor Robledo. Make her a maté cappuccino, an abomination of a beverage but a packet of which is still in the kitchen cabinet above the stove.

—I've been having this feeling lately. Nothing serious, you look so serious.

—Let's be friends, Caro, can't we be? What feeling?

—Okay... leaning forward... —Remember the Hoekstra show we went to last winter?

—Sure... barely.

—You know those pieces of his, the early abstractions, not the later stuff, how there's this order, right, this sort of control to his technical drawing but such rage in the mark itself.

—Rage? What rage?

—I saw rage.

—Sorry, go on.

—Those heavy black lines. Pressing into the paper. Do you ever feel like that?... quickly Caroline bends her head to meet a piece of sushi.

—What? Rageful?

She shakes her head, chewing.

—I don't get it. Do I ever feel like what?

Swallowing, then a sip of water... —Like within the composed out-line, the order, that there's this like, pressure that, I don't know. Lately I feel like my edges are gone, like I'm spilling over.

—You're spilling over, you, what do you mean?

—Forget it. I shouldn't say anything because you'll just make it about Darren, like he's the reason.

—That's not fair. I mean, I guess that is fair but, look, I'll stop, okay? I don't have anything against Darren... except that he has you.

—Why did I bring this up?

—I'm glad you brought it up. I want to understand.

At no time during their relationship had Caroline ever confessed to bleeding over her outline or whatever. Did she sometimes throw out a thought he didn't understand? Sure. But Benjamin always took it as Caroline's lack of clarity never his inability to understand. Every so often, once or twice a month, maybe more, in an apartment that consisted of three puny boxes strung together, Caro would be so fully immersed in her thoughts that coming across Benjamin in the bathroom or hallway was a shock worthy of a hop and a scream. Her inner life was that absorbing. Never once was he spooked to find Caroline in the bathroom or kitchen. Never once had Benjamin hopped or screamed. Were his thoughts so much less compelling? That's what he came to in the end. Caroline was even better at thinking.

Benjamin watches her gazing out the window at a woman hurrying past with a plastic armful of dry cleaning. This is not his Caroline, this heaviness, this doubt. His Caroline was always self-assured, organized, upbeat. She was the one who found their apartments, dealt with the landlords, filled out the paperwork. The one who talked Benjamin off the ledge when he thought he'd lost half his thesis, who read and edited and reread that teetering pile of pages long after Benjamin stopped caring. Slowly she turns from the window with a crooked smile, checks her cup, and picks up the teapot.

—Are you. Should you talk to someone?

—I'm talking to you, aren't I?... she laughs, it seems to come at some expense... —Hey, I'm kidding. Don't look so worried. I'm fine, Benjamin, really. I don't know what I'm trying to say. Why am I bad at explaining things? I have to get back. Staff meeting... pressing her phone to confirm the time... —They'll be waiting.

—Okay... he smiles... —I'll get the check.

—Yeah, you will with your fancy new job.

Benjamin turns to locate the waiter, waving at him with effusive friendliness, his goodwill unmistakable to everyone around him.

1:45 p.m.

—Who is it?

Armando, morose and slobby and smelling of cigarettes, stands in front of Niko, salsa verde splattered on his chef's coat.

—Which VIP?

—That's all I got, man.

—Chef.

—Chef. Three VIP lunches, Trustees Club, stat.

—Okay, but what the fuck is the order?

—I'm trying to tell you there wasn't one. Chef. Selection, the guy said, send up a selection... Armando sucks at his teeth and walks away.

VIPs in the middle of a lunch rush? Nobody mentioned VIPs this morning. Niko takes a second to stare at the cactus mat between his clogs, regain his focus. When he looks up, Jimmy is walking toward him, wiping his nose.

—Oh my god, were you doing *lines* back there?

—Allergies, Chef.

—You see we're getting slammed here, right, Jimmy? You see that.

—And I am all over it.

—Go figure out three room-temp apps. VIP order. Pull the smoked trout. Do toasts or, I don't know, something.

—Toasts, Niko? A little ambition, please.

—After that, replace me on sauté.

—Sauté? Where's Otto?

—Barfing. Out of the way, please.

—Jesus, buddy, chill. Jimmy wipes his hands and walks away.

Nikolic sprinkles fried shallots on a raviolo, peppers it, nods to the waiting server. He grabs the next ticket, turns to throw morcilla into a pan. What can he send upstairs? Salads. Gazpacho? Bad idea. The corn soup came out insipid. Niko opens the oven, flips the kale, and tongs out an oxtail, landing it on the pass. It's no good, he's going to have to fix the soup.

When this troubling side to his personality first came to light, he can't recall, this fixation with fixing things. A thousand still-dark mornings spent obsessively tinkering with a dish that given seven lifetimes would never work. But it's beyond his control. There he is, throwing more time, more money at the problem, drafting additional herbs, spices, different acids, bashing together wildly incompatible cuisines, dehydrating, slow-roasting, flash-frying, refusing to be defeated as if the dish is an actual nemesis who killed his wife, until one night he knocks back half a bottle of calvados, digs through the fridge and shoves the whole mess in the garbage, stomping it to death. Which is why, with only minutes to spare and several perfectly tasty dishes to send up, Nikolic is compelled to liven up his humdrum soup.

He tosses a fresh batch of kale with oil, throws it on a sizzle plate, and slings it in the oven. In his locker is a salt mixture Niko invented. Foraged mushrooms, dried and mixed with a blend of proprietary herbs. A shot of umami. Could work.

—Chef?... a server standing at the pass holding out two plates, burgers, bitten into, black on the inside... —Guy said these were ordered medium-rare—

—RYAN!

Fucking Ryan. Burgers, for god's sake. What's on the pass? Table five, or is it table, opening the oven, shepherd's pie dark around the edges fuck he can trim it do not lose your shit right now sweating onions hell that butter's turning black pick up the pan ditch it start another Raheem's falling behind poaching egg breaks start another into the lowboy for beans another burger sent back for refire he's going to stab Ryan after service he really is.

Back to the lowboy up with more beans jumping carrots turning to the pass to check a lobster club pickled radish touched the roll soggied it in one spot no time to redo and the printer won't let up, like the chugging of a train leaving him behind. Or the sound of Satan's metronome.

1:49 p.m.

Conrad caught her checking up on him, skulking through an ornate parlor in the American wing. Katherine was a second away from ducking behind a pair of drapes before regaining her sanity and greeting him like a normal person. Ordinarily she wouldn't let Conrad out of her sight on Gala Day but this morning she delegated oversight to the interns. She's too fragile for conflict. Must be the hormones. She feels both weary and vibrating with an erratic foreign energy. Sammy's been sending texts since she left, scolding Katherine, then apologizing, but with a bonus scolding contained within, like a squirt of vile liqueur in an otherwise decent chocolate.

—Sorry, Conrad, what?

—Your *exhibition designer*—

—Gryphon.

—When did he—

—I was about to say that last night Gryphon decided the Westwood trio was overwhelming the—

—We had a PLAN, a drawn-out plan, schematics. What's the point in, where the fuck is he anyway? Why isn't your *designer* answering his phone?... Conrad refuses to use Gryphon's name and unduly stresses the word designer as if his enunciation will turn the word into an insult.

Katherine stares into the distance with a puzzled expression, hoping to throw Conrad off the scent. After the gala last year, Gryphon brought her up to his country house where his boyfriend made cacio e pepe followed by carrot cake, then watched with startled dismay as Katherine put away tremendous portions of each. Gryphon tucked an afghan under her feet as she lay on the couch staring at leaves through the skylight. That night they let Prabal sleep on her bed despite a strict policy forbidding dogs on the furniture. She felt teary all weekend, overwhelmed by their kindness. Do not come for Gryphon, in other words. Gryphon is family.

—Do you know?

—Do I know... assessing a heavy-looking chandelier for its potential to crash on Conrad's head.

—WHY, Katherine, why your *designer* is not answering his phone.

—Um.

—He's deliberately ignoring me.

—Of course he isn't... she can hear herself rejecting the idea too vigorously and appearing collusive... —But I will track him down. Right away.

—Please do, because I have six crates of Indian tapestry—

—There could be a place for it with Patis Tesoro—

—COULD BE? There *could be* a place for it? This is such bullshit... Conrad paces from the fireplace where two mannequins stand in embroidered shifts, gypsies Griselda kept calling them even after Katherine objected, then back toward a burnished mahogany table where he plants his fingers... —This is the most half-assed museum in the country. No other museum pulls this shit. You think the Met fucks around—

—I'll get on it, right away, I promise... walking backward toward freedom, the arched doorway.

—This morning Schwebe tells me I have to relocate the bar outside Purdue. This morning. How long ago did we map this out? And I'm being told of a major relocation the day of?

—But Conrad, that's not my—

—I know it's not your effing department, okay, but what about your interns... gesturing madly... —Following me, creeping around.

—Let me track down Gryphon... the sensation rising in her throat.

—Call off your interns!

But Katherine's already off and running. Through the doorway and down the hall, taking the corner at a clip, practically wiping out a family of four, Daddy's gentle lecture on Frank Lloyd Wright. An apologetic hand wave as she skitters around Mommy and the stroller, telling herself, Do It. Stop Overthinking.

Katherine slows. Takes out her phone, scrolls through outgoing calls and selects the number. Stops next to a vitrine of animal-shaped vessels. Greek. Or Roman. Two snakes, an ox, a slender cat. A glass bottle shaped like a fish. Listening to the phone ringing on the other end. One year at Camp Pootatuck Katherine made her father an ashtray shaped like a turtle. Balancing problems rendered it useless and her father didn't smoke but the deformed turtle sat on his desk until the day he died, next to a golfing trophy filled with dried-out pens and coins the Euro made obsolete.

—Planned Parenthood?

1:54 p.m.

Curtains have been drawn in the bedroom and Clive stops in the doorway for a minute to let his eyes adjust. It's the room of a dying man. The air is close, evidence of a stream of visitors with their gift baskets of off-gassing fruit, their body odor and halitosis.

From a gap in the drapes, a single white beam strafes the room, lighting up a spindly Louis quinze table stacked with books and magazines and jammed with bottles of pills.

Walter seems to be asleep. His wife and daughter sit on either side of his bed, each holding one hand so his arms are pulled into the shape of a cross. Clive tries to recall the painting it reminds him of, gives up, coughs.

—There you are... Harriet rises, goes to him, and shakes his hand.

The horrible daughter opens her eyes, stands, and moves toward Clive... —Can't you leave us alone?

—I've only arrived this minute.

—All of you I mean, one museum after the other, begging and scrounging. Have you no shame?

—Other museums? Which ones? As you know, your father and I have an arrangement.

From Alanni comes a shrug and a disquieting smile.

—Go on now... Harriet gives her daughter a gentle push toward the door.

Together they watch Alanni leave, then turn to regard the old man. Clive hasn't seen Walter in about a month and the sight comes as a nasty shock. He looks to have lost about fifteen pounds, his lips are pale, his skin translucent. Without its jolly toupee, the old man's head seems indecently naked. Yet Wolfe has made an effort to preserve his famous courtly demeanor. He's got a close shave. His pajama top is buttoned to the neck. An elegant gold watch hangs loosely on his wrist.

For the past five decades every museum from New York to Delhi has salivated over Walter Wolfe's art collection. And to the board of each, he has politely declined a seat, accepting only the invitation of a small arts academy in his hometown of Dubuque. Diane had been director for about a day and a half before she made the trip to kiss the ring. She was a masterful toady, one of the best, and she and Walter quickly became an inseparable couple at city events: Lincoln Center openings, summer dinners at impossible restaurants. About a year ago, without explanation, the business was passed along to Clive and it became his job to massage and ingratiate. But Clive always sensed the old man's resentment in being handed off to a subordinate. As if, in Wolfe's eyes, Head Curator of European Paintings was just another dogsbody. And he wasn't wrong. With a collection like Wolfe's, stepping back was one of Diane's more baffling decisions. Equally baffling was her decision not to be here today, supplicating alongside Clive.

Wolfe stirs.

—Darling, here's Clive Hauxwell from the Museum.

—Marjorie... Wolfe says dreamily... —Is that my Margy?

—You remember, Marjorie's not coming.

—She's coming?

—No, dear, I said she's not coming... Harriet turns to Clive... —I'll give you a few minutes.

Clive watches her go, then draws up a chair, reaching over to pick up Walter's hand. The man's fingers are dry and papery. They have the weight of five cigarettes. Wolfe opens his eyes, homing in on Clive with an uncomfortable acuity.

—Sir?

—Hello, Hauxwell... Wolfe lifts his head off the pillow.

—Are you comfortab—

—Splitting my collection in half.

—Split... Clive sets the man's hand down on the comforter... —Sorry, sir, I'm not. I don't follow.

—Half to Diane, half to the British.

—Half your collection to Toby Felt? Since when?

—Played some rather nice golf together last year.

—Golf?... the old man's lost it.

—Wonderful time, nine holes. Felt's intelligent but never smug.

—But, I play golf, Walter, I play golf... never once has Clive... —Love the sport. I would have played a round with you, a round of golf, I mean, not *around*.

Wolfe smiles, alarmingly dreamy... —Felt took me to the Royal Court. The play was a dud, modern gibberish, but his house in Belgravia, I was impressed. You understand.

No, no he doesn't. What the fuck does Belgravia have to do with anything?

—I decided that instead of overthinking it, I'd go with my gut.

Clive leans back in his chair... —Felt's a dear friend, actually.

—Is that right?

—We were at school together. Father's a lord, I'm sure you know. Golf game's not exactly first rate... a safe guess, Felt got winded opening a packet of peanuts... —Dreadful, I'd say.

—Offensive, even.

—Thing of it is, Walter, splitting a collection can be, it can sometimes be seen as a sign of insecurity, if that doesn't sound terribly harsh. Now I know you, old boy, and one thing I've long admired is your eye. Some collectors have no discrimination. They spurt cash like a seminating stallion. Picasso print here, Pollock there, Mapplethorpe, Titian, Henry Moore, whatever's on the block. No cohesion. Buying prestige. Spending millions to look like they have taste. Not you. You have an extraordinary eye. One of the very best for a non-professional, I mean... a wink, a smile... —My idea, Wolfey, is to show your collection as a singular vision from an exceptional man. Name a gallery after you... fuck that's pushing it... —An exhibition after you. Walter Isaac Wolfe: A Singular Vision... with his hands Clive outlines the banner... —Make up a nice catalog for posterity, get Spinnaker to write the essay, how your life informed your vision, interview Harriet, photos of the childhood home, a biography of sorts. Because splitting up your life's work, well, it's like breaking up a family, isn't it?

Wolfe's been staring up at the ceiling but now he levels his gaze, taking in Clive with a weariness several decades old.

—What a bunch of shit you all talk.

—Sorry?

—My eye, horseshit. Singular vision? I was all over the map. Not for prestige, but because my taste changed. How will you show my Dürer alongside the Marcoussis? What do you take me for? I'm not a vegetable. You want my paintings. Have some respect and say what you mean.

—Well, sir, I—

—And stop with the sir.

Clive clears his throat... —While it's true that the Museum would love to be entrusted—

—Stop talking.

—Yup.

—Open that curtain, please.

Clive crosses to the window and opens the drapes. A pigeon lands on the sill. Possibly the same bird from this morning come to peck him to death. It could feel quite nice being pecked. Like acupuncture.

—How's Diane doing these days?

—Fine, fine... sitting back down.

—Haven't seen her in a while.

—A lot going on.

—Still a foxy little cunt?

That can't be right. Clive searches for a word that sounds like cunt but isn't. Nervous that Wolfe's mind is completely rubbished and he's about to set off on some depressing adventure in male bonding.

—God, those fuckable armpits. Always wore sleeveless tops. To snare me, I assume. Tanks, halters or what they call spaghetti straps. It's how women flaunt their vaginas without breaking the law. It's the body's legal crease, the armpit.

—Huh... hoping to keep the panic from his voice.

—I'm not as old as I look, Hauxwell.

There's no correct response, ever, to this phrase. Clive tries to sort of sidle his eye around the room in search of a clock. He has no idea what time it is or what he should do. Jump in with novel thoughts on women's underarms?

—So you want the whole collection, you and Diane? Because I'm some sort of visionary?

Unsure whether the old man is goading him, Clive goes with a mysterious grin.

Slowly, excruciatingly so, Walter Wolfe lifts his hand to his forehead and gently rubs it... —Your own dad still around?

—That's right.

—And when did you see him last?

—About ten years ago. His seventieth.

—Decade. Long time.

—Threw him a massive party.

—Fun, was it?

—Loads.

Wolfe smiles slyly and closes his eyes... —Loads.

The family gathered on a glorified river barge where they sailed in circles like an infernal metaphor. Jane's husband stood at the railing staring into the water so woefully Clive assumed the day would end with at least one tragedy. Not that Clive did anything to prevent his brother-in-law's vault overboard. He propped himself against the bar, drinking one buck's fizz after another. The hired bartender wouldn't serve a fizz sans buck, for those were not his orders. Perhaps the boat perplexed the lad, gave the proceedings a military feel such that he daren't disobey the orders of his commanding officer, the head caterer. In the end Jane's husband chose not to launch himself into the water. Clive saw them on the deck together, lit by fairy lights, swaying to Roxy Music. *Now the party's over.* Jane gazed at her husband with a love so deep it bordered on fear. *I'm so tired.* That his sister should look on this flat-faced own-goaler as if he were the heavenly manifestation of all her girlish dreams gave Clive a burst of optimism for his own prospects. In the months that followed he noticed how common it was, love. Couples everywhere. Even people starting off with a clear disadvantage. The obese, the horsey, the dense, the cruel. Those in possession of only half a body, just a torso balanced on a skateboard. But we can continue for so long, so very long, to believe we have nothing to do with the absence of love in our lives.

Wolfe appears to be sleeping. Clive stands and walks across the room to a small Cézanne still life, one of his favorites. Clasping his hands behind his back, he leans forward, anticipating his pleasure at the painting's details, the faceted brushstrokes, the emphasis on form, the tension Cézanne achieved with his flattening of space. But the familiar heaped apples and pears now strike him as hopelessly muddy. Hoping to clear his head Clive looks at the floor. Then back up at the painting. Air rushes to his ears. The groundbreaking perspective that went on to influence Picasso and Braque is convoluted and aggressive. Dizzy, Clive places his hand on the wall for balance. Why has he never recognized how noisy this painting is, how jarring. It bleats at him with bared teeth. It whinnies like a horse.

—Bought that canvas in Paris fifty years ago. Private sale. Included some hash I'd smuggled in from Marrakech.

—I seem to recall you have a number of still lifes... Clive turns around.

—Twenty-odd. In storage now. Insurance was killing me.

—We could organize a show around them. Group the pieces by country or subject matter: fish, sugar, what these things meant at the time, by chronology, politics. You have some Vanitas paintings, we could incorporate a discussion of life and death, early seventeenth century... Clive walks away from the Cézanne he now inexplicably hates... —Explain how the still lifes that were once deeply symbolic became, somewhere in the 1630s, an expression of pleasure. Or, maybe. Maybe simply point out the small but extraordinary differences between the paintings, help viewers understand the contrast between artists or the way the form changed... back toward the window... —If we can get it, maybe van Huysum's *Flowers and Fruit*, show it in relation to Caravaggio's basket of fruit, so fleshy and suggestive, or your Courbet, famously lacking sensual or tactile qualities... why is he standing in the bedroom of an ailing man who is not his father... —And, later, Morandi, you own that lovely Morandi, bringing the principles of abstraction to figurative paintings, breaking down the distinction between figure and ground. The differences in technique and materials, something we don't address enough at the Museum. When you begin to view a still life... finding it increasingly difficult to speak... —When the subject matter falls away, when you see the fruit and fish and flowers in terms of volumes, a viewer can begin to understand why Matisse was compelled to paint *Variation on a still life by De Heem*. Painting a scene not as it appeared to his eyes, but as he felt it.

Wolfe's eyes are closed and he labors to breathe.

—Sorry... hoping his intensity hasn't polished off the poor fossil... —I don't know why I... trailing off.

—Do me a favor, Hauxwell.

—Went off like, yes, a favor, of course, anything.

Wolfe waves his hand... —In the top drawer, there.

Clive goes over to the bureau indicated and pulls open the drawer.

—Toward the bottom.

Under a stack of starchy white undershirts, he finds a pack of Camels... —These?

—Good. Bring them here. Matches in the silver bowl.

—Walter. I can't possibly give you a cigarette.

—Course you can. My daughter can't. My wife won't. But your only job is to do as I ask.

—Fair point.

—One cigarette's not going to kill me.

In the silver bowl next to an unlit candle Clive finds a small box of matches advertising power tools. The box's dated design suggests a treasured souvenir. He crosses to Wolfe's bedside, pulling out a cigarette and lighting it, sucking it to catch the tobacco.

—Here you are... passing Wolfe the cigarette.

—Grand.

—Shall I open a window?

—God no. Want me to catch my death?... Wolfe takes an alarmingly deep drag.

—Easy now.

A rapturous exhale and Wolfe offers Clive the cigarette.

—Thank you but no... reclaiming his chair, stretching out his legs... —Quit five years ago.

—Then I've got a decade on you.

Since he quit, Clive has only smoked once. The night Joshua left. They argued, Joshua stormed out and Clive smoked four furious cigarettes in a row and promptly puked from the rush of nicotine.

—Hauxwell... the old man's arm is beginning to palsy from holding it out for so long

Clive snatches the cigarette and takes a hearty pull. Wolfe watches.

—Well?

Slowly exhaling... —Fucking fantastic.

Pleased, Wolfe watches the smoke float toward the ceiling... —Always thought I'd hate working in a museum. Assumed the tedium would obliterate any pleasure one might get from the actual art.

Clive hands back the cigarette... —You know how in the *Inferno* the damned have to repeat some allegorical version of their sins over and over for all eternity?... he picks a bit of tobacco off his tongue... —That's what working in the Museum is like. Except with an employee discount at the gift shop.

Walter Wolfe chokes, coughing and waving his cigarette, gesturing for water. Clive grabs the carafe from the nightstand and sloshes water into a glass, surprised to find he's enjoying himself. He passes it over, taking the cigarette so Wolfe can hold the tumbler with both hands.

—You okay?... fanning smoke away from the old man's face.

—Another puff.

Obediently Clive hands back the Camel. Wolfe sucks on the cigarette so strenuously his face changes color. Impulsively, Clive reaches out and unfastens the top button of his pajamas... —That's better.

—More dashing?

—Looked constricting.

Wolfe touches his exposed throat absent-mindedly. The skin is liver-spotted, as ridged and wrinkled as a topographic map.

—My father wore those pajamas. Turnbull & Asser. Not the fine stripe, blue Bengal, like you. With piping, of course. I don't know, can you even get them without? He had a new pair every year from his sister.

Wolfe holds the cigarette upright, bright end pointing to the ceiling. He studies Clive with an open expression, almost tender, but at the same time provisional, as if he's still compiling evidence.

—Our family didn't have much money but my dad's sister married a builder who did rather well in the housing market. It was always seen as a bit of a miracle because for ages everyone thought Uncle Rick was mentally defective on account of having a spanner bounced off his head. Every Christmas we couldn't wait to open our gifts from Aunt Posy and Uncle Rick. Saved them for last. Video consoles and Walkmen, boxed record sets and cashmere, expensive trainers, baskets from Fortnum's. Like pigs in shit, we were. It was all a bit farfetched, my mother wearing an Hermès scarf with her tatty raincoat. Shall I put that out?

Wolfe hands him the cigarette. Clive licks his finger, taps the end, gives it a conclusive pinch and shoves the butt in his pocket.

Wolfe looks amused... —Covering up my crimes?

—May I keep these?... rattling the matchbox... —Deebley's Power Tools?

—Why not.

—I've made it sound like an advent calendar, family gathered around the tree.

—Wasn't it?

Clive stares at the matchbox... —When I was fifteen my attraction to boys became obvious to my father and... turning the box over in his hands... —He handled it poorly. Nothing dramatic, nothing violent. Silent disappointment. Quite common for the early eighties. I've only seen him a handful of times since coming to New York twenty years ago. He's in a bad way now and I should really fly back, book a ticket. I should... Clive pushes the drawer of the small box in and out.

—You're busy.

—I'm. I don't know what I am.

—Ambivalent?

—That's the kind word for it.

—You're alright, Hauxwell. Better than you think.

A rasping noise is the bedroom door being pushed open. The awful daughter stands in the doorway.

—Daddy... Alanni comes into the room... —Don't let Mr. Hauxwell tire you out.

—We're fine, dear.

—Okay, but don't be naive. He's trying to make you change your decision.

—Nobody makes me do anything.

—Yes, but you're not yourself.

Wolfe puts up a restraining hand... —Stop speaking, please. And call Eunice.

—Eunice? But Daddy, it's too late for Eunice.

—Ask her to come over.

—The doctor's already said you're not of sound mind.

—That's outrageous. Sound mind. I've been speaking to your father for the last ten minutes—

—You shut up... the daughter turns on Clive.

—Really, he's sharp as a tack.

—And you... hissing at Clive... —Are vermin... the daughter turns and storms out.

—Wait, Alanni... leaping up, following her out of the room and down the hallway... —Please... marvelous ass for a skinny girl, buttocks high and round like an Uccello horse... —I'm only thinking of your father's... Clive stops. It's possible he is, in fact, vermin.

He spins on his heel and returns to the bedroom. Takes his seat next to the bed. Reaches for Wolfe's hand.

—What can I get you while we wait for Eunice? Smoothie? Protein drink?

Silence.

—Thank you. For making the changes. I really believe it's right for your legacy.

Silence. Is he asleep? Wolfe's face lies centered on the stark white pillow like a pinned bug.

—Hauxwell.

—Right here.

—I want you to know it's not easy for fathers, you understand? I have a daughter. Haven't spoken for a while. You understand.

He squeezes Wolfe's hand gently. Very gently. Those spidery fingers.

2:15 p.m.

The Trustees Club lies on the third floor of the Museum. It is filled with the inevitable snooze of highly polished wood and minor Flemish landscapes and given the osteoporotic condition of the Museum's benefactors somewhat fiendishly furnished with colossal chairs and hefty crystal goblets.

Sitting on the edge of one of these pony-weight chairs is the Japanese Ambassador, shirt open to the chest, shoulder curling forward. While unfastening his buttons, Ichimonji stared at Diane so intensely she was forced to turn and squint quizzically out a window.

—Still bleeding?

—No, no, sir. Hardly at all... Chris stands behind Ichimonji, dabbing his scapula with a damask napkin.

The Ambassador's skin seems like it would be nice to touch. Again Diane averts her eyes, this time to the other side of the room where a large seventeenth-century mirror has lost half its silver leaf and reflects the three of them with a ripple, as if they've entered a flashback. The acupuncture pills are messing with her sense of proportion. She feels tremulous, too sensitive. She nearly wept when she noticed the plastic *I* of a price tag sticking out of Ichimonji's collar. Diane stares very hard at the middle of the table, at an arrangement of white and yellow flowers she's helpless to identify. Her grandfather's cracked leather gloves retained the shape of his hands long after he died. One of the flowers is a peony.

—Your Excellency.

She looks up to see Chris examining the compress.

—Are you sure we can't call down to the infirmary? Have a nurse sent up?

Chris, dear Chris, what a wonder he is. Ignore the flare of forbidden affection. Burrow down, recall your professional duty. The Samurai show.

—Stop now... Ichimonji pulls away from Chris, standing and buttoning his shirt.

Before Diane can come up with a way to improve Ichimonji's opinion of the Museum, there's a loud creak and the door to the dining club swings open.

—Who's that?... Chris barks.

—Kitchen... a six-foot blond woman walks backwards into the room towing a cart stacked with covered dishes.

—Thank you, I'll take it from here... Chris does his best to shove the woman back out the door as he swivels the cart around... —Ambassador, you must be starving.

—Not really.

It doesn't matter because Chris has disappeared into the kitchen and returned juggling silverware and plates. Now he's pulling dishes from the cart, uncovering them, speculating merrily as to each one's delectable prospects. He's moving so fast there's a slight blur.

Diane sits motionless, hypnotized by Chris's flourishes and balletic spins. It feels as if her mouth might have fallen open, and discreetly she touches her hand to her lips.

—Look at this selection!... a note of hysteria has crept into Chris's voice... —Your Excellency, what can I give you?

—What's that?... Ichimonji points at a plate.

Chris reads off a card... —Toasts with peppery tofu, baby turnip, and yuzu, it says. Would you—

—Yes, yes. Fine.

—Delicious... placing the plate before the Ambassador with a ceremonial air... —And what about this tasty looking corn gazpacho?

—We'll see... Ichimonji says ominously.

Diane cases the plates arrayed on the table in front of her. They look like clocks. Or barometers.

—Diane... Chris pushes a plate of turbulent forestry toward her... —Salad?

Recruiting every available mouth muscle, Diane manages a broad smile. Her past hasn't included much drug use. For her thirteenth birthday she was given *Go Ask Alice*, a memoir by a former heroin addict. The book made it clear that a bong hit on Monday would have you strung-out and selling yourself by the weekend, successfully traumatizing Diane into a drug-free youth. Years later she found out the book was written not by a glamorous teenage addict but by a Mormon therapist in an A-line skirt and lace-ups. The actual takeaway had nothing to do with drugs, the actual takeaway was trust no one. Everyone's a fucking liar, was the message.

—Am I right, Diane?

—Indeed... guessing affirmation is the way to go here... —Exactly right.

The Ambassador strokes his shoulder, wincing. Overplaying it, in her opinion.

—Exactly... she repeats, glancing at Chris who is simultaneously pulling the cork on a bottle of wine and studying Ichimonji across the table.

—What a great color... Chris pours wine into a glass, expertly twisting the bottle to contain any drips... —Taste, sir?

—My teeth feel like pants... she definitely said that out loud, since both Ichimonji and Chris look over. The observation hangs in the air as the men appear to consider potential responses. She gives them a joshing smile and coughs into her fist, which she hopes looks daintier than it feels because it feels like a catcher's mitt.

—Your Excellency? A taste first to ensure its quality?

—I'm sure it's adequate.

Chris finishes pouring Ichimonji's wine, then attends to Diane, his eyes boring into her, a message: stand up, make a toast, string a few words together but Diane's slipping down in her chair. Wait, is she slipping down? She squints at the Persian carpet, trying to see if it's gaining ground. Impossible to gauge. Using all her strength, Diane pushes back the chair and stands.

—Ambassador... raising her glass... —Mr. Ichimonji. Kenichi. On behalf of the Museum, I graciously extend the warmest of. I. We. Japan. Historically... she has no idea in which order her words should appear. For a terrifying moment she has no idea if she's actually speaking English.

Chris raises his glass encouragingly.

—The honor, or is humbled a better... lucidity is within reach... —To describe how we, the Museum that is... she trails off.

—Please, Diane... Ichimonji brings down his glass... —Find a verb.

—To our continued work together and finding a home for your unprecedented Samurai show.

—Hear, hear... Chris takes a relieved sip of wine.

The Ambassador sips and looks away, out the window... —Not bad.

—A Musigny, nineteen eighty-two, Mr. Ambassador... Chris says softly, throwing Diane a glance, she must have frowned, a look to say, yes, this is the very occasion to uncork a five-hundred-dollar bottle of wine.

—I've had this before... Ichimonji swirls his glass... —Two years ago in Paris. A rendezvous had been arranged with the Spanish delegation. They were late, and as I waited I became quite tipsy on Musigny. Of course I was drinking wine sans food, a criminal act in France but I was too annoyed to care. Finally I got so hungry I ordered food, hoping to absorb the alcohol. A bit *pompette*, I misread the menu and ordered whole duck. It was enormous, as wrinkled and tan as a Côte d'Azur widow and, frankly, quite bland. I ate it anyway, every last bite... he smiles, but only slightly. A twitch of the mouth.

—Oh dear... Chris chortles... —A whole duck.

—Turns out... encompassing them both in what feels like a forgiving sweep... —I had the wrong restaurant.

There will not be a lawsuit, Diane thinks, laughing appreciatively. Will there? Ichimonji bends over his plate and starts in on lunch. He has impeccable manners. Restaurant toasts, as everyone knows, are almost impossible to eat with any delicacy since they are too brittle to saw without sending a piece shooting across the table and too overloaded with bits and pieces to pick up without showering your plate with toppings. If you do manage to successfully hoist a toast it's rarely possible to fit into your mouth no matter how wide you crank it. But the Ambassador has none of these difficulties, handling his toast with deft expertise. The acupuncture pills were a mistake, Diane thinks, as she imagines herself being handled with deft expertise.

—I must say... Ichimonji wipes his mouth with a napkin and points to his plate... —This is really one of the most extraordinary things I've ever eaten.

As one, Diane and Chris fall over themselves to exclaim, yes, yes, aren't they divine, these toasts, this peppery tofu, unbelievable, this yuzu and, oh, god, baby turnips when I didn't even know turnips could be baby.

—My compliments to the chef... the color has returned to the Ambassador's cheeks. He looks around fondly as if ready for more reminiscing.

Chris looks worriedly at his watch. All the fussing over Ichimonji's injury has eaten up time.

—Pardon me, won't you?

The men look over. Diane presses her napkin to her mouth, places it on the table next to her, stands, feels herself doing some sort of half-bow and, in an extremely ladylike manner, crosses the dining room and slips out the door. Safely outside, she rips off her shoes and sprints down the hall.

2:25 p.m.

Since leaving Clive Hauxwell in the Great Hall two hours ago Iona has spent a good portion of her time picturing sex with a man who is not her husband. Even before David took a three-week holiday from the marriage, Iona permitted herself an occasional daydream. The Swedish neighbor with meaty hands, a dog walker she used to see on the Promenade. But this time it feels less like a fantasy and more like the shaping of a plan. She takes another bite of danish and moves further into the sunflower maze, wiping sugar glaze off her lip.

One evening, not long after David returned from his walkabout, Iona sat with her elbows on the table, trying to ignore the way he ate his turkey taco. Watching a ribbon of lettuce coast to his plate, Iona didn't move but the urge to scream or run was so overpowering she could steady herself only by gazing at the salt and pepper shakers. They were ceramic frogs bought in Siena before she'd ever met her pallid, discerning husband, long before she held a yowling baby in her arms. It was a time when Iona was still entirely herself, however odd or unreasonable. Back when more than one boyfriend had named her eccentric. Before she landed in this lamentable parenthesis. The frogs, one black, one white, were enviably stable, squatting between the ramekin of sour cream and a bowl of chopped cilantro. In staring at these dutiful frogs Iona found a measure of peace. Whether because they suggested the possibility that she might one day be herself again or because in objects of any kind she can find escape, was impossible to know.

Fourteen years, they've been married. She wasn't proud of mistaking milestone for millstone.

Iona finishes the pastry. Hungry enough to risk food from the shitty café. The danish was shockingly delicious. But cyanide smells like amaretto.

2:27 p.m.

—Lovely afternoon... a nervous woman emerges from the sunflowers, licking her fingers.

—Maze is closed.

The woman pulls out her lanyard, it was hidden by her scarf.

—I see. Beg your pardon.

Henry watches the woman head toward the building, poking at the bundle of hair piled on her head. He turns to enter the maze where it's cool and dark. The sunflowers have grown to a height of six or eight feet and started encroaching on the paths. The leaves are brittle, the once in-sistent yellow has started to dull and turn brown, much as Van Gogh's paintings lost their luster over time.

The conversation over lunch rattled Henry. Jack has a way of shin-ing a light on whatever it is Henry's shoved to the back of the closet. What to do about the older kids. He tears at a leaf hoping to smell it but it doesn't come free. Instead he takes out his phone. Finds Kim's number. She picks up on the second ring.

—Dad? What's wrong?... she's breathing hard, as if he's interrupted a workout.

—Honey, nothing, hi... not the gym, he can hear faint city sounds behind her... —Calling to say hi.

—You scared me. You never call. I mean, not without, we usually we make a plan.

Henry steps back into the sunflowers... —I'm interrupting.

—No, just touring a parking structure.

He laughs, Kim's always been vague about cars, oblivious to the make and model her friends drive or the color of her rental. Even after she moved to LA and bought her own car you could still find her wan-dering parking lots squeezing a key fob.

—Visitor parking, it says. I thought I parked in B4, green, but B's not green, it's red.

—Isn't anyone around to help?

—I can't be a helpless woman right now, Dad.

—Was it a meeting?

—Shrink.

—Oh... wondering what they spoke of, dreading it might be the issue of poor parenting.

—Found it!

He hears the chirp of her car unlocking.

—Okay... the scrabbling sound of Kim opening the door and climbing in... —I might lose you.

—Right.

—Should I call from the freeway?

—I have to go but I wanted to say... what, what, what?

I was used to war, so I treated you as an adversary. The love I experienced came packaged in opposition. Unlike Colin, you fought back. I respected your defiance while despising you for it.

Instead he says... —You were a good kid.

—*Were?* Dad, what do you mean *were?*

—When you were a teenager, I'm afraid I made you feel... searching... —Like you were a disappointment or—

—Dad, stop. You're scaring me.

—I was slow on the uptake. I expected things that were beyond the capacity of an adolescent.

A long, scary silence.

—Kim, I... he feels faint... —How are you for cash? Let me send you a check.

Silence.

—Kim?

Nothing. When the phone cut out, he has no idea. Her name flashes on his screen. But he can't. He only had it in him to say once. Henry hits DECLINE

It was just an apology.

2:31 p.m.

By the time Diane reached the women's bathroom, the nausea had faded and she found herself examining the intricate tile-work next to the sink, stroking the stippled tessera with a misplaced tenderness.

The third-floor lounge is quietly plush, with flowers and pastel landscapes and a velvet armchair in the corner to ease the pain of varicose veins. Diane turns her attention to the gold-framed mirror. Her skin is sticky-looking and dry specks of mascara have flaked onto her cheeks. Why is there always a mirror where you hoped to find a window. She flicks at the black spots, trying to avoid making a smeary mess and immediately making a smeary mess.

From the woven basket next to the sink Diane selects a white linen hand towel, runs it under the water, and attends to her face.

Back in late March, when winter had lasted several weeks past sanity, and the humps of grey snow appeared to be part of the permanent landscape, an unpleasant tension emerged between she and Dominic. Like any modern person, she assumed responsibility, and set about addressing the problem.

A zendo downtown had good reviews. The guru who guided the sessions exuded an enviable serenity, always harboring the hint of a smile without ever committing to one. Diane had a gift for sitting still without cramping. But once there, her mind couldn't stop. Because of her tight schedule she took a class that met at dawn, guzzling a bucket of coffee in the taxi ride down. Was it the caffeine that made her thoughts arrive tenfold, with such laser-like insistence? Diane struggled to control her breath; she hadn't inhaled with such enthusiasm since freshman year of college when she chain-smoked Lucky Strikes. Gasping, she endeavored to observe not judge but the thoughts still came, swarming, pecking, and diving. Present annoyances, sexual cravings, an unresolved argument from ninth grade, and the Museum, the Museum, the Museum. She quit the class after less than a month.

Well, Diane moves toward a toilet, pulling back her hair as she retches, at least she tried.

2:34 p.m.

You reach a point in life when sounds like puking or someone's head hitting the floor no longer disgust you.

While walking from HQ to the ladies' room Shay was back to thinking about Henry Joles, their conversation in the gallery this morning. Shay liked the way his mind followed hers when her mind was at best these days meandering and labyrinthine. Most people can't handle themselves in labyrinths, Shay thought as she pushed open the door to the bathroom, but the lawyer was right there, meeting her at every step.

Then came the sound.

—Okay in there?... Shay calls toward the stall with its door closed.

The toilet flushes. A pause. Reluctance in the lock scraping back and the door pushing open... —Fine... out comes the girl from Costume with a shaved head, blue streaked through the hair like a bolt of lightning... —Thank you.

And she walks to the furthest sink, zeroing in on it, as if she might lose her way. The pants are tighter than appropriate, in Shay's opinion, for the workplace. The young woman has left scant mystery as to the contours of her backside. Shay watches the girl reach into her pocket, pull out a travel-sized mouthwash, unscrew the cap, and take a sip. A creaking sound accompanies all this hygiene. Underwire bra needs replacing.

Shay washes her hands... —Sounds like you got food poisoning along with the rest.

—No, I didn't go last night... the woman cups water in her hand, rinsing out her mouth.

—Flu?

Spitting... —Pregnant.

—I see... now what, what if the girl doesn't want a child... —Well... Shay rips free a paper towel... —That's some big news.

—Yeah.

God how she loved being pregnant! Carl ordered in pizza at ten in the morning, sausage and onions. She started knitting, who knew she was crafty? As the months wore on, Shay thought of her body as a building site. Her favorite dress was hazard-yellow emblazoned with an enormous palm tree. She wore this lurid tent proudly, swaggering onto the subway.

—Found out a couple of days ago. I've been in a state of shock because... summoning a story, the girl stares miserably at the silver faucets... —We broke up. My boyfriend. I don't want to get back together and he's in the middle of moving to, um, Spokane.

Girl is lying, no doubt about it. Shay goes to the garbage can, tosses the paper towel. Why in sweet jesus did she have to walk into the restroom at this exact minute? The woman has started soaping up her hands, lathering between her fingers and around her wrists.

—So I have to figure out, you know, what to do. I'm Katherine. I see you in line sometimes at the shitty café.

—Shay Pallot... they have crossed paths many times over the years, nodding or waving hello but never exchanging names... —Now, I'm going to tell you straight out, Katherine, because maybe you don't know and if you do, well, apologies in advance. THC, marijuana.

The girl looks lost, standing at the sink with wet hands.

—I can smell it on you. Got a powerful sense of smell. Now, being pregnant and all, THC could be a factor in low birth rate. Did some reading, while ago but the science hasn't changed. It's information I'm giving, you understand? Nothing to do with the law. Advice is all.

Katherine goes to the silver dispenser, pulls out a paper towel, dries her hands... —Everyone's full of advice these days.

—Thought you should know.

—Got it... the girl walks out of the bathroom.

Shay looks at her reflection. Always with an opinion. At least you remembered the word for marijuana. But she has no time for fraught white fillies and their nervy laughter, flitting around famished and over-caffeinated, taking up too much room, bursting into tears if they break a glass.

Swinging out the bathroom door, Shay's thoughts return to the lawyer. Figure out how to ask him for a favor. Harvey? Gary? Harry?

2:39 p.m.

Henry is leaving the maze when a call arrives from the *Times*. Ivy
Dygert. Staring at the screen, he debates whether he has the energy for a
journalist. Finally he pushes ACCEPT.

—Don't yell at me, Henry, I don't come up with the headlines.

—That's an apology?

—If it sounds like one, sure. Now the... a rustle of papers... —Reason
I'm calling, Henry, I have a source—

—Hang on... taking the phone away from his ear, seeing it's
Sloan-Kettering, choosing DECLINE... —Sorry, Ivy, you have a source?

—Uh-huh, talking about a major bust of a smuggling operation in
Mumbai and some objects that may have ended up in your collection.

Henry's gut seizes up. The looting affair is no longer simply a matter of negative optics for the Museum. With Kulap Stein offering to
boost Noah up the Garrett School waitlist, the situation has become
personal.

—Can I get a comment?

—I respectfully decline, thank you.

—Come on, Henry. When I was writing about your funicular or
the expansion, both times you asked me to lighten up and I lightened
up. You owe me.

—I understood that as you seeing reason.

—I'll get someone else, someone on background.

—Find me next week, Ivy. Today's—

—Next week will be too late. As you know, I assume.

—Sorry, I've got nothing.

—Okay. I'll start with Kulap Stein and work my way through his
department. Someone will crack.

Henry has always kind of liked Ivy Dygert, the Mizzou-sized chip
on her shoulder, the pony-tailed persistence, her darling campaign to
steer and prod him in Midtown coffee shops, but right now she's jeopar-
dizing the future of his children.

—When I'm done I'll circle back for comment.

He'll have to play the card he's held on to for so long... —I feel for
you, Ivy, I really do.

—Huh?

—Let's step off the record.

—Fine. What is this, you feel for me?

Henry pictures little Noah with a violin tucked under his chin, sawing away at the Garrett School Christmas concert... —I mean the pressure you're under.

—Don't worry about me.

—Even with the death rattle of print media, the pressure's still enormous, the deadlines, the stress, who among us hasn't, you know, *borrowed*—

—Where are you going with this?

—I didn't think you'd get away with it for so long, Ivy, and I didn't want to be the one to point it out. I've always hated the whistleblowers, creepy tattletales. Obviously not a Kiriakou, a Manning, hats off to them, patriots as I see it, and whatshername, the Canadian, was it Gallagher? She retired, why would she care? Chances are she's boxed up in a nursing home in Regina as we speak. Did I read that she has Alzheimer's? And it was only a few paragraphs you stole, no big deal. Or was it? Because it was a rigorous theory. The kind that requires time-consuming marination, real synthesis, not just rejiggering a Wikipedia entry. You got an entire book out of it. Yet, she never. Blew. The whistle.

Silence.

—People these days have no patience for plagiarism, I don't know what it is.

Continued silence.

—Ivy? Still there?

—Are you kidding me, Henry? Blackmail?

There's only one way to silence the nagging suspicion that his six-year-old might be at the wrong end of the intelligence spectrum. Garrett. Noah's acceptance to Garrett will mean Henry can stop spending Saturday mornings watching his son steer a train caboose end first, wondering whether the kid will make it past the second grade.

—I actually thought we had a nice relationship, a cordial one at least.

—Are we good here, Ivy? I have things.

—Okay, I was going to wait on this but, a question came up in the mayor's office... she sounds nervous... —New guy with an interest in Parks is looking into some Museum numbers that don't add up.

—What new guy?

—Your expansion budget, a budget that's, as you know, nicely padded with taxpayer funds, has construction estimates that appear to be way off the actuals, almost as if.

She pauses and Henry's balls jerk up into his body. A sour fire starts at the back of his throat.

—Looks like it could be a case of someone fairly high up lining their pockets. Creative accounting.

—The mayor's office doesn't know shit. Every day is like the aftermath of a tornado in there. People walking around wide-eyed holding a shoe in one hand.

—Check out who has access to your books, is my advice. Find out who might have his, or her, fingers in the till.

—Oh, okay, fingers in the till, I'll do that, Ivy. Grateful for the heads-up.

Henry takes the phone from his ear and presses END. Fuck. Checkmated by Ivy Dygert. He's underestimated her as he's often discounted beautiful women who wear their hair in ponytails.

Blindly, he weaves back through the maze, blundering toward the exit. He was counting on having the time to set it all straight. Before anyone did the math. It would take the Museum months, Henry figured, to find and hire an outside firm. Weeks to gather the paperwork and files. Half a year for the accounting forensics to work through it all. But some doofus in the mayor's office happens on the evidence? Blabs to a reporter for the goddamn *New York Times*?

Henry takes out a roll of Tums, peels back the foil, and pops a couple in his mouth, chewing the dry tablets with the understanding that a few antacids are not going to help. Not going to solve this problem or the Shiva problem or how to die with any sort of grace. He pushes at his thorax. Indigestion from the soppressata.

2:46 p.m.

Diane left Chris to wind things down with the Ambassador (coffee, cookies, and one final pitch for the Samurai show), while she ran down to Piquette, late for her interview with *Vanity Fair*.

—Outsiders rejected capitalism... her exhibition spiel... —In furtherance of art, philosophy, and intellectual freedom.

—That's all very interesting... says disinterested Julia Saban, video host and distinguished author of *This Bitch*... —What about you, Diane? Tell us about your bohemian phase.

Diane laughs the laugh of a public figure faced with an intrusive question. A fuck-off chuckle.

—No? I can see you in a maxi-skirt and beads.

—Bohemianism has principles, Julia, it's not just running around Coachella in a fringed vest.

—And did you ever adopt those principles?

Five of them lived in a two-bedroom railroad swathed in the fumes of garbage trucks parked in the lot below. Minimum wage and non-negotiable boozing meant living on instant ramen and rice. Four of them fought for causes with a clipboard and pen, rationalized stealing shoes from chain stores, went to Prague with fifty dollars and a bus schedule, while the fifth got carted off to detox. Then Diane's mother came to visit carrying a tote stuffed with student loan applications. A very stressful lunch took place. Across the table sat a completely different woman from the one Diane knew growing up. That woman had been a quiet, contentedly compliant presence who rarely gave the impression of fully listening, instead dreaming and drifting, her eye caught by an interesting object just out of frame. But at lunch that day her mother was fierce. Insistent. Borderline aggressive. Perhaps from the shock, Diane applied to graduate school. Months later, she was attending Romanticism in her mother's fair isle cardigan. Ready to embark on her sensible future.

—A European romp, maybe?

—No, Julia, I was never what you'd call a bohemian.

—Really?... with coy disappointment... —Certain I spotted glimmers of a wild past.

—All quite tame, I'm afraid.

—Show me a successful woman who never flirted with rebellion.

Pointedly Diane clicks her phone for the time.

—And you are one of the city's, if I may say, steeliest bitches. Women my age, we're in awe.

No, thinks Diane, you are not.

—See you as Caligula in a push-up bra.

—That's... squinting against the bright lights to see if Chris has arrived... —Certainly not how I see myself.

—But the profile of you in the *Times*. Fighting your board, saying back off, dinosaurs—

—Hold on a sec—

—Embrace it, Diane! An iron will, when most of us can't decide between like matte or gloss.

—I'm sorry, excuse me. Let's cut please.

The cameraman looks at Julia for confirmation and she nods. He steps away and stretches, reaching his fingers up toward the ceiling.

—I'd prefer not to celebrate my disagreements with the board.

—But Diane, your audacity is inspiring.

—That's, you know, extremely nice of you but...

The door flies opens and Chris stands on the threshold, looking rather wildly around the room... —Are we rolling?

—Clarifying parameters.

—Dev? Dev?... Julia beckons without looking... —Quick powder and we'll go again.

Dev steps forward with a compact and brush, a worn energy to his dispatch.

—Sorry, Julia... Chris takes up a position behind the camera... —But we have exactly two minutes.

—And let's stay on the exhibition, hm?... Diane scrunches her nose to stop Dev's powder from entering her nostrils... —I'd like to underscore how for the bohemian, life is shaped by aesthetics and, vice versa, art becomes charged with an existential force. The two are not...

But Julia is reading her phone, index finger distractedly rooting around in her mouth.

—distinct... Diane lets the thought trail off, recognizing how emphatically she has severed art from the business of living. Forgoing the pleasure paintings once brought. Viewing objects only in light of their value to the Museum. Equally, in the last year or two, she thinks, watching Julia examine a seed or something on her fingertip, life, or perhaps just life with Dominic, has become flat. Starved of exuberance and curiosity. Artless.

—We're good, Dev... Julia tucks her phone away... —Step back, please.

With a hatchet in his eyes, Dev steps back.

Ready to roll?... Julia nods at her cameraman and turns back to Diane... —Only eight years ago, this evening's cohost, Anton Spitz, was notoriously accused of disparaging—

—*What?* No... making a slashing motion across his throat, Chris steps into frame... —Cut cut cut. We agreed, Julia. No gotcha journalism, we did not sign off on, did you cut?... prodding the cameraman.

—Hey... the cameraman steps back from the tripod... —No poking.

—Time's up.

—Oh my god, did we even... Julia sinks back in her chair... —Get anything?

2:51 p.m.

Malcolm has shown up twenty minutes late with bloodshot eyes, his laces trailing.

—Not too tired?... Shay points to his shoes.

—Nope... crouching to tie them... —What's the point? I'm taking these off in a minute.

—Here late last night.

—Yeah, well, I need the money, so—

—Now don't say I need the money, Malc, when I'm pulling you onto a big event... Shay's voice echoes up the stairwell, she lowers it... —Don't say I need the money. I want to hear you say of course I'm not tired. Hear you say, I'm all rested, matter of fact I'm looking forward to working... adjusting, but her whisper sounds like a hiss... —Don't say I need the money.

Malcolm stands up... —Nah, I feel good. Worked on my music til late, that's all. D booked us some studio time so.

—Hold up... stopping at the door to -2... —Now, I'm all for art, Malc, you know that, look where we're at, after all, but making music is not a guarantee of success, not like studying business or... as if it's just occurring to her... —Law school.

Malcolm laughs, maybe thinking for a minute it's a joke. His auntie Shay having him on.

—No, really... holding open the stairwell door, following him into the hallway... —Malcolm, I'm serious.

—Law school?... he swivels to her, astonished... —I mean, how'm I gonna, I mean, *law school*?

—Because you can... stopping before they reach the door to the locker room... —Do anything you set your mind to.

—But Auntie, my grades.

—Doesn't matter. LSATs what matters.

—LSATs!... laughing that high, uncontrollable laugh of his... —How you know what matters?

—I can read can't I? I can't google?

Malcolm regards her with a pitying smile. Together they listen to the rise and fall of a conversation coming from the locker room. Shay notices, on his sneaker, a scuff mark. It must have happened on the subway. Malcolm would never leave the house with such a shoe. There's a meticulousness that could be useful, if aimed in the right direction. She looks up to see Malcolm watching her with an expression of parental affection. He gives her arm a squeeze, as if to staunch her disappointment. I'll be okay, he says, opening the door and disappearing.

2:53 p.m.

It must be the fault of that apple danish, Iona thought when the intern-thief caught her going through his duffel bag. Only one of those indigestible death lumps could have caused the mental imbalance that led to such a decision.

—You heard me.

Iona was crouched in an unflattering position, squatting like a woman washing clothes in a river. In one hand she gripped his pale blue Tupperware.

—Why are you digging through my bag?

—This isn't your bag.

—Uh, yeah it is.

—It's Dorothy's. She's desperate for a, you know, Tampax. Emergency.

—So Dorothy wears men's gym shorts?... the intern bent down, pulled a ripe-smelling bundle from the bag, and waved it at Iona. Standing back triumphantly with his long arms and undercooked face.

She replaced the plastic container... —An innocent mistake... careful not to apologize, standing up, holding out the duffel bag... —Keep this in the closet with your coat, not lying around where people can trip on it.

The intern grabbed his bag without taking his eyes off her. His expression was spiteful but satisfied, as if all along he'd expected some sort of incivility and was pleased to have his suspicions confirmed. Iona felt him watching as she walked back to her workbench. Calmly she sat down and went back to cleaning a Tibetan helmet, but her stomach roiled and she could feel a pulse jump at her temple. The temerity to go through the belongings of a coworker, where had she found the nerve? It was an extraordinary undertaking. Dorothy passed in front of her, turning to give Iona a broad wink. Dorothy also hates the intern for making it part of his workload to correct her pronunciation of words like curry, a legacy of where she grew up and not, strictly speaking, incorrect. She was supposed to keep lookout. Yet, where was Dorothy when Iona was being dressed down by a child in chinos?

Iona takes another step down the marble staircase, searching the street in front of the Museum. A yellow cab careers through the light, braking in front of a peanut vendor.

—Hey!... Clive Hauxwell steps out of the taxi, one hand on the doorframe... —Iona!... other hand waving frantically as if she's senile.

A placid smile, as if she hasn't been standing on these steps waiting for the last ten minutes. She arranges her purse strap over one shoulder and takes her time walking down the remaining steps and over to the cab.

2:56 p.m.

From an early age Benjamin's parents indoctrinated him in a false notion of romance. Repeated rentals of black-and-white classics, VHS tapes brought home with a jumbo box of Raisinets. Movies that ended with a man and a woman in a Studebaker, laughing madly, headed toward the horizon. Happy together. Veronica Lake with her blond snappy comebacks. Exciting hosiery. Who could blame Benjamin for believing that somewhere out there the perfect woman waited.

Pages from last year's budget are spread over Benjamin's desk. He's been instructed to reduce expenses. The Museum, he knows, started the film department's cost-cutting with his own salary. He crosses out the budget for the opening night reception. Then erases it, sweeping the pink crumbs off his desk and onto the floor.

But you have to be Cary Grant to hook a woman like Veronica Lake. And Benjamin killed a marriage proposal over a sink full of dishes and a half-painted wall. Sitting on the couch, surveying the wreckage of the apartment he shared with Caroline, Benjamin pulled off his shoes and thought, I can't marry into a family of aggrieved introverts. The mother with her selfish way of claiming Jesus, the father's hammy munificence. Two hangdog brothers and their moneymaking rackets. Liam's tortured artist bit. The whole gang's defiant consumption of liverwurst.

And so he didn't.

Benjamin collects the spreadsheets, tapping the edges against the desk to straighten them. Sets the stack on top of the filing cabinet and walks down the hall. But Katherine's office is empty, the lights off. What the hell does he want from her?

2:58 p.m.

The author has crazy bangs. The kind that come from picking up the nail scissors after a couple of margaritas. She arrived early, storming into Katherine's office and ripping off her coat, chattering the entire distance to the *Outsiders* exhibition as if she'd spent the last month trapped alone inside a cave.

—But honey, I'm telling you, you're green... she's become fixated on Katherine's complexion.

—This velvet jacket, I'm fine, really, was Oscar Wilde's, he wore it on his lecture circuit in eighteen eighty-two, a revival of the dandy—

—Hey, hey, listen, why don't I come back next week?

—Because you're a friend of the Museum's and I don't want to piss off the director.

—So blame me... dark pink gum dances in Clover's mouth, sending out gusts of cinnamon... —Say I freaked out and left. She'll believe it. Writers are crazy.

—I'm good. A revival of this dandy look came about in the seventies. Jimi Hendrix was a fan. Now, over in England, still in the late nineteenth century, the Rational Dress Society is promoting dress reform—

—How about giving me the speeded-up version in case you do, you know, need to puke?

—Okay. This dress, radical for its time, was designed to wear on a, Clover?

But the writer is done with *Utopia*, heading toward the next gallery muttering testing testing into her digital recorder. The camel coat drooping from one arm slips and starts dragging on the floor.

Katherine follows her through the arched doorway, hustling to catch up. In trying not to agitate the dicey stomach situation she ends up sort of waddling. There have been so many indignities recently, starting with getting knocked up by a short humorless stranger.

She finds Clover examining a Callot Souers flapper dress, coat in a puddle at her feet.

—What's your book about?

—Broadly speaking it's on, thematically I'd say it's. You know, I haven't really narrowed it yet. Still kind of casting around for ideas.

—Is that how it works?

—What, writing? I have no idea how writing works.

—Oh, I didn't... blushing... —Sorry, I, anyway, this gallery we're calling *Lost & Found*, focusing on the Lost generation living in Paris, the influence of the surrealists, uh, flapper culture, Lanvin, Chanel's jersey dress, influences from the Far—

—Wait, let's, how are you defining bohemian?

—Giselle's statement at the beginning, I guess we missed it, is a person who secedes from the conventional.

—Secedes, so purposefully.

—Right. Making choices that weren't accepted by contemporary society.

—Difficult choices.

The author's eyes bore into her as if sensing that she, Katherine, is facing a difficult choice, as if intuiting that Katherine has called Planned Parenthood four times today and each time hung up before the receptionist has tongued the *t* in Parent.

She turns to point out a Fortuny coat with Persian details, focused on keeping this tour on track but Clover is already striding away, fishing the Big Red from her mouth, tucking the gum into a scrap of paper and sticking it in her front pocket.

Katherine follows, more slowly this time, forsaking the waddle. Some nights she dreams of giving birth to a small prison. The iron-barred structure materializing on the bedsheet between her thighs. She's never faced a choice with meaningful consequences. Even when she laid into the Title IX coordinator and jumped on the first train out of Boston she always had the option of returning to college. Deciding to have a kid must be easier if you've made an irreversible decision before, like getting a facelift.

In the next gallery Clover is peering at an exhibit label and speaking into her digital recorder... —*Renaissance, Revolt, and Reds*, it's called and I'm wondering how does this exhibition trivialize or otherwise

Katherine tunes out. What the hell with her mother popping up like the Ghost of Christmas Future to talk about Susie Lenz begging in the grocery store parking lot? Bringing up the time Katherine stuffed Aunt Belinda's gift in the trash. That doll was a plastic demon with a godless smile and eyelids that flipped back in its head. The type of doll that one night sits bolt upright, rubs its hands together, and gets to work terrorizing the neighborhood.

—Hey Katherine, can you?... looping her finger.

—Right, right, so you can see this gallery includes the Harlem Renaissance, jazz, the Eckstine collar, zoot suits. Clothes for dancing that didn't restrict movement. The string tie, that was Ellington.

Clover has her phone out, lining up a picture.

—You're not going to publish, sorry, but—

—Strictly to jog my memory.

—Rebellious women start wearing pants and men's sweaters, berets, surplus store fashion. In *Morocco* Dietrich wears pants and kisses a woman and—

—Kissing, uh-huh... gazing down at her recorder... —I don't know what I'm doing... Clover blinks a couple of times and looks up... —What's the next gallery?

—*Liberation.* Covers women working during World War II, bebop, Juliette Greco's cigarette pants, the Beats, San Francisco.

—Fuck the Beats.

—Right... agreeable at all costs... —So, skip that gallery?

—The women those guys wrote about, their girlfriends... Clover stalks through the exhibit with an uneven peg-leg tread... —They were fucking ballsy, and like, artists themselves, so why did they get described as domestic moo-cows or sexpots? I am sick I said to the woodpile of doing dishes I am just as lazy as you. Maybe lazier. The top of my shoe was scorched from the fire and I rubbed it where the suede was gone.

Utterly baffled, Katherine chooses a neutral but engaged expression.

—Just because I happen to be a chick I thought... Clover folds her arms and looks at the floor... —Huh, I forget the rest. Used to have the whole thing memorized. Diane di Prima. So, it's because of the shrimp?... turning to Katherine.

—Is that, I'm confused, is that still the poem?

—I heard waiters in the café talking about poisoned shrimp. Is that why you're green?

—Oh, right, no. It's not from food.

—But not the flu.

Katherine shakes her head and starts walking backwards to lead Clover into the next gallery... —Here we have drug culture, experimental theater, women burning bras, and when we get to about 1965 elements of the pre-Raphaelites. Hendrix, Talitha Getty, Ossie Clark. Biba. This, of course, is Barbara Hulanicki, a living legend. She's like seventy and still designing.

Clover holds up her phone, snaps a picture, and tells Katherine... —Get in.

—Me? No, god.

But Clover waits so the hell with it, Katherine obeys, positioning herself in front of Gryphon's mannequins and throwing up her hands in a kind of *voila* pose.

Clover snaps the picture, checks it, and throws her phone back in her bag... —Hippies, got it. What's next?

—*Rebels*.

—How many more?

—One after this next.

In *Rebels*, Gryphon fabricated mannequins from barbed wire and installed colored lights overhead to judder and swirl. The music borders on deafening. The entire effect is horribly grating. So grating it's almost impossible to believe the gallery isn't an outlet for Gryphon's darker sentiments about the Museum.

As Katherine and Clover enter the room the Ramones express a wish to be sedated that feels extremely relatable.

—Jesus, I can't, I gotta get away from these lights... Clover hustles past the metal mannequins, glancing at the costumes as she passes, the lights turning her expression from angelic to satanic and back again, finding Katherine to say... —Better post a warning, don't you think?

—A warning?

—For epileptics or you guys are in for a lawsuit, guaranteed... pointing to a faux-brick wall scrawled with graffiti... —Sid Vicious must be rolling in his grave.

—Punk... Katherine skims through the highlights as they leave... —David Bowie, gender-bending, Grace Jones—

—Got it.

—Vivienne Westwood... moving into the blissfully silent hallway.

—Crazy to celebrate anarchy at a party where the tickets go for two grand.

—I mean, of course it's ridiculous. It's a money-raising—

—How do you think your snooty guests would react if they came face-to-face with a real bohemian?... Clover stops, clicks her digital recorder... —Can outsiders even exist in the age of the internet or has eccentricity been hopelessly leveled?

Assuming Clover's question was merely rhetorical, Katherine leads her into the final exhibition room... —This gallery, Clover?, this last gallery? focuses on the end of the twentieth century, Gryphon's calling it *Against Conservatism*.

—God those lights, I'm still... blinking and shaking her head... —What's... Clover steps toward a mannequin then steps back to regard it more fully... —This belonged to Boy George?

—Designed by Sue Clowes and over here, Adam Ant exploring a

mash-up of military and pirate, both men demonstrating the bohemian impulse of borrowing from other cultures or eras, fuck... a blast
of fatigue hits her so hard it buckles her knees.

—Hey.

—Prince's military gear... head swimming... —Influences Lenny
Kravitz.

—Sit down, Katherine, I mean it, right now.

—Madonna introduces—

—I'm sitting... Clover drops her bag and kneels down beside it...
—See me sitting?

—On the floor?

—Why not?

She wants to laugh. Clover is now sprawled on the floor as if she's
ready for a picnic, smiling up at Katherine, giving the floor next to her
an inviting pat.

Katherine sits. Her jeans are tight, the waistband cuts into her
stomach. From too much taking-out and ordering-in, she's only about
six weeks pregnant. Or along, as they say, six weeks along. Along a path
of no return.

—How's that? Better?

—So, uh... nodding... —Thank you, it's interesting how Madonna's
corset is introduced as a subversive element when, you recall from the
first gallery, restrictive garments—

—Hey Katherine?

She looks at Clover. The short bangs give her the air of a dotty aunt.

—Why not, you know, take a break?

—Okay, yeah. No, I am. I might unzip my pants.

—Do it.

She does. And the relief is delicious. They sit in companionable
silence. Mannequins displaying fashion from the eighties stand in a
firing line in front of them, a posse of misfits.

—I had the knock-off version of this guy... Clover points to a Marc
Jacobs slip dress... —Wore it to death with a flannel shirt and a pair of
ten-eye Doc Martens. Washed dishes all summer for those oxblood
boots. In a steakhouse by the highway, getting felt up under the fluores-
cents by my disgusting boss.

—My dad wouldn't let me have shoes that came above the ankle.

—Then Courtney Love went to the Oscars all dolled up in uh—

—Versace.

—Some designer shit—

—Versace.

—And stood on the red carpet mocking grunge, saying how for her it was always just fashion.

—Bias-cut silk, white silk.

—*Fashion*. Not, you know, an ethos. Fucking wrecked me. You're such a believer at fifteen, right, at least I was. All decked out in my plaid shirts. *Pretty on the Inside* was like... Clover shakes her head as if it's too much to articulate... —So when she said that, I felt like sold down the river. I mean, by then I was twenty, I should've been over grunge. Maybe I was angry on behalf of the girl I was in ninth grade when I wore that stuff to stand out... turning... —You okay?

Katherine nods. The nausea is passing. A deep breath. She needs a cold washcloth.

—But what a betrayal, right? *Et tu*, Courtney? The whole time all she wanted was to be pretty. Like every other dumbass. Are you pregnant? Is that why you feel sick?

—Did you get what you need because I could have an intern show you, an intern, um additional exhibits upstairs and.

Clover takes her hand, it's soft and cool... —Hang out for a minute, okay?

Faced with the punk tribunal Katherine is a joke. Not a badass, a child. Falling apart.

—Is there like, a father, or—

—A what?

—Someone I could call?

The Professore would love to hear from Katherine, as he's made clear in a stream of texts and voicemails. Recently he's started alluding to the possibility of a future encounter. But she has no interest in seeing him again.

The night of the fateful insemination they left the party and walked for a while in the Labor Day heat. She was curious how his tweed would stand up to the humidity. Gallantly, Professore placed himself between Katherine and the rush of the street. As they walked he told her about the year he spent in Hoboken as a teenager. Mocked his humiliating gaffes, his thick accent and mislaid antecedents. It was painful, his need to prove he was in on the joke. Katherine had no idea how to comport herself. What to do with that immoderate laugh. His weird throat-clearing. Later that night she heard Professore in the bathroom humming contentedly as he washed his hands. He came to the doorway with a big lucky smile. How dare you, she thought, how dare you be happy to be with me.

She leans back to zip up her pants... —I have to make an appointment.

—Take it easy... Clover's cold hand calming... —They're open til six.

3:13 p.m.

—Don't... the teenager puts up a hand... —If you're about to tell me how great the Museum's collection is.

—Uh, well, my—

—Because your armor holdings are shit and everyone knows it. More tea?

—Thank you, no, I'm still... Diane sets down her cup... —Drinking this.

Lucas Boone, sixteen, with inflamed skin and frizzy hair, appears to be alone in this double-wide townhouse. He opened the door nervously, voice ricocheting around the marble entryway. Since then he's gained confidence, leaning back, gestures growing grander... —And I don't care about your current collection, I care about how my pieces are treated. This gift, if I choose to give it, should be regarded as significant.

—I assure you—

—Armor should be treated with the same respect as, I don't know, European paintings, let's say. Armor has no less integrity than any other form of art.

—Mr. Boone, I assure you the Museum feels the same way.

—Why?

—I beg your pardon?

—Why do you feel that armor's a form of art? Is it something you were told to say?

—No, no, I truly believe... swiping at a gathering of sweat on her forehead... —That's the case.

—Because I don't want, you know, the condescension. Like I don't mind telling you I spoke to Les Invalides but this curator fed me such a line of. Bull. I knew they were trying to test me because they saw a sixteen-year-old kid who, let's face it they probably guessed was twelve. They assumed I couldn't know much, assumed they could tell me I was looking at a Negroli instead of some hackwork you can pick up on the Portobello or the Portaportese and I'd fall for it. They looked at me and thought, this kid googled daddy's stuff and thinks he's hot shit.

—I think you'll find we don't underestimate the education of our collectors... she reaches for her tea, restrained by the tight blouse... —And frankly I'm surprised a museum of that size, with such a reputation for arms would be—

—Total jerks?

She takes a diplomatic bite of ginger biscuit.

—A lot of people think that, by the way, not just me. They gossip about it on the boards.

—Mr. Boone, your gift would allow us to justify allocating to Arms significant space and a dedicated curator. At the moment, as you said earlier, we are currently, in armor, a bit—

—Shit?

—*Dispersed.* Our preference is to have it grouped together in—

—My parents are divorcing.

Diane swallows, chooses silence.

—It's the reason I'm donating, I mean, if I go ahead with the gift.

—I see.

—I'd want my mother's name, her maiden name under *gift of.*

—That's up to you. You can also change it at any time.

—Change it? Why would I change the name?

—I only meant—

—Nothing's going to change. My relationship with my father, if that's what you were implying.

—I would never—

—Because we've had exactly the same relationship for the last, what, six years, Ms. Schwebe. In a nutshell, he treats me like crap, which is followed by shame, guilt, and gifts. It's a collection built on remorse.

—Mr. Boone.

—Lucas, call me Lucas. I'm sixteen.

—Fine, Lucas, and you must call me Diane, I was merely pointing out you have options. I wasn't in any way making a reference to your relationship with your father which, naturally, I couldn't presume to know anything about.

—Okay. Are you ready to see the pieces?

Diane stands so quickly she joggles her tea, sploshing it on her too-tight blouse, annoyed, irrationally, at Chris for buying the wrong size. She follows Lucas out of the living room, back into the foyer and up the stairs.

—My father insisted on languages. French, Italian, and some German, you have to read a little German if you're going to research this stuff properly. Father, I never called him Dad, even when I was young, not that he insisted on it, he just never seemed like a Dad, um, sorry, I'm lost.

—Your father insisted on languages.

—Uh-huh...

—He believed in education?

The boy stops so abruptly she nearly bumps into him and has to careen backward to avoid a collision as he turns to glare... —My father spent three years fucking another woman.

She nods, worried both for the boy and her balance.

—For three years behind my mother's back, pretending he was in Tokyo when all the time he was fingering this nobody in the Tribeca Grand, one of the worst hotels in New York, by the way, with lax security and a bar full of hookers. The rooms are minuscule. The walls are painted the color of despair and smeared with the fingerprints of a thousand greasy businessmen. I followed him, if you're wondering, and yes, there's a pathetic *Death of a Salesman* vibe to the whole proceedings but I knew he wasn't in Tokyo because he hates Japan and every time he went he'd come back complaining about the crowds and smells, mocking the way they pronounce their *L*s and *R*s. Not once before he started banging his Human Resources manager did my father come home from Japan looking all swoony and faraway and smiling to himself at the dinner table because my mother, bless her trusting little heart, has always insisted on the three of us sitting down to the dinner. She read it in a book somewhere. It's supposed to keep families together and the kids off smack.

—Yes, I've heard that.

—I mean, you have to admire the irony of it, my father presenting me with objects designed to keep a person safe while at the same time smashing my life to pieces. Do you have children?

Following him down the hallway at a safe distance... —I don't, no.

—Because they're annoying?... stopping again to face her.

—More that I never got around to it.

Briefly Lucas closes his eyes before moving on... —I thought about selling the collection. To help out, you know, because I'm sure my father screwed my mom in the settlement. I'm sure his little tart is living it up on a boat somewhere.

—A boat?

—I don't know, a yacht? That's what I imagine. Basking in gratuitous displays of wealth while my mother darns socks. I mean, clearly she doesn't darn socks, anyway... Lucas throws open the door... —Check it out.

More of a small gallery than anything resembling rooms in a private residence, the space Diane walks into has vitrines running down the center of it with larger pieces of armor installed around the perimeter. Another room lies through an arched doorway and, by the bursts of reflected sunlight, appears to hold further riches.

—I repainted the rooms a few months ago, see how the pale yellow brings out the shine of the metal. I did it while I was still mulling over the decision to give it all away. I've always loved manual labor for the purpose of mulling and yes, of course I'm aware how absurd the idea of manual labor is, given my circumstances. My father and I built the display cases together. For some reason all the jerky qualities my father exhibits by the truckload are never present when we work together. Every other father in the world turns into a giant crabby asshole who won't let their kid hold the hammer or yells if a nail gets mis-hit, but my father always moved slowly, explaining everything, never blinking when I splintered a ninety-dollar piece of ziricote by drilling too fast even though he'd just told me to turn down the speed.

—What a lovely memory.

—Yeah, the same man who tore out Mom's heart and tossed it in the meat grinder, all the while denying his behavior even when I showed him the pictures I took with the twelve-hundred-dollar Nikon D570 he gave me for Christmas, turns into a saint when he straps on a tool belt. Go figure, right?

The boy wipes a mark off the glass case with such absorbed precision that for an alarming second Diane thinks she might hug him.

—Lucas... coughing to get ahold of herself... —Is there some kind of an order to the—

—Part of this, getting rid of my collection, is to exorcize the side of my father I remember with. I'm going to say affection. Not love. It would dishonor my mom to call it love... sensing that Diane asked a question... —Order, right. No. No particular order, or at least, there's an order that's personal to me, but not chronological or adhering to country of origin. But this is probably what you've come for... crossing to a suit of armor on the other side of the room... —One of only twelve existing homogeneous suits dating from the fifteenth century. It's German and you can see the proportions are more refined compared to like... he whirls around, pointing... —This suit, a Milanese tournament... turning back... —See how narrow the German waist is, these fluted lines, decorative touches, these are lilies, this pattern. Over here we have complete suits dating from the sixteenth and seventeenth centuries, two adult military, one adult tournament, one adult parade, and two child tournament. The large one was made by Filippo Negroli's younger brother Francesco for the Duke of Urbino. Personally I think Francesco was the superior craftsman but I'm aware I'm in the minority holding that opinion. Look at the burgonet, I mean.

—Incredible.

—These are child and adult tournament suits, both belonged to the same French nobleman so you can see the growth. I wish I had the adolescent suit that goes in between. I started looking for it at one point, then I got distracted.

Distracted. So, a child still for all his reading and research and blazing anger at the sins of his father.

—Complete suits are valuable, but I have more interesting pieces. This helmet from Greece, mid–sixth century B.C. was forged from a

single sheet of bronze. These are jousting suits for boys of about six or
eight. They're not extremely rare but they are in good condition, which
makes me think the boys weren't really training as hard as they should
have been, you know what I mean? Weren't giving it their all. This ventail is German, from the fourteenth century. Look how flexible it is.

Tentatively Diane takes the helmet from him.

—It's okay, you won't damage it.

Gently she flexes the metal, notices her polish is chipped, hands
it back.

—Articulated breastplate, couple of pieces of blackened armor, a
bird-beaked bascinet. This is a riveted mail hauberk, rare on account of
its preservation. Mail rusts so easily. My father bought this for me after
throwing a Limoges soup bowl at my head. It was after a big dinner party
my parents hosted around Christmas and I'd told a Supreme Court justice, state supreme, I thought he'd made a mistake on some recent ruling.
I was nine years old. I assume I thought I was being funny. Father
wanted something from the guy and my insubordination was not appreciated. Anyway I fell asleep on some dish towels inside the pantry and I
woke up to my father going ballistic. And I mean literally ballistic since
he was throwing the porcelain at me. My mother had gone down to see
the guests off and she lost it when she saw the two of us surrounded by
shattered wedding china. I mean, I think she always kind of hated the
service but she also didn't want to have to take me to the hospital for
stitches. That night was a doozy for my collection. A week later my father
and I flew to Texas where this oil guy with brain cancer was liquidating
his... glancing down to see what she's looking at... —Mail, you probably
know this but there are a lot of theories about how mail was made and
evolved and the divergent schools are still pretty tense about it, in particular if a separate rivet was used and if so, how it was inserted.

—Fascinating... Diane bends over the vitrine, squinting at the
objects.

—Like I told your assistant I don't have many swords or much in
the way of arms at all. I guess I'm kind of a pacifist and my father never,
well he never encouraged that side of the collection, I guess he knew,
what with his temper and all, it wasn't the greatest idea to have his kid
sitting up in his bedroom, body teeming with adolescent hormones,
diddling around with knives. He was not a dumb man, my father, I

know that makes it sound as if he's dead. The few arms I do own were given to me by my aunt Joan, my father's sister, even though she was told many many times that I'd decided to focus on the defense part of the equation but despite being brilliant, she's a professor, fyi, Aunt Joan never quite grasped that I didn't collect swords and went about buying me battle-axes, crossbows, and a wheel-lock pistol as my parents' marriage came apart and finally disintegrated.

Lucas unlocks a case, flips it open, and hands Diane a small helmet. She studies it carefully... —The detail is—

—Right? I think so... he points to another piece... —Check it out, this pauldron, along with the breastplate and gauntlet supposedly once belonged to Jeanne de Penthièvre. *Supposedly.* Aunt Joan bought the whole bundle. Now there are a lot of people who don't believe that Joan of Arc wore armor or fought and the same is true of Jeanne, aka Joanna of Flanders. You can see why my aunt Joan was a fan of these women despite never doing anything braver than chase her ex-husband for child support, which by the way she had every right to, for a hundred reasons, not only because she supported him while he went to med school, but everyone pretty much knew Uncle Derek was squirreling his cash away instead of forking over half the Andover tuition plus. Plus because my cousin kept getting suspended and Aunt Joan kept having to parcel out hush money to his RAs to cover up his weakness for nose candy.

Ex-husband, what a vile word it is. Suggesting damage and fury and pain. She can't imagine Dominic as an ex. A word she hears in her head as ax. Ax-husband. All that love and history shredded.

—When her husband died in 1335, Joanna of Flanders busted out the armor, you probably remember this was in the middle of the Breton War of Succession, and organized resistance to protect the rights of her son. She was eventually forced to retreat to England, where she slowly went mad. But I prefer to remember her decked out in this armor fighting tooth and nail, don't you?

Diane nods, entranced by the helmet she holds in her hands.

—These are my favorite pieces because they make the idea of war and battle so palpable, don't you think?

—Yes... tracing the lines of the helmet... —Is there proof that these belonged to Joanna of Flanders?

—I have a contemporary illustration. It's in my bedroom. I'm not selling it, but I can show it to you... Lucas takes the helmet from her and replaces it in the case... —It was only about a year ago that I realized of course Aunt Joan knew I didn't collect arms. It was a warning. She was preparing my mother and me. Not that Aunt Joan thought I should chop my father up but, symbolically.

—Right.

—Also, a way of distributing her assets before the marriage ended. She was smarter than anyone gave her credit for. This set of horse armor is nearly intact. Maybe ten percent is missing.

—Mr. Boone, Lucas, have you considered what your father will, I mean, how he'll feel when he finds out.

—Oh, it'll kill him. He'll be incandescent. I'm laughing because it's one of my favorite fantasies of the last few weeks. He's on the board of the Art Institute and very loyal to all things Chicago. I know he assumed the collection would end up there at some point, probably long after his death. And seeing it exhibited under my mother's name, or his friends seeing it. No, I've considered it in detail... reaching for his acned cheeks as if to pick or scratch, then dropping his hand...

—Specific detail.

Stopping in front of a case... —What's this?

—Breastplate belonging to a child but check out, see this dip, that's from a projectile. Now, it could have been a test, but kids were sent into battle on occasion, as aides or squires.

—It's so small... she looks at him directly... —Lucas, I wonder if it would be better for you, your relationship with your father if you didn't give it to us right now. What about bequeathing it?

—But then you'd be dead, too. Isn't acquiring my stuff a big win for you?

—There'll be other collections. You can't undo these things, Lucas. And your father, I mean, that's a lifetime relationship.

—If my father disowns me over a bunch of objects, what does that say about him? Why ask me to be the adult?... his hands fly to his face again... —Breastplate with flowers and patination. Helmet from the sixteenth century. See how the top ridge on the vizor is really a lion? The ventail is missing a bolt.

—Consider it? Lucas?

—Picture what your board would say hearing this.

—I'll have to trust that it stays between us.

—Gauntlet. Immaculate shape. One of the oldest in existence. The left one is in the Museé de L'Armée. They wanted this one so badly. I wouldn't budge. I imagine you'll sell to them.

—We might come to an arrangement.

They come to the final case.

—The thing about collecting, Diane, you think it's about aesthetics, the beauty of the piece. And that's what it should be, right? Or a fascination with history, looking at the concrete and finding in it a way of experiencing the abstract, almost impossible concept of lives lived hundreds of years ago. In fact it's neither of those things. It's just a sad obsession for people who live for the chase. Who can't find joy in the present. Pleasure lies in anticipation. The next object, and the one after that. Owning what no one else does. Getting there first with more money or a better story.

Diane's stomach grips and pitches and she turns away. A hand on her abdomen, hoping to calm it.

—Are you okay?

—Fine.

—You can't help but worry. What's missing? What hole are you trying to fill by possessing these things?

—I imagine.

—The theologians, St. Augustine, St. Thomas, were wary about curiosity. Mostly about where it would lead the faithful, but I have no faith, so let's exclude them. Even Montaigne talks about how we have more curiosity than capacity. Montaigne! Back in the sixteenth century. Imagine what he'd make of Google or Wikipedia, coupled with our ever-growing failure to retain any of the information we, are you okay? You look green. Diane? Diane?

But she's already out the door, cannonballing down the stairs, headed toward the bathroom she clocked on the way up.

3:31 p.m.

The two of you had been at it nonstop, like literally every time I turned around you guys were, or I guess it wasn't really fighting since you just stood there cracking your knuckles till Dad got tired of screaming. That was a time that seemed to last, from my point of view at least, for like five years but was probably more like six or seven months. Anyway, ANYWAY, let me finish, Dad decides to take us to Pistakee, like it's going to be this great bonding experience, like somehow it's going to be like when we were six or eight and genuinely excited about shit, only now we're fourteen, we're pissed and miserable. So we drive up. Remember we stopped at that diner and wanted milkshakes, but he'd only buy one, made us share. It took years for me to realize that Dad was always setting up dogfights. Anyway, we arrive at the lake and it's like a lake on a poster advertising how great lakes are, crystal blue. White puffy clouds. No one's there, it's still early in the season. We had that semi-legal place he liked to camp or maybe it was completely illegal because we always had it all to ourselves. We park the car. It's hot and we're dying to swim, but this being Dad, first we had to make camp. Set up the tents, find firewood, prep the fire, deal with the folding table, probably some business with paper towels, remember how obsessed he was with paper towels? Okay, so finally it's all ready, and we're silent because if you ever said anything like, *now* can we go for a swim? Dad was going to torture you even more. So we're like, hands in our pockets, whistling, like maybe we came all this way to hunt for a crested woodpecker or whatever. Finally Dad whips off his shirt and charges into the lake, yelling, You pricks swimming or what? We tear off our shirts, we'd been wearing our suits since seven in the morning and jump into the lake. It's cold as a heart attack but we're trying not to scream cuz that's really going to piss him off. For about half an hour we're swimming and diving, dunking each other. It's perfect, everything you thought a lake could be. And for half an hour we're eight again, all that teenage misery disappears. I still remember the look on your face. Then out of nowhere it starts raining. Not just raining but biblical pouring, like where's the hail? Where are the frogs? We have to pack up, right? I mean, our tents were ancient, no way could they handle the rain. So you and I, we get out of the water, start running around, packing away the food and paper towels, pulling down the tents, folding up the table. You remember. We never once looked at each other. Never said a word. Spinning around like *Swan Lake*. Like we'd spent a month rehearsing. Three minutes in, the campsite's a mud hole, right, a fucking battlefield. Of course we're laughing, the two of us, we're hysterical because we're slipping and sliding, the rain's coming down so hard it's painful. At one point you wipe out, feet out from under you like a cartoon. I almost pee my pants I'm laughing so hard. Finally everything's packed. We jump in the car. Sitting on towels, can't get Dad's nylon interior dirty. Now Dad revs the engine, puts the car in drive, but the wheels just spin. So you fly to the trunk, grab a cardboard box, dump out the stuff, flatten it, wedge it under the tires. That works, and we're gone. A minute later we're back on the highway heading home. Up front, Dad's all furious, wipers going, no expression, but the two of us, we're charged, adrenaline pumping. That's what this rush reminded me of, Jimmy. Orders piling up, but we're knocking out dishes, no big deal, that family from Florida, four kids, each allergic to something different, Canadian who ordered the mackerel remembering when the dish arrives she actually hates mackerel, that old dude showing off to his jailbait date, saying the wine's corked, and the whole kitchen's taking it in stride, even Ryan, a blithering asshat. Otto's sprinting to the bathroom every five minutes to puke. But we're zen, we're in sync, we're like a commercial for efficiency. Dishes appearing right when you need them. Entire kitchen operating on a psychic level. Communicating with one look. No time to think, no time to process. Like that time at the lake, you forget what it is to be human. You're just a body moving through space, plating, pulling down orders, a robot, a machine. In the zone. How incredible it feels not to feel anything.

3:36 p.m.

—Apologies for keeping you so long, Lucas... she found toothpaste in the medicine cabinet, thank god... —The Museum would love to be thought of... Diane breaks off, he's said something, she can't tell what, his back to her... —Sorry?

—I miss him. In case you think I hate him... and Lucas starts off down the stairs... —But you can have it. All of it... he turns to check she's following... —However this works, contracts, papers. My mother will sign as my guardian if that's necessary. I assume it is. You can't really do anything under the age of eighteen in this country. I'll have to choose the right time... down the hallway to the next stairway... —Like you, my mother believes I'm going through some kind of phase, separating from my father. All very Oedipal, she'll assume, but I'll win.

—Wonderful, thank you. The board... she swallows hard... —Will be over the moon.

In the wide entrance hall Lucas comes to a stop next to an antique entry table. He kicks a sneaker out of the way... —You okay? You look sick.

—Excited by your generosity. We hope you'll be our honored guest next Friday at the opening of "Warriors of the Himalayas."

—Cool, thanks, but—

—I know, I know, it's a patched-together show.

—Not that, it's—

—Which is why we're so grateful for your sizable donation, the department, I do beg your pardon, I really must, forgive my rush.

Lucas opens the front door, admitting a summery breeze and the sound of hammering down the block... —I do have one request.

—Right, your mother's maiden name—

—No, the gala this evening, I'd like to attend. With a guest.

—Not the "Warriors" show, VIP?

He shrugs.

—Children don't usually... oh what does she care... —My assistant will email you an invitation... stumbling and almost falling out the door.

—Hey, are you—

—All good... she takes the first step so they stand at eye level... —Lucas? You're sure you're ready? To give up what you love?

—Loved... he smiles at her with a kind of summoned resolve... —Past tense.

—We'll speak more this evening... and turning, she takes the remaining steps and walks toward Chris who is opening the car door and stretching out his hand.

3:39 p.m.

When the mooks appeared Henry was staring out the window at nothing in particular, a couple of clouds, one shaped like a camel, while he popped antacids from a jumbo-sized container. These were flavored, exotically, and revoltingly, in fruits of the tropics.

The news that the mayor's office was digging into museum finances already had Henry asweat and at the sight of two black-jacketed figures jumbled in his doorway, scanning the office with brazen prerogative, Henry began to double-sweat. Fisk and Travis. He could feel moisture pooling between his shoulder blades like a tarn in the mountains. The mere scent of a cop has always made him fret the jig was up, long before there was a jig. Back when he obeyed a strict code of ethics.

—Henry, I tried, I'm sorry... Audrey makes a helpless gesture... —They wouldn't wait.

—No worries. Come in, Officers, won't you?... Henry sets his tub of antacids on the coffee table and steels himself.

The agents step into the office, bringing with them the distinct smell of pepperoni and another smell, not body odor exactly, but the musk that comes from wearing one layer too many and spending too much time indoors. Badges are shown. The agents are from DHS, not here for him.

—Have a seat, please... squeezing past the one called Fisk, friendly hand on the guy's back to call out... —Audrey, mind rustling up some coffees?... encompassing the agents to ask... —Or cappuccinos? We have a snazzy new machine.

—Double expresso with lemon for me... Fisk sinks into the office couch.

—If I could get a caramuccino or anything with caramel that would really hit the spot... Travis folds her arms and remains standing.

—I'll take my usual... calling out as Audrey leaves... —And send for Diane.

—Don't bother... Fisk looks up from examining the books on Henry's coffee table... —We stopped by Schwebe's office. She's at a meeting.

—Oh dear. I'm not sure how much I can do for you without the director present.

—Let's find out, shall we?

Agent Fisk has a round pink face, short-fingered hands like the paws of an animal and too much real estate between his nose and lips. His eyes are pitch black and kidney-shaped; they look more like nostrils than eyes. Henry puts Fisk at fifty-five or sixty, making his luxuriant hair a rare find. It's the mane of a man without worries. A fellow you'd come across in a field in Greece chewing olives, tending a couple of skinny cows. Henry takes an instant dislike to him.

—Check out the maze... Agent Travis taps on the window...

—Sunflowers, I love it.

—Pulling it down tomorrow.

Fisk's partner is more like thirty with Slavic cheekbones and her hair wrapped in a tight librarian bun. Slim, almost delicate, she's trying to take up more room than possible according to the laws of physics. A bird fluffing out its feathers at the sight of a cat.

—Take a seat, Agent Travis.

—Oh, I'm happy standing, thank you... she picks up a framed photograph from the windowsill.

—As you wish.

—Cute kids.

—Kim and Colin. Out West these days, Los Angeles.

—Huh... she replaces the picture, picking up a souvenir seashell with the offhand scrutiny of lawmen on TV.

So here they are, Tom & Jerry, inspecting mementoes. What now? A quick game of good cop, bad cop?

Henry leans back in his chair, swiveling so he can fit both of them in the same frame... —How can I help?

—Wanted to run a couple of names by you.

He waits.

—Ever come across a dealer named Vauclain? Stuff from South Asia mostly.

—Doesn't ring a bell.

—What about an Alfred Langston? Owns a garden supply store over in West Orange called Art Fabrications.

—No, no. I don't have a garden, so.

—Very good. You can probably guess there's more to it than ceramic planters.

—Let me stop you there, guys. I'm afraid our curator's out with food poisoning. Kulap Stein's the one you'll want to interrogate.

—Interrogate, Mr. Joles, no one's—

—Henry, please.

—Henry, thank you, we'd love to speak with your curator when he's, uh, recovered. In the meantime, if we could toss around a couple of names. In case you get the chance to speak to Mr. Stein before we do.

—Coffee... Audrey struggles in with an overloaded tray.

Travis takes the tray and sets it on top of an expensive monograph. She ferries cups to Henry and her partner and returns to the window with a large mug and several cookies.

—So, Langston... Fisk continues... —Who is Alfie Langston with an innocent-looking garden center over in West Orange?

—I'm eager to hear.

—For one thing, he's a guy with a whole mess of names... Fisk sips his coffee... —Alfie Langston isn't Alfie Langston and he ain't Vauclain either. He's a guy named Ahmed. Stay with me, Henry, this will all make sense in a minute.

—Hanging on every word.

—So Ahmed's supply of antiquities comes from a guy in Mumbai and a jewelry store owner in Kabul. Pieces from Syria and Afghanistan go through Barumcha, where there's an unmanned border crossing into Pakistan. From there it goes to the free port in Switzerland or Dubai or Sharjah. Vauclain-slash-Ahmed has paid contacts in all three places. Most of it ends up in Brussels.

—Any two-bit gallery in Brussels will sell you a piece warm from the ground.

—Lisa, please. Don't start.

—Ever since Brussels disbanded its antiquities division... she ignores Fisk, her eyes glittering... —Galleries'll tell you right to your face you're buying loot. For the cachet... the color rising in her face... —I mean, why not? There's no downside.

—Enough.

Travis shutters, simmering. This appears to be a familiar dance. Travis: young, feisty, invested. Fisk: patiently and briskly snuffing her passion.

—Let's keep our focus.

Travis bites expressively into a cookie, snapping it in half. Kim used to get like this, flaring at instances of injustice, even as a child.

—The loot ends up at the gardening center in New Jersey with our friend Ahmed. And Ahmed, he's got friends. High up.

—He's merely an employee... Travis chews... —Not a mastermind.

—Works for the Islamic State.

—ISIS.

—ISIS?... Henry sips his coffee.

—I'm sure you're aware that trafficking antiquities is one way terrorists fund their operations.

—I don't keep up with the nuances, no.

—It's hardly a nuance, Henry. Mohammed Atta, you remember Atta, flew the plane into the Twin Towers?

—I do.

—Financed the project by trading stolen Afghan art in Germany. Now, who's buying the stuff? Private collectors, sure, but soon they run out of small-time guys. So Ahmed-slash-Vauclain-slash-Langston starts up his business... Fisk, enjoying himself, modulating his tone as if he's making his case to the jury... —Pretty soon he's eyeing bigger fish.

Henry places his cup on the desk. Objectively, it sounds a bit like he slammed it on the desk. But they've started to piss him off with this crap about Atta, the Twin Towers.

—Gotta say, Henry... Fisk, watching him closely... —This is a great couch. Where do you pick up a couch like this?

—I have no, do I look like I buy my own office furniture?

—Most couches make my hips go numb. Got sciatica from an unsafe snatch and jerk in oh-eight. Uncertified trainer, turns out. I was trying to do the right thing by my health. Goes to show you.

Fisk, sitting there with his gigantic mane, hair like a Van Gogh in its stria and variegation of color. Still marveling, the eye travels, how can it not, down to the man's hard round belly which rests on his thighs in an oddly disconnected fashion like the basketball in a team photo. What is Fisk up to with his sad tale of twitchy nerves? Some distraction technique they teach in the academy? Get people to empathize, open up, spill secrets.

—So, Henry... Travis takes over... —This guy Vauclain connects with galleries in London and Paris. New York, too, as it happens... dipping a cookie in her coffee... —Also with some museums, we hear.

—You hear. Who are you hearing that from?

—We have guys... Fisk bounces on the couch.

—You have guys. Well, it seems these famous guys of yours missed the ISIS fanatic sitting on a pile of swag in West Orange, dealing Buddhas to fund suicide bombers. Pretty sloppy. Find yourself some new guys, that's my advice.

—Now, Henry.

—We stopped by hoping you could help.

—Since 1970 the Museum has followed strict protocol on—

—Oh, come on... Travis, breaking rank... —In March you returned a statue to Italy bought in the nineties. Late nineties. Don't bullshit us about 1970.

—Before you tell us, Henry, that you have documentation your stuff left India before 1970 let me say that we have photos of the statues in situ. Taken by a husband-and-wife photography team. Evidenced rural temples in four countries for over a decade. Decade, you understand? All very tight. Now, I'm not saying we're going to find any of these pieces in your galleries, but if we did. Find them. Understand proof of their origins exists.

—As I said when you walked in, without our curator I'm useless to you... standing, enough of this shit... —I do apologize.

—Henry, Henry.

—I have nothing to add, I'm afraid, until I speak to Kulap... smiling falsely as he reaches out for a handshake... —Sorry to disappoint.

Ignoring Henry's hand, Fisk tips back his cup to show he won't be rushed, drains his coffee, and languidly returns the cup to the tray. Finally he gets to his feet. Handshakes follow, formal nods, business cards. Eventually they leave.

Henry goes to the window and returns the framed photographs to their original position. Where the fuck is Mike Decker? He straightens a picture of Kim and Colin playing on the beach. Kim in a ruffled suit, hair buffeted by the wind and ropy from salt water. Staring up at the camera. Already wounded, from the look of reproach in those black

eyes. Next to her, Colin gazes shrewdly into the distance like a specu-
lator sensing opportunity on the horizon.

—Henry?... Audrey, on speaker, jolting him... —I have Diane calling
from her car. Shall I tell her you'll call back?

—No, put her through. Oh, and Audrey? Keep the visit from DHS
to ourselves for now.

—Of course.

—How did they get up here? I mean, no warning, nothing?

—Calling Security as we speak. Also, Henry, a call from Sloan-
Kettering.

—Okay.

—No luck reaching your cell, they said, trying to schedule—

—Got it, Audrey. Go ahead and put Diane through.

Silence.

—Diane?

—It's still me. The hospital, may I set a return call? They seem
persistent—

—Audrey, Audrey.

—Putting you through.

—Thank you.

Silence.

—Henry?

—Diane, what's up?

—Did you hear back from Ichimonji's people?

—Yes and there was no mention of a lawsuit. However, were the
Ambassador to be introduced to the Disney kid... searching for his
Post-it... —Lindsey-Hailey Green, it would go a long way.

—Is Lindsey-Hailey coming?... Diane's voice fades.

Chris, faintly in the background... —Yes, confirmed. One of Noizy's
guests.

—Henry—

—I heard, but tell me, I googled this smutty child—

—Smutty, please. She's ex-Disney.

—Yes but the *ex* is rather important, I saw pictures—

—Doesn't matter. I'll truck in Las Vegas strippers if it gives us a shot
at the Samurai show.

And she's hung up. Always good with an exit line, Diane. He stabs the intercom... —Audrey?

—Yes?

—Get me Mike Decker at State, would you please?

3:50 p.m.

Diane hands the phone back to Chris and immediately he starts typing into it, muttering *Ambassador* and *Lindsey-Hailey*. Traffic is stalled on Seventy-Fourth. They wait in a long line of cars. Horace taps the steering wheel and cracks his neck.

Along the street Zelkova trees are blazed with red. Fall back still weeks away. Diane powers down her window. Maybe fresh air will temper the nausea. Two gangly teenagers cross between the cars, pushing at each other, bumping off fenders. In the brackish air you can smell the nearby river. Behind them, a driver leans on his horn.

It didn't take long for the meditation impulse to flicker out and die. Diane quit the zendo, turning instead to the famous feeders of the soul. Augustine, Epicurus. When she opened paperbacks last cracked twenty years ago, Diane expected to find old friends. But now the words struck her as reproachful. In college the same phrases prodded and shook her, electrified her brain. *Begin at once to live and count each day as a separate life.* She paced the campus, feverish and alert, too hot for the snow outside. What a firecracker she was at twenty! Well, Diane, the current one, wasn't going down without a fight. Let her younger self win? Not a chance. For some reason, this is where the contest lay. In April she sprung for audio versions. Biking across Central Park, she tried to absorb the wisdom of Pliny as she slalomed squirrels, rocks, syringes, anarchic toddlers and, more than once, a runaway thermos rolling toward her tires.

Diane starts, pulling back from the face at the window. A miniature devil with pointed ears. She watches an ample woman, South American, pick up the child's red tail, and start plucking leaves off it. The nanny notices Diane and smiles, but does not, as Diane hopes, roll her eyes. Diane smiles back. The child waits with forbearance, like a little king bored with his jester. In forty years, the devil will be a trustee and Diane will be the tail-plucker.

Dominic said nothing when she abandoned the Greeks, despite Diane's showy reading of *The Collected Stoics*. And weeks later when she lay curled on her side, beaten by Seneca, humbled by her inability to find a curative, glaring at a thriller rippled from a plunge in the tub, Dominic stroked her back until she fell asleep.

Revisiting books first read when she and Dom were falling for each other, Diane thought, might return them to a love that was hungry and forgiving. Her curiosity in Dominic used to be endless. How she marveled at his long-toed feet. Now they seem suspiciously arboreal.

On the seat next to her, Chris types into his phone, thumbs moving with impressive speed. Across the street a flock of pigeons have gathered on the sidewalk, elated to find half a sandwich. One bird is so overcome he's pecking the bare sidewalk. God, the metaphors.

Where will she find such love again? But it's not love she misses.

Her own parents never divorced. To the casual observer it appeared as if Diane's father doted on her mother. How cozy that he accompanied her on shopping trips for dresses or a new bathing suit, that together they picked out her annual summer handbag. But Daddy wasn't there for the fun of it. He was suspicious of outside influences. He treated Diane's mother, not the way you would a queen, but as you would tend a Bonsai, by steadily, almost imperceptibly, reducing her choices, pruning and guiding and restricting growth until he had cultivated a remarkable replica of an actual person.

Traffic begins to move. In the front seat Horace keeps up a gentle yammer into his cell phone. He wears the earpiece in one ear only in order to be sensitive to the cues of other cars: the honking and swearing, an unexpected motorbike.

Daddy's acerbic face and thin nose afflicted most men on the Schwebe side of the family tree but the pendulous ears were unique to her father, as were the eyes that bulged with froggy mistrust. It was during Intro to Art History that Diane recognized her father's uncanny resemblance to Giovanni Arnolfini.

Chris finishes typing and starts to pocket his phone.

—Before you put that away... Diane turns to him... —Add Lucas Boone to the guest list.

—Isn't he like sixteen?

—He's a donor.

—Yes, but alcohol—

—Put him on the list with a plus-one.

Chris punches in the information.

—Also... pulling at her blouse... —I need another one of these.

—What is that, tea?

—Yes, and order it one size up.

Back to his phone, tapping... —I have Peter asking whether he should disengage the funicular for this evening. Last time I checked it was completely dead.

—Then don't bother.

—What about Shay Pallot? Have you given her the news?

—The minute we get back.

The traffic lightens and Horace barrels toward the West Side Highway. In front of them a nineteenth-century schooner scoots past in the river, four white sails abilllow. A stunning reproduction.

—Where are we going?

—Lyle Kipsie. An issue with your dress. An assistant, never mind he was fired for it. Workshop's so close, we may as well dash in and dash out.

—How is this being sprung on us—

—There was an intimation this morning.

—An intimation?

—Here is good?... Horace pulls over.

—Perfect... Chris opens the door... —Back in twenty.

—An intimation?

—Horace? We'll text when we're ready?

—Yup, I'll circle.

Diane slides across the seat and climbs out of the car. Dark birds spiral in the sky. She closes her eyes. Everywhere there are signs.

3:56 p.m.

—Semiotics? They teach that in eighth grade?

—At the Garrett School they do... with a tight smile Miss Wendy looks up from her phone... —Surely Mr. Bjarnsen hasn't forgotten his promise to the winners of our A.V. Club's short-film contest? Jason and Pritha stayed after school specially to meet with him.

Benjamin sees that the girl he took for nine is also about fourteen, simply tiny. She wears her hair in thick black braids, one over each ear and stares down at her shoes. Jason, in huge untied sneakers, hasn't stopped moving since the three of them appeared at Benjamin's door a few minutes ago.

—This all the DVDs you got?... Jason patrols the bookcase, scanning the shelves.

—Perhaps you could send for him, Mr.?

—Rippen, but you see—

—Film department should have like a million DVDs.

—Jason, stop that this second. It's inappropriate.

—Miss Wendy, what I'm trying to say—

—I mean, even I have more DVDs than this.

—Jason!... Miss Wendy returns her focus to Benjamin... —Here's the email... tilting her phone toward him with the persistence of a woman who's been habitually underestimated... —You see we made the appointment three months ago.

—Yes, I understand but I'm afraid that—

—He's forgotten us.

—No, no—

—Where's the screening room?

—Down the hall there but—

—Check your computer.

—Can I borrow these—

—Hush, Jason. Mr. Rippen, our appointment.

—Cassavetes DVDs?

—I can't see why there's cause for confusion. We had a plan, Mr. Rippen. Check your computer.

—That won't make a difference you see—

—We've been so excited—

—Ward Bjarnsen's dead.

Silence. Even Jason falls quiet and stops moving. All three look at Benjamin with dismay as if he's told a very silly joke. He has no idea why he said it. By all accounts Ward is lying in bed sipping Ensure, watching *The Lead Shoes.*

—He's?

—Dead, he said.

—Jason.

—Yes, I'm sorry to report... Benjamin leans forward and presses his fingertips against the desk, as he's seen people do when taking charge... —Mr. Bjarnsen has... what's the polite phrasing... —Passed over.

—How'd he die?

—Jason, that's really none of our—

—I actually don't know.

—Oh dear, well... Miss Wendy pulls her chin back toward her neck like a chicken... —My goodness... from the handbag looped around her forearm she retrieves a tissue. This she gazes at, seeming to gather strength from the soft white square... —Well... collecting herself... —Since we're here, and first of all that is quite awful about poor Ward, my prayers to his loved ones but since we came all this way, would it be possible if you, Mr. Rippen, gave these youngsters some of your time?

—Sorry but, you know, I have a whole day... Benjamin points at his computer, which is quite visibly powered off. He's been sitting here for forty-five minutes ostensibly waiting for Jeff from IT to return his call but instead reliving the scene from lunch over and over. Caroline sipping tea from that doll-sized cup, so pale you could see a filigree of blue veins along her jawbone. Her fragility spooked Benjamin but also gave him hope it was related to a fatal inadequacy on the part of her new boyfriend.

Pritha is toeing the carpet as if she's curious about the prospects of it standing up to heavy use. The kid moves him. So serious in her thick braids.

—A few crumbs of advice. Promise it won't take long... Miss Wendy looks around for somewhere to sit.

—Yeah, yeah, sure. Why not? I'll answer a few questions... stepping out from behind the desk... —Please, sit... rolling his swivel chair toward the teacher.

—I'm good... Jason, in the middle of the room, clasps his hands behind his back.

—Pritha, take the armchair.

She pulls off her backpack and sits down, having to almost climb into the chair.

Benjamin leans back against his desk, folds his arms and tries to look wise... —So, uh, let's see. Winners of your school's short-film contest, congratulations. Tell me what inspired you.

They both look appalled.

—Who are your favorite directors?

—David Fincher, PTA, Aronofsky, QT, and Chris Nolan.

Benjamin takes an immediate dislike to this Jason kid. The bratty self-awe reminds Benjamin of the chumps he knew in grad school who sat around the quad squabbling about their love for Lav Diaz.

—And you... nodding at Pritha... —Do you have a favorite?

—No, not really, I mean, maybe like Agnès Varda?

—Varda, one of the very best... flooded with relief, a fellow countryman... —What appeals to you about Varda?

Pritha shrugs, looks down at her hands. In her right nostril a slim gold hoop catches the overhead lights.

—Critics talk about her sense of space.

Still focused on her hands, the girl says... —I like how in *Vagabond* the girl keeps saying no, like even when it's bad for her, even when it's dooming her to death, she never gives in to what other people want for her... Pritha's voice drops... —I kept hoping she'd accept help, but she couldn't.

—She wasn't built for compromise.

—Uh-huh.

—Why do you think Varda wanted to provoke this feeling of discomfort?

—I don't know, I'm not sure I understand her movies.

—Understanding's overrated.

—My mom thinks *The Dark Knight* is like some dumb action movie.

—After all, Bresson... Benjamin raises his voice... —Bresson said I'd rather people feel a film of mine before understanding it.

—And I keep saying, dude, you're not getting the deeper meaning.

—Have you seen her first film, Varda's, *La Pointe Courte*... mangling the French... —I'm sure we have it in the library here.

—No, not yet.

—Tell me about the film you made, Pritha.

—Like in *Batman Begins*—

—What's it about?

—a man overcomes his darkest fear—

—Not really anything. A boy goes looking for his dog.

—triggering his alter ego... on and on Jason jabbers... —Chris Nolan, can I say—

—It was called *Timmy's Tale* and people cried... Miss Wendy, interjecting... —They really did. Quite an achievement. Only nine minutes long.

—But can I say, Mr. Rippen, Chris Nolan—

—Cried? That's wonderful.

—Chris Nolan thinks—

—And does Timmy ever find his dog?

—I read somewhere—

—No, Timmy's brother killed it.

—Oh dear.

—maybe in *Sight and Sound*—

—He hated that Timmy had something to love.

—that Chris thinks most movies—

—HEY... Benjamin wheels around to face Jason.

The boy steps back, bumping into the wall behind him.

—Do you actually *know* Christopher Nolan?

—I mean, not personally but—

—Then. STOP. Calling. Him. CHRIS.

Jason's lip quivers and he stares down into the cardboard box where *Bettina!*'s swollen breasts peek out from under the scattered plant dirt.

Benjamin kicks the box against the wall.

—Jason here... Miss Wendy, speaking rapidly... —Made a short film... possibly alarmed by Benjamin's kicking... —That ran chronologically backward. Very innovative.

—Exactly like *Memento*, you mean? That kind of innovation?

—Inspired by it, sure.

—Got your eye on Hollywood, have you Jason?

—I want to make movies, don't I?

—You're aware of the pressure to make a certain box-office?

—So what?

—Sound like art to you?... Benjamin has no idea why he's needling this pimply youth.

—What are you talking about?

—Auteurs can't exist in a system built for profit.

—There's a ton of great American directors... panic rising in his voice, Jason turns to his teacher... —This guy knows nothing.

—I know incoherent editing when I see it.

—Oh please.

—Jason, be polite... Miss Wendy addresses her phone.

—Sounds like you hate America... the kid glares at Benjamin... —What's wrong with profit?

—A profit-based system—

—You a communist?

—is by definition corrupt. That's not communism, buddy, it's a statement of fact.

Engulfed by Ward's armchair, Pritha has her knees pulled up to her chin, her face buried in her elbow. He can tell by the shaking of her shoulders that she's laughing. Well, then, mission fucking accomplished.

—Jason, hear Mr. Rippen out.

—Why? He's an idiot.

—Because opposing viewpoints are vital to—

—My dad told me to steer clear of losers... Jason heads for the door... —Said they'll bring you down... and he springs from the room in his pillowy sneakers.

Miss Wendy follows close behind calling, Jason, Jason. The echoes of her voice fade away until the room is silent.

Benjamin crouches by the cardboard box, spreading soil over Bettina's breasts. He knows exactly why he was needling Jason. Not because the kid reminds Benjamin of the chumps he knew in grad school but because Jason is exactly like a person who went to Columbus brimming with the radical ideas he planned to bring the world of cinema only to jettison any idea of directing the second he graduated. A nobody who swaggered around bitching about janky tripods and the lack of authentic al pastor, asking everyone he met why the squirrels in Ohio were so goddamn fat. A person who was, in the end, nothing more than a coward.

—I liked his movie about the donkey.

Benjamin stands up... —Donkey? Sorry?

—Bresson?... avoiding his eyes... —The tortured donkey?... Pritha tells her knee... —With the girl?

—Balthazar? You mean *Au Hasard Balthazar*?

She nods.

Benjamin brushes the dirt off his hands, watching the business with disembodied interest. *Balthazar*. Thackeray showed it early in the semester. The movie upset Benjamin. It wasn't an emotional response to the film, or not solely an emotional response, but a boiling resentment that two decades after his death Bresson had the power to disrupt a stranger in a dark room. Render that person so altered and fragile he was useless to face the world. And maybe it was then, only a month in, that Benjamin's dream began to slip away.

—I'm sorry, Pritha, what?

—I said I liked his movie *Mouchette*.

—*Mouchette*? What do you, they let you watch *Mouchette* in, what grade are you in?

—It's A.V. club.

—Okay, but Pritha, that's not exactly, I mean. *Mouchette*'s a tough movie. Not that *Balthazar*'s a piece of cake.

—At least it's about a girl, from a girl's point of view, like she actually feels things not just, you know, Shirley Temple or whatever people think a girl is. We saw *400 Blows* and *Bicycle Thieves* and *Armacord*, but nothing where the girl matters. I watched *Vagabond* on my own, online, Miss Wendy said it wasn't a classic. But the classics are either about guys or pretty ladies... she pulls a braid around and inspects the end of it...

—I like them okay. *Roman Holiday*? That's a good movie. You can't say it's not a good movie.

—It is, it's a great movie.

—*The Palm Beach Story*. It's not like I don't like movies about pretty ladies, but.

They hear Miss Wendy calling from the hallway.

—I should go. She gets mad quick... Pritha struggles to get out of the armchair that appears to have swallowed her.

—Right, well... Benjamin is oddly disappointed... —Maybe you'll let me see *Timmy's Tale* some time.

—Maybe.

—Stay in touch, okay?

While it's indisputable that Pritha's short film sounds a lot like *Kes*, Ken Loach's masterpiece of the British New Wave, if *Timmy's Tale* had a genuine effect on people, the borrowing is irrelevant. Pritha won.

—Ten years from now I'll be screening your films here. Promise you'll bring them to me first, okay? Not Lincoln Center.

—I'm going to law school.

Pritha is so very little, swaddled in dark cardigans and scarves, bundled to a point where it's impossible to distinguish one article of clothing from another. The heavy braids weigh down her features, giving her the doleful look of someone three times her age. It's painful to think that Pritha would waste so much promise.

—My parents say because I like to argue... staggering as she tries to pull on an enormous backpack almost exactly her size... —I'd make a good lawyer.

—But Pritha, you moved people. Brought them to tears, Miss Wendy said. Why waste that gift by becoming a boring old lawyer?

She smiles uncertainly, as if making a great film was just another after-school activity.

—Drop by anytime, okay? Give me a chance to talk you out of it.

Suddenly young Pritha stopping by the film department to borrow Benjamin's books and soak up his advice means more to him than anything in the world.

—Promise... he tries to sound offhand... —Promise you will.

—Okay... saying it faintly, halfway out, not looking back as she pulls the door closed behind her.

4:08 p.m.

—Human Resources already feel as if they're working in a pinball machine, not to mention the grief the press gave us for the wedge which, by the way, the restrictions, ouch, sorry, the—

—Grief from the press? Have you even read the architectural reviews? Or anything that actually matters?

—Okay, forget I said, hey—

Selina yanks at the dress in the guise of making it sit correctly but perhaps also to express her annoyance that Diane's on the phone. The tug nearly launches Diane off the small raised stage and into the trifold mirror. Lyle Kypsie left Selina behind to run his studio while he gathers inspiration in Senegal and it appears the workload has begun to take a toll. Her hair is unwashed, pulled back with a cheap tortoiseshell clip. Her breath is vegetal. Once feline, now she moves in sighing flings and darts.

—Hang on, John... pressing mute... —Selina?

She looks up at Diane, straight pins pressed between her lips, eyes querying.

—Let me apologize once again for—

Selina gives her a dismissive wave.

—Thanks for understanding... Diane unmutes her phone... —Look, John, we can't keep having the same conversation over and—

—No... warningly... —This isn't the same conversation. Not at all. The last time we spoke the north wall was under discussion... a rush of water, the unmistakable sound of a toilet flushing... —This idea is brand new. It preserves the original intention of the design, solves the problematic interaction with the urban fabric by addressing the inaccessibility of connections and takes into account both the budget overrun and the programmatic needs of the space.

—When a change in design adds money to a project, that is not the definition of taking into account, John, that is the definition of ignoring.

—I respectfully disagree.

She falls silent in order to give the impression of an amiable ear, picturing John on the other end of the phone wearing one of his confusing coats. He has the architect's attraction to complicated clothing and often shows up in a shirt or jacket featuring pleats or whorls or allusions to Fibonacci, a neckline that's uncomfortably deep or weirdly high, as well as an apparent disdain for any type of ordinary closure. Last time they met, John wore a buttonless jacket so crimped and torqued Diane spent the entire meeting trying to figure out how he took it off at night.

—Furthermore.

Furthermore!

—The concessions you want are completely at odds with the boldness you requested, the argument for hiring us in the first place.

—John, please. You know where we are with our budget. The reason we even need these concessions is because of overruns that were entirely avoidable in the first place.

—Avoidable if you wanted—

—A functioning museum? Then they were avoidable? It doesn't appear as if the news has registered, John, but we're anticipating a financial contraction that makes it impossible to both operate the Museum and, you know, actually acquire the art for your addition. We're going to have a very beautiful but completely empty new wing.

—Stop. I can't even. Whatever you're about to say, don't say it.

Selina stands and encircles Diane's waist with a swatch of chartreuse fabric, winching it tightly.

—No... hissing, pressing mute... —Where did this come from?

—Diane, let me send over, if I could show you what we're thinking instead of trying to describe it over the phone, I'm sure you'd

Ignoring her protestations, Selina binds the sash, whacking the dress to make it lie flat while simultaneously and needlessly whacking Diane on the ass.

—And finally, I refuse to compromise the integrity of our firm. Backtracking *unintelligible unintelligible* the godforsaken McKenna and—

—No, John... unmuting... —No, John. No more additional costs and no more fucking curves.

Chris jerks around. He's sitting at Lyle's long white desk with rococo legs. From the matching ornate chair he shakes his head quickly, eyes open wide to signal that Diane is entering dangerous territory. Cursing country.

—Lift your arms... Selina demonstrates... —Higher, higher.

Switching the phone to speaker and complying... —Excuse my language, John, but—

—Of course... unmistakable frostiness from the other end... —But most architects wouldn't put up—

—Oh please, the Museum has bent over backwards—

—with these ever-changing—

—Not to mention, John, the regulations we've ouch, pretty much tossed out the window, the construction lawsuit, trying to get this shit past the board, okay, if you want to talk about conservative.

—Listen to me for a second.

—Uh-huh... but Diane is not, as requested, listening, except to the voice in her head screaming, BECAUSE OF YOU MY JOB IS IN JEOPARDY, and additional unsavory exegesis along these lines, while at the same time understanding that she herself was responsible for signing off on designs and budgets as well as promoting Eli Gabor to V.P. Construction, depending on him to handle operational oversight, when, more than once, he'd appeared at a morning meeting reeking of alcohol... —Right, right.

—So you see what I mean, then?

—John... she watches Chris silently mouth *hang up* and mime setting down a receiver... —Why don't we settle this early next week?

—Because time is of the—

—Monday? How's Monday?

Chris shakes his head.

—Tuesday?

—We're in Australia until Friday and I won't. Diane, I won't keep doing this on a phone that

Silence.

She looks at the black screen, bewildered... —It's dead.

Chris gets up from the fussy white chair, takes the phone from her and starts fiddling with it.

—Never even got to the brunnel. Thank god, I guess... in the mirror the dress is... —Selina, why am I wearing this waist thing?

—You lost too much weight.

—I've what? I haven't lost an ounce.

—Well, somehow, without losing an ounce, all your measurements are smaller... Selina treats herself to a smirk... —At this point a sash is our only option.

—Okay, but the color, if it could just, you know, not be this color.

A dark look from Selina who turns back to the dress, muttering... —Two hours they give me to fix this. Two.

—What are you typing? Chris?

—Emailing John to explain why your phone went dead. And Ichi-monji's assistant said he'd like to meet the chef who made his toasts. I'm figuring out an intern who won't massively fuck that up.

—He's still at the Museum?

—Big textile fan.

—Chris?

—Hmm?

—I know this is outside your so-called duties but this sash thing...?

He glances up quickly, takes her in, toe to head to toe... —Yeah, it works... back down to his phone... —You returned Dominic's call?

—On my list... staring at the top of his haircut.

—Okay, we need to prepare for our five thirty... Chris looks up, puts away his phone... —I have Horace outside... standing... —Let's go... he snaps his fingers.

—Are you snapping at m... but as Diane takes a step off the raised platform she catches her heel in the hem of the dress and trips, straight into Chris who catches her but they smack heads and Selina's grabbing at the dress wailing about ripping but it hasn't ripped it's all okay and Diane has to run into the dressing room because the vomiting feeling arises again and she has to keep it all. Tamped. Down.

4:16 p.m.

Men who wear cheap suits with unreasonable confidence usually work for the government, so Clive assumed that the idiots who barreled out of Corbeau's gallery pecs-first were federal agents. Their forceful exit made for havoc on the sidewalk; a woman was leashed to a large and obstinate shitting poodle that created a tangling confusion with lots of high-stepping and swallowed profanities. Several items were dropped and someone, Iona, Clive thought, got stepped on, but it was semi-graciously sorted out, the Feds went on their way and he and Iona continued into the gallery where Jack Corbeau stood stock-still in the middle of the room, pulling at his earlobe, and staring emotionally at a woodland tapestry. Clive had to spell out his violent need for a coffee three or four times before Corbeau finally collected himself and handed over a Styrofoam cup containing a foul black liquid. Only Iona Moore's ass improved Clive's mood. She went at the marriage chest like Martha Graham, bending, twisting, and folding, stopping now and then to ask a question or point out a detail but in general putting on a rather delightful show.

The cab hurtles into Central Park, cutting off a bicyclist grinning in the fragrant breeze, and instantly driving the twinkly gent into a whirl of shaking fists and middle fingers.

—Um... Clive leans toward the cabbie... —We're not in any hurry.

As the words are leaving his mouth, Clive recognizes his comment as the sort that forces a cabbie to abandon all rules of the road in order to teach you a valuable lesson in keeping your fucking mouth shut. Iona braces herself as the taxi takes the curve on two wheels and streaks through a freshly red light at terrifying speed.

It was an inspired idea to bring Iona Moore, with her optivisor and revivifying buttocks. She confirmed that the cassone had been almost entirely reconstructed and the lid, though likely contemporary, was not original to the chest. Even better, a few features appeared to have been added in the nineteenth century. It was all good news. Iona bit at her necklace and rattled on about man-made stenciling. Her tartan skirt was snug on the hips. Only an incurable slut would wear such a hideous skirt.

Up ahead the traffic light turns from green to yellow. This time the driver stomps on the brake, shuddering the cab to a stop and throwing Iona against the seat in front.

—Okay?

She nods, righting herself, blushing.

—You don't fasten the belt?

—Forgot... Iona looks down as if to confirm the lack of restraint, then reaches around and pulls the seatbelt across her body. Clive fishes the matching buckle out of the crevasse and together they fasten the clasp. Immediately, she returns to gazing out the window.

It's not that she's childish, Clive thinks, but that she gives off an air of arrested sexuality. With those big squishy lips. Another woman would have made something of a mouth like that. The passive mouse bit doesn't usually appeal to Clive, but he can't quite shake the feeling that fear has led Iona down this colorless path. A tiger could lurk beneath that perverted skirt. He's interested in putting it to a test. But no, he mustn't.

A young couple with a child crosses in front of the taxi, arguing. Clive rolls down his window. The breeze is warm but smells of fall, the promise of cool nights.

Iona sneezes into the crook of her elbow.

—Allergies?

She nods. He studies her profile. A couple of wayward hairs have attached themselves to her lip gloss and she's either humming tunelessly or quietly groaning. Flopped between them on the seat is Iona's handbag and as she looks out the window she plays distractedly with the strap. The bag is a defeated shade of blue with cracks along one seam and white tributaries fanning to the far corners. Embedded in the flap hanging over a side pocket is the half-moon of a bite mark. You can make out every tooth. He wonders if it came from her child or if in a fit of frustration Iona bit her own bag. She sneezes again and Clive is gripped by a surge of affection. He gets this feeling in a deli sometimes, late at night, watching a stranger search the freezer with singular focus, as if the right ice cream will clear up the truth about love.

—You know, you should really be the one to ask Tindall-Clark about his lion.

Iona turns partway, acknowledging Clive's words without actually looking at him.

—Do it tonight, why not, at the gala. I have an extra ticket.

—No thanks, I trust you.

—That's a terrible idea, for a start. Wouldn't you like to come? People say it's a fun night.

But Iona Moore of the skinny calves and Jagger lips shakes her head.

—Come.

Her fingers stop playing with the strap of her handbag. These surges of affection that hit Clive are only ever aimed at strangers.

The cab shoots out of the park and a few minutes later Iona adds to her earlier observations about the condition of the marriage chest, something about pillars with composite capitals.

4:23 p.m.

They took away Marie's beloved donkey, the one with melancholy eyes, and gave it to the local baker. In the weeks that followed, Balthazar was passed from one neglectful owner to the next. Scene by scene, they treat him cruelly, with malice and contempt. Little Marie is likewise subjugated by her owners, a terrible mirror of Balthazar's hardship. Notebook balanced on his lap, Benjamin was alive to interpretation, on the lookout for themes and allegories. At the same time he couldn't help wondering, am I the donkey? Maybe I'm the donkey.

Bresson favored a mechanical style of acting that annoyed Benjamin. It was unpleasant, the flattened-out images and over-amplified sound. But when Balthazar staggered onto a field of sheep and died, Benjamin broke down. The film bypassed the place where he could assess it critically and shot straight to his heart. And Benjamin wasn't the only one crying. The sound of sniffling filled the lecture hall. Thackeray took his time fading up the lights.

"The difficulty is that all art is both abstract and suggestive at the same time," Bresson once said. "Art lies in suggestion. The great difficulty for filmmakers is precisely not to show things. Ideally nothing would be shown."

That was Robert Bresson's idea of a perfect film. Nothing would be shown.

4:25 p.m.

The lawyer is singing. Painfully off-key. Looking out the window, pounding the air with a raised fist.

—*When they kick at your front door how you gonna come?*

A heavy-looking silver watch flashes with every rebellious punch.

—*With your hands on your head or on the trigger of your gun?*

Again, Shay coughs. Louder this time. But he doesn't flinch, doesn't move. She turns to go.

—*When the law break in*, Chief?

Shay's almost to the door, another inch and she'd be through. Absurdly, she considers making a break for it. Instead, sanely, she turns around.

Joles is pulling headphones from his ears, fumbling with his phone... —Beg your pardon I was—

—No, no, my fault, I—

—reminiscing.

—Nothing urgent, I'll come back—

—My punk days, if you can believe.

—tomorrow.

—Stay, I insist. Come in. Sit down. Have a coffee.

—Henry!... a ruckus by the door is the lawyer's secretary. Unhappy to see Shay has entered the office without clearance... —I stepped away—

—Aud—

—for one second—

—Audrey, it's fine. Rustle up two cappuccinos, would you, dear? Not dear, sorry, not dear.

—If I could, I never get mad at a mocha.

—A mocha for the Chief, and you know, I'd better take a decaf, thank you.

Shay attempts an apologetic smile but the secretary leaves without looking back.

—Please... Joles indicates one of the chairs flanking a glass and steel coffee table.... —Gala prep going okay? Anyone accidentally drill himself or take a headlong off a scissor-lift?

—Nothing reported. Red carpet's going down now. Fellow from

the precinct rerouting traffic around the install. So far so good, knock on wood... accepting his offer of a chair but perching on the edge to remind them both of the limited time she has for things like sitting... —Now, on my end, Mr. Joles, I have to apologize about earlier, the federal agents. My staff got intimidated by the badges and let them up without running it by me first. Won't happen again.

—Good, good. Glad to hear it... Joles runs a hand over his naked head... —So.

—It's a personal issue, if I may.

—Of course.

—I have a nephew... for god's sake, his name, she just had it, covering the pause with a small cough... —Working with me down in Security. Temporary type job, you know. Without weighing you down with details—

—Weigh away, I could use the distraction.

—Then I'll come right out and, my nephew could use a mentor. *Malcolm!*... then, less excitedly... —Malcolm. A good boy. On time, reliable. But now you see my sister still sees Malc as the child he was at seven. Had a speaking impediment, a limp, glasses this thick. At school kids stuck him in the recycling, tossed him around like a football. Once he grew, they stopped. Today, they're all friends.

—He forgave them.

—That's right.

—Admirable. You know, I had a stutter once.

—No one said you couldn't be a lawyer.

—That's what your sister's saying?

—There's a condition runs in our family, Mr. Joles, early onset dementia. Tasha got tested, learned it was coming for her and let the news drain her life. So with her children, you understand, it isn't that Tasha's negligent, of course she cares, it's more that she lacks motivation... recognizing only now, maybe as a result of her deteriorating faculties, that the Museum's lawyer might well wonder whether Shay herself could be on the receiving end of this hereditary nightmare... —I took the test... nothing for it, she'll have to lie... —I'm not at risk.

A loud bang as the door flies open and the lawyer's secretary enters with a tray.

—Thank you, Audrey.

Wordlessly, the secretary sets the tray on the coffee table, there's a run in her stocking down by the ankle. Flashing Henry a tight smile, she ignores Shay, stalking away in a huffish cloud.

—Sorry to hear about your sister. Sugar?

—Thank you, no... taking the cup he holds out. The liquid inside is the furious brown of a flooded river... —I thought a man of your standing could be a strong influence on Malcolm. A mentor type. He's come to a fork in the road, as I see it.

The lawyer takes a loud vacuuming sip of coffee, swallows, and sits back... —I'm honored, of course, Chief... raking his bottom lip with his teeth... —But I'm afraid it's impossible. There's the matter of time. These days I don't have much to spare. And other factors. I've been a mediocre father... holding up a hand as if anticipating protest... —My children, the older ones, speak mostly to their mother. My daughter was fourteen when I said, 'why not try to be pretty?' Her clothing was shapeless, scruffy. Never brushed her hair. Feminist of some kind. I didn't see my comment as unforgivable though I may have voiced my displeasure more than once.

Sipping the mocha, Shay waits for his point. Despite their friendly conversation in Greek this morning, she's unwilling to act as his confessor. Yet appears to have no say.

—Why didn't I teach my son chess or archery or how to steal a base? I lacked role models of my own. I was afraid of my father, my mother was institutionalized. They're polite, the kids, send a card every birthday. But, unlike their mom, I'm inessential. I can't go around aping the qualities of an estimable man. Doling out advice? Not possible. If your nephew's as smart as you say he'd see right through it. There comes a point, often late in the game, too late, sometimes, when it behooves you to recognize that the person you wanted to be, the person you hoped to be, you never actually quite managed to be.

Shay stares at her knee, the sharp crease in her pants, like a blade this morning, has begun to fade.

—And upon that recognition, stop hurting others with the sham.

If this man in purple socks had any idea what it's like saying goodbye to the life you had and the things you loved. Yesterday Shay was brushing her teeth when she heard finches cheeping outside the window.

The longer the chatter went on the more upset she became, even setting down her toothbrush to press her thumbs into her temples, as if the pressure might assist in translation. A minute passed before it came to her that nothing had been lost. She could never understand what birds have on their minds.

—I'm sorry I couldn't be of service.

—Mr. Joles, I never should have asked... placing her cup on the table next to a stack of expensive art books and other costly useless objects. Everything about his office irritates her.

—I'm happy you did. Another thing, I've been laid out recently.

—You looked unwell, I thought, this morning... standing. Enough. One favor, one, she's asked in her thirty years at the Museum.

—Yes, this morning... Joles stretches forward to set down his cup... —I enjoyed our chat. A person behind that spoon, as you said. Our mortal dilemma.

—I remember.

He stands, pulling his phone from his chest pocket... —Sorry, do you mind if I... he reads the screen and immediately breaks into a big smile... —Great, great... replacing his phone... —Forgive me, Chief, I was waiting to see whether my guest for this evening, a friend I asked last minute. Plans shifting.

—Seems like good news... Shay turns toward the door... —I should... pointing.

—It is. Wonderful news. My ex-wife. Be nice to see her.

—Well, thank you for the coffee. Museum's closing in half an hour, so I'll...

—Mm... Joles stares into the middle distance.

—I'll be on my way... but he hasn't yet released her.

—You never mentioned the boy's father... he turns his watery eyes to her.

—Passed away. A while ago. Malcolm was a child.

With a crooked finger Joles pulls his cuff away from his watch... —Where's your nephew now? Could we do it right away?

4:35 p.m.

Down in Archives, Katherine is standing in front of a full-length mirror wearing nothing but her underpants. For months she's been eyeing a suit that belonged to Jimi Hendrix, one that didn't make it into the *Outsiders* show. Blue velvet with black cuffs and collar. In a picture of him wearing it, Hendrix sits in a room that's entirely blue and green from the drapes to the armchair to a blue phone parked on the olive-colored carpet. He sucks on a cigarette, legs outstretched, staring at the camera with a kind of cool certainty. An enviable certainty.

Katherine steps into Jimi's trousers, pulls them up. Takes a piece of fabric from the cutting table, and cinches the pants around her waist, tying the material in a fat knot. The velvet is still rich despite a little fading and loss of pile. She pulls on the matching jacket and a pair of boots. Adds his black fedora, which once bore a particularly jaunty feather.

As she larks around in Jimi's clothes, Katherine knows she should be concerned with cultural appropriation. Does it count as appropriation without a witness? What if she's only here for the bad-assery? You mean, ignore Jimi's contradictions, his vulnerability, and humanity, in order to use his clothes for the most superficial of reasons, the borrowing of swagger? Yes, that might be the exact definition of cultural appropriation. But despite behaving in a way that's indisputably problematic, if not downright racist, no one will ever find out. And though that troubles Katherine, she has yet to take off Jimi's pants.

She examines her reflection. With impaired vision, you could definitely mistake her for a man, if not Jimi fucking Hendrix. Here's a world without Katherine Tambling. What a relief.

A vibration from the cutting table. She clomps over, tripping in Jimi's big boots.

—Hey, Chris.

—Katherine, hi, listen, I need—

—What's up?

—I was sent—

—Kind of busy here.

—It's about Conrad. I received a text—

—From Conrad.

—Yes, a text asking—

—All I can say about Conrad, Chris, is that here we have a grown man who's designed the gala every year for the past five years and every year for the past five years he's tried to fuck with the exhibits that Gryphon has painstakingly installed over the course of an extremely intense six weeks. Every year without fail Conrad acts as if the entire museum is conspiring against him and every year we're all forced to run around groveling that we love him best. So if Conrad's complaining about me, Chris, all I can say is. Fuck. Him... she aims a finger-gun at her reflection.

—*What?*

—What?... and shoots herself.

—Why are you, you sound weird.

—No, I'm not being weird, Chris. I'm being efficient. I know Conrad's been complaining about me and I'm setting your mind at ease by informing you that vexation is Conrad's comfort zone. When Conrad isn't bitching about something, that's when it's time to worry but if Conrad's running around whining and grousing then we know that everything is going exactly to plan and the gala design will be exactly as extraordinary as it was last year and the year before that.

—Katherine? Why are you, are you drunk?

—Of course I'm not drunk... adjusting Jimi's hat for another rush of borrowed bad-assery... —I'm sorry if my efficiency reads to you as drunk, Chris, if that's how you interpret concision.

—Uh, okay. I have to. I'll catch up with you later.

Katherine tosses her phone back onto the worktable. God that felt good. The secret to everything is not giving a fuck. Or, maybe, being a man. Jimi's trousers have lent her viability, potency. His suit is armor, she is impenetrable.

But as she stands in front of the mirror, legs wide, hands on her hips, admiring the way she takes up space, Katherine has a profound realization.

Immense.

Life-saving, potentially.

Why had she never seen it before?

4:39 p.m.

Clive is sitting at his computer working up his report to the committee when Diane knocks and walks in... —Mind if I interrupt?

—Of course not... he stands, uncertain... —Take a seat.

—No, I'll stand.

—Sure?... Clive smiles politely.

—Sorry I couldn't come with you to Walter's. Don't be annoyed. How was it? You're not answering my texts.

—He asked after you. Called you a wildcat.

This doesn't elicit the secretive grin Clive predicted it would. Diane cocks her head... —Did he? How odd.

—Anyway... electing not to repeat Wolfe's thoughts on women's underarms... —In the end he promised us the lot. We'll see. Wife and daughter appear in favor of half going to the British. They could contest any changes.

—Then, we can only hope. Thank you, Clive, for going, you know, I think I will sit... and Diane takes the armchair, pulling at her skirt where it's bunching behind her knee.

—Alright... stepping out from behind his desk, curious to learn why the director is settling into an armchair on one of the more stressful days of the year.

Diane crosses her legs, eyes roaming the prints above his flat file, foot keeping time to a private song... —Ever thought what you'll do when you leave this place?

—When I retire you mean?... Clive takes a seat on the sofa opposite... —Or, is this, have you come to fire me?

—Retire, or if you went on to something else.

—I haven't thought about next Tuesday.

—My plan is nothing.

—Sound.

—I'll wake up and laze around, spend the day lazing and go to bed early so I can be fresh for more lazing the next day. And don't say it doesn't sound like me, Clive—

—Never.

—It's exactly like me.

He has no idea what's happening right now. Why is she confiding in him? They haven't spoken about anything personal since that deadly trip to Paris. Diane considers her shoes, as if she's about to put her feet up on his coffee table.

—You like your job.

Now she's frightening him. The gala is mere hours away. Surely she has more pressing concerns.

—I've started to wonder if you're happy here.

—If I like my job?

—Yes, Clive, your job.

—Of course I like my job.

—You seem different from, I mean, recently.

He knows she can't bring herself to say, different from when we were friends.

—Distracted.

—I've become a recluse, could that be it? I rarely go out. I stopped ordering in because even the deliverymen require a level of engagement that's beyond my capacity. My entire social life revolved around a friend who, with a stunning indifference to logic, just fucked off to Berlin. At the age of forty-six I'm in the position of having to dredge up a few people I can tolerate. My sister's fed up with me. As am I, by the way... he points to the window... —I've struck up a friendship with a pigeon. It was sobering, sitting next to Walter Wolfe during his final hours. A hundred people I imagine had been through his doors to say goodbye. He was a father, a husband. Revered or reviled he was, at the very least... Clive presses his fingers into his eyelids in an effort to reboot himself... —Why are you here?

But she's staring out the window... —Which pigeon? That pigeon?

—Diane.

—Well, there are two pigeons... she redirects her attention up to the ceiling and folds her arms.

—What is it?

—I don't know.

—You do.

—Okay... Diane levels her gaze, eyes meeting his... —I'm thinking about leaving Dominic... saying it firmly, as if she's contradicting him.

Clive chooses a detached expression.

—Something needs to change.

—And you're certain it's your marriage?

—No, but I don't know how to know. Where do you find out?

—Therapy?

—I'm prejudiced against it.

—Same.

—Makes me sick.

—What, physically?

—Yes, actually... and again Diane glances toward the window...
—Sophomore year of college I saw this counselor who used to eat his
breakfast during our sessions. Balanced a plate on his knee and demol-
ished a pumpernickel bagel smeared with cream cheese. I don't know if
that's ethically permissible, I really feel it shouldn't be, because this kind
of gross white paste would collect at the corner of his mouth. He'd go
on and on, speaking through this paste about his Hawaiian vacation.
Did he really expect me to open up about my crippling teenage perfec-
tionism, or whatever, my parents' practice of benign neglect when I was
faced with this spermy substance coating his lips?

—Jesus.

—So you see, there's a direct link between therapy and nausea.

—Not therapy, then. Books?

—Oh, books. I have the books, Clive. I have all the books... she
looks desperately around the room.

—Meditation?

Diane shoots him a look that curdles his balls. But he wants to
help, he really does. Return them to a time before Paris. Clive searches
for advice, a bromide, anything to alleviate her pain. A few thoughts
about men? A priceless insight, a squeeze of the hand. It's too early for
a drink. He has a flash of Diane sitting at the bar next to Joshua,
laughing, her teeth flashing in the candlelight. They were close once,
genuinely.

—You may've come to the wrong place. My expertise in relationships is... he shrugs, gives up.

He watches her gaze as it travels his office, landing on a vulgar seascape he found in storage and hung on the wall to torture himself.

—I could be very happy living in a hut on a beach.

—You?... not meaning to sound so derisive.

—All these barriers.

Having no idea what she's talking about, Clive nods thoughtfully, fearing he'll seem unsympathetic or dense... —Could you just need a break?

Diane shifts her position, straightens. Appears to focus on her exhale, as if marshaling the energy it takes to face an imbecile... —Small favor.

—What's that?

—In about an hour... checking her phone... —Less than an hour, I'm meeting a young tech CEO to discuss a donation. Could you stop by, briefly? Deploy a bit of that famous Hauxwell charm.

He almost laughs. Too predictable. Everything about her, a calculation.

—It's a sizable chunk. Twenty million.

All that business about leaving her husband. And he fell for it.

—Five thirty in Piquette. Please come. Chat about, I don't know, Leonardo, blah blah, the origins of technology. I have young Jakob coming from Digital but I need gravitas. Cover all the bases.

—I'd rather gargle glass.

—Six minutes. Ten, tops. How's your father, better?

—My father? When, I mean, when did we speak about my father?

—Briefly. This summer.

Clive doesn't recall ever mentioning his father, or anything about his personal life to Diane, not for close to a year.

—July? August?

—Hanging in there.

—Good. Glad to hear it. So I'll see you in a bit?

—If I did stop by, could I then count on you to back an acquisition of mine?

—What's the piece?

—I'm still... pointing to his computer... —Writing my report.

—You're asking for my blind support?

—That's right.

—Typical, I mean... standing, brushing off her skirt with mighty sweeps of her hand... —I should have known it was beyond you to act out of a spirit of generosity.

Diane walks quickly to the door, opens it and leaves, pulling the door shut behind her. Not slamming, but almost. Clive stares at the stained wood and silver handle for several minutes before rising to return to his report.

4:48 p.m.

—I don't *speak* Japanese, obviously I've memorized important phrases in most languages, Nik, I'm in the hospitality business. I welcome tourists to my restaurant seven days a week. And there were no texture issues... Jimmy leans against the flat-top pulling on a bottle of Rolling Rock... —Your palate's flawed.

—It's not flawed, Jimmy, simply because it's different—

—Hey guys... Otto appears in the open doorway, gym bag slung over his shoulder, a pair of headphones hugging his neck... —I'm out... even after puking for several hours, he remains dispiritingly handsome.

—Dude, you missed the Japanese Ambassador. He was all, I loved your toasts—

—Shut up, Jimmy, no one wants to hear it... smiling at Otto... —How you doing?

—Fine yeah.

—It's crazy you stuck around. Appreciate it.

—No problem... sounding annoyed by the accusation of heroism, Otto turns to go... —Later, my dudes... this sort of parody of white broism leaves Niko certain he's being mocked but clueless how to respond.

—Good night... the words come out prim, too formal.

He watches Otto stop in front of Jimmy. The two of them perform a complicated handshake and Otto pulls up his headphones, takes out his phone, and disappears through the swinging doors.

—You two fell in love.

—Kid's got a first-rate palate, might poach him for my place. Feather-light touch... Jimmy shakes his head fondly... —You know his grandpop dated Mahalia Jackson when he was a teenager? Got some real stories, Otto.

Nikolic scrubs the worktop furiously, immersed in the accuracy required which is basically none.

Jimmy takes a slug of beer and sets it on the lowboy with a gentle burp... —Look, I didn't want to say anything in front of your guys, Nik, but that rabbit? Octopus, too, both straight-up Cyrus Fang. Why are you copying recipes? This was your moment, a walk-in full of top-shelf proteins. You could have really, but instead, I mean, smoked eel?

Maybe if Niko stays silent his brother will simply evaporate.

—Hey, Nikolic?

This could all be an illusion and Jimmy's still in San Diego, wearing his dog's bandana and driving his staff nuts.

—Niko?

—Yes, yes, yes, what?

—Fuck's this?... Jimmy points to the jar of mushroom salt sitting on the lowboy.

—Where did that come from?

—Your locker.

—Why are you, don't go through my locker.

—But what is it?

—Dried mushrooms. Wild dried mushrooms.

—Oh my god, have you become a *foraging* guy?

—Shut the fuck up.

—Some kind of Demetri Müller?

—I've been experimenting. So what?

—You. Foraging. Same guy who thought the garden hose was a rattlesnake and crapped his pants.

—I *didn't* crap, I was a kid.

Jimmy has the lid to the mason jar unscrewed. He licks a finger, sticks it in the mixture and tastes it... —Interesting. Sweeter than I would have guessed.

—Sweet? It's not sweet.

—There's kind of an anise—

—Give me that... Nikolic grabs the jar, tastes the salt and quickly wipes his tongue on the sleeve of his T-shirt.

—What's wrong?

Screwing the lid back on the jar, he slams it into the garbage can.

—Christ. Chill the fuck out.

How could he have missed it? The blood drains from his head. His stomach flips and flips again. He was running the kitchen, he was distracted. There was Jimmy to think about, for one. Niko's neck starts to sweat.

—Why'd you throw out your mushrooms? What? Your eyes are going crazy. What's going on?

—Those mushrooms, Jimmy, are not blewits.

—Who cares? Shit tastes good.

—*Who cares?* If they're not blewits then I don't know what they are. Meaning, I don't know if they're edible.

Jimmy takes an impressed step back to lean against the flattop... —*Fuuuck*. Didn't you taste the stuff?

—I've been, I haven't been sleeping. I came up with it, developed it when I, and I was positive they, the mushrooms, but the insomnia, I don't know. I get dizzy sometimes.

—Breathe, you're not—

—How could it happen, I—

—Where's your inhaler?

—I put it on the shrimp.

—You put your inhaler—

—The SALT. Can't you listen? The reception, my mushroom blend. I used it as finishing salt on the shrimp. That's why I'm running the kitchen today. Emerson got fired. Half the staff got sick from eating bad shrimp and they fired him.

—Okay. That's not good.

—Oh my god, it wasn't Em, it was me... a clicking sensation starts up in his ear as if an important bone has become misaligned.

—Slow down.

—This whole time it was me... prodding his tragus to make the clicking stop.

—Let me think. Stop fucking with your ear.

—I should tell someone... pulling his phone from his back pocket.

—Put that away.

—No, I need to... sweeping through his contacts... —Call Marjorie.

—Google first. Make sure.

—Google what? I can't remember what they look like. And now they're all dust.

—Put down the phone.

—Maybe if I come clean they'll go easy—

—Give me this... Jimmy snatches the phone from Niko, powers it off and tosses it on the countertop... —You're a tiny little boy with no brain and I'm not about to let you imperil your career and possibly mine while you run round looking to take some high road nobody cares about. Do exactly what I say, understand? Now, for all we know Emerson really did fuck up. Didn't check the shrimp, left them in the sun—

—I sprinkled it on his soup... Nikolic sinks to his knees, still trying to fix his ear.

—That floor's still wet, what soup?

—The soup, the soup. Fucking pay attention. We sent gazpacho upstairs. The Japanese Ambassador.

—Okay... Jimmy spins around, starts tying up the trash bag...
—Let's get rid of this.

Why didn't he taste the soup first? He did. No. No, he didn't. The kitchen was slammed. He placed it on the cart and sent Adrina on her way.

—Be right back... Jimmy swings the black bag over his shoulder...
—And get off the fucking floor.

Still on his knees, Niko bends over and bumps his head against the floor, turning to place his cheek against the cold tile. Bumps his forehead again. Alternating. Imagine going down in flames for copying a hack like Demetri Müller. Bumping then resting, bump

Interrupted by a cough.

—Fuck off, Jimmy.

—Who the hell's Jimmy?

Niko opens his eyes on a famously ugly chef's clog. Raises his head off the floor... —Oh, hey, Marjorie. What's up?

—Need a favor.

4:56 p.m.

—You're still mad.

—Of course not... but Iona is, in fact, pretty mad... —I mean, you said you'd be lookout.

—He's an intern... Dorothy makes a show of rolling her eyes... —He's not reporting shit. What, they're going to arrest you because you mistook his duffel bag for mine? But I love this Iona. Let's see more of this lady.

Peeling off her gloves and tossing them down, Iona steps around her worktable.

—Quick drink. I insist... Dorothy shoulders her inspirational tote... —You can tell me where you were all afternoon.

—It wasn't *all* afternoon.

—Lycheetinis at that place on Seventy-Fourth, my treat.

—Can't I'm afraid... and she edges past Dorothy blocking the doorway, wide in her coat.

—You can.

In answer Iona jerks her thumb back toward the worktable still strewn with pieces for next week's show, and heads down the hallway to the bathroom. Dorothy can be a bully when it comes to cocktails.

Washing her hands, careful not to splash her skirt. The back of Clive's head when he bent to fasten her seatbelt. The hair at his nape was shaved close and Iona had to resist reaching out to stroke it. Imagine him in a tuxedo. Dancing together. Instead of what's waiting for her in Brooklyn. Bucatini followed by an asinine comedy; the three of them sitting in a mirthless row, exhausted by the quips.

Quickly Iona dries her hands and takes out her phone. A reckless text: *What time tonight?* Leaning against the sink, she waits, unable to move, thrilled by her nerve. Exactly as her phone lights up, *Fantastic! See you here at 8*, she realizes she has nothing to wear.

Out of the bathroom, halfway down the hall, Iona stops outside the Costume Center. The door is ajar and she can hear movement from inside the room. The women who run Costume frighten her. She's nodded hello but never spoken to either the very ancient one or the pretty but sort of bitchy one who ruined her hair.

Iona takes a breath and pushes the door open.

The sort of bitchy one is standing in the middle of the office, holding an open book as if it's a hymnal. She's peeling something pink off one of the pages. Lunchmeat? Iona watches her sling it into a trash can.

—Is that bologna?

—JESUS... the girl jumps, slamming the book closed and hugging it to her chest... —What the hell?

—Sorry, sorry.

—No, no, you just, it's fine... setting the book carefully on her desk... —What's up?

—I'm Iona, I work down the hall... she walks in without waiting for an invitation.

—Right, in Conservation. I've seen you in line for coffee. Katherine.

—Nice to meet you. About this gala thing tonight...

Katherine nods, smiles. Iona takes it for encouragement.

—I've been invited.

—Have you?

—As a plus-one. So, I wondered. You're always so fashionable and I, what kind of thing should I, I guess I don't know what suits me or what's even appropriate. Could you maybe, Bloomingdale's is still open and I thought I could run over—

—*Blooming?* No, god, don't buy anything and not at fucking Bloomingdale's... Katherine sounds personally affronted.

—That's okay, I'll... Iona points at the door.

—Let me think.

She watches Katherine pace across her office with quick birdy steps. She is slight but not tiny. Iona stopped befriending tiny women. They have Napoleonic predilections.

—Okay... Katherine nods.

—Okay?

—I mean, why shouldn't I, right?... Katherine picks a mug off her desk... —Fuck this place and its stupid rules. We can find you something. In fact, I just saw... She drains the contents of the mug, wipes her mouth with the back of her hand.

—You saw?

But Katherine's rooting around in a desk drawer, taking out a nicotine patch or maybe it's hormonal, contraceptive. Peeling off the

backing with a violent swipe, she slaps the patch on her biceps...
—Ready?

—For what?

Katherine grabs her lanyard from a hook behind the door... —Let's
go get you a dress.

5:00 p.m.

Shay is standing outside Security, scrolling through texts, when she
hears conversation coming from down the hall. Looking up from her
phone, she sees Iona and the pregnant stoner leaving Costume. In a
clownish flurry, Shay spins around and dives through the door to HQ.
Anything to avoid another second of mousy rage. Imagine refusing to
ask your husband where he went for three weeks.

Shay crosses the room, heading toward her office, skirting Andy,
arms crossed, scanning the bank of monitors. The video feed shows
the second shift combing bathrooms, stairwells, and galleries with tall
display cases, like European Porcelain, where a troubled woman once
stood perfectly still and tried to escape notice by pretending to be a
teapot.

—Chief? If I could just... Denis reads off an iPad... —Currently
Dispatch has Marc with a C handling the Great Hall, Pavel and his
team in charge of the bathroom sweep... the sound of her office phone...
—Tina, she's new—

—Stop now, I have to... and she darts inside and grabs the phone...
—Chief Pallot... shutting the door with her foot.

—Shay, it's Diane.

—Everything okay?... watching Denis through the door's glass
panel. The kid's ambition, his initiative, the unswerving drive, if only
Malcolm were similarly inspired.

—I'm just going to say this now, Shay, apologize the conversation
couldn't take place in person. I won't leave it til tomorrow, I'd hate for
you to find out from someone else.

Diane sounds businesslike but regretful and the combination floods
Shay with dread.

—The board, on Monday, voted to sell off the properties bequeathed to us by the Dudley estate. It's supposed to be an anonymous process but I don't mind telling you I voted against it. Now, unfortunately I was the only nay vote—

—Excuse... Shay's voice breaks, she clears her throat... —Me?

—My hands are tied.

—*Selling?*

—That's right. I'm terribly sorry.

—But that's impossible. I mean, it was my understanding that, that, those apartments were not allowed to be sold. It was a condition of Dudley's legacy.

—There was a proviso.

—What proviso?

—If the endowment fell below a certain, uh, number the Museum could take matters into its own hands—

—To sell my home?

—Apartment, and not just yours, Shay, about twelve in all. It will be a significant addition to our coffers.

—Okay... pressing a hand to her chest, as if it will stay the panic... —But I was told, promised, that I would have the chance to purchase the apartment should the Museum ever—

—The properties, I'm sorry to say—

—I've been saving, since the day we moved in, setting aside—

—Shay, the properties are being sold to a trustee as a package, well above market rates. It's a loophole. I don't quite understand it myself, but it's a way of benefiting the Museum and at the same time—

—But why not donate the money? This trustee?

—Yes, as I said, I'm not permitted to discuss—

—My home.

—Shay. I know you understand.

—Twelve years ago, when Chief Security Officer became available, everyone knew the position was mine. I was the only one who'd put in the time, who had the loyalty and dedication, the experience and commitment, and by the way, who actually loved the job, but, as Dr. Sericko explained at the time, the job had to go to Easby because of his relationship to—

—Ralph Kade, yes, quite true but—

—Despite being wildly unqualified, serving only in military affairs, never working in an arts institution and nearly burning the place to the ground five years in.

—Yes, yes—

—Everyone knew I'd do the job for him, not get the paycheck but pick up Easby's slack.

—I'm sorry.

—Gave me the apartment, a big apartment, to shut me up, if you will, so that a Black woman who actually earned her promotion wouldn't go running her mouth to the press. And I didn't, did I? I kept quiet. So the idea that... she can't finish the thought... —It's my home, Diane.

—Shay, Shay, listen to me, okay. I will find a way to make this up to you. Naturally, your salary will be made commensurate with the cost of renting a comparable

But Shay stops listening, thinking of the drawing William crayoned onto the wall of the bedroom closet. At the time she was angry, but she grew to see it as a masterpiece. The museum will expect their apartment back in perfect condition. With clean white walls. And no sign of her son.

Diane signs off and Shay returns the phone to its cradle. Extremely gently, careful not to slam it.

5:06 p.m.

—The trustees, the wives, love to donate dresses, love to imagine their pit-stained Alaiaa is like, culturally significant. Not that I'm going to give you something like that, I'm not. I know exactly what will suit you. Perfect for your eyes with a killer décolletage.

Katherine holds open the door to the costume archives, flipping on the lights as Iona enters. The space is pristine, filled with shiny white cases split into cubes that stop just short of the ceiling.

—Ninety percent of what's down here won't fit. Dresses get donated by the designers and the designers... Katherine grabs a big hook... —Want their clothes to appear exactly as they envisioned, which is size fucking zero... she disappears down a row of cubes...
—Because, you know, *all* women are a size zero. Actually most of the

trustee ladies *are* a size zero. Over here... appearing behind Iona...
—What's normal to you and me is like whale weight to them. Lucky
for us, dresses in larger sizes never go on display. A designer would
freak if we showed a dress of theirs in like a four or something.

—Because four is considered big... Iona sucks in her stomach, regretting the pulled pork she's eaten two nights in a row.

—Where is it? I saw it earlier.

—I'm starting to think... because what will she tell David when she
throws on a ballgown and heads out for the night... —Maybe this isn't—

—I made a mental note. I don't know why, well I guess this is the
reason why... Katherine stops and rotates a crank on one side of the
cube, inching it back to make space between the cases. Still holding
the crook, she walks along this path, paging through garment bags
and dresses... —Who's taking you?

—Clive Hauxwell.

Katherine turns around, arms up but stilled... —European Paintings?... a twisted smile... —Nice one. Gorgeous, don't you think?

—Oh, it's a favor, not a date. I asked him to speak to a trustee
about a piece and he said—

—Of course it's a date.

Coloring, dipping her face to falsely check her shoe... —And you?...
she hears the dresses start up again, hangers scraping... —Do you have a
date?

—God no. I don't date.

—What never?... Iona raises her head.

—Never.

—You never date?

—Not for the last year. Fourteen months.

—Don't you get lonely?

—Yup. Here it is... stepping back with her giant crook, Katherine
fishes down a dress... —Not exactly on theme, but.

Iona follows her down the path to a full-length mirror. Katherine
hangs up the dress and steps back. The gown is exquisite. Silver-grey
and strapless, faintly imprinted with a butterfly design.

—Dior. You can't tell a thing until you try it on... unzipping the
dress, pulling it gently from the hanger, turning... —Um, honey,
you're going to have to take your clothes off.

—Is there a...?

—Here, I'll... turning her back to Iona... —Throw your stuff on the bench.

Unzipping her skirt, stepping out of it and pulling off her blouse and bra. Until five minutes ago she wasn't sure of Katherine's name, always thought of her as the bitch in Costume. Now the bitch in Costume is about to see her breasts, underpants dingy from washing with the darks... —Okay. Ready... she can't help herself, with one hand, Iona pretends to scratch her opposite shoulder, covering her breasts.

Katherine spins around, holding the dress open... —Wait til you see the back.

Iona steps into the dress, quickly uncrossing her arms to pull it up... —I've never worn a strapless—

—Suck it in!... Katherine, behind her, muscling up the zip... —Listen... swiveling Iona to face her... —I'm going to need you to own this dress. Shoulders down, ass out, strut, bluster, dominate... dropping to tug at the hem... —Fucking possess the room.

—Okay, but like—

—Ignore the trays of sparkling wine, what you want is a mixed drink. Arrive early, head straight to Middle Eastern, they always set up a bar in Middle Eastern, throw some elbows, grab a couple of martinis, not just one, okay? The lines get long, I'm talking about a couple each... Katherine fusses with the dress, laying the neckline flat, not seeming to care that her hand is stuck down the front of the dress, perilously close to Iona's, okay, there it is, *on* her breast, pulling and shoving so Iona fills the built-in support... —Stand more like... she grabs shoulders and pulls them back, manipulating her into a better posture.

—Is that where you'll be? At the bar?

—Not allowed to drink. It's our event, our department, and the boss is out sick so I'll be babysitting Anton Spitz. Making sure everything's copacetic with that nutty ocelot. Dude is seriously, like, everything in his studio is white and glossy with floor-to-ceiling windows so the minute you walk in you're like blinded. He writes notes in purple ink, periwinkle, on these tablets, not pads, tablets. Anton buys them in volume whenever he's in Paris. If they run out, he flies an assistant to France.

—Couldn't he get them sent?

—Yeah, if he was normal. Also, he eats these mints from Japan, not sure how he keeps them in stock, but he's like a rabbit with those mints. I fucking love this dress for you. Here... pushing Iona in front of the mirror... —What do you think?

As always when regarding her reflection to assess a pair of shoes or an article of clothing, Iona focuses solely on her face, wiping away a smear of eyeliner and wondering when the creases in her forehead started. After a brief inventory she steps back.

The tight fit of the dress has worked as a sort of corset, flattening her stomach and defining her waist. More unnervingly, the dress has somehow doubled the volume of her breasts.

—Do you love it? I love it.

—Does it seem a little, you know. Busty?

—You've got a great rack, of course we're going to show it off. Now, hair. A chignon, messy bun, topknot, something to show off your neck. And a smoky eye.

—A smoky eye.

—Grey shadow, smudgy, soft. A neutral lip, and a shit-ton of black eyeliner. Elizabeth Taylor. But subtle, not *Cleopatra* but like, *Butterfield 8*. You can manage?

Iona nods, thinking probably not.

—What do you think of this?... Katherine holds up a piece of oddly shaped red fabric.

—That's a...

—Rei Kawakubo... settling the dress over her arm, Katherine looks up to see Iona's confusion... —No? Legendary designer. All about what's not there instead of what is.

—Huh.

—The meaning is that there is no meaning.

Iona can only nod.

—Rei said it in an interview. Genius, right? What kind of artist tells you there's no meaning?

—That's um, genius, but Katherine, borrowing archival dresses, is this like—

—If anyone asks, maybe say Bloomingdale's... Katherine spins her around to tackle the zip.

—So it is? It is against the rules.

—A little bit.

—But I... turning her head, trying to get Katherine in her sights...
—But won't—
—Oh please. Who's going to know? Just keep your distance from Diane Schwebe.

5:15 p.m.

His conversation with Malcolm was a complete disaster. A nail in the coffin of Henry's parenting skills. In hopes of consolation, he's looking for Diane. It's his new sensitivity. Indifference is out of the question.

Was Malcolm one of these new types he'd read about? Young men with a distaste for the detached approach favored by men since the invention of fire? Because he appeared to see right through Henry's little games: the verbal prancing, a studied ignorance of the facts, the side-stepping of blame. Surely this was impossible, they'd only spoken for twenty minutes.

He finds Diane in the hallway outside her office, clamping her phone to her sternum with her chin.

—Henry... she finishes tucking her blouse into the waistband of her skirt... —What's the news on Mumbai?

—Still waiting on Decker.

—We're rushing to our Silicon Valley... Chris warns as he comes out of Diane's office, handing her a leather portfolio.

—Fun. Best of luck. I'll walk you to the elevator if you don't mind.

With a tight smile Chris conveys that in fact he does mind and could Henry please fuck off and not for one second think about delaying them. But Henry can't fuck off. He's here for absolution or comfort and he's not leaving without one or the other.

—You wouldn't believe the call I had with the architects... Diane sets off down the hall... —Hernandez actually flushed the toilet while we were speaking. The man is such a, anyway. What's up?

—Nothing really... but he can tell neither of them believes he happened to be strolling by... —Okay. Kind of an awkward, Shay Pallot asked me to speak to her young nephew. She's worried about his prospects, wanted me to give the kid some mentor-type advice. And I, I bungled it royally. I was nervous, we didn't have much time, I felt rushed. Now I feel terrible. Shay couldn't have children so her nephew's like a son to her.

—I'm sorry, Henry... Diane looks up from her phone... —What are you talking about?

—I mean, I imagine he's like a son. She dotes on the kid.

—When did Shay Pallot say she couldn't have children?... preoccupied, Diane returns to her phone.

—We had a nice conversation this morning in Greek. Waiting for the tech from Oceania—

—Ferris Finotti.

—Yes, we chatted, opened up, real nice, a confidence sharing and Shay—

—Said she couldn't?

—That's right.

—But she did.

—Did what?

—Shay Pallot did have a child, she had a son.

—William... Chris, head still bent, scrolling... —William Joseph.

—She didn't want to tell you so she fibbed. Understandable.

The acidic fire in Henry's stomach starts up again. This can't be true. He tries to remember what Shay said as she stood among the Greek vitrines. Had he invented it? No. No, they spoke about grave goods and Shay said she couldn't. I wasn't able, she said.

—Craig Potter told me... Diane squeezes the bridge of her nose as if a headache's coming on... —It was before my time. Boy was what, about three, Chris?

—Nearly three.

—Potter said she only took off about a week of work. Came back one morning as if nothing happened. Ordered new uniforms and overhauled the rotations.

The three of them reach the Reskman elevator and stop. Henry watches Chris jab the down arrow.

—How?

—How what?

—How did the child...?

—Fell out a window. Screen popped out.

—Jesus Christ.

—At least that's what Potter said. He was close to the family.

The elevator arrives. The doors open.

—I didn't know.

—Of course you didn't.

He watches Diane and Chris step into the elevator, two people who have lived with this dreadful news all along, known and digested this tragedy of which he's remained ignorant, blithely chatting to Shay as if she'd simply made peace with forgoing children. What had he said to the poor woman? Nothing human, Henry feels sure. He has no idea what his problem is. He's always avoided self-examination, regarding it as a passing trend.

—Sorry, Henry... Diane puts out her hand to prevent the elevator doors from closing... —Did you have a question?

He shakes his head.

—I'm sure Shay's nephew loved your chat... Diane smiles encouragingly and takes her hand away from the sensor.

As the doors come together, he sees Chris open his mouth and start speaking. The two of them have finished with Henry and moved on to the next problem.

After a minute Henry turns and starts down the hallway. He needs to find Shay.

5:20 p.m.

—Don't mother me, Chris, I'm perfectly fine.

—A sip of ginger ale or like

But Diane tunes him out, staring at the silver panel of buttons. An oppressive smell fills the elevator. Like rancid french fries. Never has a red emergency pull been more appealing.

Chris is saying something about saltines, a packet of which he has in his desk and a couple of which he wishes she'd at least nibble.

—Chris, please, I'm fine.

—How did Shay take the news?

Diane opens and closes her portfolio... —She was very understanding, very—

The elevator doors have opened to reveal a startled young woman wearing a long-sleeved dress in a heavy material. Circles of perspiration have darkened the armpits.

Chris watches the girl step inside... —Who are you?

—Intern... stabbing L again and again as the doors close.

—This elevator serves the Reskman tower only... Chris informs her icily... —Trustees, the director, upper management. No one else.

—Never mind... the girl's baggy wet dress endears her to Diane... —It's difficult to remember at first.

—Honestly, this keeps happening. I need to speak to Gross, these interns. Your name?

—Freda.

—Department?

—European Paintings.

Worriedly, the intern watches Chris thumb his phone.

L is reached, the elevator doors open, and the girl spills out, trotting to get away. Still working his phone, Chris steps aside to let Diane exit.

—Chris, be nice. What are you doing to poor Freda?

—Moving her to Musical Instruments.

—Cruel.

—You have to harden your heart when it comes to interns, Diane, trust me... Chris has stopped in the hallway, staring at his phone, which he holds horizontally.

—What are you watching?

—*Vanity Fair*'s posted your interview.

—And?

—Clearly they didn't get anything usable so they... phone returned to vertical, he types into it with rapid thumbs.

—Bad?

—Irrelevant... shoving his phone into his back pocket... —I've revoked their gala tickets.

—No.

—No?

She shakes her head and Chris retrieves his phone, swiping and tapping, before pocketing it and starting off down the hallway... —Shall we?... he glances back impatiently.

Together they bypass the Great Hall, taking the hallway parallel, which echoes with the whinny of drills and the intermittent ka-thunks of a nail gun and a bass line of Conrad's bellowed gripes.

—Remember to call the donor Z. Never his full name, just Z.

—Yes, yes, Z, got it... mentally scrolling through her interview with Julia Saban.

Back to reading his phone, Chris senses and dodges a woman pulling a wheeled bin of fabric rolls... —It looks like Jakob is heading home. Migraine, he says.

Diane bites her lip against the urge to scream... —How disappointing... she iterates carefully... —I was hoping Jakob would bring that wonderful VR headset to our meeting. Plus, I wanted a young person in attendance.

—This Z guy, Diane... Chris turns to find her, she's flagging... —I did some digging this afternoon and he comes across like a full-blown, I don't know, socialist or something. Like, he graduated from Oberlin. I'm not saying that's a sign of whatever, but both parents are teachers, and he started a food bank in high school. Yet no large donations until now. Why? Why start now? And why did we invite him here? Into our home. We should have flown to California, had a nose around. I can't help it, I've got a bad feeling.

—I don't.

—Okay, but, Diane, I mean, remember last year when you thought that guy on the 2 was showing you his coat?

—I need new glasses is all.

—Oh for God's... Chris stops dead, staring at the screen of his phone... —His assistant in Palo Alto says Z's headed to the roof.

—What for?

—Loves a rooftop bar, apparently.

—Isn't it closed?

—Opening it as we speak.

5:24 p.m.

Fuck fuck fuck. In a pair of panties and nothing else. Bent over. Her ass like. What the hell? What the. Shoving folders and DVDs into his backpack, trying not to think about the word *Joy* stamped across the back of Katherine's purple underpants. Spilling papers from the folders, Benjamin's reading material for the, fuck were you thinking barging into her office like

—Hey.

—I'm sorry, I... he turns around... —I really.

—It's fine... Katherine stands in his doorway in painted toenails and a tight red dress.

—I hate... and he needs to. Lean against his desk... —I hate that I barged in like that.

—My fault. Should've locked the door.

Benjamin can't quite raise his eyes to her. Because she is unquestionably lovely and he needs to take a minute to reassess. Think things through. Settle down. Get composed.

—Decided I hated the dress I brought and spotted this Kawakubo down in Archives which is needless to say completely illegal. You coming tonight? I can get you in.

—No, I have a... what, he has nothing... —You know, plans.

—Too bad. It's a pretty fun night. Unless, actually, some years it's fairly hellish.

Turning back to his bag, zipping it closed, wildly unenthused about returning to his empty apartment when he'd much rather. What. Well, what he wants makes no sense. This woman who works down the hall. A woman Benjamin once nearly loved. The sex. He can't remember her body. Keep it in perspective. Keep your cool, keep it in your pants, keep it together.

—Thanks for helping me this morning. I put bologna in Giselle's daytimer.

—Nice... straightening, he gives Katherine a businesslike nod... —See you tomorrow.

—But then I took it out, the bologna. I can't gaslight her. Picturing her face, you know... she doesn't move from his doorway.

—Sure I get it. I should...

—Need this?... Katherine holds up his cell phone... —Found it right here... pointing to the top of the filing cabinet.

Walking to her, careful not to graze her fingers, he takes it... —Thanks.

—Adios.

Benjamin closes the door behind Katherine and picks up his back-pack. Still in a trance, he tucks his phone into the specially provided pocket. Usually he refuses to submit to the coercion of Big Backpack and tosses his phone into the vastness of the bag where it works its way under water bottles and sweatshirts and a sunglasses case that weighs about seven pounds. But he has no strength left for resistance.

A last look around. With that ridiculous metal filling cabinet and pitted wooden desk, the office looks like a film set or a museum exhibit. Not that it bothers him. Benjamin has often seen rooms as sets.

A knock at the door.

—Yeah... assuming it's Katherine, he doesn't look up.

—Mr. Rippen. At last.

Benjamin freezes. His blood turns to ice. He looks over.

Five hundred miles from Columbus, Ohio. Leaning against the doorjamb with that familiar nonchalance. Avery Eccleston. In a shiny white track jacket zipped to the neck, sleeves pushed up past the el-bows.

—Hey Avery... forcing his voice lower... —This is a surprise.

With a ludicrous smile, Avery steps inside the office, pulling the door closed behind him. He has the slouchy bulk and disappointed eyes of a JV wrestling coach. His bald head and radiant skin give him the appearance of an incandescent light bulb.

—My phone stopped working. I mean, in case you've been calling, I don't know that you have been. I believe it's a coverage problem. Keep saying I need a new plan.

—May I?... Avery indicates the desk chair. The shiny jacket strug-gles to constrain the triangle of trapezius formed by pointing.

—Of course... Benjamin steps to the side... —It's broken so. I guess be careful.

Avery sits down cautiously, taking in the office.

Benjamin watches him jounce in the chair, testing it. This can't be real. He must be inventing scenarios the way he did back in Columbus when he spent hours trying to come up with a story that had a strong moral argument. His professors were desperate for themes, but Benjamin's scripts never had a point.

—So. A museum, huh?

—I was going to say I've got a great new job. Money pouring in. Getting paid now, regularly.

A flicker of irritation crosses Avery's face and Benjamin recalls what a stickler he was for manners.

—May I offer you something? A glass of water? How was your flight?

—Terrible, Benjamin, thank you for asking. The plane was small and the engines were loud. Guy in the middle fell asleep on my shoulder. Word to the allergic, airlines are back to serving peanuts. Taking a Darwinian approach, I guess... idly, Avery picks up an issue of *Film Comment* lying on the desk... —How's your girlfriend? She still around?

—No. Yes. I mean, we may get back together.

—Uh-oh.

—We're on the verge of, why, why are you asking?

—Thought maybe you got in a bind with jewelry and so forth... flipping through the magazine... —Expensive gifts.

—That money was for grad school. My PhD.

—Oh, your PhD, okay... Avery looks around the office... —In what, movies?

—Film studies.

—Twenty grand that costs?

—A lot more than twenty.

—So, no rock... tossing *Film Comment* onto the desk where it spins up to the edge and stops... —For Caroline?

—Like an engagement, no, no, I... Benjamin swallows... —How do you know her name?

Avery swivels the broken chair around to take in the bookcase... —Got any Tarantino? He's my boy. I mean, naturally I question his intentions as one must, given the thorny predicament of race, but undeniably a genius.

Benjamin has already crossed to the bookcase and pulled down a DVD. He hands it to Avery.

—Don't be an ass. *Pulp Fiction?*... tossing it at him... —I own four versions. One in Gaelic on account of dating an Irish girl way back. Adds an unexpected dimension, Gaelic, being ancient and powerful.

—A classic? Something recent?

—Surprise me.

—I'll see what I can do.

—You'll see... laughing, Avery crosses his arms and settles back... —You crack me up. Peeling out of town like you knocked up the baby-sitter.

—I didn't know what to do. I ran out of money. I panicked.

—You came into this with your eyes wide open, don't start screamin' blind man now.

—My paycheck starts in two weeks. I can give you a little every month.

—No, Benjamin... softly... —It's time for the balance. Twelve grand.

—A few payments first? Show of good faith.

—Good faith hit the road a while back. Ignoring my calls. Hurts my feelings going to voicemail.

Benjamin tries to think clearly. The museum has metal detectors at every entrance. Avery couldn't have gotten inside packing heat. So he won't be shot, at least.

—What we got here, Benjamin, is called bad faith.

—I'll get you the money by Friday. Next Friday.

—Tuesday.

—Half by Tuesday.

—Listen up, dickhead. Hard to believe but the man sitting before you once tipped the scales at three-twenty. Couldn't play with the kids, couldn't climb two flights of stairs. Day came when I took a long naked look at myself, literally naked, and identified the trouble. What the head docs call emotional hunger. Finding comfort in spaghetti and dough-nuts. Thai iced tea and buffalo wings. So I took care of it, Benjamin. Dropped the weight in six months. It's why I got no time for messy peo-ple. My dad was a derelict, Ma left cigarettes burning all over the house. I'd love to view your situation with compassion but because of my his-tory, I'm afraid it's impossible. I don't make deals with desperate people, Benjamin, crackheads or moms. I deal with those who got choices. College guys. Dentists, shrinks, motherfuckers with PhDs. That way there can be no excuses. No one can say "I was jacked up on meth, I didn't compute the terms." Everyone understands. So I can't see there being any hard feelings should, you know... Avery sighs... —Push come to shove.

—Push come to, I can't pay you if I'm banged up.

—Banged up? Anyone here holding a tire iron?... performatively checking the room... —Because I see two guys sharing personal philosophies.

—There's a subtext.

—Oh, okay, *subtext*. Subtext what you get for twenty grand?

—Implied, then. There's an implied threat to what you're saying.

—If I want you to feel threatened, Benjamin, I'll come right out and threaten you. As the great Samuel Beckett once said, If I'd meant waiting for God I would've fucking called it *Waiting for God.*

—Well... Benjamin picks up his backpack, impatient to leave the suffocating room... —Looks like we're clear on the timetable and so forth.

Avery unzips his white jacket two inches at the neck, as if he's releasing something... —I don't like to say it, Benjamin, but you're an ill-mannered person.

—I apologize. It's my first day.

—Apology accepted... staring into the eyes of Humphrey Bogart... —So you come up with the movies they show here? That your job?

—One of them.

—Bounce some ideas off me.

—I haven't really sat down and—

—Come on, Benjy, let's have some fun. Can't we have some fun?

—The calendar is booked through the end of the year—

—Prostitutes.

—Sorry?

—Idea for a theme. French movies, Italian. Europeans lose it for broken women. Nymphos in pussy bows. Your typical Bordelais butcher believes Mrs. Dubois from down the road wants a whole lot more than a nice pork chop.

—Sure, like women sell their bodies for their own enjoyment. That's the male fantasy, right?

Avery's face sours. Benjamin has not been invited to the game.

—You have until Tuesday at five... Avery stands up, roughly pushing back the damaged chair... —I fly back Wednesday morning and I go with eight grand. Understand?

—Half of twelve is six.

Avery stares at him.

—Got it... nodding... —Eight. Eight grand. Got it got it got it.

5:26 p.m.

—What about the new film hire?

—Benjamin Rippen. Started today.

—Bring him in to replace Jakob. I'm sure he's about the same age as Z.

—If he's even still here... Chris types into his phone.

The tendrils of a headache begin to twine and stretch behind Diane's eyes. She pinches the bridge of her nose, holding it until the elevator arrives at the roof.

The doors open. The evening air is still warm, a relief from the museum's ferocious air-conditioning. Beginning to pink, the sky is punctuated with one lonely cloud. The young billionaire stands with his back to them, studying the skyline. He has the hood of his sweatshirt pulled up, giving him the profile of a modern druid. Zedekiah Willington. The person who holds Diane's future in his uncalloused hands.

—Hello there!

Slowly, as if mesmerized by the setting sun, Z turns, pulling his hood away from his face. He's boyish and attractive, his dark hair chin-length and tousled. What a nice even tan, she thinks before recalling that Z is half Filipino. There wasn't time to do more than skim Chris's information packet. Diane walks toward the investor, handing Chris her leather portfolio which functions only as a prop.

—Welcome Mr.—

—Z... Chris, at her heels, correcting... —This is Diane Schwebe, director of the Museum.

Z smiles. His mouth is packed with expensive teeth. He wears skinny black jeans and blinding white sneakers.

They shake hands and Z reaches out around Diane... —This is my bodyguard... pulling into view a shifty-looking young man in his thirties... —Liam.

—Bodyguard? Goodness.

—Pretentious, right? There were disturbing emails.

Liam shakes Diane's hand, avoiding her eyes.

—And I'm Chris, nice to... staring at Z's bodyguard... —We've met before.

—No. Pretty much impossible... Liam turns away... —I'll be over here... tossing the words behind him as he wanders to the far side of the roof, a bench facing the Henry Moore.

With narrowed eyes Chris watches the man walk away.

The second elevator bings its arrival and the bartender steps out, Daniel or Stanley, wearing that unfortunate fedora of his. He moves swiftly to unlock the roll-down doors enclosing the bar.

—Cocktail?... Chris gestures to the seating options, chairs or a bench... —Our gin martinis are rather famous.

—Lovely.

—We'll have three dry gin martinis.

—They're not served... Z tweaks his jeans at the knee to sit, the action of a much older man... —In those massive cones, are they? Because I'm a spiller.

—I do believe it's the eight ounce... Chris, apprehensive, looks to the bartender who is moving at high speed, rattling ice into a mixing glass... —Is it a coupe, the martinis?

—Eight ounce, conical.

—Can you give us a sour glass?

The bartender shakes his head.

Chris gets out his phone, stabs at it... —Let me find you the right...

—No, no. Please don't bother. Anything is fine, really.

—What about Liam?... Diane sits next to Z on the bench... —Would he like a cocktail?

—Oh, no, we'll give him water. I need him in fine form tonight. Fine fettle... Z laughs as if certain words are fun for him.

—Three martinis coming up... calls the bartender.

—God, I love New York... Z takes a quick glance around... —What a nutty city. And the gala, we've heard about it for years. Sara's spitting with jealousy but she has a human trafficking paper due. Her studies always come first. I need, Diane, another invitation or, Liam, is there a list?

—Oh, easy, easy enough. Chris?

—Yup, yup, sending right now... he bends over his phone.

Diane smiles at Z, trying to look relaxed and hip but also wise and commanding.

—Three dry gin martinis... the bartender walks toward them holding a tray.

Diane selects two glasses, handing one to Z. Chris takes the third and walks away, assaulting his phone with his thumb... —Excuse me, I have some work... arranging himself on a stool at the bar, setting his cocktail out of reach with painstaking precision as if, were the glass three inches closer, he'd be obliged to drink it.

—Mr. Willington... Diane swings her glass toward Z... —Welcome to the Museum.

5:32 p.m.

The Piquette salon is a depressing holdover from Tiz Sericko's reign when the ex-director spent his time drumming up restricted areas for donors and trustees, even installing a private elevator to prove the Museum wasn't intolerably earnest about the whole egalitarian bit. Bernard Daedalus Piquette was a renowned archaeologist and, understandably, less renowned wife-beater, dipsomaniac, and slaveowner. For seven years Diane has promised to rename the room but it remains so named, remains decorated in clashing contradictions and, critically, at this moment, remains completely empty.

Clive walks over to the sealed window. The room is stuffy with the fug of a little-used space. Why had he let down his guard? It was all that talk about her bagel-eating therapist. Quickened his sympathy. He watches a man walk down the street holding a hotdog.

Or maybe because for a few minutes it felt like old times. For months after Diane first arrived at the Museum Clive would find any excuse to drop by her office. They'd sit with their feet propped on the coffee table and talk about Olympic trampolining, fecal transplants, or echolocation and what it's like to be a bat. Flirting wantonly and irresponsibly before one of them remembered the time and rushed off to a meeting. On cold days they'd walk down the corridor to the Trustees Club, where Diane made spicy hot chocolate in a clay pitcher, frothing it with a molinillo. Rituals always made Clive uneasy but this choreography held a sacred appeal. The ceremony was composed of several steps and she treated each one with the gravity a child at the beach brings to the business of measuring sand. Her solemn expression excited him. Everything about her excited him. She was merciless and flinty with girlish blouses and clipped fingernails. Her hair was golden-red and shiny like the skin of an onion; her exasperated taming of it he found charming. The possibilities were suddenly infinite, filling Clive with strange ambitions. He replaced all his vitamins, bought a yoga mat, and ordered several promising body washes.

And then they flew to Paris.

5:35 p.m.

Chris is staring at her from his stool at the bar, eyes wide, signaling that the natural pause in their conversation is turning into an awkward silence.

—Thrilled the gala will give you a chance to look around this little museum of ours... Diane leans forward to demonstrate enthusiasm... —I think it will give you a sense of our mission.

—Saw quite a bit of the museum this morning.

—Did you? Today was unusually hectic what with the—

—Food poisoning, wasn't it?... Z sips his martini... —From the restaurant?

Over at the bar Chris swings around and leaps off his stool. Diane slugs her drink, skittering drops down her new size S blouse.

—Who told you that?... Chris strides over, fingers white where they grip his phone... —Who said it was food poisoning?

—I overheard a couple of waiters—

—*Waiters?*

—Trying to guess which customers could be spies from the health department.

—The *health* depart—

—I had an egg dish and about twelve cheesy biscuits with I guess scallions on top... distractedly, Z taps his glass... —Sara is begging me to quit carbs but really. Life's too short, don't you think?

—Yes, yes... Diane and Chris fight to endorse the idea that life is indeed rapidly over, in a blink over.

—She's the reason I'm here, Sara.

Chris spins around and trudges back to the bar.

—Her mom believed that solitude sparks creativity. Saturday mornings she'd drop Sara off at the Museum, pick her up in the afternoon. She was eight or ten.

—Leave a child here? Alone?

—It was a different time.

—Was it?... Diane tries to calculate. Not the seventies, but nineteen-eighty-nine or ninety.

—Sara adores this place. The donation, if I go ahead with it, would be in her name, a wedding gift.

—And you're thinking naming rights or—

—It's not about publicity, Diane.

—Of course not, sorry, jumping the gun. You were talking about a gift.

—Here's the thing... Z searches the rooftop as if looking for a way to put into words an unpalatable thought... —Where are the brown people?

—The brown...?

—Because all I saw was a sea of white. A great big white-out.

—That's a, we have a number of programs addressing diversity.

—And these *programs*, the people leading them, are they all white? Because I read an article—

—Yes, yes, you're speaking of, and you're quite correct, of course, mistakes were made. That issue is being remedied as we—

—Your guards look suicidal, the docents are stuck-up, and your entrance fee is despicable. How do you expect a family of five to afford twenty bucks a head?

—Technically... taking a breath and addressing it to her sphincter...
—The fee is merely a suggestion.

—Access to the arts remains out of reach for most Americans, even the middle class... Z is staring at something behind her shoulder.

Diane turns around. Liam is stretched out on the wooden bench, one arm draped across his eyes.

—Don't you think?

Turning back... —I understand, of course, and we have made substantial—

—You run an antiseptic mausoleum that's hostile to people of color. What about recent immigrants?

—Our audio guides... snapping, refusing to let it all slip away...
—Are available in fifteen languages.

—But more than racist, your museum feels classist. To me, anyway.
—*Classist.*

—Beginning with the suggested donation, which you only know is a suggestion if you're an insider. All the signs, Diane, say, in large print that your admission fee is twenty dollars. Then there's the intimidation factor. I feel intimidated and I went to Yale.

—My mother grew up poor... Chris has appeared next to them, gesturing with an alarmingly empty glass... —And she was never put off. She felt at home here, she—

—Thank you, Chris.

—Refill? Anyone?

Diane copies Z, shaking her head. In truth of course she'd like at least one more drink, if not several. Ahead of her lies a long evening of this cheerful abasement.

Chris disappears. Z savors the last of his martini.

—Z... reaching out to touch his knee before, why is she touching him for god's sake, snatching back her hand... —We're open to any suggestions on how to make the Museum more approachable.

—It's not about pandering, cooking up shows like "graffiti is actually the oldest form of art"—

—I mean, could Silicon Valley be any whiter?... Chris, back, and still annoyed.

—Right... Z, serenely amused... —But I'm not giving Silicon Valley twenty million dollars to solve the problem... he stands... —I should really get back.

5:42 p.m.

Clive presses up.

In Paris Diane tutoyed those who should have been vousvoyed, speaking with such vigor everyone took her for German. Clive's teeth were newly bleached and sensitive, he couldn't stop running his tongue around the inside of his mouth. The meeting was a bust, both paintings minor and in worse condition than promised. Afterward the two of them wandered the city, passing pastries back and forth, ignoring the shower of laminated flakes falling down their fronts. If you'd happened to notice these two tall people licking their fingers and colliding gently as they strolled, even stepping into a doorway briefly when it drizzled and the streets turned to silver, you might have assumed they were minutes away from a blazing fuck. Instead Clive went with Diane to one of those impeccably curated Parisian shops filled with perfect T-shirts and offbeat magazines and pricey leather doodads you were, until a moment ago, innocent of a homicidal desire to own. And here's where it all gets muddy. He made a teasing comment about Diane's sense of style. A pair of mystifying boots she bought. His only intention was to make her laugh. Facing each other outside some nothing brasserie on their way to lunch. Diane held the shopping bag, overjoyed at her silly new boots. Clive made that comment, whatever it was and when he looked up her mouth was a straight humorless line, her cheeks flushed pink. Without a word she walked away. The next day they were adversaries. Flying back in near silence. Now maybe he's invented it. Maybe the tension between them is due to something else. On the other hand, he's never seen Diane wear those boots.

The elevator doors open. Lucy was right all along. He really is a killjoy.

5:44 p.m.

The three of them turn at the sound of the elevator doors. Stepping onto the roof is a lanky young man of about thirty, the whitest man she's ever seen, a backpack hooked over one shoulder.

—Here's Benjamin Rippen... Chris walks over to collect him...
—Our brand-new head of film... looping the air with one finger in the direction of the bartender... —You remember Diane.

—Wonderful, wonderful... coming forward to shake... —Benjamin, please meet Z, visiting us from San, that is, Palo—

—Alto... Z, sticking out his own hand... —Pleased to meet you. Film department, huh?

Rippen stays silent, rooted to the spot, shaking hands with Z but staring at Liam, who has finally roused himself and is walking toward them.

—Do you two know each other?... Diane looks from one to the other as Liam approaches.

—Of course not. I'm the bodyguard.

—The *bodyguard*?... the film hire looks incredulous.

—That's right... Liam, roughly... —The bodyguard. Liam Stuck.

—I'm. Benjamin. Rippen... as if he's being strangled.

The two men shake.

—Diane, can you point me to a bathroom?

—Down one flight and opposite Tapestries.

Liam nods at her and saunters toward the elevator. Benjamin stares after him.

—Film is our newest department, you may, Z, have heard of Ward Bjarnsen who set up the program... buying his cred, knowing his health was rocky, desiring the imprimatur of a legend... —Simply one of the greatest film minds of all time... where is the bartender... —But when Ward decided to retire, we thought, let's go a different way... raising her voice over the sound of Chris dragging a chair... —We asked ourselves, how can we shake things up, not by, lovely... the bartender, thank god... —Benjamin, have a martini, surely not by hiring the old guard, the Academy, absolutely not. I, we, insisted on hiring someone young, fresh. A whole new perspective.

The three of them pivot appreciatively toward Benjamin, who has his martini lifted to his mouth and is currently, most unfortunately, poking the olive-bearing toothpick straight up his nostril. Over the rim of the glass he notices their stares and lowers it, swallowing conspicuously.

—That's right... appearing to gather himself, perhaps spotting things heading rapidly downhill... —I was very glad to be afforded the opportunity... smiling at Z, swiveling to encompass his audience... —To introduce a contemporary buzz or energy... so Chris has briefed the kid though there is, Diane thinks, a somewhat robotic quality to his words.

Z sits alone on the wide bench facing the others, who sit on chairs semicircled around him like supplicants. It's galling, the power held by this underfed putto.

—And what type of movies are you programming?... Z asks politely.

Benjamin wipes gin off the sleeve of his disgraceful windbreaker... —My own calendar won't start until January. Ward had the fall season planned so I haven't... he catches Diane's blistering stare... —One thing I have been thinking about, and tell me what you think of it, Z, maybe it's too... now what, the kid inventing on the spot, bleating random words... —Too outlandish or, but I've always wondered about... Benjamin pauses... —Prostitutes.

Chris coughs, almost spitting, hand to his mouth, doubled over. She feels her lungs contract like a popped balloon. The hand holding the stem of her glass turns into a fist.

—Prostitutes?... Z laughs. Good. His first laugh.

—Starting with the French, *Belle du Jour* and Deneuve's bored housewife, then there's *2 or 3 Things I Know About Her*, *Vivre Sa Vie*—

—Godard's kind of a perv, no?

Diane stares at this Benjamin person, willing him not to answer, perhaps even fall to the ground with a mild heart attack.

—Godard? God, yes, complete perv.

—Branching out to other countries, we have Fellini's *Nights of Cabiria*, Kiarostami's *Ten*, *The Life of Oharu*... Benjamin appears to have hit a stride of some sort... —*Happy Together*, *Mamma Roma*, *Accattone*—

—But surely that one's more about the pimp.

Diane has no idea how to stop the runaway insanity of this conversation. She hears the chuckle of a cretin and identifies it as her own.

—You're right, strike *Accattone*. Now we have the Americans—

—*Pretty Woman*... Z says happily.

—But we'd go less commercial, *McCabe and Mrs. Miller, Taxi Driver, Butterfield 8*, and of course the films about men, *Midnight Cowboy, My Own Private Idaho.*

—*American Gigolo*?

—Maybe, maybe.

—I love Richard Gere... Z looks around brightly.

—Who doesn't?

—A national treasure... she offers, feeling the ground to be safer...
—Richard Gere.

The men smile tolerantly at Diane.

—You know one of my favorites... Z has become a completely different person, animated, leaning back, leg crossed at the knee, one arm flung along the back of the bench... —*Risky Business.*

—Love it!

Can the film hire possibly be tipsy from half a martini? She glances at Chris, he catches her eye, nods.

—Perhaps not right for your series.

—I think probably not but definitely transgressive in many ways.

—And Blaxploitation?

—Different festival, I think.

—So, what's your like, thesis?

—Not quite there yet but... Benjamin leans in toward Z... —What about taking a movie that on its surface appears to serve male fantasies, presenting it with or against the sort of lived banality of, say, *Jeanne Dielman* or—

—Oh my god, with the towels.

—Benjamin... Chris scoots forward in his chair... —Might we put a pin in this?

—Of course... deflating, blinking as if he's waking up.

—But what a fascinating idea... Z tilts his head, musing... —Could it be part of a larger show, incorporate paintings and sculpture?

—A museum-wide show about prostitutes?

—Mary Magdalene, geisha, and are they called hetairai? Trying to remember my art history.

—Hm... Diane tilts her head, picturing Ralph Kade's expression upon being asked to sponsor a show about whores.

Z brings his gaze up to the cloudless sky, closing his eyes, skinny neck sprouting from the cowl of his hoodie like the stem of a plant. How pleasant the setting sun must feel on your face when you're a billionaire. When not in jeopardy of losing your job, that warmth must feel pretty good.

—Gentlemen... Chris pushes back his chair and gets up... —I'm afraid Diane needs to prepare for this evening.

—I'll see you tonight?... standing, Z offers Benjamin his hand.

—Do come, Benjamin... she says warmly... —In the meantime stay up here as long as you like, have another drink... joining Chris to walk silently across the roof, waving and saying thank you to the bartender as they go.

Once inside the elevator, Chris goggles at her, eyebrows raised.

—I mean, Z seemed to like him. But what the hell with prostitutes, what the everliving?

—I can't even... Chris types into his phone.

—We'll have to give him a ticket.

—Sending it this minute. Obviously I can't come out and *say* don't you dare attend.

—But your email makes it clear.

—Crystal.

Diane leans against the elevator wall. The martinis have dissolved her headache. I can get another job, she thinks. How hard can it be? Suddenly she wants Dom, his bearish form, his arms around her. Whatever transpired in the kitchen last night, it's Dominic she wants, the marriage she needs... —What time does my husband arrive?

—Email from him... Chris looks up from his phone... —Says you have yet to return his call. Maybe there's an issue with his tux?

—Okay... closing her eyes... —I'll take care of it.

5:54 p.m.

Wildfire season. Henry drove east from Los Angeles eyeing the horizon for smoke, arriving late with his tank on empty. He was nervous on the drive, obvious from the constant minuscule adjustments he made to the radio and air-conditioning. He had spent little time alone with Colin, almost none while he and Annie were still married, when she was the placating sun around which the three of them made an aggrieved orbit.

Waiting in Colin's dorm room as he showered, Henry found books on astrophysics, the bewildering concepts highlighted in yellow marker. Why had he never bought Colin a telescope, or stuck phosphorescent stars to the kid's bedroom ceiling? It struck Henry that he didn't know his son, perhaps had never known his son. Had he tried? He combed Colin's boyhood, searching for evidence of effort. He remembered high-spirited ribbing with Colin's friends, and squinting concern around his teachers, but with his son, only small talk, silence, or reprimands.

They went to a diner where their booth quickly filled with the scent of tough-guy cologne, a gallon of which Colin had slapped about his jaw and neck. Breakfast for dinner, they decided, a blueberry stack, bacon on the side. Then, silence. Colin stared across the room at a case of rotating pies. Henry unfolded his napkin and placed it in his lap, feeling the full weight of his parental shortcomings. He could stop it right then, he thought. Reach out to Colin, admit his failings, offer advice, apologize. Put an end to the bumbling. But the words didn't come. Desire itself was not enough. Instead Henry grumbled about the artificial syrup. It was indefensible. But what could you expect for six dollars and fifty-five cents.

Henry finishes his search of the second-floor galleries and swipes into the back staircase, hollering *Shay* up the stairwell as he tromps down.

The memory of this long-ago dinner came to Henry as he waited for Malcolm, wisdom and compassion at the ready, as if years of distracted parenting could be wiped from the record by acting fatherly and helpful to another man's son. The Museum is too short for a real view. From the roof, you stare down on treetops or into the midriffs of other buildings. Yet Henry felt closer than ever to death. Brought on by a proximity to heaven, he thought, absurdly. The sky was an almost painful blue, broken only by a hot-air balloon in the distance, bobbing over New Jersey.

—Those things hit power lines... Malcolm observed when he arrived.

The kid was tall and shy, with Shay's wide forehead and a trick of glancing around warily as if someone might pop out from behind a potted shrub.

Henry was unprepared for the quiet strength and cool intelligence of a young man not yet twenty. He couldn't help but see himself through the eyes of this young stoic. Look at the cabbage-eating dotard in the middle-management suit. No doubt has pebbly strips stuck in the tub to avoid a slippy-slidey cropper into the faucet. Never before had Henry seen with such searing perspicacity into the mind of a complete stranger. Meanwhile, Malcolm had done nothing more revealing than bury his hands in his pockets and regard Henry with a polite expression.

—I advise, Malcolm, that you live with an eye toward regret.

—Sir?

—Try to imagine what it will feel like looking back.

—You mean, while I'm living, like in the present, I should imagine myself in the future thinking about the past?

It only got worse from there. With sweeping digressions, Henry spoke for longer than either of them wished, quoting *The Inner Game of Tennis* and mentioning time spent abroad. It's possible he was still giddy that Annie had agreed to come to the gala on such short notice. Overjoyed at the prospect of confessing. Clouds scudded in from the west. Is this how I go, Henry wondered, thrashing around in this murk of misunderstanding? He would have guessed that clarity, a kind of liquid grace comes over you as you approach the endgame.

It was the end of Malcolm's break. Tired of thinking, Henry unbuckled his watch, pressing it on the kid, insisting he take it. A vintage Submariner to atone for his mentoring failures. Or, Henry thought as he left the roof, an inane attempt to scrub the history books.

He takes a right, into the warren of smaller galleries that surround American. Where the devil is Shay Pallot?

5:59 p.m.

Ascending, Shay maintains perfect control of her emotions. After his conversation with Henry Joles, Malcolm returned to HQ. Told Shay everything. A waste of time, he said. The old man talked about tennis and some trip he took with his ex-wife. He kept staring at the sky and I kept looking where he was looking 'cause I thought he was looking at an actual thing. To Shay's follow-up questions, Malc said, it don't matter. I don't want to study law. So her one chance was ruined.

Eager to learn exactly what Henry Joles was thinking, Shay is heading to his office.

The elevator stops on the second floor, the doors open, and a white man of about thirty-five gets on and presses the button marked roof. Instantly Shay's simmering internal monologue stops. The man raises a hand, pinches his eyelashes. She's seen this person before. Early afternoon, lunchtime. Musical Instruments. Speaking with the new film hire. Voices low and urgent.

—Museum closed to visitors at five o'clock sharp... checking her watch... —An hour ago.

The man shows her the laminated GUEST pass hanging around his neck... —I'm with Zedekiah Willington? Big donor. Meeting with the director. Bodyguard, hi... dropping the pass and holding out his hand... —Liam. Just ran to the bathroom.

Shaking his hand reluctantly. A bodyguard. What kind of fool does he take her for?

—Z's very rich, Silicon Valley. Required protect—

—Don't bother. I'm not someone you need to lie to.

The young man's expression falters... —Sorry?

But the elevator arrives at the fourth floor, and Shay disembarks without looking back.

6:02 p.m.

Naked and stepping into the shower, Diane remembers she forgot to call Dominic. It isn't, as Chris guessed, a matter of his tux. It will be about last night. Words exchanged as they faced each other over cold grapes. Bending to adjust the water temperature, she sees the two of them at the kitchen table, faces lit by the stovetop light. Between them was the metal colander which, despite the painful symbolism, looked very much like a discarded piece of armor.

Diane reaches for the shampoo. Focus on this evening. Not your marriage, not a pile of grapes. But her mind swerves from the gala back to Dominic and the day they bought the kitchen table.

6:03 p.m.

A short distance down the carpeted hallway, Shay slows and comes to a stop. Speaking to Henry Joles in her current mood would be a mistake. Not because she might lose her job, though that's definitely a risk. More, that she can't bear these people to see her as anything but even-keeled and emotionless.

As Shay reviews her options, she hears a sound coming from the reception area outside Diane's office. Creeping forward a few steps, she pokes her head around the corner. It takes a minute to figure out what it is she's looking at.

Chris.

Sitting at his desk, folded over, arms around his head as if steeling himself for the emergency landing of a doomed jetliner. He has a sports coat draped over his head and the muscles in his back are rigid with tension. Suddenly Chris lets out a blood-curdling scream, howling into his coat, pressing it against his face to dampen the sound. Shay turns on her heel and sprints down the hall to the back staircase, throwing herself against the panic bar and flying down the stairs. This fucking circus.

6:04 p.m.

Fourteen years ago at a store in SoHo that specialized in midcentury design, Dominic was in full Scandinavian stride, swapping arcane trivia with the shop's owner when Diane came upon a table she liked. It was handsome, but oddly shaped and too small. In a word, unrealistic. Be practical, Dom suggested. He had his mind set on utility and any objections she made regarding beauty would be discounted as beside the point. With that in mind, Diane agreed they should buy the one he wanted, all the while thinking she had never set eyes on a less inspiring table.

But over time she came to appreciate the table's dimensions, how generously it fit a fruit bowl, flowers, and settings for six. It was the sort of sensible outlook her mother encouraged. A way of being Diane slipped into the day she started grad school and, over the course of their marriage, one that Dominic has come to expect.

Diane leans back, rinsing conditioner from her hair.

Pragmatism is, inarguably, a vital quality in the running of a museum but all that common sense has entered her bloodstream. Infected her with reason. And it's possible no marriage can withstand two reasonable people.

Flipping her hair to one side, she squeezes it, watching the water run down her arm.

No easy answers. No answers at all, she thinks, pulling back her hair and placing her face directly in the spray. The water needles her cheeks and eyelids.

6:06 p.m.

—Needle thin. This is garbage.

—Yes, Chef.

—Do it again. And wait on those or the bottoms'll get soggy.

The Events kitchen swarms with caterers recruited from the North Fork of Long Island. They are part-time actors and wannabe models. The presently lost and formerly addicted. Disaffected college kids and middle-aged failures.

On the surface Nikolic is effortlessly managing the food prep. Meanwhile, his brain's exploding. What kind of prison time comes from poisoning dozens of people and a foreign ambassador? How much does it cost to hire an even marginally competent lawyer?

—What's with the gay hat?... Jimmy walks up, wiping his hands on a side-towel.

—Required... the toque is farcically tall and keeps slipping off his head... —And don't say gay like it's an insult.

—No one heard.

—I heard. I'm a person.

—Are you... mildly. Then... —Check out these losers. Think any of them cooked before?

For a minute, Niko and Jimmy stand together and companionably shit-talk the temporary crew. An older woman butchering basil. A sleepy kid in moccasins slopping crème fraîche into a pan, a curious move since none of the recipes actually calls for crème fraîche. The girl tempering chocolate keeps touching her nostrils and appears to be crying. How good it feels to slander and demean, to identify flaws, cluck over the problems of inbreeding and guess at inherited wounds. Some good old down-home defamation. Is the tall kid's gonzo dicing a precursor to a stroke? Could the weirdo in the corner be one of those Russian orphans who doesn't get enough hugs and ends up microwaving the family cat? Even the sex life of a gawky innocent grating cheese doesn't escape their scholarship.

—Okay... Jimmy pulls out his phone and checks the time... —I gotta go get ready. Don't answer your cell. Any unknown numbers, anything with an area code—

—Yeah. I get it.

—You promised. Remember... Jimmy points at him and spins on his heel.

Niko watches his brother saunter across the room, pausing only to slide his eyes toward an attractive brunette bending to read an oven dial. He swipes a macaron off a tray and pushes through the kitchen door.

6:09 p.m.

The man crashes into Shay as he barges out of the swinging doors ass-first and chewing... —Whoopsie... hand over his mouth to stop food flying out or to disguise the fact he's laughing.

—Pardon me... she's only just caught her breath from galloping down the back stairs.

He picks up the notebook that flew from Shay's grasp and holds it out... —My fault... saluting in the tiresome manner of a person faced with an authority figure he doesn't respect.

—You with the catering crew?

—I am, yup. Hey, have a fantastic evening.

Shay pockets the notebook, checks its safety, watches this person disappear into the Great Hall. Is it the disease? She's beginning to suspect everyone of lying.

—Finally!

The voice of Henry Joles. Slowly Shay turns to face him.

—Been looking all over for you... Joles is rumpled and breathing heavily... —Made a whopping hash of my talk with your nephew. Came to apologize... his skin has an unnatural cast, cheeks red and waxy like an ornamental apple... —I was ineffectual, at best. But I didn't know, at the time, about.

—About what?

Joles squints unattractively... —All the details.

—All what details?

—Nothing... he pushes at his chest. Snowy wisps of hair emerge from his cuff.

—What were you... Shay tries to stop herself but... —*Tennis?*... she practically spits... —Your *ex-wife?* Some trip to Slovenia, Malc said.

—I apologize. The conversation took a turn.

Over the lawyer's shoulder, across the hallway in the entrance to Egypt, Aaron slumps against the wall. He should know better. She's been abundantly clear about posture in her emails.

—Chief Pallot, Shay.

She brings her attention back to the lawyer. Doesn't bother to hide her irritation.

—Let me take another crack at it.

—I can spot your wallet in your trouser pocket, Mr. Joles.

—Where's Malcolm now?

—I recommend switching to an inside jacket pocket this evening with the crowds.

—Couldn't find him down in HQ.

—It's not best out of three, Mr. Joles. The young lose patience.

—Understood... Henry moves his wallet, as instructed... —But this morning—

—Earlier you were wearing a watch, fancy thing. On your right wrist.

—Remember when we were waiting for the tech—

—I recall inferring you were left-handed.

—That's correct, yes, but Chief, Shay, this morning, the two of us, we spoke about the past, leaving behind a legacy. What was that? Not a joke, not to me, at least. Give me another chance. Mouths on spoons, remember? Those miniature items, leaving a part of yourself behind. Today was, I had so many, the Mumbai problem is only one. Tell me you understand. I've got my own trough of shit to manage.

—Mr. Joles?

He looks at Shay hopefully. But she refuses to join him in recalling this morning.

—What happened to your watch?

The lawyer's expression doesn't change, and she makes a wide arc around him, heading back the way she came, angry now only for letting herself get carried away, fabricating a mentor for Malcolm. What was she thinking?

6:13 p.m.

As soon as the elevator doors closed behind the director and her assistant, Benjamin offered Z his polite regards and fled, hurrying to stake out the museum entrance. For the last twenty minutes he's been pacing from the fumes of a peanut vendor to those of a hot dog cart. Forming in his head both a pleading argument and a snide little monologue.

Finally, Liam shambles down the wide marble steps, laughing, the tech investor by his side. Benjamin watches them man-hug and part, Liam heading downtown, Z going up. Once Z has safely disappeared around the corner, Benjamin takes off, sprinting.

—Wait!... the backpack kicks against his spine... —WAIT!

Liam turns around, sees Benjamin, and appears to sigh.

—What the hell?

—Hurry up.

—What was that business on the roof?... the short jog has taken a toll on Benjamin's breathing... —How in christ do you know a Silicon Valley billionaire?

—Whatever, I went to college with a guy who knows a guy. Turns out Zedekiah Willington identifies as a progressive.

—Oh my god.

—Super into nonviolent protest. And smart. I showed him pictures of my work. Gave me great feedback.

—I'm going to throw up.

—I really think we'll be friends after tonight.

—Just walk away, Liam, please. Don't fuck with the Museum.

—Why do you care?

—I care about Caroline. How's she going to feel with her brother in jail?

—Yeah, right... Liam starts walking... —As if it's about Caro. You're more selfish than that.

Benjamin falls in next to him, ignoring the dig, he can't afford to get distracted... —I have money problems, okay? My landlord's a minute away from tossing me on the street, my student loans are killing me. I get a thousand calls a day. I've started hallucinating. I can't lose this job. At the very least, I need Museum insurance in case I have a full-blown nervous breakdown.

—How're you gonna lose your job? No one knows we know each other.

—They'll find out. This is how it goes with me and if you're dicking around with this protest—

—Prank, Benjamin. The word I used was prank.

—Whatever, someone's going to find out we know each other and it's all going to turn around and bite me in the ass.

—Stop it with the persecution fantasy, will you? Everything's, hang on... Liam fishes out his phone and holds it to his ear... —Hey! Great... a pause... —In Duane Reade picking up a plunger. Bumped into Benjamin... listening, then moving the phone aside... —Clover says hi... back into the phone... —Yeah, we're just, you know, chatting, fascinating, actually, Benjamin's been telling me all about Robert Altman—

—Fuck off.

—How Altman edged up to the brink of chaos, kissing incoherence before, what? Okay... over the phone... —Clover says not to disappear.

—I won't.

—Benjamin says he won't. Yup. Uh-huh. See you soon... Liam shoves the phone back into his pocket... —Look, I gotta go... taking Benjamin by the shoulders and shaking him, a way Liam has of expressing affection... —I have to go shower and change. I'll see you tonight. And for god's sake, stop worrying.

Liam gives him a friendly punch and continues down the street, crossing against the light, patting a doodle on the head, overtaking a group of teenagers and fading into the distance.

6:19 p.m.

Darling, Jane says on a voicemail left three hours ago, Dad's been asking for you nonstop. He's in a bit of a state. Probably the painkillers. Perhaps a brief phone call, after all? A few words? We'd keep it short.

Clive plays the message through twice before deleting it as he walks down the corridor to the office kitchen. All he's eaten today is half a yogurt and two bites of birthday cake.

6:20 p.m.

—I don't understand... Diane stands stock-still, naked but for a pair of restrictive underpants. One minute out of the shower and halfway through turbaning up her wet hair... —What do you mean you're not coming?

The door to her office eases open... —Diane, I've got hair and makeup—

—Hang on... grabbing a towel from the couch, wrapping it around her torso... —What is it?

Chris sticks his head around the door... —Didn't know if you were decent.

—On the phone with Dominic.

—Hey, Dominic.

From the speaker... —Hey, Chris.

—Hair and makeup's in the building.

—Fine, fine. I'm going to put on the dress now, so.

—I'll leave you to it... Chris pulls the door closed behind him, saying faintly as he goes... —Bye Dominic.

—We've had this plan for months... she tells the speakerphone... —Together we decided this could be—

—A fun night, yes, I know.

—Your tux arrived?

—This isn't about my tux.

Her gown was delivered less than an hour ago, hanging dismally from its own small rack. Paralyzed, she stares at it.

—Still there?

—I'm listening... forcing herself to drop the towel and remove the dress from its hanger. She fights through layers of muslin and tulle, trying to find a way in. And then there's the sash. Why on earth had she agreed to Selina's ugly sash?

—How can I stand there pretending?

—This is crazy. We should talk. Shouldn't we? Don't people talk?

—But, darling, we did. Last night in the kitchen.

—That was the beginning of a conversation.

And the details she still can't bring to mind. She remembers telling Dom about buying fish and cheese, flummoxed by which way to walk, facing what appeared to be an insurmountable ascent. And the expression on his face, as if it wasn't just a funny story.

—We were just beginning, Dom... hoping the firmness in her voice might convince him.

—Why dance around for another six months? When was the last time we laughed?

—We laugh all the—

—No, Diane, we don't.

—I'll think of a time. Give me a minute.

—I want to fuck and be stupid.

—*I* want to fuck and be stupid. Don't make me the one who doesn't want to fuck and be stupid.

—You don't have the courage to say we're done. I'm doing this be-cause you refuse.

—Stop, please. I can't think, I can't... half-falling, half-sitting on the couch, the dress pouffing up around her like a parachute it so regretta-bly is not.

—We're speaking past each other.

A bolt of fury blazes through her. The anger is so swift and savage Diane is forced to recognize it, sadly, as mere melodrama.

—It would be dishonest to pull on a monkey suit and stand by your side as if... he coughs... —As if everything's normal.

So all these weeks she's been Hamleting about the marriage Dominic's been waiting in the wings with a vial of poison. God, how blind she's been.

—Diane.

—I'll quit. The board meets next week. I'll give them time to find a, a... speaking in a desperate rush... —An interim director or—

—Stop, please.

The door to her office creeps open.

—What is it, Chris?

—The ladies are here.

—Give me a minute.

The door remains open several inches.

—Come tonight, Dominic, please. We can talk.

—You're not listening.

—Please... frantically, what can she offer, what can she promise.

—Come on now. Come to your senses.

Two figures enter her office with bundles and cases. Her senses are the last thing she'll come to.

—Good luck tonight.

And the phone goes dead. She feels the life drain from her body, leaving her digits and limbs cold and useless. Lying on the carpet in front of her is a staple. Her eyesight has become superhuman. When was the last time she used a stapler? She doesn't appear to be breathing.

—Ma'am? Is that where you'd like to sit?

From her dead place on the couch, Diane looks up. Two impossibly chic women stand before her, clad entirely in black, holding bags and small suitcases. One woman unshrugs an elegant backpack. Who are these people? Why are they in her office?

—I'm Marcy, this is Famina.

Diane watches as they take over the room, setting down cases and making clicking and zipping noises with clasps and buckles, pulling out tools, compacts, and pots.

—Ms. Schwebe? Let's put you over here.

With extraordinary effort, possibly even grunting, Diane gets to her feet, shuffles across the room and collapses in the desk chair.

—What a pretty dress... Famina unfolds a hairdresser's cape with a sharp flick, and Velcros it around Diane's neck.

—Too tight.

Famina re-Velcros... —Heat protection oil?

—Whatever you think is best.

Famina removes the towel turban and begins combing out Diane's wet hair with rough disciplinary strokes. Across the room Marcy is setting bottles on the credenza, adjusting them so the labels all face the same way. Out comes the hair dryer and round brush. Look at these professionals. Marcy sets to one side a monstrous emery board, takes Diane's hands and examines her chipped polish and ragged fingernails with a mother's disappointment.

6:28 p.m.

Still wearing jeans but in full evening makeup, Katherine walks through the bowels, out of the employee entrance, down the loading ramp and up onto the street. An hour ago her phone dinged with a text from the Professore, the first in several days. *I hope if we were to see each other again it wouldn't be too unhappy for you.* As with all his texts and overly intimate voicemails, she did not reply.

A brief wait for the light before she's charging across the intersection, overtaking a man pushing a two-year-old in a stroller. As she passes she looks down at the child as if to find in its small face Katherine's own or the Professor's sharp chin and caterpillar eyebrows.

Planned Parenthood closed half an hour ago. At this rate the decision will be made by failing to decide.

6:30 p.m.

The journalist appeared at their apartment one day last April along with a thousand bracelets and rings, several scarves, and some sort of knitted shoulder bag. Her name was Lydia Swann. She wore a sweater with tassels and a pair of fringed suede boots. Each piece of clothing came with footnotes.

At the time Diane didn't question whether Lydia and Dominic had ever been a couple. Aristocrats weren't Dom's type and Lydia came across as a blueblood. She had an aquiline nose, a long slender neck and wore her hair in a low poofy bun. When she turned to the side she looked like a pilcrow.

While Dominic was busy digging out a jar of olives and rosemary flatbreads, Lydia wandered the hallway, examining framed photos of last year's trip to Cairo. Unsure where to go, Diane hovered, suppressing the urge to justify what were clearly unspeakable acts of tourism. She wanted to compliment Lydia's fragrance but wasn't sure whether it was actually perfume or a sort of natural ambrosia Lydia typically emitted.

Marcy massages cream into Diane's forehead and cheeks, fanning it dry with a manila folder.

The two of them repaired to the living room and a few minutes later Dominic came in and set down the crackers while Lydia positioned herself on the couch, arranging her long legs so they were crossed and aslant. Once she was assured of her comfort or, perhaps, of her appearance, Lydia plowed through the flatbreads, speaking in great paragraphs of sound. With labored humility she spoke of the political friction she encountered abroad. And though her tales were fascinating, these were not countries torn up by war, Diane made sure to ask. She wasn't being shot at, for god's sake. Safe nations, that was Lydia. The old human interest. Flying in for the flood or earthquake. Dashing around in a safari jacket, befriending refugees and bullying widows.

Famina burns her neck with the hairdryer. Diane barely flinches.

Could Dominic be leaving her for Lydia Swann? He didn't seem exactly smitten that night, though he did laugh louder than usual and raise his eyebrows excessively. They are beginning to thicken and spurt grey hairs, as well as take on a more pronounced arch. Tomorrow will he dye them? Buy nasal strips to combat the snoring? Plenty of unchartered territory lies ahead. Territory Diane will know nothing of.

She watches Marcy flatten the nail polish brush against the mouth of the bottle, carefully ridding it of superfluous color.

But this is fiction. Dominic is incapable of lying. A strict Catholic childhood, a forbidding grandmother who brooked no funny stuff. To this day he blushes to the scalp if he's forced to tell a fib.

Not an affair, then.

So, why?

Because they sold the place upstate?

6:35 p.m.

The television hanging in a corner above the counter is playing a baseball game with the sound muted. The match is an important one in the playoffs, so Clive tried chatting with the pizza guy, pretending he too had stakes in its outcome, all the while thinking, have I won? Or lost? Won? Lost? The guy frisbeed a cold slice into the far reaches of the oven. He'd been forced to end an intense phone call to take Clive's order and was not in the mood for chit-chat, crashing together metal containers of onions and peppers and wiping them aggressively with a frightful grey rag.

At an orange Formica booth littered with crumpled napkins, Clive sizes up his slice. Despite preferring almost any topping to pepperoni, his order was never in question. No slice is more straightforward than pepperoni. Especially cupped pepperoni. And if your pizza is without pretension, it stands to reason that you yourself are an honorable man. Going about your honest, maybe even virtuous, business. Not a terrible person with a calcified emotional life. Certainly not the type to ignore a broken father. That is the unstated law of pepperoni.

6:37 p.m.

Behind the house was an old barn stuffed with the previous owner's cat miscellany. She and Dominic spent a week piling tchotchkes high in one corner so Dom could build a workshop using wood from a bureau he found at the dump. He was suspicious of the store-bought cabinets that promoted order. Workbenches, he thought, should be handmade and half-assed. Crude, wooden, spattered with paint and gluey blobs, that was the proper backdrop for creative thinking.

During that time, the time of the workbench, Dominic looked at Diane differently, as if he were surprised to find her there, but it wasn't an unpleasant surprise, quite the opposite. For his birthday she gave him an expensive plane for shaving wood and he gazed at it with the devotion of a father meeting his newborn son.

—Don't do that with your forehead... Marcy stands back with her palette and brush.

—Sorry.

It was a heady time, being seized by the good life. In the summer they woke late to the sound of cicadas and a morning thick with green heat. There was no air-conditioning, they kept the windows open at the bottom and shaded at the top. In late spring a circle of maple trees sent down showers of tan apostrophes. They had a long flirtation with solar panels, a shorter one with composting. Farmers' markets for apricot jam and exotic mushrooms. Discussions, both sober and drunk, about beehives. The world is running out of bees, the two of them were on hand to help. Also, honey, they thought, could be a pleasant accessory to the country life. But a neighbor dissuaded them from beekeeping with a long anecdote involving his genitals.

After a few fires filled the house with smoke, a meth-head of a chimney sweep drove down from Albany to pronounce the fireplace dead. Sitting back on his grubby boot heels, picking his teeth, *no point in fixing it*. He comes to mind, on occasion, in the middle of the night. But she and Dominic were upbeat and vigorous from all that country air. Defective fireplace? No problem. They ordered a pellet stove and when it arrived, had sex on a mildewed horse rug, spread out romantically before the heat.

In the country Dominic baked bread and built shelves. He wore espadrilles, as only a confident man can. And Diane discovered the power of diversion. A promising tag sale had her setting the alarm. The haggling was addictive, she brought a woman to tears over a chipped Crock-Pot. She clipped back vines, ordered seeds. In a pair of chic rubber boots she dug a trench to lure rain away from the house. Quests of various sizes filled their weekends. Painting a bathroom, finding a rain barrel, correcting the balance of their soil's pH, it was absorbing stuff. The sense of purpose was gratifying. And then it came to an end. One night Dom went downstairs for a glass of water, flipped on a light, and found a possum staring back at him, sprawled on the counter like a saucy odalisque. Museum work began consuming more of her weekends. Raccoons chewed through the eaves. They couldn't rid the den of an unappealing odor of vinyl, sour milk, and horse. After a year on the market the house in Tivoli went for a loss.

6:43 p.m.

The downtown subway platform is packed, the air heavy and human. People wait with Soviet resignation, cradling armfuls of coats and sweaters, staring blankly into the middle distance. Benjamin bends his knees. Recently they've begun to ache for no reason. On the wall opposite, a poster advertises body lotion in hysteric pink letters. Six women in white panties leap in the air with expressions of ecstasy. Katherine looked less happy about being caught in her underpants. The word *Joy* was stamped across the back. But it was not a joy, walking in on her. Frankly, it was the opposite of a joy.

His life is unraveling. This morning he needed a thousand dollars to avoid being evicted. Twelve hours later, eight grand stands between Benjamin and a pair of cement shoes.

Maybe he's misread the situation. Exaggerated the danger of Avery Eccleston. That time he stood in a Salvation Army dressing room in Tennessee wondering how many customers the shop assistant had butchered when the shop assistant was doing nothing more menacing than sucking sugar-free candies from a bowl by the register. And his suspicions about Nigel, his grad school officemate who used to appear unexpectedly around corners, had wet fingers, and was never normal about the office supplies. Nobody but Benjamin assumed Nigel spent his free time writing manifestos and buying ricin on the dark web. Caroline was right. The movies he directs these days are in his head.

Across the tracks, the uptown train blasts into the station. Before Benjamin can second-guess himself he's shoving toward the stairs, climbing them two at a time, sprinting across to the other side, flying down the stairs and pitching through the closing doors, heading back the way he came.

6:46 p.m.

As long as Clive sits in this orange booth, eating his pizza and glancing at the baseball game with an expression of investment, everyone will assume they have an emotionally healthy person in their midst, and so it will be. Consensus will insist that of course it's not unreasonable to remain three thousand miles from your father while he writhes in an NHS rehab unit, undermedicated and alone.

The fat-necked patriarch of a family of four stares at Clive accusingly. Your father only ever provided for you, never reacting when, at the age of nine, you chose to support Liverpool over Newcastle because Liverpool is the enemy of Newcastle. He brought home headphones for your record player, nice ones, the sort he couldn't afford, so you could lie on your bed singing your treasonous Bronski Beat songs. *Run away, turn away, run away, turn away.* He took it all in stride, your dad did. As you marched around deceiving him and despising him and behaving, in the end, as if you were too good for him, he waited with his clumsy love, watching from afar, allowing you to be spiteful and truculent, understanding he had done nothing very terrible to deserve such treatment. All he did was conform to his upbringing. One that feared art, falsettos, boys in makeup, and, especially, boys liking boys. All he did was not be you. You hated the ways you were different and you hated the ways you were the same. And maybe that's to be expected from a fifteen-year-old, but you fucked off to New York and your feelings about your father never matured. Your soul cauterized. At the age of twenty-two. The letters he wrote in his inky schoolboy script, blotted and blotchy, scattered with Irrational Capitalization, you ignored. You didn't give a fuck about his Blighted Courgettes. Giles cartoons ripped from the *Sunday Express*, sent in translucent blue envelopes. He was dead to you, years ago. Over nothing. Nothing! The way he wrung his tea bag, the clicking of his jaw, the punitive pub lunches. Grinding the gears, bellowing on a long-distance call, it drove you mad, all of it. And these days when you look in the mirror and watch yourself pull on your coat with a secondary flick exactly as your father pulled on his coat with a secondary flick, you hate yourself exactly as you hated him.

There was an important transitional phase on the road to this indifference, nights when drink made Clive soppy and garrulous. He'd pick up the phone and call Jane. It would be early morning in Swindon, she'd be feeding the dogs or feeding her legs into stockings and Clive would remind his little sister of some trifle from their childhood, a piece of mischief not worth recalling. How, in school, his little black dictionary defined fart as "an explosion between the legs," and how, even as a ten-year-old, the definition had struck him as horribly, perhaps even fatally, imprecise to someone, a nonnative speaker, for example, who'd gone to the dictionary in hope of elucidation. Jane always let him blather on. Who was that friend of hers, the one with the frozen eye, he could never remember her name, she was a terror, a real klepto, Teresa, was it? But that phase ended, so now, even with drink, Clive remains reliably unsentimental.

He's always preferred Auden's correction: We must love one another *and* die. Not *or*. People, some, wanted the word to be *or* but *or* makes no sense. We all die. There's no fucking *or* about dying.

Clive detaches a cup of pepperoni from its bed of cheese and eats it. The father wipes red sauce from his daughter's face and orders his son to pipe down before he takes out the belt.

We try, of course we do. But in the end we do the thing that keeps us lonely.

6:53 p.m.

—The hypocrisy, of course, what do you think? That's why I'm...
Iona finishes the sentence by ratcheting the belt on her bathrobe.

—But it's one night. I can't see the harm in one night.

—Really? When three or five or however many hundred people are
looking at it, trusting that it's genuine. I mean, really, you can't see the
harm?

Iona has been on this tear since she unlocked the door and saw
David standing by the fridge. He was wearing a pair of slippers wrapped
in duct-tape and eating peanut butter off a saucer with a fork. His benign smile brought Iona to the boil, all the lying she was being asked to
overlook.

—Innocent guests, appreciating the Museum.

The release of venom was somehow related to the girl in Costume,
the way she had so casually committed a crime. Borrowing dresses from
Archives, as if the world was hers for the taking. What a way to live.

—Meanwhile, in the middle of the crowd, is this... squirting foundation onto a makeup sponge... —You know, *statue*, mocking those of
us who value truth.

—Then why go?... David leans in the bathroom doorway watching
Iona at her makeup.

—You have no understanding of the legal implications.

—Do you?... he snuffles a glass of red wine.

A vein begins to throb at her temple... —So you agree that museums should just display whatever, call it authentic even if—

—Of course not.

—Then you're being naïve. They're not going to bury a piece in
storage when they've spent a boatload of cash on it, and no visitor's going
to know the difference... too much foundation, whatever, powder...
—Wake up.

—I'm so confused. Is this about—

—No, David. It's not.

—Last year.

—Didn't I just say no?

—Because you hit a bartender.

—God, I did not hit, I was being expressive, I didn't know he was right behind me. And it's not about one small Cycladic sculpture that anyone with a brain could recognize as fake, okay? I was annoyed for a minute but I let it go. Never told anybody.

—You dropped your... he bends, handing her the eyeliner she accidentally flung.

—Thank you... moving to her eyes, a picture of Elizabeth Taylor pulled up on her phone... —Did I lose respect for Ian and Jenny? Of course, I mean, really. But I kept quiet.

—I remember... David sloshes his wine, falsely aerating.

—But that was one small figure... blowing shadow off a brush, applying it up to her eyelid... —In a large case.

—That's a lot of eye—

—This is different, okay? A whopping great statue plopped in the middle of a central hallway.

—So say something.

—What?

—Stand up and say what's on your mind.

—Oh please.

—What are they going to do? Fire you? When Ian returns from Italy take him out for lunch and—

—Take him out for, I'd like to... leaving it unsaid as she grimaces, targeting her cheek for blush... —He signed off on the installation without ever laying eyes on the lion.

—Either say something or suck it up.

—I'm allowed to vent, okay? I'm allowed to air my feelings.

—Why not air them to his face?

She opens the medicine cabinet, takes out a cotton swab, and carefully fixes her eye shadow, blending the color.

—Take a sip of this... David holds out his wineglass... —It might relax you.

—Don't you ever feel like you've had it with lies, lying by omission and whatever?

He takes back his glass, his expression unreadable. She watches David; he watches his wine.

—Excuse me... pushing past... —I have to find a barrette.

6:59 p.m.

—Thanks... accepting the paper plate, yanking a bunch of napkins from the silver dispenser, too many, as always. And she can never get the extra ones back in.

Running naked down the state highway. The man behind the counter wipes his hands on his apron and reaches across a plastic fern to turn up the volume. *In the middle of the day,* he lip-synchs, heartfelt, hand on his chest.

Katherine grabs a jar of red pepper flakes, and turns to find a table. Beneath a grease-spattered poster of the Coliseum, a teenager has his arms stretched along the back of a booth, legs spread obscenely wide, as if to advertise a pair of horse-sized testicles. He juts his chin at her, an invitation, and she turns away.

Give me your heart I'll give you mine first.

At a square table a family of four eats in defeated silence. The father glances up at Katherine, tonguing his teeth.

Give me your time and I'll give you

7:00 p.m.

My trust. And we're buck naked now. Like when we were born.

Sounds like David Byrne. Lucy always loved the Talking Heads. Clive checks his phone for the time. She'll be inflating her travel pillow or drinking a can of Bloody Mary mix. Before Giuliani outlawed dancing in bars, Lucy would go berserk when "Road to Nowhere" came on. She'd pinwheel her arms, go full Pentecostal. One night she wind-piped a Hell's Angel. The gentleman was very decent about it, considering.

When will we find out? And why does it take so long?

Christ, is he going to cry? Feels as if he could, right here and now, start blubbing, the fault of this harrowing—

—Clive?

Song.

7:01 p.m.

He's chewing, taking her in while he finishes. Swallows. And indicates... —Sit.

—No, you're lost in thought.

—I insist.

Sliding into the booth, dropping her paper plate heavy with pizza onto the table and setting the jar of red pepper flakes beside it, wondering if it's too late to sit somewhere else.

—How are you?

—The usual, stumbling around... Katherine reaches for a jar of oregano, raining green onto her slice... —Dragging innocent people into my private hell. I may look like I'm sitting here eating pizza, in fact I'm on the floor, knees to my chest, you know, whimpering.

Clive wipes his hands on a paper napkin, throws it on the table and leans back... —I read the paper this morning. Is that why? Bastovic?

—Partly.

—What happened?

—No idea. I thought it was a lock. We spent an entire weekend playing bocce, forcing down his child bride's pink chicken, pretending to swim. Giselle can't get her hair wet. And he goes and gives his entire archive to the Met?

—And that spells trouble for you?

—Depends.

—On?

—A decision I make. If I go one way, they can't fire me. It would be discrimination... Katherine picks up her slice... —They can't terminate you if you're pregnant... reading his face... —Oh my god, you're doing the math.

—Certainly not.

—That was eight months ago... she takes a bite... —I'd be out to here.

—I assure you I wasn't. Anyway, congratulations. Or, contingent congratulations?

—Contingent thanks... chewing, observing a couple at the counter ordering, suddenly aware of Clive watching her... —What?... she turns back.

Those unfairly blue eyes. He shakes his head.

—I never really trusted Bastovic... Katherine sets down her slice and licks her fingers... —What kind of artist lives in a place with bare walls? Nothing about the guy makes sense. I think his first wife was the real genius. When she died, so did his designs.

—You're inventing now?

—Doesn't make it not true. Fitzgerald used to copy chunks of Zelda's diaries into his novels and when she complained, threw her in the bug-house. There was a crushed quality to Bastovic's first wife, I met her once. She died from a head injury, which is obviously... reaching for the red pepper flakes... —Suspect.

—So now he's killed her?

—Right, that doesn't make sense. He was dependent on her ideas. I don't know what I believe... Katherine finishes pelting her slice with pepper flakes and replaces the jar... —I guess I don't want to get fired. I mean, if I decide not to... she points toward her abdomen.

—And when do you make this decision?

—Soon.

—If it's any consolation, the science says you'll be exactly as happy either way.

—But won't I be happier... picking up the pizza... —Knowing I won't die alone?

—We all die alone.

—Yes, but I'd have a son or daughter holding my hand.

—Not if your son or daughter is doing ten to fifteen, or robbed you blind and fled to South America or... Clive glances up at the television... —Less dramatically, hates you for no reason. As some do.

Katherine sets down the oily slice she's massacred with oregano and red pepper. Again, the bitter sensation rises in her throat. Her stomach is a Jacuzzi of acid. Not from pregnancy, not from nausea. It's the indecision. Bubbling up, refusing to be ignored.

—Alright there?

—Late... standing up, wiping her hands on a napkin... —Gotta go.

He grabs her hand... —Wait.

Reflexively, she starts to pull away. Then softens. There's a sadness to Clive, a gravity that wasn't there before.

—Have a coffee with me... pressing his thumb into the back of her hand... —Next week.

—If I still work there.

—Even if you don't.

—Sure.

—That doesn't sound genuine... he won't let go.

—I will, really.

—We can talk.

—Yeah, coffee, I know how it works... gently she extracts her hand.

—Katie.

But she has to go. She has a dress to put on.

7:08 p.m.

—What would I what?... struggling to clip the barrette closed...
—Think of what?

—Sketching again. You used to sketch when we walked around Rome, remember?

—Barely.

—You were so happy drawing.

—I was twenty-five, of course I was happy, I was a moron.

—But, Iona, haven't you noticed, I mean, look, I know it sounds, whatever, but since I've been working on my play I have a new, I don't know, it's as if I have a sense of purpose or—

—I have a sense of purpose, David. We have a child, for one... gathering strands and retwisting her chignon.

—But, when I'm writing...

—I hate the theater.

—So you've said, but you don't.

—I hate how audiences giggle and snicker through the whole play because no one can stand to go unheard for a single second.

—Everyone... smiling patiently over his wine... —Hates that.

—I swore I wouldn't go back after they chuckled through *Lear*... shaking out her hair to start over.

—So you're going to skip my opening night... David makes a face suggesting he's in on the joke while at the same time wildly hopeful he will, one day, have such a thing.

—It should bother you that only rich people can afford tickets and how much they love plays about racism or the struggles of the working class or anything they don't have to like actually live through.

From David comes a raspy sound, almost, but not quite, a sigh.

—Is that what your play's about? A shopworn struggle?

—No... watching her try to again close the barrette... —It isn't. Would you like help with that?

—I'm fine.

The hair clip continues to fight Iona and she continues to fight the impulse to hurl it like a throwing star. Finally the barrette closes. Iona steps back from the mirror, adjusting her décolletage. David sets his glass on the bureau and comes to put his arms around her, exhaling warm wine breath.

Iona tries not to flinch.

—When are you going to wear this for me?... he buries his face in her neck... —Let's have a date night. Go to a fancy restaurant.

—Like the place we went with Kent and Gail? Your close friends. They seem to know a lot about your life.

David releases her and stands back. Does something to the sleeve of his glass-holding hand, folds it back or arranges it in some special way... —When do your rings come back from cleaning?

—Not sure. I won't kiss you goodbye, lipstick will smudge.

She slips past him, switching down the hall, hoisting the top of her dress. Strapless, her first. In the kitchen Emily stands in the maw of the open refrigerator, scornfully assessing its contents.

—Emily.

—Uh-huh.

—Tell me what you think.

Reluctantly Emily closes the door to the fridge, holding a tub of cream cheese in one hand. Oddly unsurprised to see her mother in a ballgown. A slow, cold appraisal... —Where'd you get that weird dress?

—I borrowed, what do you mean weird? How is it weird?

—I don't know. There's a lot of material.

—It's a classic design. Dior.

—Okay.

—Classic.

—Whatever. Calm down... Emily rips the lid off the tub and smells the cream cheese... —It's just my opinion.

—Get your nose out of there.

—Wot 'appened to the 'ummus?

Iona doesn't mention that the accent Emily has been practicing sounds more Oirish than Cockney and that her drama teacher should be working harder to fix it.

—Mum? Did you finish the 'ummus?

Iona wills herself to say it, fuck the hummus, say it, fuck the...

—Lock the door behind me... she wheels around, goes into the hallway, pulls a coat from the rack, and leaves.

She's never asked why the school chose *My Fair Lady* as the fall musical given that it ends with Eliza Doolittle having to choose between life with an abusive tyrant or utter destitution. Off she trots to fetch his slippers! What kind of message is that for a teenage girl?

7:15 p.m.

The elevator opens directly onto the small private lobby of the Tindall-Clark apartment where Eleanor's assistant waits. With her triangular skirt, flat-ironed hair, and coat-hanger shoulders, Jenifer looks two-dimensional.

—So how are you?... Benjamin tries to smile... —It's been a long—

—Follow me, please.

Obediently, Benjamin follows, wiping his hand on his pants, heart drilling in his chest. Horrified to notice, on the front of his shirt, the ghost of this morning's lentil stain.

A battalion of Marlon's marble lions used to run the length of this hallway, leaving only a narrow alley to walk along. It was always a precarious negotiation, the journey to the living room. But the lions have vanished.

—Look who's come to see us... Mrs. Tindall-Clark walks toward him, hands outstretched. She's shockingly thin. Benjamin can't believe how thin. And unsteady. Wearing a floor-length gown covered with shimmering beads which seems far too heavy for her emaciated frame...

—You disappeared on me... she takes his hands, clouding Benjamin in old-lady perfume, as she leans forward and kisses him on the cheek...

—Naughty boy.

—I wrote, you got my—

—Yes, of course I did, sit down, I'm teasing. I'd offer you a cocktail but we're on our way out. Maybe a glass of mineral water... nodding at Jenifer waiting flatly in the doorway.

—Sorry if I interrupted.

—You should be sorry about disappearing to study movies.

He feels his face get hot... —It was kind of a rash decision.

—Weren't we doing good work together?

—Yes, ma'am.

—I don't know if you heard but our water project was a great success... she goes to the mantelpiece, where she picks up an earring... —After a few stumbles, of course... and fixes it in her ear... —It's so difficult to work around the local bureaucracies, but you remember that. All the time we spent huddled over paperwork, gosh it is good to see you, Benjamin... another earring, another ear... —Your hair is different.

—There's less of it.

—Well, that's life, isn't it? Sit down, please. I'll sit too, will that help?

They sit next to each other in upholstered chairs. Nestled between the chairs is a low table displaying a silver cigarette box and a carved African head. He remembers the Tindall-Clark apartment as a minefield of dangerous knick-knacks. There was always some provocative trinket you were being asked to overlook. Like a disembodied black head.

Eleanor waits for him to speak. On the other side of the room Boris lies on the windowsill, tail swishing. Decrepit beast must be at least twenty. The cat gets up and stretches, bowing between his front legs and leaning back to present Benjamin with his ass.

—Here... Jenifer, abruptly holding out a tall glass of seltzer with a square napkin wrapped around it.

Benjamin accepts it gladly despite the unpleasant sensation that his throat is closing and he's moments away from suffocating. He watches Jenifer leave the room. There's no way to spin this request to make it sound halfway normal.

—So.

—I'm in trouble.

—Oh dear.

—I didn't mean to, I don't know exactly how it happened but I was in Ohio, as you know, in grad school, and I needed money for my second year. Financial aid, it's a long story, my timing was off. So I asked around, found a local guy to lend me twenty thousand dollars. For a year I made the payments regularly, every other Monday. I had a couple of jobs, working as a TA and cleaning the library, only, when I finished school, after graduation, I skipped town. Never told him. That sounds bad, right, I know, unethical, but I had no money left for the move and I needed cash for a deposit on an apartment here. Nothing fancy, a crappy walk-up with leaking windows. I don't know what I was thinking. That he'd forget about me? Well, he didn't. This afternoon the guy shows up at the Museum, the guy who lent me money, and, Mrs. Tindall-Clark, he was not happy, in fact, I'd say he is pretty displeased. He's insisting on eight grand by the end of the week or else he'll, I mean, I'm pretty sure he'll put a hit out on me.

At the words "hit out" Eleanor's fingers fly to her earlobe, where she calms herself by confirming the security of her sparkly earring.

—It would only be a loan, of course. I'm sorry, I'm incredibly embarrassed, but I have no one else. I don't know anyone with, you know, that kind of money.

Silence.

Eleanor can't look at him. She stares at the uncurtained window where Boris contemplates the night. Benjamin curses everything that's brought him here. He had potential once. At eight he was a whiz at math, knew all the flags and dazzled grown-ups with his drawings of horses.

—Let me see if I understand... Eleanor searches his face... —You would like me to give you eight thousand dollars.

—God, no, not give, Mrs. Tindall-Clark, lend. Lend. And not even eight. A couple of thousand should get the guy off my back, give me some breathing room so I could, I don't know, take out a bank loan?

—You have a job now, isn't that right?... she speaks slowly, with a girlish lilt.

—Yes, at the Museum, a great job, film curator. But I don't get paid until—

—And how do you think you got that job, Benjamin?

—I beg your pardon?

—Your job, how did you acquire it?

—I applied. I guess I don't understand the question.

—You never wondered why the Museum would hire a newly minted PhD, a young person with no accomplishments to speak of, to run their film department? Some nobody waltzing in from grad school in Michigan?

—Ohio.

—Why would they do such a thing? Out of charity?

—I mean, I thought I had a pretty good interview.

—You did have a pretty good interview, Benjamin. You had a pretty good interview because Tony Thackeray told me you were applying and I strongly advised Diane to hire you.

—You know Professor Thackeray?

—We have people in common.

Benjamin tries to process this information... —But, I mean, they wouldn't have hired me if—

—For over thirty years Marlon and I have been the Museum's most reliable benefactors.

He places his water glass on the table and stands.

—Sit down, Benjamin.

He sits.

—I tell you this not so you might question your credentials or your right to be there, but to demonstrate that I have helped you in exactly the way I was supposed to help. Not by handing over my wallet as if I were being mugged in an alleyway but by picking up the phone... she lifts Benjamin's water glass from where it sweats beside the troubling African head and places it on a coaster.

—If I'd known I would have sent a note or a box of chocolates.

—I don't need chocolates, Benjamin.

—But you have my gratitude, enormous gratitude, you must know that.

—When we worked together, do you remember, we'd sit at the dining room table with our laptops, brainstorming and emailing, coaxing my friends to write large checks. Do you recall how badly you wanted to go over? Nothing very useful could be done on the ground in Kaolack and we had people in the field. You and I were doing good work here in my dining room, yet all you talked about was going over, going over. I thought you must have some vision of yourself in a flak jacket surrounded by grateful villagers. I couldn't believe it when Mr. Thackeray said you were applying for a job at the Museum. My Benjamin? There must be some mistake. The Benjamin I knew had a far grander idea of himself than working nine-to-five.

—I mean, it's hardly corporate or.

—I got you the job because I heard you wanted the job and I consider you a friend. But what is all this with money lenders and men threatening you? Putting a hit out. This isn't real life, Benjamin. What are you doing?

—I have no idea.

—Flailing around.

—Pretty much.

—Why aren't you in Hollywood becoming a film director?

—You say that like it's a breeze to up and start directing. You need connections, financial backing—

—You're scared.

—Yes, ma'am.

Eleanor stands and glides across the room, her gown whispering against the carpet. When she reaches the door she turns, hand on the knob... —I'm sorry to say, Benjamin, the risks you're taking are not the useful ones... and out she goes, pulling the door shut behind her.

Benjamin sits in the chair, small and still. He's lost all notion of time. How long has he been here? An hour? Ten minutes? He can hear murmuring in the hallway outside. The cat turns his head, regarding Benjamin with a cold stare.

—What?

Boris blinks slowly several times before returning to his rumination. Even the cat is disgusted with him. Nothing in Benjamin's life suggests he is worthy. The job he was so proud of landing was handed to him as a favor. He takes the wrong risks. He lost Caroline. His mother never calls. Bathing in this pity soup feels delicious. He's an odious human being, the very worst, there's no way around it.

After a few minutes, half an hour, a decade, the door swings open and Mrs. Tindall-Clark walks in holding a cream envelope.

Benjamin stands and picks up his backpack.

—Be careful, it's cash... she hands him the envelope... —Two thousand dollars. I'd have to speak to Marlon about a figure as sizable as eight and he's in no mood. He's been going down the street every morning for kouign-amann and now he can't button his tuxedo trousers.

With a weak smile, Benjamin unzips his bag and stuffs the envelope under a sweater and his new-employee paperwork... —Enzo said you weren't well. I'm sorry. I hope you feel better soon.

—How kind... she smiles as if she's tired of people hoping things... —Good night, Benjamin.

—Good night.

Jenifer appears and he follows her silently back down the lionless hallway. She closes the door without saying goodbye, leaving Benjamin to take the elevator down to the lobby. With his remaining strength he bids Enzo a cordial good night. Then Benjamin continues on, into the October evening where the apple smell of fall hangs in the air and leaves rustle in the gutter and dance down the street, borne by the breeze.

7:33 p.m.

Niko sucks on his inhaler as he paces the Events kitchen. Stopping to urge his Mattituck soldiers onward as he tries to keep the food prep from going entirely off the rails.

—Again, don't stack those tartlets. The bottoms get soggy.

Uneasy lies the head that wears the crown. In sixth grade Niko chose the monologue for drama class. For extra credit he cut a sword out of cardboard, covered it in foil and stuck it through his belt. He always dreaded coming to the line, *O thou dull god why liest thou with the vile in loathsome beds.* All those *th*'s were a real test for his dental work.

—You, what's your name?

—Alex?... the young man is about twenty-five with a pierced ear that's become infected.

—Alex, tell me, have you ever worked with goose liver?

—Yes, Chef.

—Then why does that foie look like feces?

Alex considers... —Because it's brown?

Before Nikolic can respond, there's a loud crash followed by a cry. He whips around in time to see the swinging door bounce off the face of a shy redhead. A sweaty man storms into the room.

Emerson.

He's bending apologetically to the girl clutching her nose... —Oh honey, are you... but he stops himself, turns gruff... —Who the fuck's running this clown parade?

Niko raises his hand.

—Peša?... Emerson walks over... —Is this a fucking joke? The guy who underseasons and crowds his pans? Hell's Otto?

—Puking, Chef. At home.

—So we're left with Nikolic Peša running the kitchen... on a normal day Emerson has the crimson complexion that comes from prolonged exposure to heat but, right now, his face is inching dangerously toward eggplant... —I hired you hoping talent ran in the family, your brother hot shit out in California. They told me your wife offed herself so I—

—Heart attack, Em, it was—

—showed some compassion.

—cardiomyopathy.

—Where's the loyalty? Peša, I thought, will have my back. He'll quit in protest. But here you are, first in line to take my job. Ingrate. Take off that toque, you fucking ingrate.

Nikolic tosses the hat. He doesn't care enough to argue with Emerson. An hour ago he wrenched his back slipping on a patch of hollandaise. All he wants is a hot shower and a pack of frozen peas for his coccyx. Confident Emerson couldn't have found out about Niko's special, conceivably poisonous, seasoning, he's happy to let Em berate him and leave so Niko can get on with his night.

—You think I didn't check those shrimp were fresh?... Emerson gives Niko a hard shove, sending him into the stainless steel counter.

—Hey! Don't push. Why are you pushing me?

—There was nothing. Wrong. With. The shrimp.

—Yeah, and I told them that, Em. I said it could be a number of—

—Shut the fuck up.

—The walk-in, I said, maybe the thermometer was off, gave a faulty reading.

At a prep station, Emerson picks up a cleaver. With his thumb he tests the sharpness of the blade.

—And what about the purveyor I asked what do we know about the temperature of Rizzo's truck?

Emerson tosses down the cleaver and picks up a chef's knife.

—Everyone knows Rizzo's... with his eyes on the knife, Niko positions himself between Emerson and the Mattituck crew, as if he means to take a bullet for his men... —Incompetent, hey, Em, want to put down the knife?

—What the?... distracted, Emerson surveys the tray of mushroom tartlets... —Why are these stacked?

—Those are being remade, Chef, as we—

—SHUT UP... Emerson whips around, holding the knife under Niko's chin... —I got fired.

Shut up? Nikolic stares into the purpling features of his former boss with the sort of bone-deep weariness that gives rise to unsound ideas. Shut up? This is what he gets after the hours and insomnia, the pressure and kowtowing, the complaints about early-morning smells from the jackass in #3F, the hateful *Hello my fren'* from the deli guy downstairs? Jimmy showing up wanting favors, goading him to death. Shut up? No.

Emerson brings down the knife and suddenly, seemingly without electing to, Niko lunges, hitting Em hard, shoulder into chest, spatch-cocking him, sending the chef's knife skating across the floor as Emerson falls backward, hitting and catapulting the tray of foie snacks. In a rain of liver Nikolic throws himself on top of Emerson, trying to pin him down. But Emerson struggles, pitching and twisting, fuck he's strong and, really, none of these Long Island motherfuckers can jump in? Punching wildly, Niko catches Em on the jaw, christ that hurts, don't break your chopping hand. He tries again, this time a slap like a fucking schoolgirl. But Emerson ducks and twists, his head lowered, angling to get his hands around Niko's neck, grabbing blindly while Niko hammers Emerson's temple with the bottom of his fist as if he's pummeling the wall of a noisy neighbor, screaming a karate-ish *Hi-ya* with every thump. Undaunted by the flurry of erratic punches, Emerson manages to get hold of Niko's throat. He starts squeezing. Tighter and tighter. The room starts to dim. As Niko feels the strength leave his body, he hears the distant sound of a familiar voice. Emerson lets go. And Niko opens his eyes.

—Oh, okay. The brother... Emerson gets up, stumbling backward, tripping over Nikolic's sprawled legs and pitching heavily against the lowboy.

Jimmy reaches out his hand but Niko ignores it, coughing for breath, scrambling to his feet... —I had him. I didn't need you, I had him.

—What's up, man?... Emerson, righting himself, sounding almost awestruck... —I've been to your place in San Diego... on the syllable *go* he flings his arm around Niko's neck compressing it with the crook of his elbow... —Big fan of the three cheese maca... he pants in Niko's ear... —Roni.

—Thanks, but... Jimmy grabs a pair of tongs from the counter and poleaxes Emerson in the armpit.

—Fuck!... releasing Niko, Emerson roundhouses Jimmy with his free arm... —Sorry... adding a testicle-aimed mule-kick for good measure... —Caught us at a bad time.

Jimmy staggers back, recoiling as Emerson throws Nikolic to the ground and pins him down. There's a muscle-memory speed to Em's dispatch of these moves. Varsity wrestler? MMA fan? Niko struggles to break Emerson's hold, and in his frenzy sees the kitchen door swing open to reveal a pair of black-suited legs.

—Okay, guys, settle down. I don't want any sudden movements... a woman's voice, commanding but calm... —This is the Chief Security Officer speaking.

Instantly, Emerson releases Niko, rolling off him onto the floor. Niko stays where he is, flat on his back gazing up at the Black woman for further instructions.

—Why don't you... she motions to Nikolic... —Go ahead and stand up.

Niko obeys, lurching to the safety of the wall, pressing himself against it, brain rattling in his skull. He grips his wrist, which has started to throb. Oddly, his lower back feels a lot better.

The security guard moves toward Emerson holding a set of white zip ties... —Roll onto your front there, friend.

Emerson flops over, pulling himself into a sort of sprinter's crouch.

—I didn't say kneel. On your stomach.

With a terrifying cry, Emerson pops to his feet and dives toward the guard. In a flash, she drops the flex cuffs, steps aside, snatches his arm, twists it, and brings it down sharply against her thigh. He screams, crumpling back down to the floor.

—And here I thought I asked you nicely... she picks up the cuffs, yoking them tightly around Emerson's wrists.

Emerson, fetal, snotty and cuffed, lies immobile. His eyes are glassy and staring, as if he's reviewing the circumstances that led to this moment.

—Your arm's not broken. Might feel like it is, but it isn't... she crosses the room, picks up the chef's knife lying on the floor, looks at it and calls out... —Okay, guys. *Guys?*

Two uniformed security guards charge through the door, barreling over each other to get at the action.

—Calmly.

Elated, her men haul Emerson to his feet.

—Careful, looks like he may've hurt his arm.

—What'd you do, Chief? Knock the fuck outta him?

—I can't imagine why you're cursing... the security officer reads a text on her phone, types one back... —Remember where you are, please... glancing up... —Escort this gentleman to the holding cell on minus two.

The guards prop Emerson between them. As he leaves, Emerson seems almost relieved. He doesn't look back.

—Holy shit... oh, okay, so *now* the catering staff comes to life, talking over each other, full of... —Oh my god... and... —Did you see... and... —I'm texting my boyfriend... and... —What a psycho.

—Shay Pallot... she places her hand gently on Nikolic's arm... —Chief Security Officer, as I mentioned... speaking in a low voice... —You did well. Go wash your face now.

—I'll do that too, wash my face... Jimmy breathing hard, affecting exertion... —Whew, boy. Guy was strong.

But Shay Pallot doesn't take her eyes off Niko... —If you need someone to talk to, I'm here all night. Extension three-oh-one, they'll patch you through. Otherwise it looks like you've got a lot of food to make and some people here... indicating with a nod... —In need of leadership, understand what I'm saying?

—Yes, ma'am.

—Go on with your night now... addressing the goofs from Long Island... —Might ask for a statement from some of you shortly... and she strides out through the swinging doors.

Nikolic picks a tray up off the floor and sets it on the counter, hand still throbbing. With his other palm, he flattens out his chef's coat where it remains bunched up from Emerson's grip. The remaining foie bites still look like shit.

7:48 p.m.

We're all sort of revolting, Henry thinks, as he scrapes dried chocolate off his tuxedo cuff with a letter opener. We're essentially cavemen, what with our shitting and puking and scraping food off our clothes. In our dying. Henry's last run-in with death was burying Maude out in Montauk. He dug her grave, buckled her into a thundershirt, and set squeaky toys by her head. It was sadder than he guessed, losing the dog. Alone, he wept. She'd been a part of their lives for so long.

Henry takes a clean handkerchief from the desk drawer and wipes off the letter opener. Fashioned to resemble a Napoleonic sword, it was a Father's Day gift from Kim when she was nine or ten. While he unwrapped it she bounced impatiently and spun in a circle. Henry was being persnickety about unsticking the tape, striving to preserve the silver paper printed over and over with the words *world's best daddy*. It stayed in his desk drawer for years. Despite being several furlongs from anyone's idea of a good daddy, not to mention the world's best, his daughter thought he was doing okay.

7:50 p.m.

Shay's first instinct was to grab a gun. Trespasser demonstrating malicious intentions, Malcolm radioed about the chef bulldozing through the employee entrance, using the curiously formal tone he adopts at work, as if the job requires a concision or haste that leaves no time for articles, definite or indefinite. Trespasser? Shay went for the safe. The combination has been etched in her memory for twenty years. It's a sequence she knows as readily as her social security number. But not today. She stared at the safe, feverish, skin tingling. Not a hot flash this time, but pure adrenaline. Digits popped up, one after the other in rapid succession and varying order. But Shay knew none of them were correct. She left the gun safe for the bank of monitors, trying to pinpoint the intruder's location, willing the numbers to come. But her mind was full of static. Glaring at this gallery, that hallway, the mezzanine. As she scanned the screens she ran through digit after digit with mounting frustration, betraying none of it to her staff. Time was running out. Then Amber screamed. There! she pointed to a monitor. There he is! And so Shay sprinted toward the Events kitchen empty-handed, positive only of one thing. Her time at the Museum was over.

7:52 p.m.

—Walked in, cool as day, and kicked some fucking, hey, you're in like a stupor... Jimmy snaps his fingers... —I'm talking about that security guard. Seriously hot.

—Shut up. God, please, just.

—Get your head straight, Niko, I'm appreciating a powerful woman. She cracked Pitt's arm like it was kindling. Foxy Brown, am I right?

—That's racist.

—Is it buddy, the fuck would you know?

Niko walks away, across the Events kitchen to the prep sinks. He wants to focus on his heroics, replay the moment he stepped between a knife-wielding nutjob and the terrified kitchen crew.

On the subway this morning Niko spent half his commute trying to gauge the exact percentage of a straphanger's sneeze he had intercepted, assessing the angle of the spray, its spread and velocity. Nervously calculating his odds of getting sick. But tonight he has proved to be more than a germ-fearing nebbish in soft pants.

—Hey... one of the caterers from Mattituck is standing in front of him, whiskers bundled in a beardnet like a knot of trawled dulse... —Here... holding out the toque Niko threw to the floor... —I brushed it off for you. Should be fine.

He has earned the respect of his men. Yeah, you heard. Go call the Earls of Surrey and Warwick.

7:54 p.m.

As soon as she rounds the corner and starts down the hallway Diane senses something is wrong. Sounds coming from the Great Hall are strangely muffled and faraway and appear to become more muted the closer she gets. And when she reaches the hall, it takes Diane several minutes to understand what it is she's looking at.

The entire space has been stuffed with a boggling assortment of beanbags, daybeds, hammocks and leather footstools. All draped in a blizzard of patterns. Stripes fight florals, paisleys crowd out swirls. Pergolas drip with tassels and beads. Where there wasn't previously a nook or cranny, nooks and crannies have been created. Clashing kilims cover the marble floor. Bolts of diaphanous tenting hang from the ceiling, softening the light and piling onto the general confusion. There's a sense of motion, of shuttering and flickering, as if the whole room is going in and out of focus. Searching for safe harbor, the eye of a guest might land on the thirty-foot lava lamp sculpted from thousands of white daisies that stands in the middle of the room before realizing it is, unmistakably and quite distressingly, the spitting image of a giant penis.

Conrad's initial drawings and schematics did not allow for this degree of madness. And while Diane walked through the hall two or three times this morning, the final blitz of textiles must have occurred while she was up on the roof with Z and couldn't temper Conrad's vision.

After closing her eyes briefly to compose herself, Diane sets off toward the main entrance where a sea of black tuxes and gauzy dresses is beginning to form. Among them will be guest of honor fashion designer Anton Spitz, undoubtedly still pissed he couldn't bring his dog. Diane holds her breath as she penetrates a particularly dense billow of nag champa being pumped out by a Ganesh-shaped diffuser. She was outvoted on the incense. Conrad swayed the organizing committee by repeating the words olfactory delight until the idiots hooted and clapped like a bunch of cymbal-bashing monkeys. No one paid any attention when Diane suggested that incense would have the place smelling like high mass on Sunday and was that, really, going to impart the chill vibe they were hoping for.

—Hey... Chris rushes up. He takes her elbow and speaks ticklingly in her ear... —I've assigned an intern to follow-slash-escort Tiz Sericko around the event this evening... guiding her toward the entrance... —That person is under strict instruction to basically throw herself between Dr. Sericko and the questionable lion should he at any point approach it. Plus, the bar's been moved and the lighting dimmed.

—Great. Great work, thank you.

—Here he is!... Chris announces, standing back to present Anton.

Anton gives a pretty spin, as if he's presenting an outfit on a catwalk. In lieu of a tie, he wears a silk scarf knotted at his throat. His brown flecked suit is rolled at the cuff to reveal a pair of hospital-white ankles. He looks like a tinker.

—Hello, you... Diane holds out her hands.

The designer finishes closing a small tin and tucks it into his jacket pocket... —Darling... taking her hands, squeezing them... —And who's this?... stepping back, keeping hold of Diane's hands, appraising her dress.

—Lyle Kipsie.

—That sash is, wow, what does Lyle call that color? Apologies again, honey, that we couldn't accommodate you. I found a dress in your size yesterday that would've been perfect but I thought, oh, Anton, it's too late, don't bring it up and cause a whole thing.

—That was extremely kind.

—Have a mint... retrieving the tin from his pocket.

—Is it drugs?

—No, it's a mint.

—I'll resist, thank you.

—Mr. Spitz... Chris places his hand on the designer's back... —Let's find you a drink before the guests arrive.

Firmly he steers the designer toward the bar and Diane turns to the trustees, grinning and air-kissing to save her lipstick. Cheek-pecking when no escape is possible.

Rosey Rosenbloom pushes past, heading to the bar with his fund-raising wife who wears a gossamer Spitz gown so flimsy and ethereal she's one strong breeze from complete nudity. Arriving behind the pair is the team from Noizy. The firm's president, Alessandro, has one arm flung awkwardly around the shoulders of his much taller head designer, james.

—Alessandro, welcome.

—Your people never got back to me... Alessandro allows his cheek to be kissed... —I'm not happy about the size of the Noizy logo.

—Oh dear, well, I'm sorry to hear it, hello, james... directing her attention to the malignant goth standing beside him.

The designer nods since a deep ennui makes speaking too arduous. He's sixty or so, with jet black hair scraped into a pompadour that shivers when he moves. james's career in high-end couture ended when photos emerged of the designer standing by a bonfire, lit like the devil, dispensing sieg heils like business cards. Fortunately for james, Italian fast fashion was untroubled by his ugly behavior, even relishing the controversy.

—What do you gentlemen think of the lava lamp? Isn't it marvelous?

The men shrug, mutter, and escape into a clutch of trustees.

Nod, smile, kiss. Don't think about Dominic. Nod, smile, kiss.

—Here we are again... diaper tycoon Norm Whitstuff brushes Diane's ear with his lips... —Another year over... evidently resenting Diane for time's passage.

Norm's wife, floating lethargically next to him, presses her breast-bone to show off her rings. One result of Chris's enthusiasm for facts is the knowledge that beneath Debbie's hand beats a heart fed by pig valves.

Having exhausted his quota of harmless observations, Norm wanders off, grumbling inaudibly like a wind-up toy, mistrusting pleasure as a form of socialism or an insidious plan to separate him from his money.

All these fucking traitors, Diane smiles a radiant smile of welcome, these malevolent power brokers and sore winners the Museum depends on to run. Artless and smarmy, sporting uninspired evening wear, whispering their terrible plans in low voices. But I shouldn't despise them. And she thinks back to her Pilates teacher who always recommended compassion when he wasn't addressing her sphincter.

A number of arriving older men appear visibly alarmed by the hippie drift, the anarchic mess of pattern, a blanket sense of disorder. A few of them have hit on the unfortunate idea of wearing bell-bottoms, failing to grasp that the gala is not a costume party, that one's outfit should be a contemporary take on the theme, not a literal embodiment of it. The men look lost and uncomfortable in their poet-sleeves and scarves, staring around the hall as if wondering how their attendance tonight might result in some horrible, difficult to predict consequence.

Diane leans forward to accept a cheek kiss from Evan Chessanof, her favorite trustee, who has possibly misunderstood the evening's theme and wears, angled lewdly on his head, a red velvet tarboosh.

Straightening, she spots Henry coming around the corner from the elevator bank. He stops by the entrance to Egypt, and holds his phone straight-armed before him, squinting at the screen. A surge of relief, even love, courses through her. Henry knows Dominic. He'll assess the situation impartially. Good old Henry.

8:07 p.m.

Shay watches Diane walk past at a serious clip, making a beeline toward Egypt in a big green dress. Determined and inaccessible. Not the time for a briefing on Emerson Pitt and the Events kitchen scuffle. Instead Shay takes out her phone, composes a brief but calm text and presses send. As she does, a message pops up from Rob.

Need you at East asap

Texting *on my way*, Shay crosses the hall and goes out through the arched doorway. She passes Purdue and the fake lion, walks around the corner, and down the short hallway to the VIP side entrance.

Marc with a C is positioned beside the magnetometer guiding guests toward and through it, offering his hand to elderly ladies. Around the corner Rob waits with two men. The so-called bodyguard Shay met in the elevator a few hours ago and a tall man of Southeast Asian descent. Nice teeth, ugly waistcoat. A necklace with feathers.

—Z Willington, special guest of Diane's... the man in the waistcoat sticks out his hand, bringing it down when Shay ignores it... —And this is my bodyguard, Liam.

—We've met... turning to Rob... —What's the problem?

—Bodyguard's got a briefcase... Rob indicates... —I told him we don't allow nothing but phones and small purses. He says as a potential donor or whatever he's allowed.

—What I said was—

—No... Shay shakes her head and the Willington man stops speaking... —What's inside the case?

—Digital projector.

—Follow me... Shay leads the two men around the corner, swiping them into the back offices. She points to a darkened conference room... —If you would... following them in, flipping on the lights... —Unlatch the case... indicating the table... —And remove the contents.

The man called Liam sets the briefcase on the table, pops it open and takes out what appears to be a projector.

Motioning to an outlet... —Plug it in and turn it on, please.

He does. And it is indeed a digital projector.

—And you're bringing this into the gala, why?

—Last-minute video installation... the man called Z, speaking like someone who is rarely contradicted.

Shay looks from one to the other. Did these two really think the Chief of Security wouldn't be wise to every detail of the night's schedule: the number of guests and musicians, the quantity of canapés, the conditions of the restrooms? Can they possibly believe she wasn't consulted about a video installation? The fake bodyguard squeezes his eyelashes. Earlier today he stood in Musical Instruments and spoke of burning the museum to the ground. So this is how he plans to do it. With a film.

For thirty years this job has saved Shay. It saved her when William died, when Carl got restless and had an affair. They worked through his mistake, salvaged the marriage. The constant throughout has been the routine, the power of her own fiefdom, the respect of her staff, the guards who loved her and hated her but always came back to visit, plying her with cupcakes and picture frames. But the Museum has never let Shay forget she is an outsider. It forced her to endure years of perky condescension. Made her wait years to be promoted. Allowed the disrespect of fools like Tapestry Todd. Even Henry Joles couldn't follow through with one small favor. Shay thinks back to the phone call with Diane, how she seized Shay's home as if it was just one more thing to cross off her to-do list.

—All about the art, right?... Z unplugs the projector.

Shay studies him, this smiling man with brown skin, in too much of a hurry for a full name. What has he been through.

—Doesn't the night require art?... he stares at Shay, willing her to join their game.

The bodyguard takes the projector from Z and packs it back into the case. Shay watches him snap the latches closed. The men look at her expectantly. Her heart is pounding high in her chest, almost in her throat. Ten or so years ago, visiting Belize, she and Carl hiked to a waterfall where tourists lined up to jump over the falling water and into the pool below. One by one they took the plunge. Carl lost his nerve and turned away. They were in a fight. Carl had forgotten the camera Shay reminded him several times to pack. She was snippy and annoyed and when it was her turn, she balanced on the rock that served as a diving board and thought, let the whole world go to hell.

—Art certainly belongs in a museum... she hears herself say, leaping into the void.

—Yes... Z smiles, all those teeth... —It certainly does.

8:17 p.m.

—You look upset.

Diane pulls Henry into the darkened gallery where they can hide in the shadows.

—What's wrong?... he lets himself be pulled... —Is it about the massive dildo?

—It's a lava lamp... positioning Henry so she can see the arriving guests over his shoulder but remain hidden from view... —I had a call from Dominic.

—And what? He's not coming?

—Not only not coming. Leaving me.

—Leaving, like leaving?

—Yes, gone. End of discussion. Done.

—Marriage over?

—That's what he said.

—No.

—Henry, I'm telling you, it's over. Fifteen years... she tries to snap her fingers but can't.

—Because of your London trip?

—I have no, what London trip?

—Back in March. I figured you had a fling. The medievalist. You kept talking about his hair.

—Who, Anthony? Of course I didn't, because I liked his hair? No.

—Talk to him. It'll blow over.

—It won't. You know Dom, he never acts until all the math is in... actively biting her lipstick so she won't cry.

—Weren't you talking about leaving him?

Several weeks ago, as the day was dying down, Henry appeared in her doorway with a bottle of Blanton's. Going by the set of his mouth, he had serious topics on his mind. She found two glasses, sat down, waited. Henry spoke for almost an hour. He described a disappointing pozole, a movie about Queen Victoria he'd seen and hated. All the while, he stroked his stomach absentmindedly, as if his gut were protesting the effort to avoid whatever it was he'd come to discuss. Henry peered into his glass, baffled by his bourbon. Had Diane noticed more dog shit on the streets? Nothing deeper surfaced. So Diane opened up instead. As the booze demanded. Admitted doubts about her marriage, a feeling of being dampened or curtailed.

—So what you wanted... Henry says, with the cruel expression he gets when drumming home a point... —Was to fantasize about leaving Dom but to never actually leave.

—I wanted, I don't know.

—Excitement, freedom, butterflies. This is on you.

—*Me?*

—How's a sensitive man like Dominic not going to pick up on your doubt and ambivalence? Wake up. Did you honor what you had? No. This is what happens when you dither. This is what's left to you.

—Why are you yelling?

—You wanted to be alone, now you're alone. Free to have some space, find yourself, whatever it is you ladies are looking for.

—Ladies?

—Whatever. Women.

—So this is about Olive, or, what, Annie?

—Neither. This is about you acting like a mooning schoolgirl spewing your, whatsit, Virginia Woolf, when the entire time you had a great thing going. Did you hide the money?

—Hide the, jesus, Henry, he only told me an hour ago.

—Here... handing her his glass... —It's water. Get a grip. Dig deep. Then go out there and secure the funding so at least you have a job to get up for.

—I feel like throwing myself off the roof... she sips his tepid seltzer.

—Well, jump on in, the water's fine.

—Last week my friend Elise, remember Elise? You met her at New Year's, gorgeous, but you know, just turned fifty.

—This is relevant, I assume.

—She goes to this bar in her neighborhood, she's lived in Brooklyn for thirty years, goes to this new place with her friend, they walk over to sit at the bar but these two guys in like their early thirties tell them the stools are taken. Elise and her friend look around. There are no drinks on the bar-top or anything, but the guys insist. They point to a booth by the bathroom, tell them to go sit there, acting like they own the place. Elise is a bar hound from way back and she likes to sit at the bar so she's not about to be shunted over to some stupid booth. Then the bartender comes over and says, that's okay, you can sit there. That's when they realize—

—Diane.

—The seats were never taken.

—Stop, please.

—The seats... stepping closer to make her point... —Were never taken. Don't you get it?

—Yeah, I get it. Can we not pile on the despair here?

—These guys decided Elise and her friend weren't hot enough to sit near them so they—

—I get it.

—Tried to force them into a dark corner where their gross fifty-year-old faces wouldn't contaminate—

—DIANE.

—I'm nearly fifty... gripping his sleeve... —I have five years before thirty-year-old men start telling me where I can and can't sit.

—No one's got it easy, okay? I'm like Goya's poky little mutt paddling up a waterfall of shit.

She releases his jacket, patting it back in place.

Henry softens... —Stay with me and Olive. The spare room's got an en suite.

—No... handing him back his glass... —But thank you.

8:26 p.m.

This is the definition of trudging, Benjamin thought as he slunk down Fifth Avenue. Most of the stores he passed were lit up and decorated for Halloween. Kids were dressed as cats and superheroes; their parents looked content, not too beaten by life. One might guess it was soothing, all this autumnal cheer, to a person only minutes from one of the more humiliating ordeals of his life. It was not. It felt as if his skin was being removed with a pair of blunt tweezers. Benjamin had just identified the sensation when he looked up and saw on the corner one of those charmless chain bookstores, the type he usually boycotts for killing off the independents. Tonight the bland fortress was a welcoming beacon; the toys and puzzles were signs of levity instead of the dying gasps of a literate culture. In he went, through the shuzh of sliding doors, up the escalator to the second-floor. He gathered a stack of self-help books, treated himself to a peppermint tea with a chocolate swizzle stick, and camped out in the café. It was all an effort to compose himself. Smoke out a little self-respect. Also, evidently, to eat a cranberry muffin that tasted like a Christmas candle.

Benjamin flipped pages, tested the heat of his ginormous tea, glanced around from time to time at a couple of men sitting bundled in coats and a fortyish woman in lopsided glasses. The guides to self-empowerment were useless. He kept recalling the look on Eleanor's face when he asked her for money. I'm the donkey, Benjamin thought dully, I'm the goddamn donkey.

All the books had the same depressing advice. Act without fear. Waffling is for losers. Decisive action is the only way forward. There were no entries for a bold decision that turns out to be totally fucking stupid. His stomach twisted into an acidic pretzel, his mouth felt like sand. Neither condition was helped by the desiccated muffin.

The woman in glasses began to weep, big silent tears plashed onto her cake plate. When she saw Benjamin watching, she collected her coat and left. A couple of minutes later he grabbed a protein bar and headed home.

Once he's on the subway Benjamin relaxes, soothed by the grimy darkness rattling past. At least he got the money.

8:30 p.m.

They met downstairs at the employee entrance. Clive stepped back to take her in, complimented her dress, appeared to make a conscious effort not to linger on her cleavage. The crisp black of his tuxedo brought out the color in his lips, the alpine cheekbones, and severe shoulders. His eyes sparked with an erotic British cruelty.

When they came to the Great Hall, Clive took her by the elbow. The room was stuffed with furniture and covered in zany fabrics so that the whole space shimmied slightly. It was like viewing a 3-D movie without the proper glasses. Iona kept her eyes glued to her feet, anxious not to trip on the Turkish carpets laid across the marble.

—Fucking Ottoman lobotomy... Clive looked around the room, waiting for her to battle her dress and sit down.

Once she was settled he instructed her not to move and left in search of alcohol. Watching him walk away, Iona pulsed with desire and felt both excited and worried for the night ahead.

She leans back on the velvet fainting couch. Above her, a forest of popped-open parasols form a low ceiling. One could wiggle loose, succumb to gravity. Impaled, she'd have to go home.

—Hey... Katherine collapses next to her, wearing the weird red dress from Archives and a pair of back-breaking heels... —I'm already over this night and it's barely begun.

—Why are you, I mean, are you running around for your boss?

—I'm not doing shit.

—Ah.

—Your eyeshadow looks great. I saw it from over there. What a charade the whole thing is.

—What whole thing?

—Being a woman, I was ma'amed at the pizza place. I mean, how to ruin a night. Guy's all, here you go ma'am and I literally blacked out. Ma'am? I'm thirty-five. Today's been a fuck from beginning to end, I'll spare you the details. I'm afraid if I relive it I'll go into a fugue state and Anton Spitz will have to wait unduly for his second vodka soda which I am supposedly on my way to procure... she makes no move to go.

Frantically Iona tries to think of a clever reply. In the wake of Katherine's tumultuous sexual presence she feels timid and disapproving.

—I saw you come in with European Paintings. Pretty cozy. Sure you're not together?

—God no... Iona holds up her left hand, fanning out her fingers.

—What am I looking at?

She tells Katherine that she forgot, that her rings are out for cleaning but in fact she's married, to which Katherine smiles knowingly, staring past Iona to the room beyond. Her hand plays abstractedly with the material of Iona's dress, where it lies on the couch but also on

Iona's thigh. Katherine reminds her of the women she met when she first moved to New York in her early twenties, a loose gang of self-assured women who wore cheap T-shirts slashed at the neck, men's boots and buckets of mascara that lay clumped on their lashes. Drawing up in a sloppy-jointed wooden bar chair, they spoke with quiet fervor, so close you could smell the whisky on their breath, regarding you intensely, as if everything you said was brand new. It made you feel the chances were fifty-fifty you'd end up in bed with one of them by the end of the night. You might never before have considered a woman in sexual terms but it was impossible not to. They were soft and magnetic and when making a point would graze your scarred knee with a strangely seductive nicotine-stained finger. Often they were Irish girls slumping in corners, pretending to be plain in oversized sweaters but secretly gorgeous with creamy skin and soulful eyes and though fragile-seeming actually quite adamant with their facts and Marxism.

—What about kids? Any kids?

—One. Daughter.

A woman in front of them takes furtive measures to arrange her breasts more attractively.

—She's thirteen.

—Does she hate you yet? I hated my parents at thirteen. Maybe that was fifteen. Actually, now I think about it, I was kind of a hateful child. I hated everyone. My sister. But she was very self-righteous, even at ten. Ever regret it?

—What, having a kid?

Katherine nods, wedging a finger down the side of her shoe to scratch her foot.

—Never. Okay, not so much regret as like. Raising a kid is like every day carrying a piano up a new flight of stairs. There's a lot of navigation, a fear you'll injure it, the understanding that the whole endeavor could kill you. Some days the stairs are spiral and made of glass. Occasionally you get an elevator but it's still a piano and you still have to shift it.

—But in the end you get a piano.

—Exactly.

—Do I need a piano?

—The love is immense. You can't question the love.

Katherine leans in close so Iona can smell her fragrance along with a pleasant dose of body odor... —You don't find it manipulative?

—What, love?

—Nature blasting you with chemicals that stop you from... licking her thumb, reaching out to fix Iona's eyeshadow... —Dumping your kid at the bus station the first time he throws a fish stick at your head... leaning back to check her work... —Parents are all, having a kid re-shaped my heart. It's like, dude, read a book, it's called oxytocin.

She watches Katherine wipe her thumb on the couch... —Kids give you a sense of purpose.

—Okay, well, I could definitely use that.

—You might have a baby?

—I might quit the Museum, move upstate, start a goat farm.

—Don't do that. Goats are disgusting.

—I could see having kids in the country, human kids, I mean. Running around barefoot, three or four, each from a different father.

—They pee in their own mouths, I heard. Goats.

Katherine turns to her with a big fake grin... —Any lipstick on my teeth?

—You're good.

—Give me this... she takes Iona's phone, starts typing into it.

—I hope you stay. I like seeing you take on Amar when he adds vanilla syrup to your coffee.

—Okay... Katherine hands back the phone, not having heard, or maybe unsettled by Iona's affection... —You have my number. I need to locate vegan snacks for Herr Spitz before he freaks the fuck out... Katherine stands up, scooching her dress back down her thighs... —By the way, Clive Hauxwell?

—Yes?

—Careful with that one.

And Katherine walks away, sashays really, across the hall which is beginning to fill with arriving guests. Why does everyone fantasize about raising goats? Katherine, her ass magnificent in that peculiar red dress, high-fives a security guard as she walks past, disappearing from view behind the lava lamp. Or is it exclusively women who dream of goats and goat farms?

8:42 p.m.

—The money they throw at farmers is fucking outrageous, subsidies, they call it and no one blinks an eye. Corporations get their goodies filed under tax breaks. Two years ago banks got five hundred billion dollars, no one gave a shit. Federal bailout, quote unquote, but we have a word for free money, it's called welfare.

With a fixed smile Diane waits for the bodyguard's jeremiad to reach its unsurprising conclusion. It's vital to make contact with Z early. She'll need plenty of time to drive home her appeal. Z is dressed for the evening in a paisley waistcoat and a snarl of beaded necklaces, one of which sprouts feathers. He doesn't appear to have noticed Diane and Chris. He listens to his bodyguard, enthralled, murmuring *right* and *exactly*.

—Think about public land, *our* land, handed over to coal companies.

—I know!

—Given away! Why call it public leasing? It's barely leased! They rent it for pennies.

Maybe she'll get a dog. An Australian shepherd? Those haunting eyes. But too much grooming. Short-haired would be better, brindled or ticked.

—Of course the second you whisper the word welfare

A breed suited to Manhattan apartments, nothing too frisky. Affectionate.

—Pardon me... Chris steps forward with a petrifying smile... —Z?

—Moaning about government handouts.

—DIANE IS HERE.

The bodyguard stops speaking.

Pulling back his hair, Z appears to see them for the first time... —Hey there, Chris, Diane.

—Thrilled you could join us... she leans forward to kiss Z on each cheek, wondering as she does whether a handshake was the better way to go... —Look at your wonderful necklace... turning to include... —And, uh, your b—

—Liam.

—Yes, Liam, I was going to say. Have you been enjoying the city?

Z affirms that he is, in fact, having an excellent time and starts describing an accident he witnessed down on Broadway minutes after leaving their meeting when a cab knocked over an elderly man. Onlookers flocked to help and Z says how surprised he was that New Yorkers, folks he'd always heard described as rude and callous, were so solicitous and kind, offering to take the man to the hospital and digging out cell phones to contact his family. Worry was also expressed about the taxi driver, who was Dominican, and didn't speak much English. No one wanted to see what the police might do. During the entire commotion, Z stood on the sidewalk with a bag of Doritos, completely riveted, shoveling in corn chips, until he was suddenly horrified to realize that he was treating the crisis unfolding before him as if it were happening on television.

—Similar thing happened to me once... Liam takes a sip of wine and appears to suck it through his teeth... —Man fell off a hotel roof from thirty stories up, landed half a block in front of me. Pretty much exploded. I crossed the street so I could keep walking, I was late, okay, not unfeeling, and there was his foot lying in the gutter. Still wearing a shoe. Loafer, I think it was.

A horrified silence.

Chris coughs... —Has anyone tried the mini chalupas?

—They really are sublime... Diane looks around for a waiter... —Let me find you one.

—We don't need a chalupa... Liam says in a strained voice... —We don't need a fucking chalupa.

—Liam's joking, this is how he jokes, but seriously, we already ate.

—Well you're missing out on some real treats... twinkling with conspiratorial amusement to show she's up for being cursed at... —Chris?

With the starchy diplomacy he deploys at such a time, Chris brings things to a close, mentioning the many guests still left to greet. He places a hand under Diane's elbow to steer her away. Z waves good-naturedly, Liam glares at them and chews his ice.

As they go. Chris speaks rapidly in a low voice.

—I can't hear you.

—Guy's not a bodyguard.

—Of course he is.

—Bodyguards don't run at the mouth like that. My dad had a

couple the summer he was prosecuting mobsters, and this Liam guy? Lacks the simmering psychotic itch which in my experience is a total requirement.

—Maybe it's different out West... tired of this paranoia Chris regards as insight.

—Okay, that's the other thing. I've met him before.

—Met who before?

They take different routes around Norm Whitstuff waving his drink and confidently boring everyone in sight.

—The bodyguard, the bodyguard, you're not listening. He's from New York. I remember that habit of his, pinching his eyelashes like he had bugs in his eyes. It'll come to me. I've definitely met him. Wait, wait, wait... Chris clutches her arm.

—Ow, why—

—Are you seeing this?

—I don't know where you're looking.

—Over by the front door. Tiz Sericko walking out of coat check.

—You confirmed the lights—

—Lowered outside Purdue, yes. There she is now.

—Who?

Chris points... —The intern I put on the case. Watch. She's double-checking the picture of Sericko I texted. Isn't she darling. Recognize her?

Diane shifts... —The girl from Reskman? The one you wanted euthanized for taking the wrong elevator?

—I knew Freda was special when I hated her. Anyone I dislike at first sight invariably becomes a lifelong friend.

—What are you talking about? What about Z and his bodyguard?

—I don't *dislike* those two, Diane, I *distrust* them. I'm always right when it comes to trust. Check out Sericko. Totally charmed. He's not getting anywhere near that lion.

Tiz really does appear captivated and she hopes they haven't incited some wildly inappropriate bond that could expose the Museum to litigation. Freda has changed out of her sweaty dress into the sort of glum tunic Florence Nightingale might have worn to amputate a gangrenous leg. The girl puts her mouth up to Tiz's ear, whispering something that prompts him to toss his head and roar with laughter.

—I need a drink. You?

Diane shakes her head. Momo and Abbas stand half-hidden on the other side of the lava lamp, sharing a small plate piled high with appetizers.

—Not even seltzer?

—No. Be right back.

8:53 p.m.

—Rippen.

When he hears his name Benjamin is standing between floors two and three, one foot on the stairs leading up.

A shadowy figure down the length of dark hallway raises his arm...

—Look who it is.

—Look, Ruben? How can I see anything when the light is out again?

—Oh, okay, Mr. No-coconut in his granola bars.

—Sorry about the, but listen, it's not enough to change the bulb, the problem's the fixture. Anyone could be lying in wait... Benjamin stops speaking because the door to 2R has opened, flooding the hallway with light and a second man stands in the doorway. He wears dress pants and a white collared shirt with the sleeves rolled up to a pair of impresssive biceps.

—That him?

—Yes, sir, Benjamin Rippen.

—Who are you?

—Who am I? I'm the man you're fucking. Nice to meet you, Benjamin Rippen.

Benjamin suppresses the urge to giggle in a high ninny voice. It's a thing he does when he's nervous, become insane.

—I'm the person you've been scamming for the past two months... the stranger continues... —Pleasure to make your fucking acquaintance. Why Ruben hasn't evicted you remains one of life's great mysteries.

Ruben opens his mouth, closes it again, and slips past the man back into the apartment.

—Come here, please... the man pushes open the door to 2R, he's not particularly tall, but stocky with strong shoulders, a barrel chest, and the shrewd eyes of a workaday assassin. A great deal of care has been directed to the man's goatee, a conspicuous but futile effort to slim his great ham of a face.

Obediently Benjamin retraces his steps along the hallway toward the landlord, heart beating high in his chest, wondering what manner of violence the two men plan to unleash.

2R is smaller than his apartment and empty of furniture. The walls are scuffed with grey marks and edged at the ceiling and floor with blue painter's tape.

Benjamin cases the place for weapons. A leather portfolio sits on the kitchen counter alongside a Styrofoam cup and an orange tape measure. Further down the counter is an open bag of pork rinds the size of a pillow. No doubt a creative person could inflict deadly harm with a pork rind.

—Perhaps you failed to notice my name on the signage down-stairs. By the mailboxes? No? Tom Reggio. My name up there means this building ain't owned by some fat corporation, one that might be incognizant of a few missing rent checks. This building is owned by a real person. My grandmother bought this place sixty years ago and I grew up, Benjamin, on the ground floor. That's where I took my first steps and said my first words. It's where I beat the shit out of Richie Gomez down the street, backstabbing sonofabitch that he was, and continues to be, no doubt. So you see this building is my home. This place warms the cockles of my fucking heart. Now tell me how I'm supposed to feel when some kid moves in with his pretty girlfriend, acting like a big shot, wanting a new fridge, chipping the stairwell paint with his fancy couch and one month it slips his mind to pay the rent. You tell me.

This appears to be a rhetorical question. Benjamin looks down so he doesn't do anything weird. He stares at his hands which are clasped to-gether like a schoolboy's and suddenly seem abnormally small, like the hands of a raccoon.

—Mr. Redge, before the girlfriend moved out she signed the lease over. Now, she always paid on time. Always put the garbage in the right bin, too.

—I told Ruben this morning I can get you the rent in two weeks. The minute I get a paycheck I'll sign it over to you.

—Not good enough.

—Give me two weeks, please. I promise I'm good for it.

—You know what I can ask for this place?... Reggio makes a circling motion with one finger... —Two hundred more than you're paying. Maybe two-fifty. So if you leave, that's not so bad for me. I get a nice rent increase. On the other hand I gotta go through a whole eviction caper only to acquire some new asshole chipping my paint and bitching about a better fridge. And how can I be sure this new guy's not gonna smoke or have loud parties or leave urine in bottles on the stoop?

—I don't smoke or have parties. Or do that with urine.

—Okay, I'll give you another shot. Grab your checkbook, gimme a month's rent.

—But it would bounce.

Tom Reggio looks at him sadly... —If you need boxes, I think we got some in the basement, right, Ruben?

—No, sir, it's a fire hazard.

—Well, try Key Food. Friendly advice: start packing now you won't be overwhelmed by the weekend. At the end of which, Sunday night, you'll be out of my apartment, understand?

The self-help industry always advises living in the moment. But there are so many moments Benjamin would rather skip. He watches Ruben kick a glue trap under the refrigerator. It's nice to see that his crisis has in no way affected Ruben, who whistles softly as he washes his hands and dries them on a rag.

Surrender. The books also advise surrender.

—Wait... Benjamin digs through his backpack, finds Eleanor's envelope and hands it to Reggio... —Here. Should be two grand.

—What's this?... Reggio takes the envelope. He opens it and pulls out several hundred dollar bills... —Cash? Are you a drug guy?

—No, it's, look, it's a long story. Does it matter? I swear to you it's legal. It was a loan. From a normal, ordinary person.

—He don't take cash. Check only... Ruben extracts a carpet tack from the sole of his boot.

—Just this once I will... Reggio shoves the bills into his pants pocket and hands back the empty envelope.

Benjamin takes it, folding the paper into neat squares, fixated on the spot where the cash disappeared, then forcing his eyes away from that spot since it lies in the neighborhood of Tom Reggio's penis.

—Now scram, Rippen, before I change my mind.

He directs his gaze to his landlord's earlobe... —Mind if I... a dry cough... —Could I get a receipt?

—A what?

—I handed you two thousand dollars in cash, I'd like some uh, proof, you know, that I gave it to you.

—Fuck you accusing me of?

—Nothing. I'm—

—Get out of here. Go upstairs, get a shower, you look like hell. Bags under your eyes the size of marshmallows. Drop the booze, friend, or you'll be a basset hound by forty. A receipt... he turns to Ruben... —Believe this guy?

9:05 p.m.

The street outside the Museum is jammed with taxis and idling town cars belching exhaust. Under the temporary press awning, a bunch of peaky photographers stand in a complaining mass, sharing cigarettes as they wait to snap red carpet B-listers. Henry stalks up and down the block, sidestepping guests and peering into car windows as he searches for Annie.

Suddenly the idea of confessing to something witnessed over a decade ago strikes him as complete madness. How degrading, this thirst for exculpation. He should run home with his dignity intact and delve into the gouda he hid in the crisper. Turn off the emotions, have some cheese. Make a plate with apple slices and a glob of cherry chutney. He's debating sweet mustard when he spots Annie, toward the end of the block, climbing out of a taxi. Henry takes off, sprinting down the sidewalk, thoughts of cheese thrown to the wind, darting into the street to avoid pedestrians, dodging side mirrors as he fights his way toward his spectacular ex-wife. A bike shoots past, handlebar grazing Henry's arm. The cyclist looks back and screams... —ASSHOLE, you're wearing BLACK. And it's true, Henry is wearing black and is most definitely an asshole but down the street he goes, eager to confess.

9:07 p.m.

—Are you like even listening?

—Gentleman on the dance floor grabbed your quote ass cheek... Shay reads from her notes... —Tall with a silver toupee unquote.

—Not a hundred percent sure it was purposeful since he was elderly, like maybe he was lurching because of bad balance, but I'm saying keep an eye out, you know? Because maybe he's doing it to others. In which case that is really not cool and if he's doing it in a place like this... the woman looks around... —What's he getting up to on the subway?

—A very good point... Shay shuts her notebook... —I will keep my eyes peeled. And you have my number if you spot him.

Shay turns to go, dismissing the woman and her complaints, mind back on the men she allowed into the Museum carrying a digital projector. She'd allowed her emotions to get the best of her. She was still reeling from the news they were confiscating her apartment. That Henry Joles had flubbed the one small favor she'd asked of him. An hour later, it's clear she made a mistake. She needs to find Diane immediately, admit what she's done. Let the director deal with kicking out a VIP.

9:09 p.m.

I was terse but polite, Diane thinks. I believe I requested their departure, but it may have been more of a command. She watches the brothers weave through the crowded hall toward the exit. Momo's head abruptly disappears from view, as if he dropped something. Stilton macaron, no doubt. One of a small stockpile he munched on while casually smashing her dreams.

—You should see the... Chris appears next to her, out of breath... —Line at the bar, I couldn't, hang on a second, what just happened?... trying to follow Diane's glare... —Who was that?

—The Khans... her voice sounds surprisingly gentle, almost forgiving... —That was the Khan brothers saying no.

—*No?* They said no?

—Correct.

—But they were taking the week.

—Momo can't keep a secret.

—You're joking.

—No. They let me down kindly, which was obviously—

—Infuriating.

—So, no satellite in Abu Dhabi.

—After you flew out there? And chose the site, the problems with, I mean, what reason did they give?

—They wouldn't at first, said it was all on their end.

—But you insisted.

—Yes.

—And?

—After the tour they stuck around. Snooped. Chatted to the staff. Saw some things they didn't like.

—Things, what things?

Diane shrugs. Your museum, Abbas said, has taken humanity's greatest triumph and defiled it with staff squabbles, useless committees, petty rivalries, and a turf war over photocopiers.

—But they strung us along for like, it seemed like a dumb deal, done deal. Were they playing us?... Chris holds what is either a very large vodka or a normal-sized glass of water... —Were they? Oh my god, they were... a cloud of paranoia appears to descend over Chris, confirming that the glass does indeed hold vodka... —I need a Coke. What was I going to, oh, the architects are over by Ramses, hoping for a quick word.

—Aren't they on a plane?

—Delayed. Sorry. I would never have invited them if I thought they could come.

—Has Ichimonji arrived?

—What's that?

—The Ambassador?

—Ah.

—Oh god. What now?

—Nothing, nothing at all. A brief, informal I'd call it, email from his people regarding a delay due to, looks like a bout of something, nausea, not sure if the Ambassador vomited exactly or... Chris stops speaking to brightly acknowledge someone over Diane's shoulder.

—Vomit? Because of us?

—Impossible. From dry toast and, what, a couple of bites of gazpacho? No.

She brings her gaze to the center of the Great Hall where the lava lamp daisies are visibly wilting. And closes her eyes.

—My father, Diane.

She opens them again.

—Knows people. I heard you earlier talking to Dominic. My dad will find you a jackal. Take Dom for everything he has. Does he have anything? Asshole... Chris glares around the room, bristling and unkenneled, looking for a taker, someone spoiling for a fight.

—Chris.

—I'll go get that Coke.

Diane watches Chris force his way through the crowd, smiling vaguely and clapping Mayor Greenberg a bit too pallishly on the shoulder. Her mind wanders to the apartment she'll face later tonight. The empty closet. No blue robe drooping on the back of the bathroom door or size fourteen shoes planted across the living room like land mines. For years they've kept a small brass Buddha on the windowsill above the kitchen sink. Diane bought it for Dominic at a flea market on their honeymoon and together they decided it was their lucky object. Often they've tucked Buddha into a pocket or backpack, bringing him to an event where they've figured they might need some luck. Will Dominic have taken Buddha with him? And what will it mean if he has? That there's hope?

Chris has stopped to speak to Lucas Boone, head canted, arms folded, leaning toward the teenager with actorly fascination. The quiver in Diane's stomach starts up again. She lifts her dragging hem, moving toward Egypt and the offices beyond. She should have agreed to Chris's saltines.

—Hello darling... squeezing Ralph Kade on the arm as she glides past... —Find me later.

9:16 p.m.

Clive is trying to force his mind off Katherine Tambling, her nipples and easily bruised skin. She wore tan makeup that ran down her arms in the bath, exposing plots of crosshatched scars. In the pizza shop, for one deranged second Clive wanted to propose settling down together and together raising her child. What a glorious few weeks they spent

—Clive!

He stares at Chris's hand until it is removed from his sleeve.

—Sorry about this afternoon.

—This afternoon regarding Walter Wolfe or this afternoon when Diane asked me to stop by Piquette and was nowhere to be found when I did, as requested, stop by Piquette?

—Clive, listen, we were relocated at the last minute. Totally my fault, let me introduce—

—Can't stop, sorry... indicating the cocktails he holds, Iona Moore having drained her first martini in record time... —Mustn't keep my friend waiting, terrible temper, liable to—

—Lucas Boone, an important new donor to Arms & Armor.

Hunched into a question mark beside Chris is an adolescent in an ill-fitting tuxedo. The boy looks horrified to be present. Or alive, for that matter. Great fluffs of untamed hair surround his face and its rosy map of acne. Sheepishly, he offers Clive his hand to shake and the sleeve of his tux rides up. Clive switches one of the glasses to his other hand. Shakes. The boy's hand feels like wet bread.

—Clive runs European Paintings.

—And this is Bianca Moretti.

A bronzed pixie beside the boy offers Clive a hand three shades whiter than her face. Clive gives it a brisk shake.

—Cool drip... the boy blushes.

—Thank you... Clive starts to go.

—Your tuxedo, is it bespoke?

—Bespoke? What, on my salary? Fuck no, off the rack.

—But it's a famous designer.

—No idea. Bought it years ago.

—And you wear like a bracelet. Dope. Vintage watch.

—Clive is our resident fashion plate... Chris's vowels sound a bit sloshed.

—That's right, now I do have to zip off, I'm afraid.

—Could I speak to you?... the boy steps in front of Clive.

—To me?

—Yes. Privately. Just for a second.

—Come on, Clive... Chris starts to give Clive a razzing punch but stops himself midair... —Spare a minute for our new donor.

—Awfully sorry but—

—You'll see, Lucas, we're like one big family here.

—Friend who's dying of thirst.

—A family that supports one another whenever one of us needs support, such as acquisition meetings, and so forth.

—You're speaking, of course, of Diane's support. Because yours doesn't mean much.

—Correct.

—Understand I'll hold you to this.

—Such a team player.

—Right... to Lucas... —Follow me.

The kid nods formally to his date.

—This way... leading the young donor through the hall, around the preposterous lava lamp, through a gallery of sarcophagi to the hidden door in Egypt where he... —Hold this for a sec... swipes the pad, pushes the door, and retrieves the glass from Lucas to lead him through the unlit corridor to an alcove between offices where a printer, a photocopier, and several recycling bins have been stashed.

The place stinks of stale coffee and microwave popcorn. On the printer table a dried-out teabag lies nestled in a spoon. Clive sets the glasses on the photocopier and faces the kid.

—So, what's on your mind?

The boy rubs the back of his head... —I'm not sure how to put this—

—Find a way.

—Currently, as well as like in the foreseeable future, I'm estranged from my father and there's no one else as far as father figures go. No uncles or—

—Now, hang on. I am nobody's father figure.

—No, but it's clear to me, to anyone I would think, even after only seeing you for a minute, that you know what you're doing when it comes to sex—

—Whoa whoa whoa whoa.

—You have a kind of—

—No.

—charisma.

—Stop right there, Lucas, is it?

He nods.

—First of all, I'm bisexual.

—What does that have to do with it?

—Apparently nothing. Moving on... fortifying himself with a swig of vodka... —I'm fairly certain... returning the glass to the top of the photocopier... —That even hearing you say the word sex violates the morals clause of my employee contract.

—Please. A few questions. Two.

—What about school? There must be a teacher.

—There are no teachers. What are you talking about? Nobody talks to teachers. How about one? One very small question.

—Regarding sex? Not going to happen.

—Okay... his entire body asking to disappear.

—Look, don't—

—No, no, I get it.

—Don't take it personally... taking the dry teabag and pitching it in the bin... —I'm genuinely sorry to hear about your father, your troubles with him.

Lucas shrugs.

He should warn the kid that fathers aren't always what they're cracked up to be. That Clive's own dad smacked him on the ear when he came across the postcards in Clive's pencil box, reproductions of Leonardo's *Adam* and David's *Patroclus*. The images of naked men frightened his father, a conservative man, wary of the Lord's judgment and that of the neighbors. But there was nothing uncommon in the eighties about a smack or two. It was a loving reminder not to be strange.

The child is a thundering mess. That hair, for one. What do the boy's classmates make of him? The taunting must be endless. And the orange-faced girl, why did she agree to come? To laugh at Lucas with her friends?

—Alright, here's the deal, no sex advice but anything else is fair game.

9:26 p.m.

By the time she reaches Egypt, Diane's face has frozen into a smiling rictus. Through the gallery to the hidden door, barging it needlessly with her hip, moving into the warren of offices, pulling the door behind her. Back in the early days she and Dom had a squeaky, rather disrespectful, actually, Buddha voice they used to put on when the other person was being stubborn or tetchy. Sometimes Dominic went for an overwrought Italian accent that was both illogical and offensive, turning the enlightened being into a cartoon pizza slinger. Could Buddha have retained some token meaning for Dom after all these years? Surely he noticed the statue as he grabbed his vitamins and thought, our special object, we brought it with us when we went to Big Sur, I'll throw it in my bag. I loved our marriage. But as Diane stops to strip off her heels, she's struck by a painful truth. That, when she gets home, Buddha will still be there, squatting mutely on the windowsill.

9:28 p.m.

—So it started about six months ago, seven maybe. I was on the subway coming home from debate when I realized that, you know, authenticity can only be achieved through stagecraft.

—What does that mean?

—Like to understand truth first you have to embrace artifice. So I started doing these things, right, like I wore my dad's golf glove for a month straight then I'd only wear different shades of green. Yellow on Tuesdays. Used slang from the thirties I found in a book. Also, I read and I'm afraid quoted Voltaire and Montaigne.

—Christ.

—I know. One day I realized I was just excluding myself before anyone else could. I'd become the architect of my own disastrous social status.

—I see.

—How do I recover?

Clive takes a sip of his martini, considering the boy's options...
—Have you tried not giving a fuck?

The boy, hands in his pockets, looks unconvinced.

—No?

—No.

—Alright, different approach, go back out there, get your photo snapped with a celeb. Social currency.

—Please. Like half my class has famous parents, but that's good advice, really... Lucas smiles encouragingly... —Don't give them power, I get it. I'm taking it all in. Don't think I'm not listening. What about my appearance? Any tips?

—You look fine.

—Bullshit. I'm no one's idea of fine. Give me pointers. Really, have at it. I have no pride. You know those volunteers they bring onstage at a state fair, strap to a spinning wheel and throw knives at? Occasionally they piss themselves but not always.

—What on earth are you talking about?

—It started off as an analogy.

Clive takes the boy by the shoulders and looks him over... —The hair is a problem, this freshly-shampooed puffiness.

—It's disgusting.

—No, but don't wash it so much and personally, I would shave your head, inmate-style. Your eyes aren't bad and it will bring them out a bit.

—Great. What else?

—Your skin. Stop eating sugar.

—I take Aczone.

—Stop eating sugar.

—My doctor says—

—Your doctor's getting courtside seats from the Aczone rep. What do you think he's saying?

—Got it. What else?

—This looks like something you'd use to wipe gravy off your chin...

Clive plucks the pocket square from the kid's jacket, snaps it, refolds it and replaces it... —Much better. You know how to dance?

—No, but I wasn't planning to.

—If the little lady's focusing on her feet she's not thinking about your spotty face, now one here... placing Lucas's right hand on his lower back... —The other here, no, no... untangling... —Stop... slapping away the clammy hand... —No interlacing fingers. You're not a child.

—But what about the steps? I don't know—

—Copy the older men. Silver-haired gents are best. Make sure you're leading, that's critical. Do one of these... spinning Lucas... —La, la, bring her back in. If you fuck up, pass it off as if you meant to. Got it?

—What if Bianca doesn't want to dance?

—Doesn't want to? All the action's on the dance floor. Now, when's the kiss?

—Kiss? I wasn't—

—End of the night? In amongst the crowd?

—You don't under—

—Ah, in the cab home, nice one. Lights of the city reflected on the windows, all that lovely neon.

—I'm not kissing her and there's no neon. Do I live in Times Square? I'm planning to impress her with my chivalry.

—False.

—Back in the fifteenth—

—No.

—century.

—No, not the fifteenth anything. Stay here. Back in a mo... Clive strides down the hallway, swipes his ID, pushes through the hidden door, emerges into Egypt.

9:35 p.m.

Diane crashes into the ladies' room with such force that a woman standing at the sink whips around with a little scream. Katherine Tambling. She was scrubbing her teeth with her finger and that finger is now held aloft as if she's requesting the check.

—Sorry to... Diane darts into a stall... —Startle you... slamming the door but it bounces open, smacking her on the ass. She pushes it to and slides the lock across.

Silence from the sinks.

There's not much you can do to cover the sound of dry heaving.

—Okay in there?

—Uh-huh. You should maybe go.

—Hang on a sec.

A scrabbling noise and a hand appears under the stall's partition gripping a wad of damp paper towels. Diane takes it... —Thank you... wiping her mouth.

—They say charcoal is good for nausea, but I wouldn't know where to get it up here. Also, ironically, good for whitening teeth, charcoal. Is it food poisoning? From the shrimp?

—Not sure... Diane straightens, trying to guess what her stomach will do next. Feeling steadier, she unlocks the door and goes out.

At a sink, Katherine Tambling has moved on to her lipstick, mushing her lips to blend the color. She wears a familiar red dress, tight, with a humped shoulder, a puzzle of a gown.

—Cheers for this... Diane holds up the wad of paper towels as she crosses to the trash can.

—Ever look at your face and think, god, this thing again?

—All the time... tossing the paper towels... —It's Kawakubo, isn't it?... doubling back to the sinks... —Your dress. Looks like one Danita Philips donated.

—Here... Katherine hands her a travel-sized bottle of mouthwash... —Finish it. I have more in my office.

—Lifesaver, thanks... Diane swigs, swishes, spits. Glances in the mirror. Her hair is very strange. And Marcy has overplucked her eyebrows, giving Diane a skeptical expression. All her air-kissing and groveling this evening has been undermined, if not completely scotched, by a pair of sarcastic eyebrows.

—People keep asking about dinner.

—Who, Anton?

—Yeah, says how's he supposed to metabolize alcohol on a couple of cheese straws?

—Oh for god's, we've never served dinner, never. If one more person mentions the Met Gala I'm going to, sorry, what?

—It's ripped.

—What is?

Katherine points... —Your dress. Maybe you caught your heel when you ran in?

And it's true, Diane checks, her dress is indeed ripped up to the thigh, revealing the black girdley thing Selina insisted upon. The indignities never stop.

—Downstairs and I could—

—Sorry?

—I can fix the tear.

—Stand there and sew?

—No, I have a magic tape down in my office. If we take the service elevator no one will see us.

—Is my... trying to see over her shoulder in the mirror... —Underwear showing?

—Hold it together.

—The dress?

—Yes, your dress.

9:40 p.m.

Clive could never imagine himself as a father despite several discussions with Joshua about having children. Once, memorably, when they were lost in the Shawangunks, hiking in circles until the sun went down, empty bottles clunking in Clive's rucksack. The wine was expensive, which made Clive suspect a proposal was in the works. It was a moment he anticipated with mounting dread until it didn't come to pass when, predictably, he was deeply disappointed. As the two of them walked they discussed adoption and surrogacy, interspersed with brutal verdicts of their women friends: were any of them stable enough to approach for an egg? Eventually they found their way out.

—Here we are!... holding up the glasses as he makes his way back down the hallway to Lucas.

—What is that?

—Bubbly... handing him the prosecco... —Drink up.

—But I don't drink.

—Down in one.

—One sip?... with a dubious look Lucas takes the champagne from him and raises it to his mouth.

Clive places his finger under the foot of the flute, and gently tips it. When Lucas seems as if he might spit up, Clive snatches the glass away... —Alright, now then. Here are two full glasses. Go back to your lady, "Bianca, let's find a cozy spot," and so forth.

—That's not cool. Plying her with drinks so I can take advantage of her? That's not okay.

—Good god, child, *plying*, I'm not suggesting, what have you been reading?

—The internet.

—Well, stop.

9:43 p.m.

The Kawakubo is far too tight to walk this fast. Up ahead, Diane is hustling down the dark office hallway, hips swinging, busted ball-gown whipping around her legs. Katherine hitches her dress around her thighs and trots to catch up. The hallway smells of ripe bananas and old coffee.

—What the... Diane stops so abruptly Katherine barrels into her... —Is that child drinking?

At the other end of the hallway Clive Hauxwell is speaking to a gangly teenager. The boy holds a champagne flute in one hand. At the sight of Clive in his black tuxedo, Katherine has to turn away. Too much.

—That's our new donor.

—Sorry?

—The kid... Diane's voice rises an octave... —And Hauxwell's giving him alcohol. I'll kill him.

—No, no... forced to keep the operation on track, Katherine hooks her arm through the director's... —It's not what it looks like... semi-dragging her boss down the hallway toward the service elevator.

Hormones.

It was a rush of hormones, Katherine's impulse to fall into Clive's arms at the pizza place. Flashing back to those three weeks in February. The mind-bending sex. The baths they took, entwined in his enormous tub, reading or eating. On a wooden caddy he balanced mixing bowls filled with health-promoting cereal that was suspiciously delicious, or more modest-sized bowls of chicken soup which, like many of his compatriots, Clive ate at a reckless temperature.

Don't imagine him naked, not right now.

9:45 p.m.

—First of all, no one, not even an eighteen-year-old—

—Sixteen.

—Sixteen? Really?... Clive takes a step back, inexplicably peering into the empty glass.

—Yes, really.

—Oh dear, well, sixteen-year-old is going belly-up from one glass of prosec, half a glass, in fact, since the Museum's too tight to fill their flutes to an acceptable level. What's this?... pointing to the kid's neck... —What's happening here?

—My bowtie was flopping so I fixed it.

—Fuck no... Clive sets down his glass, flicks the tie... —Where'd you get such a soggy rag?

—My dad's sock drawer.

Clive yanks one end of the bow, pulling the tie out from Lucas's collar.

—What are you doing?

Handing the tie to Lucas... —Pocket.

—Why?

Clive undoes his own tie, pulls it off and fastens it around Lucas's collar, retying it twice to make the sides perfectly even.

—What about you? What will you do for a tie?

—Never mind me... unbuttoning the top two buttons of his shirt... —How do you feel?

—Kind of cocky.

—Good. Great, in fact.

—Like I might punch someone.

—Okay, but not that.

—I'm kidding. I don't know how to throw a punch.

—A lesson for next time.

—Really?... he notices Clive's expression... —No, there is no next time.

—Right. Get out there. Make me proud. Remember to lead.

—Copy the silver gents.

—Well done.

Collecting the now-warm martinis from the top of the photocopier, Clive steers Lucas down the hall toward the door. It's given him a real Pygmalion skip to his stride, polishing up this teenage failure. Now it's time to locate a trustee and lock down the acquisition. Ralph Kade, maybe. Or Norm Whitstuff, fabled nappy king.

9:48 p.m.

Conversation with Tiz Sericko is like wandering into Borromini's forced perspective folly. Your first impression is one of depth, but once you step inside you understand how shallow it is. The colonnade is thirty feet at most, and you can only walk to the far end if you duck. Borromini went on to kill himself, Henry remembers, which is not relevant to the metaphor.

It was only when Tiz moved from cost overruns to questions of self-improvement and assorted mythopoetic theories that Henry finally managed to extricate himself and return to the column where he'd arranged to meet Annie.

Was it his strenuous reminiscing that drove her away? She was telling him about Kim's new heartache, a boy who declared his love and promptly vanished. Henry offered concern and asked a number of questions. But then he interrupted. Remember Koper? he asked. Titov Trg in the drizzle? What about that one-eyed cat materializing from the fog? Thinking as he spoke how desperate he sounded. He waited for Annie to chime in with a memory of her own. Once they'd been almost painfully in love. Instead she futzed with her purse, smiling vaguely, maybe even hopefully, at guests pushing past. A few minutes later Annie excused herself and left for the ladies'.

9:51 p.m.

Illicitly clad in a Museum-owned Kawakubo, Katherine would have preferred not to advertise a second fireable offense but she couldn't walk away, not when Diane started with the dry-heaving. Okay, she thought, I'll commiserate, hand over some paper towels and my travel-sized mouthwash, make a break for it. But then she noticed the rip in Diane's dress. And was thereby fucked. Because you don't walk away from a woman unwittingly parting the curtains on her underpants, even when you yourself are in the throes of committing a crime. That's basic feminism.

—In here somewhere... knocking aside a box of nicotine patches, scattering the butterscotch candies she keeps in reserve for Giselle... —I used it on Monday.

—My husband's leaving me.

Katherine looks up.

Diane has sunk. She's still leaning against the wall but now sitting back on her heels, one hand over her mouth as if she's trying and failing to stop herself from speaking... —He called earlier.

—He told you on the phone?

—Speakerphone.

—Yikes.

—No one was in the room, he's not a monster.

—Still that's, I mean, I'm sorry. Did he give a reason?

Silence.

This type of thing used to happen regularly to Katherine, this sort of bearing witness. Strangers mostly, but sometimes acquaintances or colleagues, use to confess all kinds of things. This was back in college or before, in tenth grade, for example, when a man sitting next to her at the DMV admitted that every morning he fantasized about tossing a carafe of hot coffee at his boss's face. But somewhere along the way Katherine's expression or attitude must have changed because she is rarely, these days, prevailed upon to hear a stranger's private revelations of defeat or difficulty, even criminal activity, as a woman in a bar once admitted to buying herself a chest freezer with church funds set aside for the poor. The woman in question was very drunk so she may have spilled the beans to anyone, even the couple playing a video game, because it was that kind of bar, one with video games. Certainly the bartender seemed unfazed.

Diane Schwebe is staring at her hands, really scrutinizing them as if trying to determine where they came from.

How comforting to be assured that yes, it's not just me here bungling along, whacking flying objects out of my face, but many of us whacking away. And simply because she, Katherine, might lose her job and/or require an abortion, doesn't diminish or mitigate the everyday tragedies of other people, this beautiful woman in front of her, for example, sunk into the folds of her quite awful dress, coping with a husband's change of heart.

—Ready?... Katherine holds up the repair tape.

—To be honest, I was thinking about a separation... Diane gets to her feet, smoothing the crumpled dress... —It was on my mind.

Katherine goes to her, kneels and starts lining up the two edges of fabric... —Don't freak out, I'm putting my hand up your dress.

—But I would've given it another shot. I don't know why he had to burn down the whole village.

Reaching up into the director's gown, Katherine sets the material against the adhesive... —You don't have kids.

—No.

—Is that something, do you ever regret not having... realizing too late that the question is far too personal, even with one hand up the woman's dress.

—Sure that tape's going to hold?

—Sorry, I didn't mean to, I, when you sit down make sure the tape doesn't pull... Katherine arranges the gown, flattening the creases...

—Maybe your husband razed it to the ground so you could start fresh. See each other with new eyes.

—Danita Philips... Diane slips into her heels, at some point they came off... —The Museum hosted a lunch for her last year. I remember she talked about a villa she owned in Europe. Greece, I think... opening the door to Giselle's private bathroom to access the full-length mirror... —A house painter demanded double his estimate and when Danita refused to pay, kidnapped the family dog. Or so she believed. A tragic story. It's why I distinctly recall the dresses she donated.

Katherine stops breathing.

—Giselle gave you permission to wear an archival piece?

—No, ma'am... instantly regretting the ma'am.

—The reasoning behind it?

In response, a sort of shruggy headshake.

—And you, a guardian of... with an expression of disgust... —Clearly you should be fired.

—Clearly.

—However.

And Katherine allows herself to exhale.

—I refuse to burden Giselle with finding a new curator or promoting a person who aggravates her. Arrange and pay for the cleaning and return the dress before she finds out.

—Of course. I mean, that was always my—

—What about the back?... Diane looks over her shoulder at the dress... —Is it okay?

—Great, yup.

—You're not married.

—What, me? No.

—Boyfriend? Girlfriend?

—Nothing.

—Thought so. You're one of those tough girls. Uncompromising. Happy to be alone.

Oh brother, Katherine thinks, picking up her phone. This again.

10:01 p.m.

---

so tedious

no celebs

yr not missing anything

He's a thoughtful husband. He sticks his phone back in his jacket, glancing down the hallway for any sign of Annie. In the lowlit area outside Purdue, two men are admiring the Museum's new lion statue. Next to them, Marlon Tindall-Clark is pointing out details. The ears, the tail.

One of the men turns to the side and Henry recognizes the chinless profile of Agent Fisk. Which means the shorter man is in fact a woman. Agent Travis.

Immediately Henry's breath gets short and his temper flares. Up he scuttles, a glass in each hand, trying to keep the prosecco from spilling and feeling ridiculous for it.

Travis and Fisk have finished with the lion and walk to meet him.

—Mr. Joles... Fisk thrusts his hand out for a shake, notices Henry's hands are full and instead pats him on the shoulder.

—Are you kidding me with the tuxedos as if you were invited, are you kidding me?

—Now, Henry—

—Security let you in without—

—Why're you getting bent out of shape? We're just—

—Asking a few questions... Travis, hands in her pockets, a sardonic little smile.

—Nothing anyone will have a hard time answering.

—Nothing to put a damper on the night.

—And what is it that can't wait til morning?... Henry sets the glasses on the tray of a passing waiter.

—People these days don't pick up the phone. And Tindall-Clark, Ralph Kade, Whitstuff, they've all bought from Vauclain.

—You've identified yourselves as cops?

—Like to show Kade a couple of pictures, see if he recognizes anything.

Not here. Not now... Henry tries to keep his voice at a reasonable volume... —And why are you fucking around with Tindall-Clark's lion? The thing's Greek. Nothing to do with Vauclain.

—Merely chatting.

—Making conversation.

—Legally, you two—

—Don't get heated, Henry.

—Damn it, of course I am, this is... rubbing his chest.

—Are you, should I call some, why are you clutching your heart like that?

—Could it be the incense? I feel a little woozy myself.

Henry leans toward Fisk... —Think I don't know who you are with your shiny tuxedos and practiced slang? A couple of crude hustlers who fancy themselves cultural wardens. Please. All you're doing is exploiting a legal way to bully innocent people.

Fisk looks amused, his fleshy lips trying a variety of expressions in search of something apt.

—Don't underestimate me. I'll take a raised voice and turn it into a case of harassment so fast it'll detonate your dick... Henry has no idea what he's saying, already he's walking away.

—Mr. Joles!

10:07 p.m.

Jack Lemmon is straining spaghetti with a tennis racket when Benjamin wakes up from his slobbery nap. He dozed off around the time of the Christmas party. Baxter and Fran were discussing her cracked mirror.

After the horrible encounter with Eleanor Tindall-Clark, followed by a shakedown from his landlord, Benjamin ran to *The Apartment*. He climbed into bed with his laptop, a magazine, half a box of cereal, and two giant bags of chips: one potato, one corn. The movie's familiar dialogue mumbled in the background as he ate snacks and flipped through *Triathlete*. Afterward, he drank liberally from a family-sized sports drink to replenish the electrolytes that get depleted by reading about elite athletes. Twelve minutes later he was sound asleep.

Baxter walks into the living room where Fran stands by the table wrapped in his plaid bathrobe, lighting candles. *You know I used to live like Robinson Crusoe.* Benjamin reaches for a Frito across the cereal box lying on its side. Trails and hillocks of honey O's are spilled across the bedspread. His teeth feel flocked. *Shipwrecked among eight million people.* It's one of his favorite lines of dialogue and often persuades him to do something unwise like call his mother. He picks up his phone. Before she got sick Benjamin would have described the gyoza he had for lunch and his mother would have wondered about ordering chili peppers off the internet. Food was safe. Cozy, but guaranteed not to take any hairpin swerves toward an emotional province. Then his mother went back to school and made it clear she found the subject of lunch an enormous waste of time.

Benjamin is surfing these waves of sentiment, focusing on what he's lost, relishing the comfort of weeping, or the occasion to weep, even if no tears actually surface, when his cell phone lights up.

A text from a 646 number he doesn't recognize.

shit's getting weird

Benjamin stares at it for a second, then types back, *who is this?*

...

He waits.

Katherine

Still disoriented from his nap and the onslaught of carbohydrates, Benjamin ploddingly untangles the facts: Katherine from seven years ago doesn't have his new number. He checks Outgoing. There it is. Called herself from his phone. Standing in his office doorway, watching him pack his bag. Only minutes after he'd burst in on her wearing nothing but a pair of purple underpants.

Slowly Benjamin processes the evidence in front of him.

Katherine.

Wanted.

His.

Number.

Slamming his laptop closed, Benjamin smothers Shirley MacLaine, rips off his T-shirt, and stumbles to the closet, sliding hangers back and forth, combing through dress pants and shirts he thought were cool back in Ohio. Katherine's ass in that red dress. Oh my god, your teeth.

Down the hall to the bathroom, wheeling around, tripping, jogging back to the bedroom to grab his phone.

fun weird?

Texting it as he races back to the bathroom where he slaps cold water on his face and brushes his teeth so hard his gums bleed.

His phone buzzes.

weird weird

lets put it this way

...

a minute ago I had my hand up the director's dress

Benjamin returns to the bedroom, tosses his phone on the bed. He's not going anywhere without an invitation. Not without Katherine's clear intention if not like the actual words. He takes off his sweatpants. Puts on a pair of black jeans and a clean white shirt. Caroline gave him a sports coat for Christmas last year. The coat looks as if it was tailored to perfection then dragged behind a horse for two miles, giving it a louche appeal that somehow still reads as formal. It's a contradiction he's only ever seen in clothes he can't afford.

Benjamin pulls on the coat, a fresh pair of socks. No new texts. He ties his shoes. Too tight, he reties. Lint-rolls his jacket. Checks the phone again. Rerolls. In sixth grade he went through a phase of lint-rolling his clothes every morning, socks to collar, right to left. When his mother found out why he kept missing the bus she threw his rollers in the trash and set the cans on the curb. The next day Benjamin had a panic attack during the Pledge of Allegiance. After lunch he stole a three-pack of masking tape from the art room, brought it home and hid it in the attic.

He picks up his phone and stares at the screen, trying to manifest an invitation from Katherine.

Finally a chirp: *come back here and hang out!*

A very persuasive exclamation point. Benjamin grabs his keys from the kitchen table, drops them, picks them up, texting as he goes: *maybe.*

10:15 p.m.

Clive wasn't a killjoy as Lucy charged. Quite the opposite. Decent, generous, kind. Compassionate. Too much. Decent. Good enough. As he was savoring the high that came from helping young Lucas get his shit together, Clive realized that Iona Moore's plummeting neckline could potentially help his cause. Spilling out of her dress like some trollop from the jiggly period dramas of his BBC youth. Just the ticket. At a furious pace he steered Iona around the Great Hall and its peripheral galleries hunting for a trustee from the acquisitions committee.

And there he was. Ralph Kade. With the ruddy complexion and broken veins of the professional sot. Alone in a corner, tapping his toe to the jazz.

—Kade!... Clive shouted when they were still several meters away, going for a hail-fellow-well-met strategy.

At the noise Kade started. He smiled short-sightedly, squinting to locate the origin of all this bonhomie. When he spotted Clive, his smile stalled, faltered, and turned into an apprehensive frown. He stared down at his hand. It held four miniature tarts.

As chairman of North Peak, a boutique New England chain that metastasized in the past decade to become one of the country's largest consumer banks, the trustee commands a healthy amount of respect from Diane, Sericko, and other members of the Museum's board. Kade's support for the cassone acquisition would be meaningful. But first Clive had to let Ralph rib him for several long minutes about his unbuttoned collar and missing tie. It was sad commentary on what passes for entertainment in the life of a priggish plutocrat. The man's elderly zingers were not fired rat-a-tat, but launched in a slow arc, as from a trebuchet. Clive focused on the oily grey curls that sprang from the man's crown and formed a perfect circle around his head like a medieval nimbus, wondering who on earth cut it and where the barber was located, if it was in fact a barber or even a hairdresser.

Finally Kade fell silent, placing a tart in his mouth with a trembling liver-spotted hand.

Clive elbowed Iona who took the cue, hoiked the bust of her dress, and dove in.

She began quite sanely with a lovely description of the Sellaio. No one could have suspected what was to come. The panel depicted a hunting scene from *The Decameron* and Iona formed claws with her drink-free hand to bring to life a bloodthirsty wolf. Kade giggled as she pretended to attack him, ducking to sneak a lecherous glance down her dress. Then, without warning, Iona took an unexpected detour. Clive's heart sank as he heard the word symbolic.

Now, Iona, he said with a nervous chuckle, no need for that sort of thing. He tried to steer the focus back to camera figures as the earliest, but no, she wasn't having it. The cassone might have functioned as a symbol of love, she said, but it was also a warning. Clive heard the perilous word metaphor. Something about containment.

At which point he stood back and watched as Iona Moore proceeded to lose her mind. Was it the drink? She was off to the races, pilfering Baudrillard, lighting on notions of cassoni as interior spaces vis-à-vis Titian's *Venus of Urbino*. Alarmed, Clive interjected, trying to steer the conversation back to the quality of the painting. But Iona Moore would not be swayed. Back and forth they went. She insisted on contemporary anti-religious this and fleshy that, Clive pushed back with brush strokes and composition. Kade looked from one to the other as if he'd scored front-row seats at Wimbledon. They were a team, working together, riffing, their excitement rising, becoming palpable, even sexual, when suddenly Iona, in making her argument, mentioned, and mentioned quite emphatically, the word vagina.

Kade flinched as if he'd been struck. His eyes grew wide and fearful. His eyelids fluttered. One of his tarts fell to the floor. Clive felt only awe. You were forced to admire the audacity. It was a ludicrous remark. Her disgrace was promising. Recovering as best he could, Clive came up with a few anodyne comments, patted Kade's sleeve in a manner he believed to be comforting, and dragged Iona away.

As they sped off, Clive looked back to see the trustee gazing mistrustfully at his remaining tarts. How would the old man explain it? I was eating a pastry when a curious woman appeared before me and shouted the word vagina.

—So now you'll introduce me to Marlon Tindall-Clark?... Iona asked, checking in with the neckline of her dress.

No. Because that performance, whatever it was, got Clive riled up. The rapid back-and-forth, tripping over each other, working together one moment, fighting each other the next, has him terrifically aroused. He's not about to introduce Iona Moore to anyone, Tindall-Clark or otherwise. A more urgent need has arisen.

10:26 p.m.

With the exception of appreciating Chris's jawline, and his triceps when they're unveiled in August, I don't look twice at other men. I can't even recall a time before Dominic.

Except for a French man, junior year abroad, who gave Diane expensive jewelry along with some type of rash. Diane mistook the wheezing and burping for the ravages of age, failing to see he was not yet forty. The gold trinkets didn't fit into her life as a student, which didn't prevent her from accepting them. A slim devotee of Robbe-Grillet, Renaud moved with little grace, crashing into the coffee table and assorted chairs. It was an apartment full of chairs. His expectations for company were grandiose. Where is he now? Still in Lyon bumping into things? He must be creeping up on seventy or

—Diane!

Jolting at the sound of her name, Diane whips around... —Shay, hi, ow... bringing up a hand to massage the crick in her neck from her violent about-face.

Shay comes closer, expression worried... —I wanted to discuss a small matter with you.

—Oh, Shay... because she can't right now, can't deal with Shay fussbudgeting about non-urgent matters, details about some squabble in the Events kitchen or, even worse, further discussion of the museum apartment... —I'm so distracted right now. Can't it wait?

10:28 p.m.

Wait? Shay does something stretchy with her mouth, a shape she hopes will come across as polite acquiescence. For the past hour, in and among a dozen interactions with guests and guards, she's had one eye out for Diane, planning to confess. Testing out plausible reasons for allowing a stranger to bring a digital projector into a crowded gala. Unwilling to approach Z herself in case the donor flew into a rage. She's imagined how the exchange would go, how she would apologize, how Diane wouldn't care that Shay had overstepped, only that the mistake had been caught in time.

—Wait?... bile in Shay's stomach churns as she purrs... —Now, *of course* it can wait.

Taking a step back, she pivots sharply on her heel and pushes into the crowd. Let them all go to hell: Diane, Henry Joles, their despicable tuxedoed pals, the useless wives with their exhausting vanity.

Shay escapes through the other side of the throng, storming down the hall to a side exit where Troy holds open the door. She slips out into the cooling night where for a minute she can look at a tree, its silhouette, or the dim suggestion of a star.

10:30 p.m.

—You keeping an eye on these dipshits?... Jimmy leans against the prep counter, champagne flute in hand... —Because your guy back there is making a total hash of the foie. I believe he's high and may have eaten most of it. Too much liquid... he watches Niko remake a batch of gougères... —They'll lose loft with that much milk. Look at this king. Guy kicks some ass then whips up choux like an angel's kiss. Why aren't you running things? Tell me you're going to fight for head chef, Nik. I didn't see Marjorie Whoever take down a whacko like it was nothing.

Niko grates cheese, trying to ignore Jimmy. His hand still aches from punching Emerson. For the past two hours he's swaggered around the kitchen, puffed up and thrumming with adrenaline, addressing his staff with the pronounced humility employed by those who occupy a higher moral ground. He's had a wonderful time being an admirable person.

—Let me ask you this, Nik, when was the last time you had a raise?

—I don't know... he clatters several sheet pans onto the worktable.

—Yes, you do, buddy, yes, you do, and the answer is never. Fucking stick up for yourself. When did you become such a knee-knocking little coward?

—When my wife died.

—Forget Sandy for a second, Niko, this is your time. Help yourself to some testicles. Think she wouldn't want this for you?... Jimmy catches sight of something over Niko's shoulder... —That her? That the boss?

The doors are still swinging as Marjorie unwinds her scarf... —Take this... she throws her jacket at the redhead and strides through the kitchen, tasting, touching, judging... —What's this? I hope it's not the dipping sauce... and over to a set of cabinets.

Niko watches her pull a folded chef's coat off the shelf, shake it out, and pull it on. Walking toward them, Marjorie looks a decade older than she did this morning. Her usually scrupulous bun has started to sag.

—That took longer than I thought... she glances at Jimmy without interest.

—No problem... which is what Niko always says to her not-quite apologies.

—James Peša, Chef, nice to meet you... Jimmy reaches out for a shake.

But Marjorie's occupied with tearing out the elastic holding up her hair and scraping back the wayward tendrils... —I've eaten at your place... she re-forms her bun... —Food's not bad. Didn't know you were twins.

—Niko likes to pretend I don't exist.

This fails to charm Marjorie. She scans the kitchen... —Out of anything?

—Chive twists. Macarons are running low.

—And the little thingy cones?

—Good so far.

Jimmy examines her face, his curiosity shameless... —You've been crying.

—Shut the fuck up.

But Marjorie's expression doesn't change... —Go home, Nikolic. You must be exhausted.

—I can stay.

—Are you kidding?... Jimmy toasts the door with his champagne flute... —Boss is telling you to leave... to Marjorie... —Chef, my brother, I don't know if you know, his wife died and now he can't deal with women. I'd like to get him out to the party so he can hone his social skills. God knows he's not getting any practice going from work to home to work. Mondays spent in bed watching football highlights. He hates football but can't risk watching a show where men and women get friendly.

—Is that true?... Marjorie pulls the bowl of dough toward her... —Your wife died?

—Yeah.

—Nik's been like this for two years.

—How did she die?

—Heart attack.

—Alright, Jimmy, fine. Let's go... Niko rips at the buttons of his coat.

—She was only twenty-six.

—Let's go.

—Came out of nowhere... Jimmy adds.

—I'm going.

As he walks past, Marjorie grabs his arm... —Nikolic.

Jimmy's right, she has been crying.

—It's brutal, I know. My dad died. I'm sorry.

Niko pulls away, tossing his coat as he makes for the door. Marjorie's compassion infuriates him. He swings through the kitchen door into the hallway, suddenly desperate to punish her. Why don't people get how maddening it is to be understood.

10:37 p.m.

Henry watches the DHS agents cozy up to Norm Whitstuff and the mayor with performative chortles. Fisk even throws in a few sympathetic shakes of the head. Deferential for now, sure.

Another slug of prosecco. Annie must have bumped into an old friend or acquaintance. She's a notorious overstayer. Always asking one last question or puzzling out a lapse in logic no one particularly cares to set straight.

—What are you, like, deliberately hiding?

Henry turns around.

Kulap Stein.

The curator's skin is alarmingly glossy and his enviable golden complexion has turned the color of dishwater. As he looks around the room, he gives his dinner jacket compulsive little tugs.

—What are you doing here, Kulap? Last I heard you were face down in a toilet.

—Like I said, there's a conversation to be had.

—Not right now there isn't. You need to leave... over Kulap's shoulder he spots Agent Fisk lifting an appetizer, opening his mouth wider than necessary... —Immediately.

—This will only take a minute.

Henry drags Kulap out of sight behind the column... —Friend, believe me when I say your timing is far from ideal. Go home. We're handling the situation. Get some sleep.

—Sleep? How am I supposed to sleep? You talked about prison.

—It won't come to that.

—Everything I bought from Vauclain, I made sure we had plausible deniability.

—Not now, Kulap... he hisses.

—Heritage sites are getting smashed in Syria, Afghanistan. Isn't it up to us in Western—

—Syria, Kulap, Syria. No one's smashing shit in India.

—I can't go to prison. I have food allergies and zero resolve. I'll crumble... Kulap looks away, perhaps reluctant to picture further atrocities... —And what about Garrett? Unless maybe you want your kids going to PS Dumbfuck? I know parents ready to chop off a finger to get boosted up the Garrett waitlist. Strangers try to slip me cash. In the men's room, once.

—Believe me, friend, I'm working on... peering around the column... —Hell... he's caught the eye of Fisk who grimly signals Henry and starts walking toward him.

—Imagine my kids, Henry, visiting me in prison. Papa stuck behind plexi like a bug on a windshield.

—Kulap... taking hold of his thin shoulder... —I'm going to need you to breathe.

—Don't throw me under the bus, Henry, don't do me like the Getty did Marion True. I'm begging you.

—Let me do the talking here.

—Why, what—

—I'm serious. Shut it.

Kulap clenches his teeth, bringing his gaze to the ceiling.

—Mr. Joles... Fisk, tucking his phone into his jacket pocket... —Thank you for your cooperation.

—And what cooperation is that?

—It appears the department will not be pursuing the Mumbai matter after all.

Finally Decker has come through. Henry regards Fisk with a flat expression, privately ecstatic that Noah and Echo will go forward to lead lives of consequence and Olive will stop pestering him at night when he's trying to read. He'll need something truly exquisite to thank Mike. A Greek head from deep storage, maybe. The guys at State always appreciate a noble head.

—What do you mean... Kulap swings from Fisk to Henry... —What does he mean?

—What Agent Fisk means is... Travis fights her way around her partner, who appears to be trying to keep her at bay... —A deal was struck. The traffickers will be prosecuted, the looters locked up, but the issue between countries, repatriating antiquities? India's agreed to drop it. So go ahead and sleep at night.

—How about that.

—Oh please. This was all you, Henry... Fisk, permitting himself one jab... —You knew who to call. Well done.

—In exchange... Travis, turning pink... —The U.S. is dropping its litigation against Acudote. Remember Acudote? Their shitty drugs killed twelve diabetics in the Midwest... a nerve jumps in her jaw... —You understand that without disincentives like prosecution those factories in India are going to keep churning out defective drugs, keep killing people?

—Okay, Lisa, let's—

—In return, the matter of another country's heritage getting ripped from the ground and displayed in your museums? Gone. As if it never happened. Because, you know, let's ensure this cycle of looting and reward goes on in perpetuity since there are never any consequences. Except for the locals, the ones forced into crime to feed their families, those people we'll punish. The ones who had no choice. But the institutions? No. A nation? Never.

—So we're off the hook?... Kulap says... —Like completely?

—We can't even make our case to the media. We're under a gag order.

A small war won. Henry turns from one to the other... —Agent Fisk, Agent Travis... hard to believe he used to live for such triumphs... —I can't say it's been a pleasure. Now if you'll excuse us—

—Power always wins.

—Lisa... Fisk puts out his hand but doesn't touch her, letting it hover in the air.

—Annihilates anything you try to fix or—

—Okay... Fisk takes Travis by the arm... —Good evening, gentlemen... and leads her away still muttering.

Kulap whips around... —Did you make that happen?

—Go ahead home... Henry pats his back... —Get some rest.

—The relief is just... Kulap goes in for a hug, thrusting his shoulder into Henry's chest... —I'll talk to Samantha first thing. About the waitlist.

—Sounds good.

He watches Kulap make his way through the sea of tuxedos, head held perhaps an inch or two higher. It's the right kind of win, a paternal triumph. He's secured a future for Noah and Echo. Sure, there's the matter of school fees, something to worry about later.

With a sweeping hand, Kulap steps aside to allow a beautiful woman past. Finally. Annie.

10:48 p.m.

As she leans back in the hammock, Iona notices Shay up on the mezzanine scanning the Great Hall with a contemptuous expression. I should go tell Shay I don't give a blind fuck about Tindall-Clark's fake marble. No, really, I should leave, Iona thinks as she accepts a fresh prosecco from a waiter. He bends to present it because she can't get out of this hammock without risking a face-plant onto the Moroccan rug below. The pressure of Clive Hauxwell's thigh against hers has not let up and continues to thrill. I'll go home as soon as I finish this glass. As soon as I drink this I'll go home to my husband the unscrupulous playwright and my daughter, Eliza Doolittle. Tomorrow I'll run lines, buy more hummus, and volunteer for the fucking whatever Climate Fair.

10:50 p.m.

—Our interim cook, Nikolic Peša.

The young man Chris presents is moist and blinking as if he's been recently unearthed.

—You remember, Shay's text about the Events kitchen, Emerson Pitt—

—Nikolic, oh my goodness. How are you, my dear... why is she speaking like a fading dowager... —Chief Pallot gave us a brief rundown of the attack. Is your staff okay? What a monster, Emerson.

—No big deal, really.

—And you kept working... Diane shakes her head, marveling at his commitment... —We're very grateful.

—I mean, there was no one else—

—Surely you're not on your way home?

—Yes, but first I wanted to ask—

—Stay... ordering him... —I insist. Have a drink, a little fun. You deserve it.

The chef glances down at his T-shirt. It has a stretched-out neck and advertises a cowboy-themed bar in Moscow.

—No one cares. At least I don't and it is my party, after all.

—Diane, we should...

—Wait... the chef puts out his arms as if he's corralling loose animals... —I want a shot at head chef. By rights the job belongs to Marjorie Wolfe but I'd like a crack at it.

—Stop... Chris sticks up a flat hand.

—I deserve it after today, I deserve.

—Not. Now.

—I have a better palate. She's a smoker, for one.

—Really... Chris snaps... —Not now.

—Why not now? When I ran the Globe on two minutes' notice, supervised Events, got jumped by a psycho? When I made sure a bunch of snot-nosed yuks from Mattituck didn't send out food covered with their own blood because they're too stupid to work a paring knife. Have you heard people talking about the food? Because they are. They're crazy for the macarons. We ran out of chive twists an hour in... he takes a step back, saying to Diane... —You don't believe me.

—No, I do believe you, it's my eyebrows, they make me look... she can feel Chris staring at her, horrified... —Skeptical.

—All I'm asking is to be considered.

The chef has started breathing heavily through his mouth. His teeth are too small. He brings an asthma inhaler up to his mouth but takes it away without using it. Diane feels for him. He's staring at a spot behind her, rubbing his biceps distractedly with his opposite palm, as if to comfort himself. The young man is so anxious and out of his depth she wants to give him a hug. She won't, of course. The smell of sweat and grease is incredibly off-putting.

—It's a reasonable request, Mrs.—

—Diane, and I appreciate the candor, I do. You handled a couple of challenging situations and I hear Ambassador Ichimonji loved your toasts. Unfortunately—

—We really, Diane, we need to—

—a promotion... quieting Chris with a hand to his arm... —A restaurant promotion is not a decision that I—

—I'm not asking for a decision. I'm asking to be considered.

—Mr.... no idea what his surname is... —I will bring up your name when we convene. You have my word on that.

Perhaps sensing there is no further ground to be gained, the chef spins on his heel and walks away, sweeping a glass of champagne off a tendered tray.

—I cannot believe the nerve... Chris seems equally repelled and impressed... —Fishing for a promotion during a *party*?

But it doesn't matter. Nothing matters.

—His wife died, I heard... Chris goes back to his phone.

10:57 p.m.

I was thinking this sensation feels like sinking into a warm bath but it's actually more like floating in a swimming pool. In a bath there's always some critical body part sticking out, but in a swimming pool and let's say, for the sake of argument, it's a pool that's been sitting in the sun, you can submerge yourself in warmth. Limbs weightless. Hair tentacling like a sea plant, back when you had hair. Floating underwater is like being held in an enormous hug only without the psychic distress that so often accompanies an enormous hug.

—Katherine!

She opens her eyes. Heading toward the loading bay is a short man with a self-assured stride, backlit by the haze of streetlights. Instinctively Katherine squeezes the burning joint in her fist, but christ that hurts and she flings it, grinding it into the cement with the point of her shoe and fanning the air wildly to disperse the smell of skunk.

—Good evening!

To block out the glare she puts her hand up to her forehead, gazing-out-to-sea style. Dark and short with square shoulders and lips like a thread.

Professore.

10:59 p.m.

It was Katherine. Katherine's buzzcut and tight red dress that had Benjamin sprawled across his bed this evening, one hand down his sweatpants. Not Caro. Not Shirley MacLaine. Three short texts and he's on a subway, unshowered and vibrating with desire, blind to the ways

Katherine disappointed him seven years ago. Their relationship exists so far in the past, she may as well be an entirely new person.

Benjamin steps back as a group of girls in their twenties pile in, obliviously knocking into passengers with their bags and elbows. Katherine in that tight red dress and bare feet. Her gold toes like jewels on the industrial carpet. He rocks with the train as it swings around a corner. Only a few months ago he was in the same feverish state traveling in the opposite direction. On his way to Brooklyn, ready to propose.

He and Caroline had returned to New York a few months earlier, bringing with them painted furniture from Ohio yard sales and Benjamin's worthless degree in film. What they neglected to bring was a realistic plan for the future. Since their arrival, Benjamin had been temping at various firms while he figured things out. Figuring things out was his standard line to friends and relatives as he drifted and fretted. The days stretching before him felt as endless as Kerouac's famous scroll of paper, only Benjamin's paper was filled, not with groundbreaking literature, but with tasks to cross off, emails to send and errands to run. An unbearable ten-hour stretch lay between coffee and beer during which he took direction from staggering imbeciles, hee-hawing at their unfunny jokes, strolling the halls with a terrifying smile papered over his resentment, all the while comparing himself to Caroline, who received a job offer from a prestigious legal defense fund two weeks after returning to New York and was busy befriending colleagues and taking everything in stride. As she always did. Suddenly it seemed miraculous that a woman as whipsmart and well-liked as Caroline had ever agreed to be his girlfriend. Men on the street still checked her out. Once a point of pride, now he worried she had options. She could easily ditch him for an Ivy grad with better hair and a stock portfolio. Back in Ohio their life together was centered around his situation at grad school. Benjamin was the focus. Here in New York he was nothing.

Benjamin decided to propose while soaping up his hands in the men's room of a Midtown data analytics firm. Watching the lather build, it hit him that he'd never do any better than Caroline. He wanted children, a rascally mutt named Bosley, bookshelves built with his own hands, and Caroline. He needed to lock her down. Immediately. The minute he got home he'd fall to one knee and make his case. To hell with a ring, Benjamin thought, staring at himself in the bathroom mirror. It was a life-altering moment and he was curious to see what he looked like during a life-altering moment. Bucking his congenital uncertainty during a mindless trip to the men's room was intoxicating. He could scarcely get through the rest of the day and on the way home, got off the train a stop early, wrenching his knee as he tore up the station stairs, exactly as he's tearing up the station stairs now. Every action recalls a similar discrete action from his past or a movie he's seen.

Heart pounding, he dug for his key, unlocked the dead bolt, flung open the door and stepped inside. Immediately his heart stopped pounding and started to sink. The room was a disaster, burgled and tossed, as if a bunch of gangsters had come looking for their microchip. A towel, two sweaters, and the business section were draped across the couch. A sandal with a broken strap lay in the middle of the floor. A brush caught with Caro's hair was huddled against it like a dead animal. The kitchen faucet dripped onto a tower of dirty dishes and Caroline had evidently begun painting a wall she'd lost interest in halfway through.

Benjamin cleared a space on the crowded couch, sat down, and unlaced his sneaker.

He would, he decided, revisit the proposal at a later date.

11:06 p.m.

—A stunning portrait... Professore kisses her cheek, left, right, stepping back to appraise... —Like Ophelia, painted by Millais.

—Don't be, I have no hair, for one.

—But beautiful.

—She's drowning, for two.

—What about me?... tugging his lapel... —What do you think?

—How did you get back here?

Actually he doesn't look too bad. Less toady than she remembers. A cummerbund works wonders on the stout. Still grinning, the Professore reaches into his jacket and pulls out the cream-colored invitation.

Katherine doesn't take it.

He shrugs... —My family... waving a hand toward the Museum as if it's the ancestral estate... —Has been involved... replacing the ticket, hands back in his pants pockets... —In different ways.

Annoying how he sneakily solicits her approval. Dignity, where's the dignity? Act your age. Be better than me, you're an educator, for god's sake. She doesn't care about his family, clearly he's rich, which is never interesting. His name, on the other hand, she wouldn't mind learning.

—Six weeks I've been trying to reach you. Are you feeling better?

—Better than what?

—Your father. You were sad about your father, crying.

Katherine spins around as if trying to identify a noise coming from the trees.

—All night.

—Doesn't sound like me.

A hand on her arm forces her to turn... —Hey.

—My dad died two years ago. Trust me, I'm fine.

—You ordered me to leave. Said if I didn't go, you'd call the police.

She scans the ground for the crushed joint, trying to figure out how much of it she squandered.

—This is why I've called you so many times.

—Okay, you win. I had a vulnerable moment.

—I'm not trying to win.

—You're saying we shared some great emotional whatever... stooping for the joint, picking it up and turning it toward the light to see if it's worth anything.

—Don't do that... he takes the roach from her and flicks it away. Katherine tracks its flight into the nearby bushes.

From his interior pocket the Professore pulls out a silver cigarette case. He flaps it open to reveal three tightly rolled cones. She selects one, carefully drawing it from the case.

—Swipe me in, please... he nods to the security door... —It's too much, the scene out front.

—Don't you want to smoke this?

—No need, it's a gift.

Silence. She's a jerk, this Katherine understands... —I've been sick. The flu, I think.

—Then you should be in bed. Taking oregano oil. A licorice poultice is also very good.

—Don't save me.

—Why not?... he sticks out his hand. What is she supposed to do with it? Return the joint? Present him with her palm like royalty? He places his hand on her cheek.

—Because... she can't remember why. Because half the men who want to save you are themselves children.

—Why shouldn't I save you with your silly hair? All that crying, the dead plants and damp crispbread? Who else do you have? Your dead father? Your foolish mother?

Jesus, how much did she confess that night they spent together.

The Professore takes her face with both hands, he is slightly shorter than she, teeth folded on each other, breath bready, and before Katherine can think clearly, make the rational decisions for which she was once known, perhaps a while ago, middle school, Professore is kissing her in a rough sort of way, a way of ownership that is not undesirable, really, but suggests that the man's dignity is one hundred percent present.

11:12 p.m.

His shallowness stunned him. Shutting down a marriage proposal because of a cluttered apartment. He still loved Caroline, Benjamin thought later that night, as he got into bed beside her. But the following week they had an argument about hula-hooping and found themselves in the middle of a breakup.

Crossing the avenue to the Museum, Benjamin slugs whisky from a silver flask. Mere months after that almost-proposal, months during which all he's thought about is Caroline, her milky skin and sailor's laugh, one look at Katherine in her underpants and here he is. Like a dog to the whistle. The vacillations make him sick.

But not so sick he leaves.

Out of the shadows, invigorated by the shot of booze, the night air and the promise of Katherine Tambling, Benjamin jogs down the access road toward the

He stops.

Lit by the orange blast of a security light. Two figures. Kissing. A man grips a woman's waist. The woman in a red dress and stratospheric heels. Hair short as a boy's. Katherine's waist.

Benjamin steps back into the shadows, taking measure of the situation. Yes, that grinding is undeniably consensual. The stranger mauls Katherine's neck, hands moving down to her ass.

What the hell? Why invite him if she has a boyfriend? Benjamin heads toward the side entrance. Was it her plan to toy with him? Too bad. He's not leaving. Now he's pissed. Some sort of gauntlet has been launched.

—Rippen.

Benjamin is rounding the corner of the building, his mind on Katherine, or more precisely, the stranger's hands molesting her ass, when a bulky figure steps in front of him.

Avery.

11:15 p.m.

The mentality you had at fourteen is the perspective you need to fuck again. Back when you didn't regard girls as entirely human with humanish interests and needs, or physical powers like farting. In his current state, Nikolic thinks, as he speculates aloud on vegetables that take to a quick pickle, he needs to sleep with a woman he actively dislikes. Any engagement of the emotions right now feels grotesque.

Prattling on about kimchi while picturing a woman naked is a skill Niko hasn't made use of in a while. You're saying cabbage is only one of several cruciferous options, while estimating the heft of her breasts and the chunk of her thighs, envisioning a scenario where you grapple together in a swanky hotel room, slipping around on white sheets with an astronomical thread-count, lit by the lit-up city as you take her from behind, all the while shutting out the image of your actual mattress which never keeps its fitted sheet in place and lies slapped on the floor where the movers left it.

The woman glances up from her phone and looks straight into

Niko's eyes. Perhaps she reads his dastardly intent because she takes a stumbling step back, mutters a few indistinct words, and flees.

Nikolic watches her disappear through the crowd. It was beautiful while it lasted, he thinks, flipping on the lights and reaching for the remote.

—Guess who I met in the men's room?... Jimmy appears next to him, eyes darting... —Director's assistant. Name's Chris. A little square, but he warmed up. At first he thought I was you. Couldn't figure out where the tux came from.

—Jimmy, don't, why are you, these are people I work with. The director gets the final decision on head chef. Don't bug her assistant.

—Jeez, Niko, I put in a good word for you. Don't act like all I do is mess things up.

—Could you leave? Please?

—Don't be rude... throwing an arm around Niko's shoulders... —Let's find you a girl.

—God no... he knocks back the rest of his wine... —I'm going home.

—Wait... Jimmy checks his phone... —Story's not up. I keep hitting refresh, nothing.

—And what if I refuse to lie? Maybe I'm drawing a line in the sand, Jimmy. This is it, my Waterloo.

—Okay, technically, that would be my Waterloo.

He stares at him, willing his brother to disappear.

—It might be your, like, what, Agincourt? Your, wow, what would that be? Saratoga?

Nikolic walks away.

—I'm telling you... Jimmy calls after him... —This can all be solved with sex!

11:21 p.m.

It is while speaking to Eleanor Tindall-Clark, noticing as she often does, the trustee's air of capitulation, so reminiscent of her mother's, that last night's conversation snaps into focus.

Dominic set down a grape, rolling it on the table with one finger.

It's not that I mind, he said, doing the cooking, organizing the finances or managing our calendars, but at some point you've stopped being moored to our marriage. You've become a passenger.

Diane remembers silently remarking on the mixed metaphor, a tactic she's employed since college, rejecting a valid argument because of how it's put.

—How are the children?... she asks Eleanor, thinking of Dominic leaning on the table, his triangled elbows.

—Well... Eleanor says, and again Diane returns to the kitchen.

The daily shit, Dom said, matters. The daily shit is what, arguably, comprises a life. When you say you'll be home at seven but don't turn up til midnight... he stopped, pressed two fingers to his forehead, a course correction before setting off again. Domestication is not the enemy, he said so quietly she had to lean to hear it. His fingers had left a divot in his skin. Our homelife is not a prison. It's debilitating, this need of yours to prove self-sovereignty. If I tell you I get it, will you stop?

Diane smiles, nodding at Eleanor.

Revealing this appeared to pain Dominic. He must have hoped Diane would come to her senses on her own. Why was she putting him through this now, fifteen years in, a gentle man who liked to read. He didn't sign up for this willful erratic. Tivoli was different, Dominic continued. You let me love you in the country. Dinner together every night, talking non-sense, is the dill about to bolt? But in the city. He set aside the grape. You are not turning into your mother and I sure as fuck am not your father. Diane remembers his tooth getting caught in his lip when he said the word *fuck*. He wasn't much of a curser.

So that's what it was.

The entire time a Larkin poem was staring her in the face.

—Diane?... Eleanor touches her hand... —Everything okay?

—Yes, fantastic, in fact... glancing away and immediately regretting it.

At one of the small café tables, two men are staring at Diane. The architects. Goldfarb wiggles his fingers in a sarcastic wave.

She glances at the band for help, the saxophonist stands with his legs wide, as if preparing to bear a weight.

11:26 p.m.

Those first startling notes of "Someday My Prince Will Come" pierce the muggy air and a man dancing next to Henry winces and frowns, as if the high notes are a sign of bad taste. Spotlights pick up beads of sweat on the sax player's forehead as he leans back, letting the music carry him outside the museum walls.

Henry pulls Annie closer, inhaling her scent. That night in Slovenia, hysterical with new love, they leapt screaming when a one-eyed cat surprised them in the fog. The trip was impulsive, premature, they'd only been dating for three months. At the hotel Annie pulled from her suitcase the sort of filmy nightgown Henry had only seen in black-and-white movies. Was it satin? Chiffon? It's possible the nightgown clinched it. Years later he fucked the marriage, sleeping with that waitress. Catching his wife in the arms of her best friend had done a number on him.

Henry bends to murmur in Annie's ear... —I have a confession to make.

Annie draws back and looks at him directly, killing Henry's plan to avoid eye contact. Frou frous on her dress scratch his palm.

—I saw you that night. With Millicent.

—What night?

—Our party for Jordan's book. You made cassoulet.

Annie takes a second to locate the memory over his shoulder... —Okay, yeah... finding him again... —Trevor brought that horrible woman.

Henry nods.

—She kept telling stories that forced us all to picture her naked.

Again, he nods. Several dancers shoot looks of irritation in Annie's direction. He wants to say shh but he's learned to never say shh.

—And you saw...?

—Millicent and you down on the street... staring at a spot on her ear... —Kissing.

—Millicent Dawes.

—Yes, but—

—And I was *kissing* her?... Annie laughs.

—Don't, why are you, you were in her arms. I don't know what to call it. Canoodling. Were you in love? It doesn't matter. I wanted to tell you that my affair, you see, was a reaction. Not revenge, nothing like that. But I was, I acted out, as they say. Like a child. I'm not saying infidelity was—

—Oh, for god's sake, Henry. You're impossible... Annie takes a step back... —I need to... she turns, squeezing past a young man, too young, an adolescent.

Henry follows, pushing and shouldering, receiving a sharp elbow in the ribs from a woman's sloshed jitterbugging. The pain feels utterly fitting.

Small tables have been set up along the edge of the dance floor. Annie doesn't sit, turning instead to face him. A couple of tables over, Diane is making a show of listening intently to the architects. A toothy grin, never good.

—I remember that night... Annie shakes her hair away from her shoulders... —Millie'd had a miscarriage the day before, her second, she was crying. She was almost forty-three and she'd reached the end of positive thinking. And sure, maybe I was looking into her eyes, but I wasn't, listen, if I were going to be with a woman it sure as heck wouldn't be Millicent Dawes.

He stood at the window holding a French dish towel. Below him on the sidewalk his wife and Millie fused into one person. They were positioned like lovers. No light showed between their bodies. Henry has never doubted what he saw that night. Never once questioned it.

Annie puts a hand on the small of his back... —Let's find a quieter spot.

—But the waitress, my affair, it was—

—I see a place over—

—Stop.

—I'm simply trying, Henry, you seem worked up.

—Of course I'm worked up. I never would have screwed another woman if I hadn't seen you groping—

—But darling, you're wrong about the time frame.

—As I understood it, you'd moved on to better things. Why else would I have... what to call it... —Strayed.

—Our party for Jordan was after you and I went to Aquavit.

—What does Aquavit—

—It's where you told me about the waitress. Becki.

Henry tries to think, tries to bring the scene to mind. The sound of scraping forks. A murmur of conversation. Stark Nordic music. Annie sitting opposite. Her expression changing from disbelief to wounded shock, then to anger.

—Forever ruining flødekager for me, by the way.

—Don't be flippant, Annie, please. Jordan's party was before, surely, why would I, I mean, I wouldn't have.

—But you remember how awful that dinner was. You and I were barely speaking, the beans were chewy, Jordan wouldn't stop reviewing his reviews. Milly, I mean, openly sobbing into her salad.

—Sobbing? No.

—Trevor and his date fighting about the best version of "Sunday Morning Coming Down." Trevor wasn't budging on Johnny Cash even though—

—This makes no—

—Anyone with a brain—

—Why?

—knows it's Kris Kristof—

—I DON'T REMEMBER.

—Okay, okay. Don't yell, Henry, people are staring.

—I need you to listen. Why would I do such a thing? We had the kids and. Maude, what about Maude? The hours we spent. How many times did we change her food from wet to dry to wet again? It makes no sense. You and I were good together. Why would I cheat?

—I have no idea. I assume... Annie regards him, resigned but unforgiving... —You thought it would feel good.

11:36 p.m.

—Shay!

She starts. The director's ambitious young assistant has appeared by her side, eyes raking the crowd.

—Chief Pallot, I've lost Diane. Have you seen her?

—Not in the last—

—Wait!... he swipes at Shay's arm... —Check it out... nodding toward the other side of the hall... —There, see?

—See what?

—Tiz Sericko headed toward the hallway with the fake lion by the way we're not supposed to call it fake but look, here's little Freda intercepting him.

Shay watches an attractive young woman in a dumpy dress take Dr. Sericko affectionately by the elbow. At first the ex-director puts up a front, shaking his head in protest, then, with what appears to be a giggle, he gives in and allows himself to be led toward the dance floor.

—God, she's good... he searches Shay's face for approval, pupils dilated... —You can't teach that. That's innate. You either have the gift or you don't. I'm calling Gross first thing in the morning.

A number of points. First, the director's assistant is addressing Shay far too casually, she has no idea who Gross is, for example, also, Chris has called her by her given name, something he has never before attempted and, though quickly corrected, reveals flagrant disrespect and is entirely unacceptable given Shay's position. The second point, shedding material light on the first, is that the director's assistant is quite clearly coked up to his eyeballs.

—A natural. Complete natural.

—So this young lady is successfully keeping Dr. Sericko away from the statue, as you planned. Well done.

—Diane says she doesn't keep track, you know, of my ideas, which ones work, which don't get off the ground or even fail altogether, but I know she does. Like she alludes to them with crazy specificity.

—Mr. Webb.

—There's a spreadsheet somewhere. Confidentially, I've looked for it. You know, poked around a little, nothing illegal, nothing intrusive. After all, I know her passwords. Who do you think set them?

A maternal warmth takes hold of her. This poor dumb child... —Let me find you a coffee.

Chris stares at her, astonished... —A what?

—Is it possible for you to clock out? Go home, get some sleep.

—Leave the gala?

—At least sit down for a few minutes.

—No can do, Shay-Shay... he spins on his heel, almost clocking a full 360° but catching himself at about 300°... —Later.

She watches Chris fight through the crowd, worried by the pulse that throbbed in his forehead, the sight of him sitting outside Diane's office screaming into his coat. No good will come of this.

11:41 p.m.

—You need to relax. Calm the fuck down.

—Who's not calm? I'm calm.

—Okay then.

God he's hot. Benjamin wipes his forehead. Out by the loading dock, there was Avery looming in the shadows. Threatening him. Wasn't he? Shoving Benjamin up against a dumpster. A sharp punch in the face?

—Have one of these delicious tidbits.

—Do I have a bruise?... he tilts his face to the light.

Liam squints, brushing Benjamin's cheek with his pinkie, the rest of his hand occupied with a cheese puff.

—You shouldn't have to squint. Like from being punched?

—Nope.

—Nothing?

—Nothing. But you have very small pores, I've never noticed... Liam pops the appetizer into his mouth.

—It's not even red?

—Not even red... turning away, Liam takes in the crowd, chewing intently... —Look at these assholes. Plundering the world.

—There was a guy, a guy with a gun.

—What are you talking about?

—Outside.

—There's no guy, Benjamin.

—Listen... pushing against his cheek, it feels fine, not bruised... —There's something wrong with me.

—Like what?

—I don't know but it's bad, it's... how to define it... —Bad.

—Benjamin... with a small square napkin Liam meticulously wipes his mouth and fingers... —Remember a couple of years ago when I flew to Amsterdam for that group show?

—Not really.

—I stayed about a week, it was a great show, completely crazy, a wild time. On the way back, my flight got delayed. I ended up getting home at like three in the morning. As I'm getting undressed Clover wakes up so I start telling her about my trip, the show, this dirtbag on the plane with bare feet. I take off my shirt and something flies out the pocket, lands on the floor. Clover reaches out, picks it up, looks at it. Hell's that? I ask. Well, she says, it looks to me like a sheet of goddamn microdots. So I traveled back to New York, through customs and all, security, carrying a bunch of acid. Tucked in my pocket! And still Clo married me. Think about that. How it relates to Caroline.

—But this has nothing to do with Caroline. This is, I'm losing my mind. Like, I'm serious. I think I really could be.

—Listen, I'd like to help you out, I really would, but I'm kinda occupied at the moment... with his thumb Liam points behind him to where Zedekiah Willington is lecturing a couple of nymphs in transparent togas.

Benjamin slides behind Liam, hoping not to be noticed. He can't take a powwow about prostitutes right now... —So you're really going through with it, this protest thing?

—I mean, that's a little condescending.

—I apologize. My mind is melting.

—You're fine. Cool jacket, you look good. There's nothing on your face.

—Don't do it. Please. I'm literally begging. Let things be.

—Have a drink... Liam grabs a glass of champagne off the tray of a hovering waiter and passes it to him.

The drummer gives the high hat a jazzy smash. Benjamin drains the glass in one swallow and replaces it on the tray while the waiter is still struggling to hand him a cocktail napkin.

—Can that be good for you?

—I don't know, Liam... wiping his hand on the back of his sleeve... —I need to find Katherine Tambling.

11:47 p.m.

The day Henry's life changed course was a cold Tuesday in March. It was overcast and windy with fits of freezing rain. Angry torrents rushed in the gutters, snatching up candy wrappers and plastic straws. On his way to the diner Henry had plunged into a curbside puddle up to his shin so it was with one wet leg that he sat in a pleather booth holding aspirin for his elbow, waiting for a glass of water. Even before the puddle, his mood stunk. His ball toss was all over the place and Jack, in a bid for scorching winners, slammed a bunch of easy overheads straight into the net. Henry replayed the match, his mood growing more and more foul as his coffee cooled in its fat-lipped cup. Then from around the corner came Becki, a water pitcher braced on her hip like a sulky Vermeer. And something in Henry shifted. Up went his dimpled plastic cup, like the supplication of a man parched beyond reason.

Becki was silent and watchful and smelled of old bacon. It was possible she despised him, Henry thought, once the affair was over. A shallow forehead, miserable lips and cutting jaw gave Becki a severe quality. From this tangle of sharpness her eyes appeared rounder than ordinary eyes and full of wonder when in fact they were normal-sized and suspicious. In the abstract he found Becki's angles tantalizing and mysterious but the sex was lousy. Hoisting, pumping, rocking and mashing, not to mention spooning or caressing, well it was all far too much like rolling around on a hill of coat hangers to bring Henry to a full boil. And yet he continued. He craved love from unexpected quarters.

Annie remained innocent of his double-crossing. She addressed him with the same trusting affection, adding chicory to his coffee, and taking his hand when they walked to the movies. Her trust roused in Henry a smoldering anger which he predictably aimed at Annie rather than the rightful target. From his twenties he knew nothing is more infuriating than continuing to be loved long after you've stopped deserving it.

On the striped ottoman Annie has left a two-inch no-go zone between their thighs. That Henry's affair was not a pained response to his wife's romantic dabbling but instead, wholly of his own creation, is inconceivable. He can feel the news knocking at his brain, trying to get in. Above their heads a pile of clashing passementerie has been fabricated to create a dome. The bonkers decor is not helping him find his footing.

—Maybe I sensed you were unhappy.

—Would that make you feel better?

An ache in his bones travels up his skeleton toward his chest. Yes, yes, it would make me feel better to know I didn't draft my own despair. Henry bats away a tassel that's swung into his face.

—Is this about Olive?

—Olive's fine.

—Then what?

He's been careless and profligate, a coward. How comic, to think he could amend it all in his final days.

—Henry?

11:53 p.m.

Clive told himself to be patient and spent twenty minutes spiriting Iona around the dance floor while she gazed up at him with shining eyes. Unchecked in that silver dress, her breasts clamoring to escape. The whiff of dissolution was exciting. He recalled the way she pressed against him on the bench this afternoon and pulled her closer. But when the band started "Someday My Prince Will Come," Clive led her away. The song was too slow for Iona, who appeared to be emerging from a chrysalis or something.

—I haven't been this happy in a long time.

The sort of admission that sends a reasonable man into a panic.

The two of them are lodged in a hammock woven from the type of material ordinarily deemed unfit to support the weight of two adults. Iona chattering and downing prosecco; Clive eyeing a piece of gaudy plaited rope that's begun to fray. He knows enough not to hurry her, a woman who never speaks but feels unheard.

—The band's unbelievable, don't you think?... daring him to disagree.

—I do. Come to my office, we'll discuss music.

She gives him a dirty look. Like a child, her feet stick straight out, parallel to the floor. He feels confusedly bewitched by her tawdry shoes.

—Time for a nightcap. I've got a bottle of scotch in my desk. Single malt. Imagine tumbling into a bog and having to chew your way out.

Primly, she sets down her glass on some sort of garish hassock...
—I've had enough to drink.

Clive glances at the fraying rope. Five minutes, tops. With some difficulty, he gets to his feet, snatching Iona's hand from her lap.

—Wait.

—Right now... he leans back and tries to lever Iona out of the hammock, desperate to possess this odd woman. She makes a pretense of resisting and Clive pulls her up violently, drawing her close. Her breath is vodka. He bites her neck and walks away. She'll follow.

11:58 p.m.

Henry is trying to breathe normally or at least look as if he's breathing normally. The end of the marriage was entirely his fault. What a creep, ginning up a revised timeline, looking to shift the blame. He can feel Annie watching him, assessing his state of mind. He reaches for her hand but Annie moves it to his back, giving Henry the absentminded pat she used to give the dog.

After his treachery, Annie moved on and found Bruce, a man she loves despite his mortifying second serve. Her memories of Henry were not of their trip to Slovenia, that pivotal nightgown, their shared pets, but only of his deceit. All these years he had allowed himself the fiction of heroism. Saving Annie the heartache of what he saw that night. The distortion disgusts him.

—What about seeing Dr. Shulman?... Gently she touches his knee... —Bruce's sister had a lot of luck with Zoloft.

Midnight

—You always did send mixed signals... Benjamin, flushed and handsome in a Rick Owens jacket... —I remember that from seven years ago.

—How do I send mixed—

—Inviting me here. That weekend in Miami. You're impossible to understand. Even after eight months I never got access. I tried. I helped your dad with the roof. I ate your mom's liverwurst. I fantasized, okay, you want to know, I fantasized about us ending up together. I thought there was a possibility. You think I don't want to get married and have kids? Indecision isn't a form of sadism.

—Who said it was?

—Your hair's too short and the blue reads as desperate... Benjamin won't look at her, keeping his eyes on the crowd.

And he's right. Her hair is awful, the blue bolt a feeble attempt to redress it, but she's also aware that to a person listing your flaws nothing is more enraging than being agreed with.

—I was in love with you. I might not have said it seven years ago but I lived in a constant state of self-refutation... he glances at her, expecting a reply, it seems.

This morning when Benjamin found out she'd messed up the Bastovic archive, he didn't ask a bunch of dumb questions. He got to work fixing things. His seriousness moved her. How refreshing to have a predicament of hers matter to another person. To Benjamin it was probably just a fun diversion, checking Giselle's keyboard for passwords, fumbling at desk drawers, but to Katherine it meant something. She remembers relationships. Two people tackling the troubles of one.

The silence grows longer and starts to become awkward. Benjamin has returned to staring straight ahead. She remains at a loss. He admitted to loving her once.

—I do know how an eggcup works, as a matter of fact... a tall woman in vintage Missoni walks past with her date.

—I saw you, you know. Out by the loading dock.

—Did you.

—Is that your boyfriend?... finally he looks at her.

Katherine shakes her head, impulsively pointing bellyward with her
empty glass.

—Huh?

—Baby daddy.

—You're *pregnant*?

—Shh. Jeez.

—So you're with this guy, having his baby?

—I'm not with anyone. And I have no idea what I'm doing. There's
no formal plan, as such.

Benjamin takes a flask from his inside pocket, unscrews the cap and
takes a rough swig.

—Thank you for earlier, helping me.

He ignores her, making a business of replacing the cap and pocketing the flask.

—Sorry that I... she trails off. She doesn't want to risk apologizing
for the wrong thing.

—What's with the wine? If you're pregnant.

—One sip. I was having a tiny, tiny... suddenly she wants to laugh.

—What's so funny?... Professore appears, squeezing between them,
handing Katherine a glass... —I guessed Pinot Noir.

Politely he introduces himself to Benjamin. His name is Dario. She
was convinced his name started with a G. Benjamin looks anything but
happy to make his acquaintance.

Katherine steps back to set her empty flute on a kilim-covered
table. Holds the glass of red wine up to the light. So pretty. Like a
garnet.

—Planning to drink that one as well?

—Don't, Benjamin... with a side glance at Dario.

—Then put it down.

—Why shouldn't Katherine choose for herself whether to enjoy a
glass of wine?... Professore smiles benevolently at Benjamin... —Are you
her brother, or... employing the eye-twinkle the humorless use to indicate a joke... —Perhaps her father?

—They say there's no safe amount.

—Stop.

—Safe?

—I know it's different in Europe and all—

—Benjamin.

—but in this country pregnant women don't toss back booze like they've hit rumspringa. Why aren't you watching out for her?

She braces for Professore's reaction. She can feel the dumb smile pasted on her face.

—Ah, I see... with no change in expression, Dario clears his throat... —Since she is carrying my child, you mean?

—Yes, because, clearly she... waving toward Katherine... —Has no self-control.

Both men look at her. And she. Continues smiling vacantly.

—You know, Benjamin, I think is your name... Dario, with chilling kindness... —It is true what you say that things are different in Europe regarding pregnancy and a little wine. Maybe we are more. Tolerant than perhaps you are here.

—Low birth weight, for one.

—Perhaps another way we are different in Europe is we don't infantilize our women.

Okay but you did just say *our*.

—If Katherine believes it is fine for her health to sip a little wine then I must defer to her common sense.

—Obviously, I mean, I am a feminist, you know. I'm not. Pushing for the, whatever, state control of women or something. I was only saying. Also, possibly, in Europe, you might not have the science we do in America.

—We have science.

—Look... Katherine hands her wine to the waiter who's been standing impassively to one side listening to their conversation... —All done... showing empty hands as if she's being frisked... —Can we have a fun night, now?

—I'm, I have nothing more to say... Benjamin walks away.

This leaves the two of them in silence, interrupted only by the gentle rumble of Dario's throat-clearing tic. Side by side, staring into the crowd.

12:10 a.m.

Annie squeezed his hand, pressed her cheek against his. No kiss, no hug. She was fine, didn't need his help finding a cab. Henry watched her work her way past a group of television actors. Coat draped overarm, the woman who was once the love of his life walked out the museum's front door and disappeared.

And Henry turned back to the gala, pushing deeper into the crowd as if he could give himself the slip. How dearly he'd love to go home and crawl into bed. Spoon Olive, even as she bats him away. But Diane likes him to stay until the night is over. Two more hours.

—You're the one who had to have dew explained... a tall woman in a colorful knit tells her date as Henry passes... —To my eternal embarrassment.

Or maybe the woman said internal.

Henry stops at the bar, tired of evaluating and taking stock. It's murderous, the taking of stock. Weighing your decisions, your paths and mistakes, the people who crushed you and the ones you double-crossed. Jesus, how exhausting it is, the business of dying.

12:12 a.m.

With a flexibility she doesn't recall owning, Iona has one arm wrenched halfway up her back to get at the zip of her dress. Clive's ripping off his shoes, slamming the door with his foot and unbuckling his belt with an urgency that borders on comic. Sweeping books off the couch, jogging to a speaker, scrolling his phone for music. He starts taking off his shirt and Iona tries to look as if she's seen it all before. But she hasn't. Only in ads for French cologne. A stomach that's all muscle, those two furrows that form an arrow helpfully pointing the way.

Clive crosses the room, briskly unzips her dress and tussles it off, pulling down her chignon and tossing hairpins on the coffee table with a practiced underhand. She can feel her hair frozen in place, stiff with goop. She tries mussing it, scrunching, praying for the spirit of Bardot.

But Clive doesn't care. He spins her around, spanks her once, hard, and pushes her onto the couch.

12:14 a.m.

Far from the columns of delicious jelly he'd hoped for, Iona's legs are firm and horribly athletic. He's ripped off the frock of a juicy harlot only to be faced with a Victorian schoolmarm. Sturdy hips, a narrow waist, long-distance calves, those spilling breasts. Clive hesitates, steps back but Iona reaches down, pulls off a flimsy shred of satin or silk and, staring into his eyes, flings her underwear across the room.

12:15 a.m.

Not thin but gaunt. Well Enzo said she was dying. Implied it, anyway. Said the cancer was back.

—I had no idea you were attending this evening, Benjamin. What a treat.

Mrs. Tindall-Clark looks so fragile standing before him in her optimistic sequins that Benjamin has to suppress the urge to take her by the elbow, stabilize her somehow.

—Now, not a peep about our meeting earlier, promise? Marlon is hovering.

Benjamin nods... —I like your dress. It's so spangly.

It's rare in New York for a woman of means to forgo plastic surgery. For her income bracket, Eleanor's face is uniquely creased and dappled with sun spots. Her wrinkles prove, or rather, her face reveals, no, *betrays*, the life she

actually it's becoming more and more difficult for Benjamin to organize his thoughts, what with the alcohol and all.

—One night when I was three... he finds himself saying... —I fell into a pool, sank like a stone and lay on the bottom staring up at the sparkly lights.

—My dress reminds you of drowning?

—I mean, in a good way.

She laughs... —I've missed you, dear.

Not long after Benjamin started working at the Tindall-Clarks', when he was still wary of cursing or breaking a glass, he came across a framed picture of Eleanor on the bookshelf. The photo was taken in a park of some kind and she was wearing a pair of madras shorts and a tight red halter top. Golden hair blew across her face and sunglasses. A wicked mouth laughed at the person holding the camera. God she was divine. That was the word that occurred to him. Divine. Benjamin gazed at the picture with unbridled lust, which was disconcerting given that Eleanor was at that very moment sitting at the table behind him in a turtleneck sweater and double-strung pearls.

—What is it, Benjamin? What's bothering you?

—I'm not sure... he stares at his hand where it grips his drink. For some reason he wants to tell her, or try, at least... —I can't see with any clarity. I can't make anything make sense.

—Oh dear... she pets his arm, her gnarled hand heavy with splashy rocks... —You're all mixed up.

—I guess that's the way it crumbles, cookie-wise.

—A line from a movie, I take it.

He nods, hating himself on many unidentifiable levels.

—You're too much, Benjamin. So dramatic. Exactly like my son when he was six or eight. A real silly billy.

Oddly enough, Mrs. Tindall-Clark's breezy dismissal cheers him immensely. The waves of doubt and self-recrimination that wake him at night drenched in sweat is nothing more than run-of-the-mill histrionics. Silly-billiness. Nothing that requires medication, a new personality or a prolonged hospital stay.

—Now tell me you're going to keep writing movies, Benjamin. Even with a job you'll still make art. Tell me some ideas. I'm an excellent sounding board.

And he wants to say, Well, Eleanor, talk about dramatic, I make movies all the time. I never stop writing. Only by inventing dialogue can I contradict myself endlessly and still remain on the right side of sanity.

12:21 a.m.

—Dad... Colin picks up on the second ring... —What's wrong?

—Wrong? Nothing.

—Kim said you sounded weird.

—Nothing could be further from the truth... standing in the quiet hallway outside the American galleries, Henry swirls his glass, encouraging the ice to melt... —I'm completely normal. How's work?

Colin's job is beneath him but he's a good kid, not as prideful as his old dad.

—Fine. Where are you?

—Museum Gala. I read the book you recommended... Henry hadn't, but he'd flipped through it and noted its thrust.

—And?... Colin sounds as if he's walking... —What did you take from it?

—Gratitude.

—But, Dad, are you practicing it?

—All the time... Henry sucks the ice-melt from his glass... —You sound like you're en route. I'll let you go.

—Walking to a friend's.

—Girlfriend?

—A friend who's a girl.

A typical Henry stumble, sounding, even to his ears, as if he's worried Colin might be gay. It's no matter to him. He tries to show he's the kind of progressive father a kid could confide in, then turns around with a conservative question like *girlfriend?*

—Hey, Dad...?

—Remember when I visited you out in Palmdale, took you out for pancakes?

—You never came to Palmdale.

—I did... please, Henry implores, let me review my failings without contradiction... —We ate pancakes in a diner painted turquoise. The waiter had a lazy eye.

—I'll take your word for it.

His word for it? The dinner was etched in Henry's memory as the moment he assumed the full weight of his shoddy parenting. To Colin, it meant nothing.

—Dad?

Of course, Henry hadn't copped to anything that night. Only recognized his inadequacy. It was a first step. If only, in the ensuing years, there had been further steps.

—I'm just arriving.

—Yes, yes, you need to go... Henry's already walking back toward the Great Hall, past a pretty blonde in conversation with a young man who has ignored the directive of black tie and wears a stained T-shirt advertising a bar in Moscow.

—Love you.

—Love you... Henry chokes it out, pressing END as he does, looking around to see if anyone overheard.

—Usually I react badly to depth... the blonde is telling the man in the T-shirt... —It makes me contrary. But an hour after your lecture I was standing with my sister in one of those big white tents tasting your scallops and I realized, hell, yes, food *is* the only constant and I felt this release, like I was finally letting go of the whole ordeal.

12:26 a.m.

And Maya describes the ordeal that brought her to those white tents in Aspen: the fiancé who fled the morning of their wedding, the bedridden weeks that followed. Niko nods sympathetically. He wants to tell Maya he's never set foot in Colorado, but she smells like crème brûlée and the shyly reverent way she flutters up at him is making it more and more difficult to come clean.

—You're such a good listener, James. I bet you've been told that before.

Stop imagining the feel of her skin, silken hair falling through your fingers. Maya wears very little makeup, the confidence of which excites him. Unless it's a lingering effect of her depression, in which case it excites him slightly less. Niko hasn't been touched by a woman since March, when a joyless TSA agent pulled him aside for a patdown.

—James?

—Call me Jimmy.

—It's weird but I feel like you really see me.

In the past Niko's always gone for brunettes. Sandrine had Turkish blood on her mother's side and Grandpère was Algerian, but it's been so long, women, can he even claim to have a type? Maya here is very, very blond, her hair's practically white it's so blond, her eyelashes scarcely visible. The entire effect is of something papery left in the sun.

—Niko!

Maya's anemic eyebrows draw together. Jimmy is walking toward them, holding up his phone. She swivels to look at Niko, then back to Jimmy, trying to make sense of these two identical people. Jimmy calls his name again and Niko watches Maya register the truth. Her face grows hard and bony. Her eyes ice over.

—Maya, wait.

But she's gone, flouncing into the crowd. Niko finishes his drink in one swallow and sets down the glass on a confusing surface. The mere proximity of his brother brings out the worst in him.

—Buddy... Jimmy's breathing hard, hand gripping his phone...
—It's up. It's online.

—Not now.

—Yes, now... pushing his phone toward Niko... —Read it.

With that special dread he hasn't felt in the last decade, Niko skims the interview. The article captures Jimmy in all his glory. A spew of bloviated rambling, punctuated here and there by spasms of false modesty, capped off with a brazen dive into straight-up fiction.

—I get carried away in interviews.

—I don't care... he passes the phone back to Jimmy, tired of everything.

—But you'll back me up?

—Lie for you.

—Niko, be reasonable. Think how much I've sacrificed for my career. All those nights, the hours spent away from, I mean, my marriage is crumbling.

—You invented a whole childhood.

—And you poisoned a bunch of people and let your chef take the fall.

—You're the one who said to keep quiet!

—Because your life's already so pathetic. Look, I don't give a fuck about the mushrooms. All I'm saying is everybody lies... throwing an arm around Niko's shoulders... —Welcome to the party.

12:33 a.m.

Maybe they thought she'd take it better with a couple of drinks in her system. Or maybe the architects rightly assumed she wouldn't explode in public. When they told Diane that the brunnel she believed was still under discussion is in fact halfway through construction in a factory near Hoboken, Diane bit the inside of her cheek, looked Hernandez dead in the eye, winked, marched over to Chris and ordered him to hand over his acupuncture pills.

And finally the pills have taken effect, galloping through her system and sending bolts of electricity to her fingers and hips. Come on, she urges herself, get control of this night. Because she feels wolfish and mean. At the end of her reserves and slightly unglued. As a child she used to hear her mother on the phone, clinking a tumbler and laughing to a friend, *just to take the edge off*, mocking the phrase as if she were repeating a popular television commercial. Today might be the first day Diane understands that there is an edge. Yes, a sharp and hazardous edge that, right now, she needs filed the fuck down. Or she will hit her goddamn forehead on it and get carted to the hospital, spurting blood like a tapped hydrant.

—The Kleren models left early. I'm told there was a dust-up in the ladies'... Chris, suddenly next to her, so handsome and intense, adorably jabbering away... —Also, Ralph Kade is still waiting to have a word.

Look at this beautiful person. Assistant, confidant, protector. The battles they've fought, side by side. But he works too hard, kid needs a vacation. Don't say anything about beaches or... —Wouldn't you love to drive along the ocean right now? Roll down the windows, inhale salty air. Cape Cod, the PCH.

—Snap out of it, Diane... Chris leans in, unamused... —We've got donors in need of coddling. *Donors.*

—Donors, right. Then, hell, we better go coddle... she feels dangerously agreeable.

—We'll start with Chessanof.

—Excellent plan.

Chris wheels around and starts scooting guests to the side, creating a path through the ruck. Diane grabs hold of the hem of his jacket. She is a pilgrim in this unfamiliar place. People loom into her line of vision, then fall away. Beaky men, rabid women with savage mouths. Her second tour of hell today. Out of the shadows, someone barks her name. A tall man with a face like a skull feeds his date a large strawberry. A sound like flapping wings. Jangling keys, a harp, splashing water.

Suddenly Chris stops. In front of him, a group of guests, five or six, are entranced by something taking place behind her. Chris turns around, Diane does the same.

High up on the opposite wall of the Great Hall, a film is being projected. White letters on red rectangles, a poor man's Barbara Kruger. OUTSIDERS, the word spells, followed by BOHEMIANS, then MISFITS.

The production values are sharp, professional. Muddily, Diane tries to recall organizing an audiovisual component to the evening. GYPSIES, the title spells out, then HIPPIES, DISSENTERS. Now an image appears. Seven or eight white men in tuxedos sporting identical broomish haircuts and the expressions of men born on third. Behind them, a tipsy evergreen is draped in lights, a yellow star wobbling on its topmost branch. It's the notorious Goldman Sachs Christmas party from two years ago. In celebration of their lavish bonuses, the bros swig jeroboams of Cristal, dancing terribly as hip-hop thuds in the background. Two of the men rap along with the music, neglecting to omit those words that require omission by white people. The camera-phone footage showed up minutes after the bank received a government bailout when it was roundly criticized by afternoon pundits and nobodies on the internet and then thoroughly ignored. The men onscreen are punchy. They're strutting and roistering, shooting champagne corks with no discernible effort to avoid one another's eyes, an excellent vision plan presumably one of the many perks of Goldman employment, skidding as the pricey foam hits the floor, crashing into each other, cackling and punching deltoids.

In the Great Hall, conversation slowly peters out. There's an eerie quiet as guests stare up at the projection. A few laugh, as if recognizing friends. The image changes, showing what appears to be a protest. A middle-aged Latino man speaks for the disgruntled group standing behind him holding hand-lettered signs. "Look at us," he says angrily, "we're nurses, policemen, firefighters, teachers, and our life savings are gone. Down the drain."

—Chris?

He's bent over his phone... —Texting Shay Pallot.

Everything is moving in slow motion. At the most ten seconds have passed but it feels like twenty minutes. The movie cuts to a shot of Bugs Bunny sitting with his back against a tree, strumming a banjo. Remember Bugs, Diane thinks affectionately, briefly sidetracked by the sight of the affable rabbit before plunging back into the present, the hellscape of her gala being hijacked by some. Some what? Polemic? Agitprop? A bedraggled hobo walks up to Bugs carrying a bindle over one shoulder. "Help out a fellow American who's down on his luck?" Bugs flips him a coin, saying, "Now scram." Titters ripple through the room. The words OUTCAST ECCENTRIC VAGRANT appear on the wall.

With narcotized deliberation, Diane turns to locate the film's source as a recorded voice puckishly asks, "Why would we charge for checking accounts when we earn twice as much with overdraft fees?" The nasal sneer of Ralph Kade. "Of course," Ralph continues, with an unfortunate giggle, "charging for overdrafts does work as a tax on poor people, that can't be helped." The entire hall falls silent. No coughs or scrapes. No more titters. Ralph's giggle has landed much the way Cruella de Vil's would, mid puppy-flaying.

It's the bodyguard.

On the roof of her funicular carriage. Legs dangling like a Rockwell hayseed fishing off a pier. He's taken off his tuxedo jacket to reveal a white T-shirt printed with a phrase she can't make out. Next to him on the roof is a digital projector the size of a briefcase.

—CHRIS?

—Shay's headed over... Chris pockets his phone... —Let's go.

He grabs her hand and starts shoving aside hypnotized guests, trampling feet. They pass Debbie Whitstuff and her pig valves, mouth open, eyes huge.

"The upside," Kade continues, "may be billions of fees, but there is a downside." The trustee's bubble face towers above them. Evidently he's speaking at a luncheon. Chandeliers and tables. Pushed-aside plates, rumpled linen napkins. Tablecloths in the dried-blood family of red. "The downside is *millions* of fees." His onscreen audience roars, there's even a squall of appreciative applause. But here in the museum the mood is horribly tense. A precarious undercurrent is beginning to brew, rippling among the guests. Much more of this and she'll have a full-blown riot on her hands.

—Keep moving... Chris tugs her arm

The pills were a mistake. She focuses on Chris's black-jacketed back as if zooming into its darkness will trigger a cut to another time or location, following him as he struggles past guests who seem to be cemented in place. From the film comes Mayor Greenberg's baritone. He's speaking at last year's infamous press conference, "of course I'm going to put more cops in low-income projects," he says, "that's where the crime is."

—What the hell?... a woman asks her date... —This some kind of joke?

12:47 a.m.

Jogging down the stairs from the mezzanine, for fifty-whatever, Shay can still move. Conveying a sense of urgency and concern. Advancing, yes, but not too quickly, toward the funicular station.

The film is bitter and accusatory. Funny. Exactly what the Museum needs. Count Shay a fan. She feels a part of the hijinks and, having never been a part of any hijinks, the feeling is exhilarating. She's spent too long being dutiful. Trusty and faithful. Putting others first. As Shay hustles across the hall, she allows every obstacle to delay her twice as long as it should. She weaves through a group of gawkers, puts out a hand to stop a young man from tripping. A suggestion is projected on the wall in massive white-on-red type: KILL THE POOR.

12:50 a.m.

The words dissolve into a medium close-up of two pasty reptiles, text stamped across their tuxedoed chests: *Koch brothers, American Plutocrats*, which at first Diane misreads as *Pederasts*. A narrator says, "These billionaire brothers believe the minimum wage is crippling America."

Diane resolves to stop looking back. Ahead of her she can hear Chris ranting, I knew that bodyguard was fake.

A soprano hits the high notes of "Happy Birthday." This will show the time Lindsey-Hailey Green, beloved pop star and former Disney kid, feted Charles Koch, Marilyn Monroeing breathily into the mike as she undulated in orange spandex.

Using Chris as a sort of battering ram against the guests, Diane keeps her head bowed, hoping to avoid detection as the ringleader of this circus. The birthday song ends abruptly and is replaced by a reporter's voice calling, "Hey, Senator," a beat, then: "your vote yesterday means ten thousand of the nation's hungriest families will no longer qualify for food stamps." It's an old clip. She can't imagine anyone here is seeing it for the first time. Rosey Rosenbloom saying, "Then let them get jobs."

As Diane turns to look back at the projection her hand falls from Chris's shoulder. Familiar documentary footage plays onscreen, footage everyone in this room has seen every other day of their lives and become one hundred percent inured to. Factories in China and India, brown people seated in rows, bent over sewing machines, stitching purses. A fact that no amount of first-world awareness has ever changed. INDIGENT. IMPOVERISHED. INSOLVENT. Back and forth she turns as she makes her way to the funicular station. Chris has disappeared, swallowed up by the crowd. The Indian factory dissolves into a clip showing Anton Spitz's Workcamp collection from Spring 2002. Models with their heads shaved stomping down the runway in grey smocks and twelve-hundred-dollar boots. Should anyone fail to grasp the allusion, painted on each woman's wrist was a row of black numbers. Eight years ago it was a scandal. Anton apologized, did a lap of contrition. The media forgave him.

CULL THE POOR

12:54 a.m.

Now his mouth is on her thigh. His hands leave her breasts and move down her body. On his biceps, a vanitas tattoo. Skull, candle, entwined with, dear god he is, has she ever been with, holy god, she's losing it. Calm down. Maintain some fucking composure. Clive's hands are strong, gripping her ass, he'll leave bruises. Close your eyes. Clive moves with a certainty you might call routine if you were into belittling yourself during foreplay. How much sex has this man had? Knowing exactly what will feel. Tremendous. He is utterly lost, you can tell. No editing, no out-of-body critique. No worrying about cellulite or stains on his couch. Clive's hunger incites in her a mushrooming wildness. Iona takes his head in her hands, drawing him up, wanting the full weight of him. He kisses her, biting her lip. She wraps her legs around his waist. Try not to get unusual. Don't rip him apart with your teeth. Display the correct amount of passion. Dial it down. Bring on the theater of sex. Moaning softly, as she knows is fitting, when she wants to digest him or become him.

12:57 a.m.

—Please not this... Diane stabs the funicular's call button... —Not this right now.

If she can simply stand here whaling on the control pad she won't be forced to face what happens next. Wrapped in this sash like a hideous gift, poking and jabbing. The bodyguard squats on the carriage roof, soaking up the mayhem he's unleashed.

—Shay? Where are we?

—Peter's on his way... with a calm that manages to both comfort and antagonize, Shay tucks her phone back into her jacket pocket... —We'll bring down the carriage manually.

Onscreen three young women are crouching next to a dumpster, savaging dresses and blouses with a pair of gardening shears. A darling widdle puffer jacket gets decimated, a cute T-shirt torn up the middle. Overstock. The women are shredding brand-new clothes in the name of overstock. Text arrives on the screen: IN MANY COUNTRIES

CLOTHING IS SHELTER. The women laugh, dancing in a blizzard of falling feathers as if it's their first snow. A close-up shows the name on the label. Noizy.

—Of course... Diane mutters, or thinks, it's impossible to tell at this point.

The bodyguard was thorough, you have to give him that. Finding a way to provoke every one of the Museum's allies. Kudos. Did Z know about this? Endorse it? Even mastermind the whole thing?

Diane turns to look for Z. Instead she finds Shay. She's watching the bodyguard with surprising concern. Motherly concern.

—Shay?

—Mmm.

—How did a projector get in here?

Shay pivots slowly to look at her... —What's that?

—How did a deranged activist get into the museum carrying a digital projector? One of your guards—

—No.

—But they must have.

—No one on my staff, Diane, allowed unauthorized equipment into your museum.

—*My* museum?

—I did.

—What do you mean, *you* did?

—I gave the two men, one of them a donor, I believe, permission to enter with what I ascertained was a portable digital projector.

—But you knew we weren't showing any films.

—Correct.

—Help me, here... Diane shakes off a horrible feeling of foreboding... —Help me understand.

—My resignation will be on your desk first thing.

—Your? But I don't want your... stepping toward her... —For an oversight? It was a big night, hundreds of guests.

—But you see... Shay looks almost sorry for her... —It wasn't an oversight.

—Of course it was.

—No, Diane... stating her name sternly, as if bringing a child to order... —I assumed the men were planning to show a film of some kind. The physical risk was next to zero. None of your guests were likely to get hurt. Physically.

—But I, my... trying to... —This is humiliating, Shay, I mean, all these people, our trustees and benefactors.

—I didn't know the exact details of the plan.

—But you're head of Security. You. We rely on you.

For the first time Diane can see the woman's age. The skin beginning to sag at the jawline, lips thinning. Those eyes she always identified as warm and kind, are actually hollow. Tired. Shay's friendliness, the rapport she believed they had, was nothing more than the natural deference of a paid employee. They were never friends.

—We always assumed you were on our side.

Wearily Shay sights someone over Diane's shoulder... —Here's Mr. Joles now.

1:04 a.m.

Katherine makes her way across the Great Hall, searching for Anton Spitz. The designer unearths offense like a truffle-hunting pig. A genuine disgrace, and such a public one, could destroy the man. She turns to scan the crowd. Projected on the wall is a screenshot of an email, the helpless sap who tried to flag his higher-ups: *The subprime mortgage is the most dangerous product in existence.* The words dissolve to show footage of mommy and daddy, two crying children, and a dejected basset hound gazing at the sign stuck in their lawn: FORECLOSED. Cut to Bugs Bunny. *Hey you big gorilla, didn't you ever hear about the sanctity of the American home?*

DISPOSSESSED ITINERANT DISPLACED.

Katherine makes it out to the hallway, but instead of turning right to search for Anton in the small galleries, she swipes herself into the back offices. Clive. By this time on gala night Clive will be in his office cradling a bottle of single malt. In a rush, it comes to Katherine that Clive is the person she needs. She starts down the hall toward his office. But she can't ask for anything real. Back in February Clive made it clear he only has relationships with men. To stress his point he stopped kissing her clavicle, and pulled back to meet her eye. This can only be for fun. And she'd agreed. Fun only. And they did have fun. A lot. But to-night in the pizza place, the look on Clive's face as he pressed his thumb into her hand. Coffee with me next week, he said. Only Katherine can't wait for next week. She needs him now. As she takes the corner she hears the faint sound of music down the hall.

1:08 a.m.

The swell of the chorus turns a cheap fuck on a too-short couch into a romance from great literature. *Pride and Prejudice. Tom Jones.* Or a seminal movie. *A Brief Encounter.* Never consummated, doesn't count. *Last Tango in Paris. The Scarlet Letter.* No, christ, what's wrong with you? *Don't Look Now.* Real sex in that one, apparently. *Lady Chatterley's Lover.* Iona read it the summer she turned thirteen, unsticking her sweaty legs from a plastic lawn chair over and over, too engrossed to eat. By the time she went inside she was lightheaded from hunger and pink from the sun, a lattice pattern pressed into the back of her thighs.

The scent of Clive's cologne is losing to his human smell. Lemons, sweat, vodka. Slipping her hand into the cleave of his ass. He's holding a handful of her hair and yanks it.

—Sorry.

—It's fine.

—Not too much?

—No, no... and then, from somewhere... —Do it again.

1:11 a.m.

So he does, tearing at Iona's hair, pushing into her, trying to stop his hateful mind from wandering, stop imagining he's fucking Katherine Tambling. What happened earlier when they were eating pizza? She stared at him while that song was playing. Byrne's voice full of throaty despair. It was only a couple of weeks, back in February. Then why was he so happy to see her? He fucks Katherine hard and Iona comes.

1:13 a.m.

Katherine stands frozen outside the door, one hand raised to knock. In the pause between songs, she heard groans. A rustle, the sound of sex. A quiet ballad starts. She can hear bodies shifting. A woman's laugh. What a stupid idea to go looking for Clive Hauxwell. It's impossible to take him seriously. A man who looks to art for his feelings. His words, not hers. He can lose himself in a painting of strawberries. But not much else.

From inside the office comes Clive's heavy tread. The music is lowered. Over it, she can hear his deep murmur. The other voice, higher pitched. Definitely a woman. Katherine presses her ear to the door. The drone of the dreary conservator. She spins and walks quickly back down the hallway.

Of course, Clive wants you to believe that he's loveless and ironic. Removed from the human pleasures of intimacy or vulnerability. But in the bath one evening, the concealer washed off Katherine's arm. And Clive reached out to touch her scored skin. He was not going to pry, ask what on earth she'd done to herself, as others had. Does this hurt or feel nice? he asked, stroking her arm. And, as it happened, it felt nice.

Katherine reapplies her lipstick. Swipes herself into the Egyptian galleries and heads to the bar. Still, she won't forgive him for Iona.

She'll get another drink and go find Anton.

No more thoughts about Clive. It's masochism to think about a person who never thinks about you.

1:17 a.m.

There's a reckless air about Diane, the hand by her side is making spasmodic twitches like a gunslinger itching to shoot. In her eyes there's a look of downright instability. Henry keeps glancing at Shay, who leans against the far wall of the funicular station, tapping her phone with one finger and refusing to acknowledge the remorse he's trying to beam her way.

—It's not like the carriage is going to, like, shoot into the air. You're overreacting.

—No, Diane, I'm introducing you to the notion of exposure. And the exposure you're... Henry pulls out his phone, hacking into his other fist... —Pardon me, this is ridiculous. I'm calling the fire department.

—In all their heavy gear, with ladders and, no. Peter will be here any second. He's planning to winch the carriage down manually.

Hostility crackles in the Great Hall. Guests are four to six drinks in and this business, whatever it is, has gotten them riled up and skittish. They are good people, they believe. Charitable, justifiably wealthy, and, despite a few missteps, on the right side of history. Why are they being subjected to bummer footage of Midwesterners queuing outside a food pantry in the rain?

Suddenly Henry feels the fight leave his body. He is dying and none of this matters. Not Diane, not Shay or Malcolm, not even Annie. How incredible it feels not to care. Watching Diane stooped over the call button in her big dress, a wave of compassion hits him. Poor thing. Like Henry, her days are numbered.

—Okay... raising his hands in surrender... —I won't make the call, promise. You take the lead on this.

—Thank you... she looks past him... —Is it over?

Henry turns around. The wall is back to being a wall. The young man sitting on top of the funicular carriage has turned off his projector and is busily packing it into a case... —Looks like it.

—How did it end?

—No idea but I imagine it involved the word complicit.

Diane smiles briefly. Briefly grateful. He smiles back.

—Peter!... Shay calls out, needlessly specifying... —Peter's here.

—Will you excuse me?... Diane lifts the hem of her dress... —I need to find Chris... and she turns and walks away.

1:22 a.m.

The minute Liam's film started playing, Benjamin whipped around and hurried out of the Great Hall. He didn't run, which might draw attention. He moved like a sprightly guest with a powerful thirst who is quite justifiably headed to the less crowded bar in American. This is where he's spent the last half hour, listening to the rise and fall of voices coming from the hall, making conversation with the bartender, who recently took up surfing and was eager to describe and then exhibit several startling scars.

As often as Benjamin silently mocks Liam as someone who complains about the spaghetti he's eating until his fork scrapes the plate, he actually envies him. Liam's single-mindedness is pure. Benjamin is single-minded about nothing. Anything Benjamin loves, he also sort of questions. Forget vision, he has no stamina. No perseverance. Lacks faith.

He isn't ready to go home, back to his pulverized cereal and money problems. Benjamin heads down to his office.

1:25 a.m.

—Never called, never texted. Three weeks later he just shows up.

Iona lay back on the couch for exactly thirty seconds after Clive withdrew. He still had a handful of tissues, attending to his condom, when she took off on the journey of her marriage.

—Standing at the mailboxes like he never left.

—Did you ever ask your husband where he went?... Clive finds her underpants, hands them to her.

Iona steps aggressively into the leg holes... —Apparently he needed to write plays. Every morning he's up at five, waking everyone up and

As Iona's temper increases, Clive turns to pull on his trousers, recoiling from her specifics. It's become the sum of his life, this teeming mass of details. Maggots swarming the carcass of a moose. He's mired in a close-up when what he wants is the bird's-eye view. Mountains and a lake.

—Bitching at me about bagels... with a struggling face, Iona zips up her dress.

—Maybe your husband needed a new passion. It's not unforgivable, is it? We all get tired of our lives. He got tired of his.

—Tired of me, you mean?

—Instead of silently resenting your husband for fucking off... Clive shoves his shirt into his trousers... —Have it out. Ask some questions. Scream. Or, conversely, book yourself a secret holiday.

—You are truly vile, aren't you?

1:29 a.m.

With an expression of forbearance that fails to mask his true contempt, Peter winches the carriage down the track toward the terminus. Every so often, he snorts, as if fine-tuning a monologue for his buddies at the bar, lampooning the brilliant minds found at the Museum.

—Careful... Shay says it knowing it's an impossible order. There's no way to control the halting movement of the funicular's carriage.

Peter doesn't bother to acknowledge the senseless instruction and Shay turns away.

So that was it. Her great subversive act. Her time here at an end. When she gets home, a letter of resignation. Good. Excellent. More time with Carl before it all disappears.

A bouncing glow catches Shay's eye. It's coming from the darkened hallway leading away from the alcove. A figure kneels next to Tindall-Clark's fake marble, holding his phone to light the lion's malformed feet.

Tiz Sericko.

Shay laughs. A rough bark that causes Peter to spin around in alarm. She puts up a hand to reassure him. It's all too much.

1:32 a.m.

—Fucking wait, will you?... jogging to catch up as Iona rustles down the hallway... —Your zip's undone.

Instead she speeds up.

—I'm trying to apologize.

Advising a holiday, he concludes, as Iona disappears around the corner, was not the right approach. Clive follows at a clip. Down the hall, Iona is waiting by the door leading into Egypt.

—Swipe me out, please.

—If you'll listen for a minute.

She holds out her hand, palm up... —ID?

—Look... positioning himself between Iona and the door... —I simply suggested you allow yourself to be angry—

—No. You said, or insinuated, that David leaving was my fault.

—Did I?... he tries to recall... —No, I didn't.

—Get my zip... she turns around and points to her back.

So he is a killjoy, after all. The proof is standing before him in a big grey dress... —Stop all this... Clive fights the zipper closed... —Take hold of the steering wheel... he spins her around to face him.

But Iona takes a scornful step back. She lets her eyes rove his shoulder and chin, dropping to the tuxedo jacket held in his fist, then up to his white shirtfront and finally his face... —Do you even have rheumatism?

—What?

Iona points to his copper bracelet, making a conspicuous effort to avoid touching him.

—Belonged to my mother. Worn it since I was fourteen.

A second for her to process that. Yes, a dead mother. Goody, it's all making sense.

—Anything else?

—You think you're... Iona stares down the hallway... —But you're not, you know. You're cruel and unreliable.

—I'm not unreliable.

—You might have tried harder with the Greek lion. You promised to help.

—Okay, that's true, I sup—

—I mean, I did—

—I could have—

—help with your—

—For GOD'S sake.

She flinches.

—Nobody cares, understand?... planting a hand on the wall behind her, leaning in... —Tindall-Clark's marble is one insignificant piece in a collection that contains Dürer, a Cranach, Rubens. Do you really think, I mean, you can't possibly be so naive to think anyone in this madhouse gives a toss whether his stupid lion is authentic or not. No. One. Gives. A. Fuck.

Silence. He reaches out, takes hold of Iona's face and licks her on the mouth.

1:37 a.m.

—A bit of bohemian mischief, Ralph, befitting the evening's theme. A real Happening.

—No, Diane. I was around for the sixties and that... nodding at the wall where the film was projected... —Was not a Happening. It was an act of war.

—Mr. Kade, the film, video, whatever, was not museum-approved... Chris has appeared, thank god... —There was a mix-up.

—A mix-up... Ralph's eyes turn narrow and mutinous... —Four hundred people just watched me fuck the middle class. Do me a favor... he spins around... —Extract your knife from my kidneys.

—Now, Ralph—

—You don't get beautiful things without a smidge of ugliness.

—Sir, there was no... Chris glances up and stops speaking.

A woman standing on the other side of Chris is shaking her friend's shoulder, pointing. Slowly Diane lifts her gaze.

—Fuck... very much not meaning to say this aloud.

The funicular carriage is still only about halfway down its descent to the station and, perhaps out of boredom with the dragging pace, the bodyguard has risen to his feet and stripped off his T-shirt. Bare chested, he's lassoing his shirt around his head in a parody of burlesque. It's a small stage, the roof, but Liam makes the most of it, sticking out his ass and gyrating his hips, all the while keeping the digital projector safely planted between his feet. His belly is carpeted with dark hair, and with an inviting hand, he begins to stroke it, his tongue sweeping back and forth across his upper lip.

—Show us your tits!... a man shouts unnecessarily.

Liam drapes the shirt around his neck and reaches for his zipper.

From Chris comes a strangled cry. Both Kade and Diane whip around to check on him before quickly whipping back to the action.

Liam turns his back to the crowd and begins to pull down his pants. An animal instinct propels Diane forward. She pushes through the crowd, frantically gesturing NO up at the carriage. She can feel Chris behind her, flagging and waving, shouting STOP.

In a pair of underpants that are more saggy and beige than tighty or whitey, Liam shimmies a surprisingly muscular ass.

—That's as far as he'll go, right?... Diane circles madly to find Shay, Z, someone to end this... —He won't... but as the words leave her mouth, Diane stops, arrested by the sight of Chris, ashen, his hand to his face and she knows.

Rotating slowly, nervously. Yes. As she feared. Z's bodyguard has dropped his briefs and is now panning his naked ass from side to side, ensuring everyone below gets a fair view.

—Be right back.

Diane hears Chris's words distantly. She can't tear her eyes from the circumference of ghostly flesh suspended above the crowd, praying that this bodyguard person can not, does not, will not, but yes, of course he does. He turns. The crowd laughs, clapping and hooting, shaking off the video's buzz-killing rebuke. In the middle of the audience, Diane spots Julia Saban and her *Vanity Fair* editor joyfully holding up their phones, filming Liam's dance.

1:44 a.m.

Cock in hand, Henry stands at the urinal, willing himself to piss. Heart stuttering. He's finding it increasingly difficult to breathe. The familiar anxiety? Or is this it? The end. Can this be how he goes? Sloping into death apologetically, like some doofus in the theater groping for his seat after the lights have gone down. What happened to exploding into death like a Christian martyr? What happened to newly-hatched sagacity? A little wit? *Either these curtains go or I do.* A fantastic last line. Endlessly quotable. Dizzy from staring into the white mouth of the urinal, Henry zips his fly. He lacks a parting line.

1:46 a.m.

Liam has zipped up his pants and pulled on his T-shirt. Show over, guests have turned from the funicular and started to move toward the bar or the coat check. Chris is nowhere to be seen. Ralph Kade has also disappeared. And there's been no sign of Henry since their earlier fight about the fire department. As Diane scans the thinning crowd, a flash of paisley catches her eye.

Zedekiah Willington.

Standing at the perimeter of the hall, sipping from a coupe with a tickled expression.

—Z!... her voice is hoarse.

Still on the lookout for Chris, Diane starts making her way across the room to the baby billionaire. And comes within an inch of smashing into Ambassador Ichimonji. He's darted in front of her, blocking her path, and smelling of hair gel. Annoyingly resplendent in a sharp black tuxedo.

Diane takes a step back... —Kenichi! Where have you been hiding?

Ichimonji holds up his hand to traffic-stop her gaiety... —How could you?

—Could I what?

—Lindsey-Hailey. She's a delicate soul and that, that... pointing to the scene of the crime... —Was an atrocity.

—Ambassador, the film was not museum-sanctioned, it was a guerrilla—

—Doesn't matter. I'm afraid I can't—

—Yes, yes, I know... trying to edge past him... —Don't bother saying it. I have to keep moving.

But Ichimonji insists. The Samurai show will be awarded to the Metropolitan Museum. Diane presses her lips together and waits for Ichimonji to stop speaking. She regrets lunch, the wasted bottle of Musigny.

—Congrats to the Met. I'll make sure to send Jim a fruit basket.

Diane gives Ichimonji a farewell flap of her hand and continues speeding toward Z. An ex-MMA fighter the size of a toolshed steps out of her path and into it steps Lindsey-Hailey Green. Surrounding the pop star are several identical young women. Incensed young women.

The squad takes a sort of collective step back.

—Lindsey-Hailey, let me say—

—Are you fucking kidding me right now?... the singer has a mafioso spark in her eye that clashes with her dewy skin and juvenile jawbone, the kind of features, Diane could mention, that won't last forever, especially if she insists on parcelling out cutting stares... —I was like a teenager, okay? Think I knew that fascist banker? No one told me anything. My manager was popping Oxy for breakfast.

—That film was not museum-sanctioned—

—I don't give a rat's piss about sanctioned. I. Plan... she points at Diane's face with a terrifying talon... —To. Destroy. You.

Lindsey-Hailey and her entourage pass in a huffy train. Diane smiles warmly at the women, pointlessly disavowing the threat and continues on toward Z. Thankfully, here comes Chris, approaching Z from the opposite direction.

1:52 a.m.

—I'm a laughingstock. A stooge, a, I forgot your name.

—Katherine.

—I'm like a fat Otto Griebling.

—You're not fat, Anton.

—I have a fat soul.

She found Anton in a small Greek gallery hiding behind a kouros. In a large glass of whiskey, he was locating the courage to make his way through the crowd to the exit.

—I came to New York City and I became this... he trails off... —Despising anyone who reminded me of Gelsenkirchen. A place where no one had taste or wanted better things. Like that man in the tight T-shirt.

—What man?

—With the movie. Standing on the little train. He's a symbol. A warning. Because I like only pretty people. And pretty things. I tried to forget where I grew up. The pants I wore. I tried to leave chubby Anton behind. But it's impossible. You can't hide from your past. Your past will always find you.

—Oh, please. Some dumb stranger isn't—

—Don't. Don't you dare.

—Dare what?

—Do this shit of yours.

A terrible cold crawls up Katherine's spine and spreads across her back... —Sorry, Anton, what shit?

—Patronizing shit... the designer's face has gone frighteningly slack as if some vital guy-lines have been snapped... —You come to my studio, dragging your feet and rolling your eyes. When you leave, I always ask Benoit, do you think being so mean makes that office girl feel better?

—Anton.

—And here you are, I ask you to your face. Does it?

—Listen—

—Does it help, feeling superior?

—No.

This appears to lift Anton's spirits.

—Of course not.

Anton dabs his eyes with a handkerchief, glancing at the fabric to check it for eyeliner.

—I'm a jerk, I know. I'm sorry. I want to be different, Anton. I want to help. You don't have a fat soul. And that dumb movie, it wasn't a reproach or, whatever, divine retribution. A random chubster is not punishment for scorning your past. Wait, where are you going? There's no such thing as symbols, Anton! He's just a guy.

1:57 a.m.

—Who also functions as a symbol... Z swoops his glass as if to illustrate his point... —The idea of dropping an outsider, an actual bohemian, onto the heads of the very elite who keep the poor poor, was too delicious to resist. A provocateur! The Museum is hungry for this kind of interrogation.

—So you're like a man of the people or something?... beads of perspiration have collected on Chris's upper lip. His skin is the color of a pencil shaving... —Like, how are you not part of the elite?

—The better question is, do I have a conscience?

—Where was this conscience when you chose to publicly humiliate me?

—But, Diane, you're overreacting. It was a naughty prank. I admit the mooning came as a surprise. For the record, I don't condone non-consensual nudity. I imagine Liam got caught up in the moment. Would you like me to take you through it?

—Please.

—This afternoon, touring your museum, I had an open mind, I promise. But I started feeling, you know, creeped out. This place is so archaic, so removed from anything real. I'm trying to relax, check out the little relics and whatnot, but when I see these intense paintings, depictions of revolution, labor struggles, poverty and everyone around me is, all, you know, hands clasped behind their backs, oooh, what an *accomplishment*. I mean, it doesn't bother you? Those paintings were a call to arms, a scream of protest. Revolution! Yet here they are, here we are, behind glass in this corporate crypt.

—Corporate! What about... Chris wipes his face with his hand... —Your massive company with its bloated campus and fifteen kinds of cereal, that's not corporate?

—I understand you feel betrayed, Chris.

—Sickened, more like. Disgusted.

—I think if you take a step back you'll find that I'm actually trying to help.

—Pardon me, I can't... Chris interrupts himself by walking away.

Z sighs to see Chris go, as if it's a continual source of frustration for him, being misunderstood.

—You were never considering a gift. This was all a joke to you.

—But, Diane, who said—

—Your friends back home getting a kick out of this? How you came to New York, made fools of us all?

—Who said I'm not making a gift?

She stares at him. Z smiles with those bright teeth.

—After tonight there'll be some buzz about the place.

—I'm sorry, what?

—Tomorrow you and I will put out a statement announcing the gift and contextualizing Liam's performance.

—Context—, you're committing?

—Of course. Now your museum has a bit of life to it.

—Twenty million?

—Twenty, twenty-five, sure.

—And the conditions?

—I hope you'll be open to some ideas on diversity. Other than that, at your discretion.

She examines Z's face for clues, trying to determine if this offer is simply one more jape in a protracted comedy routine. One of his necklaces loses a feather and Diane watches it drift away.

—Deal?... he sticks out his hand.

They shake and the vice around her ribcage loosens. Finally, some good news to bring to the board. Z's gift will ease the disappointment of losing Abbas and Momo. And finding a new location for the satellite won't be difficult. She'll draw up a list before the next meeting. She needs to tell Chris. The tension in Diane's shoulders begins to melt. The news is not yet a joy but a relief. An enormous relief.

She and Z look up at the funicular carriage as it inches back down the track. Liam stands on the roof, hands on his hips, fully dressed. His T-shirt is printed with the words *Degenerate Artist* and, above it, a red arrow pointing up. He notices Diane watching, waves, bends at the waist, and bows.

—What would you think about hiring Liam?

—Hire your bodyguard?

Z smiles patiently.

—I mean, I know he's not your bodyguard. Clearly. Who is he? Hire him for what?

—Consulting?

The funicular carriage judders and Liam slips but recovers.

—He's smarter than he looks. He's an artist. A good one.

—An artist... as if she's never heard this mysterious word before.

—That's right. Oils mostly. Liam said you canceled a show—

—What? I didn't cancel any, I'm not a curator.

—A group show, of contemporary art. He had a couple of pieces in it.

—What, 1072? The DUMBO kids?

—That's right.

So Liam is a disappointed artist from the Brooklyn collective. And his video, a chronicle of the horrors of capitalism is, what, payback? Revenge for the failure of a capitalist exchange. It couldn't be more absurd.

—Liam showed me some pictures of his work. I'm thinking of buying a piece.

She and Chris visited 1072 last summer. The day was scorching; the studios were airless and rank. To Diane, the sweaty kids from DUMBO seemed alien and slightly forbidding, with a secret binding agenda, like members of a disputed religion.

—His new series is inspired by the Armenian genocide... Z drains his martini... —Abstracts, naturally.

Chatting to the artists, Diane thought they seemed obsessed with money. Not pushing new ideas, or expounding on old ones. Not even reputation or glory. Just cold hard cash.

—I'd love a painting in the lobby of our new headquarters... Z hands his glass to a man who is not a waiter... —What if I provide an endowed position for Liam, how about that?

—On top of the twenty-five?

—Of course.

—I'll alert Security we won't be pressing charges.

The carriage reaches the end of the track and Liam jumps down, digital projector clutched to his chest. Artists are sensitive, Chris warned this morning. And it's true, as Diane took her virtual trip through *The Garden of Earthly Delights,* she forgot that the painting contains what many experts agree is a portrait of Bosch himself. The artist is the one stabbing himself in the groin.

—Okay... she pats Z's arm... —Let's circle back. I have to find my assistant.

—Good idea. He looked upset, poor guy.

As Diane starts off across the Great Hall, she hears her name being called. Tiz Sericko, fighting his way around the reunited cast of a nineties sitcom. Luckily a group heading toward the bar obstructs his path and she can make her getaway.

2:09 a.m.

—Are you with me, Mr. Tindall-Clark? I understand it's a shock but I don't see the information penetrating... in the small gallery off American Iona has the trustee pinned against a wall... —If you look where the marble's cut you'll see the drop-off in the lion's claws, how squashed his back legs are. Never mind that, go by the feel of it. He's not regal, he's constipated. No one at the Museum will come out and say it, Mr. Tindall-Clark, so I will. Your lion is fake... catching the alcohol on her breath, Iona takes a step back... —I understand the statue probably has sentimental value, but you of all people would want to know the truth. It's a crime to display it. I mean not like a real crime but, you agree with me, I know you do. It's an insult to visitors expecting to see actual objects from actual antiquity, right?

Iona grips her phone tighter. Google provided her with the donor's picture and she hopes his face isn't peering out from between her fingers. Overhead, the lights flicker: the end of the party.

Marlon Tindall-Clark, eyes wide, remains silent. His cummerbund has ridden up to expose a large safety pin in the waistband of his trousers. The pin straddles a black expanse, the button unyoked. He appears shaken, even frightened, and Iona observes that in her enthusiasm she has expectorated on his glasses.

2:12 a.m.

Believing he's spotted Iona disappearing down the hallway to the American wing, Clive takes off at a clip. Exactly as he realizes that the woman he is chasing is not Iona Moore, Clive understands he has underestimated the suicidal slipperiness of the tuxedo shoe. He skitters, knocking into a pergola covered with vining flowers and lopping out one of the legs. For a long and horrible second the whole construction teeters. A group of lazing sylphs gaze up at Clive, first wonderingly, then with mounting alarm. With a professional mutter he shoves the wooden post back into place and gives it a little shake to prove he's established the security of the structure. The overhead lights blink on and off and Clive continues on his way.

2:14 a.m.

And again Shay texts Peter to stop flashing the lights and turn on the overheads. All bars should have closed fifteen minutes ago but Roberto has communicated, with an army of exclamation points, that the bartender in the Great Hall will not pack up. Every year the company sends one of these showboats, a Broadway ham who can't bear to quit the attention. She'll have to close the bar herself. *OVERHEADS*, she texts Peter. *NOW*.

2:15 a.m.

—Now, Anton... Diane says... —I can explain.

A ghastly silence. He's materialized before her, popping mints in a furious blur, eyes blazing, back rigid, demanding a public apology as well as a show of personal contrition.

But Diane can't bring herself to agree that the screening was a mistake. With Z's funding guaranteed, she can privately admit she got a kick out of Liam's film. It was the sort of public action she worshipped in her twenties. So, a degree of her former wildness remains. But like a plant in a terrarium, it's pushed at the constraint. Growing tangled and confused. The cage she assembled herself, as people so often fashion what they most fear.

And maybe it's the effect of this realization, or the overwhelming relief at the influx of money, but a burbling sensation starts in Diane's chest, and before she can assert any semblance of control, it turns into a ripple, a ripple that gathers momentum, morphing into a powerful wave that overtakes her, filling her sinuses, prickling her eyes and burning her tongue until finally it bursts out in a delirious explosion of laughter.

Anton Spitz flinches, halting his mint tin halfway to his pocket. His eyes get wide and his head turns too far on his neck like an owl. Diane covers her mouth, trying to smother the offensive noise, but she can't stop her shoulders from convulsing. Snot bubbles into her palm as she struggles to catch her breath. The German's pique is the funniest thing she's ever seen. Has his face always been so round? He looks like a snowman with those cold staring eyes. The hatred in them becomes more piercing. She has to leave. His coal-eyes are freaking her out. Mustering some dignity, Diane nods to indicate her exit from the scene, turns, and pushes through a snag of guests, hiding her face. It seems sensible not to get caught giggling like a maniac after this evening's provocation. They'll think she was in on it. Stop laughing.

Your beautiful husband has fled. You are dogless and alone. Wearing a dress held together with tape. Diane runs through a sorry list as she walks across the hall, dodging donors, searching for Chris. There's nothing funny here, no reason to giggle. Consider aging. A turkey neck, chin sprouting hairs like a Chia Pet. Skin like a ball of paper pulled from the trash and smoothed out. Picture spending your new solitary nights overly invested in a hospital drama. Eating wet baby carrots from a plastic bag. And with that, the urge to laugh evaporates.

Katherine

The bar is crowded. Guests elbowing and pushing. Everyone wants one last drink before the lights come up and Security gets serious. The woman next to Katherine eyes the bottles of alcohol with a collusive expression, as if she's run into a group of old friends.

The bartender jerks his head in Katherine's direction... —What can I get you?

—A glass of...

But a strong hand appears on her upper arm.

And Dario speaks for her... —Water, perhaps.

—I was about to say. A seltzer, please.

The bartender whirls around, snatches up a bottle and glass, and pours the water from a height, staring into Katherine's eyes like a magician showing off a trick... —Anything for you, sir?... he asks, without taking his eyes off her.

—Thank you, no.

Katherine takes the glass, toasting Dario with a kooky flourish. With that, a person she can't see among the press of bodies, merely a tuxedoed arm reaching for a cocktail, collapses.

There's an artificial break in the chatter, as if someone's pressed pause. Then the crowd leaps into action, pulling back, spilling drinks, and tripping over each other. Yelling variations of *give him space* and *get a doctor!*

—LET ME THROUGH... Dario erupts into action, diving toward the body.

Diane

Suddenly the atmosphere around her changes. The air turns heavy, almost metallic, and there's a kind of whooshing suck. The crowd has thinned enough that Diane can see, up ahead, a group gathered in a circle. Others move toward it, seemingly against their will, like iron filings being dragged to a magnet.

—Excuse me... she pushes between two guests... —Excuse me, please.

Through a gap she notices a pair of black dress shoes pointed toward the ceiling. A figure, sprawled on the floor. A collage of shapes she can't organize into a recognizable form. She struggles to understand, her thinking is still gluey. Why is Chris taking a nap? Who are all these people? Finally Diane registers the man giving chest compressions, the fear evident on the faces around her. No. No, no, no, NO.

Katherine

—CHRIS!... Diane appears, pushing guests aside... —Can you hear me?

—Nobody talk, please... Dario counts to himself as he pumps Chris's chest.

As Diane bends to him, she resplits the tear in her gown, the repair tape starts curling back. Swiftly Katherine pulls the dress closed, trying to retape it. Diane sort of flails around, hitting, but Katherine ignores her, guessing the director would be happy for help if she knew she was exposing her stricken guests to a great deal of thigh and was only minutes away from parting the curtains on her underpants.

—GET HELP.

—Please... Dario says, looking up... —Everyone stop talking.

Shay

Hurdling a bench, Shay swerves, knocking into a pile of floor cushions, and kicking them aside. In her wake, two gaunt models tumble like bowling pins. But Shay doesn't look back. She rounds the corner, hydroplaning across a puddle of spilled liquor.

—STEP ASIDE... what she would give for a Taser... —Move back, sir.

—Stop that... the man replies, windmilling from her shove... —This is outrageous. You can't put your hands on me. I'll take you for everything you've got.

But Shay's already left the walrus behind. If the man only knew how little she has left.

Diane

The entire point of staging paramedics in the building is so they will arrive in fewer than ten fucking minutes. Sitting on the floor frozen, but the world won't stop rocking. Chris lies stretched out before her in a slapdash cross. Diane squeezes his hand. For the second time tonight she finds she is praying. Really. As in, dear god.

Guests knock against her. Katherine fusses at the back of her dress. Tiz Sericko has appeared and is making a valiant attempt to disperse the crowd, barking crossly and pushing people away. A doctor has been located, a prominent cardiologist, Tiz relays, but he's passed out in Publications. When a young internet star holds up her phone for a selfie with Chris, Tiz's imperious hand closes around it and the love Diane feels for him is infinite.

The world beyond Chris's felled body is out of focus. Faces without features squabble and call out advice. A wattled man, silver hair grazing his collar, stabs a finger into Sericko's chest.

The man giving CPR sits back with a defeated expression.

—What is it?

—I get his heart but then it goes again. Where the devil are the EMTs?

Diane pulls Chris into her lap, cradling his head in her arms. With his shirt ripped to the navel, his bare chest damp, the smell of him, the Chris of him drifts up to her. His nostrils are caked with a white paste.

—Oh, Chris... she whispers... —What have you done?

A flicker from behind his eyelids. Slowly he opens his eyes. There's a film across the pupils, like that of a lizard. He doesn't register Diane, doesn't focus.

—Darling.

But his eyes close again.

A wave of sound and movement from the crowd signals the arrival of the paramedics. Diane moves Chris off her lap. Katherine, still holding her dress together, remains attached to her back like a remora.

—Let the medics through... Diane shouts... —MOVE... shaking off Katherine and standing... —Push these assholes back.

Shay

Pulling guests out of the way of the arriving paramedics. One of them is Terry, the other has a forgettable name but resembles a young John Kennedy. Between them they wheel a gurney.

—Malcolm, start moving people out... Shay, speaking low into her walkie... —Keep everyone away from the situation in the center. I want a wall of Security preventing guests from coming within three feet of this mess. This minute, please.

She turns back to find Diane is looking up at her, asking for something, reassurance she can't give.

Henry

Basking in the relief of a fantastic piss, Henry strolls down the hallway toward the Great Hall. He's looking forward to going home, accidentally waking Olive to relay the news about Garrett. You done good. Where's that from? Maybe a show, or a movie, or

A wave of noise. Henry looks up.

And stops.

In front of him is a scene of sheer chaos. He can feel his brain short out as it tries to make sense of what he's seeing. Tables overturned. Drinks abandoned. Guests shouting. Security guards trying to shepherd angry VIPs toward the exits. Overhead, the lights flicker and Henry's heart, unsteady to begin with, begins to beat double-time. Even his bowels feel unpredictable as he swivels back and forth, identifying hotspots of possible litigation.

Shay

Terry prepares the paddles to try again. He and JFK exchange a silent look heavy with meaning. This time the paddles jerk Chris to life. He blinks a couple of times, eyes wide and staring.

—Chris... Diane lurches forward.

Shay grabs her before she tumbles... —Let the men do their work, ma'am.

The paramedics lift Chris onto the stretcher. Terry squeezes oxygen from a football-shaped bulb into his mouth. JFK raises the gurney and unlocks the wheels. Shay lets go of Diane. Instantly, she grabs Chris's dangling hand. He doesn't appear to notice. Or register a thing. His face is yellowy-green, like the flesh of an avocado.

—Ma'am?

And Diane steps back. Terry and JFK turn the gurney toward the exit, escorted by Malcolm on one side and Shay on the other. And here's Roberto, thank god, substantial bulk to that kid, up ahead clearing a path. As they leave the Great Hall, wheeling and jogging to the service elevator, the overhead lights finally come on in a terrifying nuclear blast.

In the elevator, Diane again has hold of Chris's hand... —He's okay... she's asking Terry... —He'll be okay?

With one look Terry communicates, at least to Shay, that Chris is very much not okay.

—He's breathing again... JFK, he's the one you look to for comfort... —So we're moving in the right direction.

The doors open, they rush out, pushing the gurney down the hallway, out the exit onto the loading bay, into the night where an ambulance waits, lighting up the trees red blue red blue.

2:38 a.m.

He finds Iona outside one of the side exits. She's sitting at the top of a short flight of marble steps, heels in one hand, cigarette in the other, watching a man trying to pack his plastered date into a black car. A small knot of guests stand at the bottom of the steps, smoking and observing the couple with lazy interest. The woman has turned to rubber. She keeps sinking to her knees or getting a long white arm caught in the window frame. Her consort seems ready to cram her in the car and be done with it but remains mindful of his audience. *Helena*, he keeps saying, glancing around, *Really*.

Clive knocks away a crumpled paper cup and sits down. Iona

ignores him, tapping ash and exhaling a thin grey stream. Her smoldering expression makes it appear as if the smoke is escaping from a private inferno.

—I could use one of those.

Iona ignores him, regarding the drunk woman with a wistful expression, as if she would like the chance to be a pliant spectacle.

Clive picks up the hem of her dress and brushes off the dirt.

—Don't... she coughs and inexpertly flicks the half-smoked cigarette. They watch it bounce down the steps, scattering embers.

He thinks about apologizing but it's clear the window for forgiveness has closed. Clive tries taking her hand.

Iona pulls it away.

—I can't touch your hand?

She wraps her arms around her knees, squeezing them. The pressure makes her forearms bulge like the peach ham-hocks in Bluestein's painting. The girl imprisoned by Renoir's lopsided perspective and unjust use of color. Why has he come to pester this poor woman? What a joke, an obscene joke, that little Lucas would look to Clive for advice on the ways of sex. He's an idiot about human things.

—I didn't mean truth doesn't matter, Iona. I was being, you know. Dramatic.

Finally the man gets the boneless woman into the black car and slams the door. He picks up her dropped purse and bumps fists with the driver who's been watching the entire business unfold with an expression of humored disdain.

—Your husband—

—Stop, please... Iona examines the back of her hand... —I've made a decision.

—Have you... very much not wanting to hear it.

—I'm filing for divorce.

Why had he ever started with Iona Moore. With her self-denial and air of shot prospects. Reeking of that useless pride common to the timid. Refusing to demand accountability, choosing instead to revel in her mistreatment. Clive has no patience for the lethal story she's told herself.

—Why else would I sleep with you? Subconsciously I must want my marriage to be over.

—You decided this, what, in the last hour?

She nods, distracted.

—Could it need further marination?

—No... saying it softly to herself as she gets up and dusts off her dress. She starts down the steps.

—Iona, stop. Let me find you a cab.

Putting up a hand to indicate she's fine, Iona wanders past the waiting cars and disappears into the night.

2:45 a.m.

—That was a lingerie model you scared off, okay, Nik, *lingerie*, not some catalogue skank.

—I don't care. This is important.

—That was important.

—Shut up and listen.

—Let go... Jimmy bats him away... —You're wrinkling my, this is a rental.

—Okay, okay... Niko releases his brother's lapels and steps back.

The underwear model disappears around the corner, leaving the two of them alone in the hallway.

—Do you have any idea what's going on out there?

—I heard a commotion... Jimmy continues to make a show of straightening his tux.

—A *commotion*? People are losing their minds. The director's assistant had some kind of heart attack.

—Really? A heart attack? That sucks.

—Yeah, it does suck. Apparently he snorted a mountain of cocaine.

—You don't know that.

—I saw him, Jimmy. Zipping around with nostrils like igloos. An hour later, guy has a fucking coronary. Not hard to do the math... Niko digs his nails into his palm.

—Why can't people handle their drugs?

—Was it you?

—Was what me?

—Did you give that Chris guy cocaine? When you saw him in the bathroom?

—No... Jimmy makes a smirky expression... —Not in the bathroom.

The urge to haul off and punch his brother is overpowering, tempered only by a simultaneous desire to collapse on the floor.

—You know how I feel about drugs, Niko, it's uncool not to share. Was I supposed to know it was the kid's first run? He didn't let on til he'd returned three or four times.

—Three or four!

—It was a long night. Crazy to work these hours without a little boost.

—And what if he dies? What then?

—Dies? Kid can't be more than thirty. Nobody dies from cocaine at thirty.

—They do if they have a weak heart.

Jimmy looks down, gently kicking a balled-up napkin... —Hey, come on.

—What?

—Don't give everyone a weak heart.

In his pocket, Niko takes hold of the inhaler, pushing at the canister with his thumb... —Why are you still here? You couldn't leave California for one day to come to her funeral, suddenly you've got all the time in the world.

Silently they watch an older gentleman come out of the men's room and walk past them toward the hall, drying his hands on his pants.

—You know, Nik, you've always had this idea of me, like it doesn't matter how well I do, you're still up there taking the moral high ground. Sure, I asked for twenty grand and like a sap you gave it to me. Nothing in our childhood, nothing you know about me, has ever suggested I'd pay back twenty thousand dollars. You gave me the money so you'd have one more thing to hold over my head.

—That is some rich inventing, Jimmy. That's, I'm worried about you now.

—Sandy was too good for you.

—I know that. Think I don't know that?

—But you fucked—

—Don't.

—A hostess, for god's sake. Don't shit where you cook, the only rule that matters.

—Once. It was once. Eight years we were together and I made one mistake.

—Man, I'd hate to be you, I'd hate to have, because of how guilty you must've felt when she died.

—Felt? I still feel guilty. I don't know anymore what's guilt and what's grief. I want a drug that will knock me out for a year so I can wake up different.

Jimmy takes a step back.

—So if you're trying to make me feel worse, you can't. Nothing can make me feel worse than I do every fucking morning in the shower.

—I'm sorry to, I'm sorry it's so bad.

—You know how desperate I am to leave behind these miserable buildings and head West? Things could be different in Tucson or LA. But I can't stand to be within five hundred miles of you. You've been dead to me for a decade. Here... Niko rips out his phone... —I'll call the journalist. If it means you'll leave I'll spew some crap about us living wherever.

—Don't wherever, Niko, it can't be wherever, you have to say the projects. And be specific, for god's sake. You gotta be specific when you're lying. Details are important.

—Tell me exactly what to say.

Jimmy looks away, up at the ceiling, shoving his hands in the pockets of his pants.

—Cabrini-Green? Government cheese?

—You know what, forget it.

—No, I'm ready. Dumpster diving? Holes in our shoes? Chim Chim Cher-ee?

—Put the phone away.

—When you've been hounding me all day? Tell me what to say.

—Let them write what they want. I'm probably moving to Japan anyway... Jimmy reaches out and presses his finger against the wall, watching it whiten with scientific interest.

—Japan?

—I bumped into the Ambassador in the bathroom. He wants to put me in touch with his good friend the Prime Minister. Said he'd hook me up with a gig in Tokyo.

—What about Kia? The kids?

—We're getting a divorce.

—A divorce? You didn't say you were divorcing.

—What did you think I meant by my marriage is crumbling?

—That you were working on it.

—Kia knows who I am. There are no unplumbed corners. No encouraging signs of a better person.

—Sorry. Jesus, Jimmy.

—Yeah, well.

The hallway is empty but for the crumpled red napkins strewn across the floor like tossed flowers. The roar coming from the Great Hall has subsided. The muffled sounds are of guests moving away, out into the streets.

Niko feels oddly empty, struck by how crushed his brother sounds. Even in defeat Jimmy's always had the bearing of a victor.

—Hey, Nik. I'm starving. What do you think?

—I could eat.

2:56 a.m.

Once Diane and the paramedics left the Great Hall, Shay took charge, swiftly organizing her staff to herd guests toward the coat check and ordering the dawdlers to make it snappy. They obeyed. Slowly. Groggily shuffling to the exits. Only when the overheads came on did people really start to move. A flood of women rushed the main entrance. Men forgot they came with coats and disappeared. No one wished to be seen in such unforgiving light. The hall quickly cleared. Most of the guests were ready to move on, to reminisce, embellish, review the pictures. As with most things, the memory would prove twice as much fun as the event itself.

2:58 a.m.

—It's three in the morning... from the mezzanine Henry watches Shay Pallot direct the final reluctant stragglers to the exits... —Everything okay?

—Yeah, couldn't sleep... Jack sounds depressed... —You still at the Museum?

—On my way out.

—How'd it go?

—We ended the night with an employee in the ER and a political stunt that will almost certainly get us sued. So, on the whole, not good.

Henry's face in the reflection of a landscape is bulldoggish and jowly. He stretches his head back to thin his neck. A young man and his date appear at the entrance to the mezzanine, hand in hand, laughing, breathless. They see Henry and stop short.

He pulls the phone away from his ear... —Museum's closed. Go on home now.

The couple looks at each other and leaves. Henry goes back to the phone.

—I take it the insomnia's back.

—Yeah, yeah. Listen, I've been a basket case since lunch. Trying to wrap my head around your condition. I didn't tell Ellen. We're leaving for Ithaca at dawn to see if our kid needs rehab, so...

—It'd be too much.

—Exactly. But she's going to lose it, Henry. You're her favorite. I'll spend more time with Jean-Clair and she hates Jean-Clair.

—Because Jean-Clair's a dick.

—Forget Jean-Clair. The reason I called is, I want to tell you I'm here. Whatever you need.

Below Henry, in the Great Hall, an elderly couple emerges from the coat check and stops to arrange their scarves and coats. He will not see old age. He will not have time to become wholly decent, despite his last best efforts.

—Actually, Jack, there is something.

—Anything.

—Over the last year I've, uh... what is he doing, it must be the alcohol... —Dabbled in a bit of peculation. Not a ton but it adds up.

—You've done what? From the Museum?

—Yes, the Museum, where else?

A devastating silence from Jack's end.

—My kids, the little ones, at some point they'll find out Daddy was a crook. Talk to them. Tell them good things. Kim and Colin, they know who I am. But the little kids might buy the idea that Daddy was okay. At least for a while. It kills me to know someday they'll find out the truth.

—Stop this. Come for dinner Monday. This isn't phone stuff.

—Yeah, sure, dinner, but promise me now.

—I promise. Seriously. I'll make you a hero.

—Well, don't overdo it. They're smart kids.

—I can be sly. I'll take them to the movies, buy a round of hot dogs. Afterward, maybe I tell a story or two that has you coming out on top. And if they find out their dad splashed around in ethically dubious waters, well, he did it for their sake. Their future, their happiness, their well-being. He was a flawed man, but he did his best.

—Thank you.

And for a few minutes Henry takes comfort in listening to Jack breathe.

3:04 a.m.

As Chris was being wheeled away, Dario took Katherine by the elbow and insisted they find a private place to speak. She knew it would be useless to point out that the museum was emptying and everyone was preoccupied with finding their coats. "We're fine right here," was not the way to go. The Professore was displaying the sort of gravity that requires a small dark room.

Dario leans against Giselle's printer with his arms folded. He looks as if he's conducting a military tribunal. Where had he come from, this lipless pedagogue?

—Should I assume, Katherine, from your abandoned drinking that you don't plan on keeping our baby?

—Don't say *our*. And it wasn't abandoned. I had maybe two glasses of wine.

—And marijuana.

—That's like folic acid for pregnant women.

A groove has formed between Dario's eyebrows, etched there by his efforts to save a man's life. Or the discovery that he may have fathered a child with a lunatic.

—Will Chris be okay, do you think?

Dario nods, shrugs, equivocating, reluctant to be distracted... —How old are you?

—He'll be fine... finding she has to say it aloud as if warding off a curse.

—Thirty-seven?

Katherine pulls out her desk drawer, roots around for a nicotine patch, peels off the backing and slaps it on her biceps.

—Thirty-eight?

—In horror movies... picking up her mug of water... —Why is it always children who get demonically possessed?

—Answer me, Katherine.

—Kids make ideal demonic vessels. You see where I'm going with this.

—Forty?

—Thirty-five, but thank you for those guesses.

—So, if you want to have a baby someday... Dario clears his throat, that tic of his.

—I have plenty of time.

—No.

—You're a fertility expert?

He comes up on Katherine with his bready breath and catches hold of her wrist... —Give me this... grabbing the mug and setting it on the desk.

—You're hurting me.

—Why do such a thing?

—What?

—Fuck with people.

She looks at his hand where it grips her wrist. Idly she wonders if he means to break it.

—That boy, he comes to the museum, what did you promise him?

—Who? Benjamin?

—Everything with you is a game... casting her hand away... —Embarrassing him.

—Why are you sticking up for some guy you don't even know?... Katherine steps back... —What do you want from me?

—To grow up. To be thirty-five. To think... Dario taps his head, indicating the correct muscle for this undertaking... —To say, am I going to have a baby? Maybe I won't take wine and marijuana.

Dario sounds disappointed. He should meet her mother. They'd have a grand old time discussing Katherine's shortcomings over a half-priced Tom Collins. The many ways she disappoints men, how she's indifferent or unapologetic or doesn't live up to whatever the fuck.

—Maybe have the courtesy to inform the baby's father of your condition instead of forcing him to learn the news in front of strangers.

Dario walks over to the lateral files as if he can't bear to look at her for another second. His shoelace is untied, and this makes Katherine think of her father. Memories get dispatched from her brain like this, summoned by an image, breaking off and assailing her when all she's done is look at a shoelace.

Three years ago on Christmas Eve she sat with her father in a bar in Old Greenwich, drinking smoky scotches and waiting for Sammy. Dad sat in a cracked leather club chair, one ankle propped on his opposite knee, a brown lace in his black shoe. A few days earlier he'd complained of a sore throat and he wore a green scarf tied around his neck cravat-style. While they waited, Katherine told him a story she'd heard about a friend of a friend, a performance artist in her late fifties, how one night Pam had nearly died from choking on a piece of boiled seitan. Dad loved a good story. He settled in, recrossing his legs in anticipation. Well, Katherine said, it was all the more terrifying because Pam lived alone and there she was, banging on her chest, gagging, unable to breathe, becoming completely hysterical because an hour earlier she'd passed her neighbor on the stairs, going out as she was coming in. Quickly approaching her mortal end, Pam staggered around, trying to figure out a solution before she collapsed. Finally, on the verge of blacking out, she threw herself onto the top rung of a ladderback chair. It was an inspired idea. The self-induced Heimlich shot the glutenous nugget out of her windpipe like a bullet, freeing Pam's airway and saving her life. When Katherine told her father this story, embellishing all the good bits and using phrases like *mortal end* and *glutenous nugget*, Dad rolled his eyes and whispered, "Is there anything sadder than the aging performance artist?" He was intentionally missing the point, as he liked to. But it was a cautionary tale. This is what it looks like to end up alone. Folded over a dining room chair, trying not to die.

3:14 a.m.

The credits are rolling on *His Girl Friday*. Benjamin turns off the computer, tips back in his broken chair. He needs to get rid of *The Maltese Falcon*. A pathetic choice for such a dominant poster. He could name five better Bogart movies. *The Petrified Forest*, for one.

From down the hall comes the choppy rhythm of an argument. Katherine, so unappealing and defiant in that tight red dress. Mary Astor, there was a woman. Hair like Caroline's. That peculiar look on Caro's face this afternoon, watching a stranger struggle with a bag of dry-cleaning. It occurs to Benjamin, not without resistance, that he never made much effort to understand Caroline. What made her complicated. What it took for her to move to Ohio and put up with the sagging porch and lack of friends, the mindless job. The compromises she made were not easy, despite her habit of passing them off that way. Caro was the strong one, went his story. To see her as someone who battled doubt or fear would have meant dimming the spotlight on his own struggles.

Benjamin pushes back his chair carefully and stands up. What if he had accepted Caroline as flawed and uncertain? He comes around the desk, turning the question over. What if they had dug deep into this perplexing outline spillage? He stands, frozen. What if he had tried?

He's made a terrible, irredeemable mistake.

With that, Benjamin bolts across his office and out the door. He canters down the hall to the back stairwell, flying down the stairs and into the bowels. He races through the intersecting hallways, past golf carts and towers of orange cones. When he reaches the back door, he flings it open, and barrels down the steps, past two security officers sharing a smoke, up the loading ramp and into the street.

CAROLINE, he thinks, perhaps even shouting it, as he dodges traffic and pedestrians. Benjamin imagines the look on his face, hungry and consumed, like Redford's when he loped through D.C. in *Three Days of the Condor.*

No more waffling, I promise. You're the woman I need. He darts across the street. A taxi brakes to a shuddering stop. Benjamin smacks the hood, pointing at the driver, I'm walking here, I'm walking. Except he's not, he's running. Does it start to rain?

3:19 a.m.

The door shuts with a soft click and Diane is left alone. She sits on the edge of the hospital bed, the steady whoosh of a respirator the only sound in the room. A few minutes ago two nurses wordlessly tucked a sheet around Chris as tight as a shroud and adjusted the tape securing the plastic tube emerging from his mouth.

Diane picks up his hand. Even Chris's fingernails are pale. An alligator clip bites the index finger of his other hand, measuring a weak pulse. Wires snake out of round white patches on his chest and across the bedcovers to a monitor that displays sinuous waves and red flashing numbers and from time to time emits a series of ominous beeps.

She called Chris's parents from the ambulance. The paramedics pressed for it, which she took as a discouraging sign. On the phone Diane declined to give the exact details of Chris's condition in case his parents brought onto the highway the kind of frenzied emotions that could lead to an accident. Best for all concerned. Safety first.

In a minute she'll go through Chris's phone, determine who else should be notified. Read his texts in the most non-intrusive way she can. Find the girlfriend. A roommate. Someone.

Fear clamps Diane's chest, squeezing oxygen from her lungs so her breathing becomes rough and shallow. Her mind is racing. She tries to picture Chris as a habitual user of cocaine. It makes no sense.

She sets Chris's hand on the bedsheet-shroud and leans back to take off her shoes. Her toes are scarlet. In bare feet, she walks to the window, the torn ballgown swishing around her legs. Down below, brake lights dot the way up Park Avenue. Diane presses her forehead against the glass to cool it. She can feel herself rebelling, her vision clouding over. Entertaining alternatives. An everyday miracle. As with last night's talk with Dominic, bending the truth to her will.

Stepping back, Diane catches her reflection in the dark glass. Famina's intricate neo-beehive has turned to tumbleweed and some primitive instinct compels Diane to re-pin it, smoothing and tucking. Why try to pull this mess together? She turns away from her face.

On the other side of the room Chris lies motionless. Acknowledge the truth. Only a doctor's declaration of the hour and minute stands between Chris and death. She feels faint and folds over to get her head lower than her heart. The pain is unbearable.

The door opens and she straightens. In strides a sallow-faced man wearing soft nurse pajamas. Pink and violet unicorns prance across his tunic. The staff here wear obscenely cheerful uniforms. A classic attempt at misdirection.

The nurse takes stock of Chris, then turns to Diane.

—Everything okay?

—Well... like a game show host revealing a prize, Diane sweeps her hand toward Chris. There appears to be a large gulf between what this nurse means by okay and the widely accepted definition of okay.

The nurse with his womanly hips goes to the machine and starts marking importantly on a clipboard. The minute the man turns his back, Chris opens his eyes and gazes at her. Later she will swear it. No one will believe her. But for one second Chris gives her a meaningful look, as if trying to convey that the love Diane feels is mutual. I love you too, his look says, I do. I love you too.

3:26 a.m.

—Katherine?

She has shut herself illicitly in Giselle's private bathroom. Clinking through the collection of perfume bottles in the cabinet. Poking into the compact of loose powder with its big fuzzy puff. Under the sink a drawer rattles with lipsticks, the gluey kind that taste like stale perfume.

—Are you hiding from me?

She dabs lipstick onto her cheekbone, hoping to restore her color and instead turning herself into a psychotic clown.

—Unlock this door, please... Dario clears his throat... —I'll call Security. I'm afraid you've passed out.

—No, no, don't call Security. I'm upright.

—I frightened you. I apologize.

In the mirror Katherine uses a Q-tip to fix her eyeliner. What is she doing? Hoping Dario will go away. Yet his insistence, the entitled bossiness, even his anger or exasperation, reads as concern. Which is not unwelcome.

—Katherine?

—The word filial applies to daughters as well, you know. People think filial just means sons.

—Open this door, please.

—You think only sons spend their lives wanting to please their fathers? Why can't we get our own word? You're probably Catholic, right? You believe in hell?

—No.

—I don't either, not hell or heaven. Just purgatory.

—You can't only believe in purgatory. You can't pick or choose.

—Pick *and* choose. And that's if you're Catholic. If you're nothing, like me, you are absolutely allowed to pick and choose. My whole life is picking and choosing.

—Let me see your face now.

In the third drawer down she finds a washcloth.

—All of us live with our dead, not just you.

Runs it under cold water.

—Katherine.

Presses the chilled washcloth against her face.

—Open this door at once.

—I'm fine, really. Couldn't be better.

—Right now, I insist. Let me in.

She laughs. Let me in. Burying her face in the washcloth so Dario won't hear. Let me in.

3:30 a.m.

—Benjamin?

She's at the door in bare feet, one foot saddled on top of the other. Sweatpants streaked with bleach and cut off at the knee. She smells terrific, hair frizzed and wild.

On the wall behind Caro is the black-and-white photograph of the Percheron. In Ohio it hung above their stove.

—What are you doing?

—I came for you... he's made a decision. Fuck doubt, here he is.

—It's three in the morning.

—It couldn't wait. Are you alone?

—Yes... Caroline steps back... —Come in... her beautiful forehead crinkled with worry... —What's going on?

—I never saw you as real. I refused to recognize that you struggled too. I was afraid you'd need me or I would need you, even though of course I did, I did need you, and there was a day last March when I wanted to propose, why didn't I?... falling to his knees on the linoleum, clutching at her hand... —Who cares? I'm asking you right now. Marry me, Caroline.

—Benjamin, stand up.

—You see, I had this tremendous, this, I realized you don't stumble across the perfect person, Veronica Lake or whoever. You become perfect together. Compatibility is the triumph of love. All this time I've been looking for, but I'm smarter now. And I've been so stupid. Together we can make it work. Ditch this Darren guy, you don't love him. You love me. Don't you? Please love me. Marry me, Caroline. Please.

—Benjamin... but she's laughing, and holy hell is she lovely.

His knees are starting to ache. But this is it. She'll say yes. They'll snap up a ramshackle farmhouse near Calabash. Fix it up, paint the shutters blue. Rescue a mutt. Teach their kids science with bugs and a magnifying glass.

—Oh, Benjamin, if you're serious—

—I am. Deadly.

—HELLO?

—Then of course I'll marry you.

—SECURITY.

Except Caroline would have a better comeback. Witty, offbeat. Along the lines of *shut up and deal*. She'd have that melting look in her eye and he'd take her in his arms and say

—I hear you in there... a loud rapping on the door.

—Okay.

The door to his office swings open and the face of a tired security guard peers around it... —About to activate the alarms.

—Sorry, sorry... Benjamin stands up, nearly pitching face-first into his desk. This chair will be the death of him.

3:35 a.m.

Why and again *why*.

C.J. is about twenty-five, big and broad-shouldered, flushed high in the face and wailing. *Why?* A few minutes ago she barged into the hospital room in a pilling hairband, tripped on a chair, and launched herself onto Chris's bed. She's been lying there silently, face down, legs stuck out straight. Her rubber rain boots are on the wrong feet.

—I don't know if you should lie on top of him like...

But C.J. has already slipped off the bed without taking her eyes off Chris and landed into the chair next to him in a surprisingly limber move. Impossible to believe that this untidy woman with her wrong-footed boots, uncombed hair, and disinhibition belongs to Chris. Punctual, detail-oriented Chris? A man leery of emotion, the victor of a hard-won war against a breath strip addiction. It can't be true.

—His parents called you, then? I tried searching his contacts... but Diane hadn't tried. Not that hard. Not really.

The nimble C.J. takes no notice. She grabs Chris's hand, flashing fingernails that are chewed and ragged. Speaks softly into his ear.

—I don't think he can hear you.

Chris's girlfriend turns slowly, regards Diane... —What did his doctors say? About his recovery.

—They're waiting for his parents to arrive... glancing unnecessarily at her phone... —They'll be here soon.

—But he's on a respirator.

—Yes.

—So how can the news be anything but awful?

Diane stands... —I'll give you time alone.

3:38 a.m.

—Tastes like a dirty sponge... Jimmy stares at the half-eaten burger in his hand... —Flat-top hasn't been cleaned in a month, unless... considering... —Could it be deliberate? Tell me that palate-raping top-note isn't purposeful.

—The question is... Nikolic grabs a handful of french fries from the red plastic basket, drops them on his plate and showers them violently with salt... —Why are you still eating it?

—You know, it's oddly addictive. I should experiment more with rancid oil... Jimmy peels back the top bun and pokes at his burger fixings... —Personally, I take it as a win if a customer hates a dish of mine.

—No you don't.

—I mean, I expect them to change their minds but the idea is... reassembling his bun... —The flavor's so new they have no way of cataloguing it... fluttering his fingers near his ear... —Like, whoa, what the fuck was that? Do I like it? Let me focus on the food and figure it out.

—Pass the ketchup, can you?

Jimmy slides the bottle over and watches Niko glop too much ketchup onto his burger... —That's gonna be gross.

Niko ignores him, aware he's destroying his food. He flips the top bun back on the patty and applies light pressure.

Jimmy hums tunelessly as he eats, something he did as a child...
—Remember that carp we ate, up at Pistakee? Dad wouldn't admit the
fire was dying so we ate raw fish. You were gagging.

Niko's mouth is full of the burger he's ruined with gratuitous
ketchup.

—I gave you something, a leftover doughnut. To batten down the
hatches. Keep the fish from coming up.

Niko chases the wrecked meat with a huge swallow of water.

—Think Dad knew how nasty that fish was?

—Course.

—Such a strange little dude.

Niko gazes around the diner. The few remaining customers sit
sagged over their plates, coming off a late shift or down from drugs,
soaking up alcohol with platters of French toast. A clock above the
counter has a face speckled with dead flies. Their father was a brute.

—Could we get more fries?... Jimmy winks at a passing waitress and
turns back to Niko... —This afternoon I was thinking about the time in
high school Dad told Nate's mom—

—Enough.

—What enough? Enough what?

—I'm not in the mood to, you know, reminisce.

—You're still mad. I'm treating you to this disgusting delicious
meal, you're still pissed off? Saved your life twice, once figuratively, once
literally. Blood is thicker than, didn't one of us bleed? When Pitt went
mental?... Jimmy checks his knuckles... —Why can't we talk about the
good old days we hated, growing up.

—I don't think about the past anymore.

—You brought up the lake this afternoon!

Nikolic pushes away his plate. He hadn't thought about the lake in
years.

—See how fun it is? Let's laugh about the trauma we now call childhood. Our fucked-up family never bothered you before. I thought you
had that shit handled.

—I've been trying to live in the moment more.

Jimmy leans back in the greasy booth, biting into a pickle spear,
eyes darting over Nikolic, down to the table where his fingers tear at a
napkin.

—What?... he hides his hands in his lap.

Jimmy brings his attention back up to Niko's face... —Oh, okay, all Zen, huh? Raking a maze and some shit? I don't buy it for a second. You're not living in any moment. This is about Sandy. What does our childhood have to do with her?

—Because I remember how she reacted to those stories. I see Sandrine's face, if she laughed or if—

—Jesus fucking christ, give it a rest. You loved your wife, we get it. You're not the only person who's ever loved a wife.

—This is why I don't open up to you.

—Save it... Jimmy throws his half-eaten pickle spear into the french fry basket... —Time for a hard truth.

—I'm good.

—But you're not... Jimmy yanks a fresh napkin from the stainless steel dispenser and makes a show of wiping his hands... —You're not good and it's why you're still working the line. Got no access to this... jabbing his thumb into his chest.

—My solar plexus?

—Your truth, asshole. Yeah, I know how that sounds, go ahead and laugh. But which one of us is stuck in a museum, and which one owns his own place? Isolating yourself. Dicking around with nettles and berries. One week you're copying a Flemish dilettante, the next it's Demetri Müller.

—You done?

—Shut up. You will never, NEVER be close to great until you figure out how to access your shit. Return to the food you loved. Deeply, when you were a kid, hey thanks... to the waitress setting down fries... —Back at my place we sell a version of that sloppy pot pie Mom used to make with the store-bought crust and canned chicken. Oh my god, if I smelled that when I walked in the house, man, it was better than smashing Lori Dixon.

—You never smashed Lori Dixon.

—Obviously I meant the *idea* of, look, the point is, my customers die for our pot pie. I can't take it off the menu. Twice a week we run out halfway through service. Food is a material form of love. There's no way around it. Even Dad. Homemade ajvar and a punch on the arm was the way he said I love you. It's not going to happen for you,

Niko, not like this. All frozen up and... Jimmy clenches his arms by his sides... —Refusing to remember? That's some, I mean, you need therapy, that's some unhealthy shit. Also, impossible. Seems impossible, at least... Jimmy takes a french fry, chomping it daintily with his front teeth... —Christ, that's hot.

At the table next to them a woman types on an open laptop, her expression one of resigned disgust. A lemon meringue pie sits beside her computer in its foil tin. Neon yellow, billowed with white peaks. She's been eating it with a fork, no plate. What is she writing about, fueled by that much sugar?

—Are you listening to me, Nik?

Working her way through an entire pie, living her life. She should probably see a dentist. He's worried, rightly so, he believes, about this stranger's teeth.

—Niko!

—I think it's a myth that your food has to be personal. Plenty of chefs don't—

—Name one. One of the greats.

—Okay.

—You can't.

—Dammit, give me a min—

—Chefs draw on memories. Every single one. Think it's healthy, what you're doing, blocking out the past? Man the fuck up. She died more than a year ago.

—Some memories get through, a couple.

—Like what?

—Meeting Sandrine and the day it happened.

—Anything happy? Your wedding? High school?

—I start to, sometimes, but then I... Niko stares into his water glass. A pair of crescent ice cubes have fused together forming a pair of tiny lungs.

—What? Shut it down?

—Force myself to stop. You say access those memories or whatever, but it's an actual physical pain. Like being shanked.

—Assert some fucking control. Start tonight. When you fall asleep, instead of Sandrine, remember... Jimmy looks around the diner...

—Remember Myrtle Beach.

—The summer I got chicken pox?

—When did you get chicken pox? The time Dad stayed behind. It was just the three of us. We had that dirty cabin with bats and Mom let us eat ice cream for dinner every night.

—Every night. We were there like a weekend.

—Hot sun, salt drying on your skin. You loved being buried in sand.

—Did I, Jimmy?

—Okay, that one time the waves came in.

—The time I nearly drowned? That time?

With his french fry Jimmy dismisses this as a frivolous objection...

—We dug you out.

—After I swallowed like a gallon of seawater.

—If it was so memorable, make that.

—What?

—A dish that tastes like drowning.

The woman with the lemon meringue pie is still staring furiously at her computer screen. The last time Niko looked over, her hair was clipped up, now it's down around her shoulders. Could he? Stop the hackery and invent a dish that matters.

—The filthy cabin, Niko, mint chocolate chip. I'm giving you images to help you sleep. Myrtle Beach. A kite bobbing around or some shit. Parents calling their kids for dinner. I don't care if you told Sandy about that weekend or if after you told her, she got down on her knees and blew you. That was your childhood, ours, yours and mine, nothing to do with your dead wife. Mom sunbathing in that crazy turban. The smell of seaweed. Fall asleep tonight smelling the ocean. Promise me.

—Okay, lower your voice.

—That briny smell, the feel of the sun.

—I said okay.

—This is going to unstick you. Come to San Diego, we'll set you up. Mom in her turban, your Budweiser beach towel. Stop dancing around it, Niko. Stare into the devil's eyes. Go into the pain.

3:56 a.m.

Iona walked for several blocks after leaving Clive, zagging west to try for a cab on Broadway. She was wide awake, ready for her new life. Two women stood smoking together outside a dimly lit bar. It wasn't yet four and through the open door came the sound of a full-throated karaoke session. Impulsively, Iona pushed into the bar, her ballgown as wide as the doorway. I'll see about this singing, she thought. Clive's disdain had cut her. His contempt arriving only minutes after the seduction. It was better not to know why David left. She lacked the strength to hear it was her fault, her failures that sent him on the run.

When her name was called, Iona sang "Little Red Corvette." Her singing voice was still strong. She'd been picked for choir all through school. When she finished, three men in their late twenties screamed Butterflies! They waved her over, insisted she squeeze into their booth. They were named for cities or states. Dakota treated the table to tater tots and their little group sang a crowd-pleasing "This Time Tomorrow," dancing on the small stage, a fifties kind of shoop-shoop business. Iona was euphoric, untethered, free of the sad, silent business of marriage. She would find a studio apartment, fill it with cacti and carbohydrates. Watch foreign films. There was the matter of custody. Emily would despise her. But half Iona's time would be her own. She'd no longer have to hear how fasting would change her life. And what about parties? She loved parties as a child, running to top up Daddy's gin. David didn't like guests, they tracked mud into the house and once, unforgivably, polished off a bottle of Japanese whisky he'd hoarded for a decade.

The bar's din: drunk laughter, a wayward screech, glasses thumped down on tables or dropped, was heaven. The clamor enveloped her. Again and again Iona took the stage. Singing and sweating, the hem of her dress growing dark with dirt and spilled beer. No one in the bar suggested she have more self-confidence.

Waiting in a crowd for a round of tequila, a wobbly tenor described the athletics he could put to her, back at his place. As if what happened with Clive had reshaped her and men could now sense she was up for a good time. When Iona declined, he blew the foam off his beer and walked away. Transfixed by the white heap dissolving on the bar-top, it occurred to Iona that, like the Etruscans, she was resistant to interpretation. Lacking a Rosetta stone. Untranslatable. Then Iona was called to the stage to sing "Pale Blue Eyes." All she wanted was to be heard. Not true. What she wanted was to scream.

Finally last round was called and she left her new friends with promises to meet up the following Thursday.

Standing on the street corner, Iona finishes booking a hotel room as she waits for a taxi. She'll need clothes to go to work in the morning. Have something delivered.

A cab flies past, roof light dark, leaving the street empty of traffic. Iona finds Katherine's number and sends a text. *Coffee tomorrow?* The Costume girl's self-possession, her certainty was invigorating. Borrowing the dresses was a cementing experience. Katherine will help her be different.

4:03 a.m.

Outside an entrance to Central Park Henry arranges himself on a bench facing a Presbyterian church, umbrella laid across his knees. A rusted red beater rattles through the light. Out a muffler, it sounds like. Overhead, a dusting of stars.

Soon after the doc gave him three to six months, Henry went into the attic in Montauk and brought down a box of old clothes. Olive was at the farmers' market with the kids so Henry had the house to himself. He dumped out the box on the bed in the guest room. Before him lay the many missteps he'd made in search of a style. A leather jacket, caramel-colored, bought in a Florence flea market, he must have been twenty, at most. Four or five pastel sweaters. A polyester shirt with enormous winged collars looked like a bird trying to escape an ugly shirt. Flopped on the bed like a bag of wet meat, Henry forced the zip on a pair of flares. It was an attempt to feel his entire life simultaneously, he thought, as if that might somehow compensate for the lack of a future. He'd last worn the trousers when he was thirty, working for a nonprofit, still a good man. And he felt a surge of affection for that well-meaning rube in ridiculous pants. He was decent, optimistic. Five years later he started at the Museum. His life hadn't gone as he'd guessed it would.

Before she left the gala, Annie faced him, coat in hand. "The kids have never interested you." Her gaze, sad and reproachful, swept the Great Hall. "Not half as much as this place." Naturally Henry protested. Because his love for his children overwhelms him. But Annie's accusation didn't mention love, she spoke of what held his interest.

He's given everything to the Museum. Twenty-eight years. He was at work the Saturday Colin broke his leg. During every one of Kim's tribulations. Even as his marriage disintegrated. Annie was right. It bored Henry to push a swing. He couldn't remember the teachers' names. Family matters lacked fire. Weekends with the kids felt interminable. And like any institution, the Museum took what he was willing to give.

4:08 a.m.

The kitchen has always provided a backdrop for clear thinking. The sunny cabinets, the pacifying hum of the fridge. This is where she and Carl discuss the household finances and think up ways to distance themselves from his sister's relentless drama. A kitchen that is no longer theirs.

Her chamomile tea steeps. Shay finds a pen. For a rough draft she'll use the back of the gas bill.

The day she visited Ma at Maple Valley, Shay noticed a woman sitting by the window watching birds outside bicker on a tree branch. It was actually impossible to know what the birds were doing since all the windows are sealed shut at Maple Valley and you can only get a rough idea of the outside world, nothing of its essence, of its singular, magnificent-smelling jangly wonder. Staring out the window is not terribly different from watching television in terms of your attachment to the unfolding scene, chattering birds or a gust of wind tickling the grass. Shay couldn't help assuming that the woman slumped in her wheelchair was wondering where the hell her life went, which was unfair, after all, it was more likely the woman was wondering where the hell her lunch was or why her son was late or another concern that was much smaller and more trivial but at the same time more pressing. If the woman were Ma or the future-Shay she won't have the faculty to size up the past. Shay is on her way to becoming a creature of reflexes and needs.

~~Dear Diane,~~
To whom it may concern,

Carl will find a way to chip William's drawing off the closet wall. This wasn't your run-of-the-mill slanting house or row of stick figures. The mural was an abstract work. Explosive swirls, purple and yellow. And, in the bottom corner, above Carl's shoes, what appeared to be a set of pointy teeth. It could not be a more apt portrayal of Shay's current state. Fanged chaos.

4:13 a.m.

A small pink tree swings from the rearview mirror, filling the cab with the reek of artificial strawberries. In the back seat, from the sea of her dress, Iona turns to watch a man leave a bodega, a twelve-pack of toilet paper stuck in his armpit. Down the street a businessman staggers into a brightly lit hotel, drunk or exhausted. All these in-between spaces. States of suspension. No families out this late, no couples, just stranded individuals.

Prince lyrics repeat in her head. Iona checks her phone for a reply from Katherine. Nothing.

The taxi driver speaks rapid Arabic into his earpiece. David will be shocked at her emotional extravagance. And what about Emily, tomorrow morning, searching for breakfast.

A bicyclist shoots across the intersection. The car in front of them slams on the brakes with a piercing shriek that rings and echoes in the empty street.

Five blocks from the Radisson.

What will she do with all this free time? Hours spent looking out a window like a woman on a book jacket. Emily and David have given her purpose. Also, hours of meaningful resentment.

Four blocks.

Her beautiful annoying husband. Uneasy in the doorway in his heartbreaking slippers. All he wanted was a meaningful pursuit. At dinner last night his artist friends rolled their eyes at his attempt to find it. I'll be the eye-roller around here, Iona thought, and imagined stabbing them with her butter knife.

Three blocks.

Emily will need her mother as she moves through her fraught teenage years. Iona can still spot the fragile four-year-old under the shaky lipliner and lumpy mascara.

It isn't fear, Iona tells herself, it's a matter of responsibility. Promises and contracts.

The cab stops at a red light and Iona leans forward, knocking stupidly on the plastic shield. Her silence is incompatible with independence. Long ago she chose this state of contingency, accepted her life as one of reaction, a fleeting appearance in the lives of others.

—Sir? Could you turn around, please?

With theatrical patience, the driver takes out his earpiece.

—Sorry, could you head east to the FDR?

—You said the Radisson—

—I changed my mind. If we could—

—No Radisson?

—Yes, I mean, that's right, I don't want to go.

—Another hotel. Marriott?

—No, no, I—

—Got a revolving restaurant.

—That sounds, but, you know, I don't think I want a hotel after all.

—East?

—Yes, to the—

The driver yanks the steering wheel, hurtling across two lanes of traffic to make the light.

—Bridge. I'm really sorry, I won't change my mind again, I promise.

—What bridge?

—Brooklyn, sorry.

—Brooklyn... the driver mutters, as if there's no worse bridge in all of New York City.

Iona can't follow Clive's suggestion to stage a confrontation. But she can rebel. Bury David's duct-taped slippers at the bottom of the trash.

—Where we headed?

—Pineapple Street?

—Okay... catching her eye in the rearview mirror... —You live there?

—Yes. Fourteen years.

He starts talking about his cousin. A property in Cobble Hill.

4:19 a.m.

At Eighth Avenue Katherine changes for the L, her feet blistered to ribbons from walking the twenty blocks down to Columbus Circle. She was unwilling to return home right away. Her dinky studio with its small windows was too cramped for a big decision.

The subway doors open. On the platform a man is stretched out, asleep on a bench, one arm hanging down. The doors close; the train leaves the station. And Katherine thinks about Chris. His hand dropping lifelessly off the side of the gurney. His skin was so green. She's texted him several times: *Thinking of you. Call me when you wake up.*

During the Title IX investigation, Chris drove Katherine to the emergency room when she felt dizzy and numb and thought she was having a stroke. In the car Chris performed quite awful impressions of their Brit Lit professor reading Spenser excerpts, then sat with her for two hours in a crowded waiting room, getting up to buy her coffee and a Snickers, patting her on the knee like a chilly great-aunt.

Tomorrow she'll visit him in the hospital.

4:22 a.m.

—And if there are grounds for prosecution, well—

—Is this the time to discuss such a thing, Mr. Webb?

—He's Pribble... C.J., flashing her overbite... —Mr. Pribble is the stepfather, Chris's real father is—

—*Real* father?... the man glares at C.J.

—Birth father, I meant, birth father, is on his way from California.

—Either way, I don't see how the Museum—

—Not the Museum. We don't blame the entity of the Museum... Stepdaddy points... —We blame you.

—Diane... Chris's mother, the voice of reason... —I think what Gordon is saying is that Chris seems to, that is, he confided in us how difficult the job was.

If she's about to hear that Chris hated his job or, worse, hated her, Diane will lose it. To steady herself, she keeps a fierce eye on the mother's necklace, a polished silver cross.

C.J. lies stretched out on the bed next to Chris. At some point her rain boots were switched to the correct feet.

—You pushed him. Over and over, well past his limits... Gordon says this more to the sink than anyone in particular. Anger appears to be a refuge for him. Where he goes in lieu of pain.

—Let's all take a breath, here, okay?... Chris's mother stares down her husband.

Gordon shrugs and the mother turns her attention fully to Diane.

—Chris looked up to you.

—He thinks you're nuts... C.J. adds, from the bed.

—Quirky... the mother amends... —But he believed in what you were doing. He shared your sense of mission, he saw you were trying. He admired you and we... indicating her husband... —Trusted that you cared about him.

—I did. I do care about him. Of course I do.

—You overworked him.

—He had a serious drug problem.

—Chris? No... confirming it with her husband... —Never. Chris didn't do drugs.

—Guys, please... C.J. pulls herself up off the bed... —Can we stop using the past tense?

Everyone looks at her.

—Please?

—We have to face reality... Gordon tells her... —Chris is on a respirator.

—But we're not in the ICU. Unless it's the ICU it's not life-threatening... C.J. turns to Chris's mother... —Isn't that right?

—They haven't had time to move him... the mother reaches for C.J.'s hand but finds only air. C.J. has dropped to her knees.

—I'm going to... and moving to the door, Diane slips out.

4:27 a.m.

Clover always writes at a twenty-four-hour diner in Queens where she has room to spread out her notebooks and printouts and cupware. She likes to have a variety of fluids on hand, both hot and cold. Tonight she's at her usual booth, a half-eaten lemon meringue pie on the table next to her.

—Guess what?

She looks up, bleary from pie or the unexpected intrusion, as if she's surfacing from anesthesia, unprepared for someone to initiate conversation here, a place where she has undoubtedly always felt safe in her solitude. She stares at Liam, then to either side of him as if trying to place this particular person in this specific context.

—Guess what?... he slides into the booth, covering his concern about interrupting by grabbing the pie plate. He takes her fork, digs in.

—What are you doing here?

—I figured you were nearly done... Liam swallows a forkful of pie. Christ it's sweet, already his teeth hurt.

Clover closes her laptop, pushes it to one side.

—I got a job.

—A job? It's four in the morning.

—Yeah, it's a, uh, long story but—

—Where did you find a job at four in the morning? A bar?

—No... he watches an elderly woman across the room wrap a stack of toast triangles in paper napkins and place them in her purse... —At the Museum. They have good burgers here?

—The *Museum*?

—Yup... searching pointedly for a waiter.

—You're going to work for the Museum?

—Yeah. Cheeseburger, I think.

—I don't get it.

—What's there to get?

—That you took a job at a place you hate? A place full of crooks? You said, Liam, this morning, the Museum pollutes art... Clover takes a drastic sip of coffee... —Plus, they fucked you. Not just you, all the artists at 1072.

—Okay, but... why does she have to ruin... —I thought you'd be happy for me.

—I am, of course I am. I'm surprised, is all. Give me a minute to, I mean, it's.

—Why are you being like this?

—I'm sorry, I'm not, I'm... Clover pulls over the incomprehensibly sweet pie... —Trying to understand... she gazes at the waves of meringue as if trying to find her thoughts in an actual body of water.

Liam pushes the fork toward her... —What about changing the place from the inside? Get in there and shake things up?

—That's what apologists say.

—I could make a difference.

—And your work? Finishing your series?

—I'd be like a consultant. Work on my own time. Don't worry, I'll finish.

Clover looks at him, that expression he hates, not skepticism, which Liam could bear, but the attempt to hide it, plaster the doubt with cheer.

He stretches out his leg to extract the wadded packet of Drum from his front pocket, intent on rolling a cigarette for the walk to the subway. Instead Liam tosses the shag on the table and stares at it... —I'll have time.

—Because it's important, your work.

—We'd have health insurance, what about that?

Miserably, she says... —That would be amazing.

—You've never had health insurance.

—No.

—We could have a baby.

—A baby? Do we want a baby?

—All I'm saying is it's doable, with insurance. Send him to the Garrett School. Or her.

—We're sending our kid to private school?

—Clover. I'm kidding.

—I believe in public school, you know.

—Didn't I say I was kidding?

—I'm not sending my kid to some snobby school.

—We don't have a kid!

Staring into the middle distance, Clover pulls the fork through her lips.

—We should be celebrating. Come on, let's celebrate... he signals for the waiter.

It's likely Clover wouldn't believe it if he came out and said it, because his income was spotty well before they were married, but there exists in Liam an old-fashioned impulse, a holdover of a tenet he witnessed in his father and his grandfather before him. As much as he doesn't want to feel it, even fights against it, Liam can't help but feel an obligation to support his wife and any forthcoming or prospective children. It's odd they've never discussed having a baby, not seriously. He's wanted to, from time to time, in those moments when he's lost to love and longs to see the best of his and Clover's qualities blended into a little person. But he's always resisted thinking too much about the future. He has a feeling Clover would think it bourgeois to discuss children. Maybe even to have children.

If she had any idea what he does to impress her.

Liam looks down. Her hand slipping into his as it rests on the tobacco packet.

—Promise the Museum won't corrupt you.

He brings up Clover's hand, feeling silly but kissing it anyway.

4:37 a.m.

Down the street, the black rectangles of apartment buildings are silhouetted against a navy sky. Blocky shapes, randomly pierced by the yellow square of a lit-up window. Benjamin watches a man cycle through the intersection at fantastic speed.

Abandoned in the gutter below is a child's woolen hat, fashioned like a strawberry, its green stem bent. Time to quit thinking in frames. Stop the little movies. Forget the man he named Avery Eccleston. Return the loan officer's call. Set up income-based repayment. Get a new office chair. Let go of Caroline.

Benjamin pulls down the blind, unbuttons his shirt. Wishing for mystery and danger, he's written a more dramatic story than the one he's in. He tosses his shirt on the dirty clothes piled on the closet floor. He is unexceptional. Burdened by laundry, shackled by debt. Afraid of love.

Maybe he'll call the Robledos if he has time when he wakes up. Pretend he has more questions for the book. Be good to talk. Sofia and Victor. Eating their botifarra, holding hands, teasing each other. He believes in their life.

4:40 a.m.

Iona stares out across the river as the cab rockets down the FDR. There's little traffic and the feeling of speed is exhilarating. It's rare in New York City to feel as if you're getting anywhere. Lights from the buildings over in Brooklyn. What a privilege it is to be healthy and alive and looking at lights across a river.

The taxi driver snaps off the radio. Back to reality. Biscuit factories converted into expensive lofts. Heading home.

4:41 a.m.

Dance music plays from a phone at the other end of the subway car. Three boys, too young to be called men, sit pressed together, eyes closed. False lashes as big as a child's fingers.

Stairs and benches flash past and the train enters a tunnel. The boys nod to the music as if they're agreeing with it. An empty beer can rolls toward Katherine from the other end of the car.

Dear Mimi, Your daughter came to see me today. Announced that I drive men away, asked why I couldn't be more agreeable. It would have cracked you up. Agreeable! Katherine plans to write, the very idea makes me want to run screaming down a highway. It reminds me of something that happened when Dad got sick.

The music ends abruptly and the boys search the phone for a different song.

A few days after Dad went into the hospital, I called this man I'd been dating. We had broken up a few weeks earlier, but oddly, and quite mistakenly, as it turns out, I still felt close to him. When we parted he said call me anytime. I want us to be friends, he said. He sounded genuine, so I called. Described my father's condition, how close he was to dying. But when my ex heard the name of the horrendous disease that was in the process of claiming my father's life, he interrupted. What news, you ask, was so urgent it warranted interjection at this awful moment? If we were speaking, Mimi, I'd wait a beat to see if you could guess. No? He needed to correct my pronunciation. I pause again, and listen to you laugh. Did this man really believe I hadn't spent the last five days listening to doctor after doctor discuss my father's prognosis? That the horrific word wasn't etched into my brain? It was precisely because of the hundreds of hours I spent researching this disease and becoming conversant in its specifics that Dad's nurses assumed I, too, was a nurse. This ex-boyfriend with no medical degree to his name was positive he knew better. And he was not about to sleep on the opportunity to do some correcting.

Katherine lurches forward as the train brakes violently. The doors open. At the other end of the car, two of the club kids stand, hugging the third, who stays behind. One leans in for a kiss: a joyful, significant kiss, as if tonight was the night desires were confessed. Young beauties, churned up, fiery, feeling things.

Though I never again spoke to this informative jackass, many months later he continued to bear the brunt of my silent rage. Grief, rage, whatever you want to call it. This horrible person with whom I had once regrettably enjoyed intercourse loomed as the most villainous presence in the grief-stricken year that followed. When I found myself mad with despair I would think of this past person, his uncontrollable urge to correct and, instead of mourning in a proper fashion, I vowed to never again suffer correction. I'm not talking, Mimi, about the small adjustments we all require: the establishment of a date, what a forgettable acronym stands for, I'm talking about the violence of correction.

The unsaid assertion of my ex was: you are wrong on a molecular level. You, the fairly intelligent daughter of a dying man, cannot possibly understand what I, by virtue of my, what, self-assurance? possess the intuitive sorcery to grasp. My magic is impenetrable; your proximity is meaningless.

But I don't want to be corrected, Mimi. Not anymore. Or strive to be agreeable.

I see you so clearly, out by the pool, checking your tan lines, a mug full of hurricane. The look in your eyes. The doubt in your forehead. Katie, you're saying, you sure you want to go it alone?

But I'm prepared, you see. Falling asleep at night I figure out a way to hold my own hand. I read somewhere it's what people do when they're dying alone.

The last club kid is staring at his shoes. They're black and round-toed and covered in silver glitter. He looks up, sees Katherine watching. Waves like he's wiping a window. She waves back. He takes out his phone. She looks down at her stomach. It looks so ordinary.

4:50 a.m.

Safety standards were different twenty-five years ago. These days stickers are mandated. CAUTION the stickers scream in enormous red letters. DANGER. This screen won't keep a child from falling, they print right on the frame. But who's to say Tasha would have been any more vigilant? Warnings are easy to ignore, even in screaming red letters.

Shay puts down the pen. Carl once asked if her interest in Malcolm was some sort of payback. Are you stealing Tasha's son because Tasha took yours?

A last sip of tea. Her scrawled resignation drafted on the gas bill, one corner soaking up spilled water.

Grief becomes a roommate, they all said. A roommate that never moves out. One you'd miss should it ever disappear. They, the mental health professionals, didn't know that one day Shay's memories would vanish. A time will come when she never had a son.

Down the hall Carl calls out in his sleep. Shay takes her mug to the sink, rinses it, and places it in the drainer. The word for mug is mug. The word for drainer is drainer. The word for forgive no one remembers. The type of tea she likes is.

The beat don't stop until the break of dawn.

Chamomile.

4:53 a.m.

The limited traffic leaving the city at five in the morning has given the cab driver license to speed. Hurtling across Queens, through Kew Gardens and Ozone Park, radio set to easy listening. Barry Manilow comes on singing about Lola, yellow feathers in her hair.

Diane was walking toward the waiting room when she heard the echo of footsteps and saw the doctor striding toward her, his white coat unbuttoned and flapping. He stared straight ahead, passed her without a glance, and stopped outside Chris's room. The doctor stayed there, with one hand on the doorknob, watching his other hand stroke his tie. It was the tie-stroking. The abstracted habit of a person collecting his thoughts, summoning courage, figuring out the right words. A person about to change a family's life.

And Diane ran. Tripping on the coat she held, recovering, overtaking two nurses and throwing herself against the stairwell door. She flew down the stairs, into the lobby, out the entrance, and into the street, waving desperately for a cab.

At the Copa, the Copacabana.

The driver taps the steering wheel in time to Lola as they loop around the airport. Taxis, one after the other, take the offramp. Diane stares at the black humps of trees lining the highway, the lighted signs, gas, a hotel.

Chris.

How could she have failed to see he was struggling. An image comes to her of Chris trying to wedge a quarter between the stuck doors of the funicular carriage. His expression of focused concern. And she presses her fingertips against her eyelids. Impossible to imagine life without him. The steady calm of his pressed shirts. Feeding her aspirin and cof-fee, the details she needed, pushing people aside or bringing them forward. For Diane, Chris had only ever wanted glory. And she had loved him, really. For who he was. Or who she thought he was and Diane thinks again of C.J. in the hospital, big and braless with uncombed hair. Diane's version of Chris's girlfriend wore ballet flats and kept a papillon in her purse. Maybe he had always been a stranger.

4:58 a.m.

What about his nutty mother? Slathering his feet with Pond's cold cream. As a boy Henry had unnaturally dry skin. And then she was carted to the hospital. The two observations are unrelated. He can't think clearly. A swell of wind scatters the leaves on the path ahead. When was he last in Central Park before sunrise? Stupid idea. Streetlamps light his way in golden circles. The only sound is the steady plod of his footsteps.

How long does he have until they uncover the evidence? Embezzlement is no walk in the park, Henry thinks, as he walks in the park. The news will shame Olive. His obituary will reveal a devious bastard. There's only so much Jack can do. Echo and Noah will grow up with shame and derision for their old dad.

Or, before he goes, could he plead that cancer ate his brain? Metastasizing cells wreak havoc on a man's reason. Henry walks past a lamppost, striking it with his umbrella. Yes, there's a way. Phone Dr. Lee in the morning. Together they'll strategize. A doctor's note. Look what I did when my body was ravaged by disease. Can you believe it?

Will they?

There's still an angle to be played. Insanity by cancer. Demean a man who made mistakes while dying? They'd be animals to do so. Henry walks a little faster, letting the plan unspool in his mind. Dr. Lee, he saw Henry's agony at the news of his fate. Those nasty cells creeping around. The rotten decisions that followed. No one knows when the cancer started.

A small toy car lies on the path ahead of him, the kind Noah loves, with flashy paint and big wheels. Henry starts to reach for it, but stops and flicks it away with his foot. Stoop for a filthy toy?

Henry feels a stirring, the old fight returning. He'll figure it out so

his legacy is clean. Find the money to repay what he took. Start by selling the house in Montauk. Olive hates to drive, three hours each way,
she'll never do it, not in traffic. How dare they destroy his reputation.
He won't allow it. For the first time in months Henry has a wave of the
old giddiness. All he ever needed was opposition. One last war before he
goes.

5:03 a.m.

O sleep! O gentle sleep! Nature's soft nurse, how have I frightened
thee, That thou no more wilt weigh my eyelids down And steep my
senses in forgetfulness?

Nikolic closes his eyes, begging his mind to quiet down, stop repeating a monologue he memorized in sixth grade. He thinks of
Jimmy in the diner, bearing down on a french fry. Damaged love is
still love, Niko thought, watching his brother ogle a waitress. Even the
kind that's gone a few rounds. Even from Jimmy. No one loves perfectly. The sheet pops the corner and starts inching over the edge of
his mattress.

A memory of the beach the time Dad had to stay behind. Mom in
her turban.

He flips onto his side, pushing a pillow between his knees.

They met in Sanitary Measures. Three classes it took Nikolic to notice the girl in steamed-up glasses. Quiet, thoughtful. A presence of still-
ness. Unassailable technique.

He forces his mind back to the ice cream he and Jimmy ate for dinner in Myrtle Beach, to the smell of seaweed. Salt water. Skin tight from
a day in the sun. Mint chocolate chip.

But back it comes, the buzz of those first days, students casing the
classrooms, trying to predict who would drop out, who would excel.
Bets were placed on who would crack under the pressure, succumb to
an interesting meltdown.

Sand in their hair and butt cracks, watching the smallest TV in history, an actual antenna sprouted from its top.

The teacher lectured on chicken, salmonella, how to prevent.

Mom, turban, ice cream.

After a week of trying, Nikolic finally succeeded. He'd sprinted to the space next to Sandrine, beating his rival, a kid from Chicago with ironic sideburns. Ignoring the lecture, Niko waited patiently for his chance to impress her. He needed a perfect opening sentence. Insightful or hilarious. Memorable. Emotionally stable. A sentence that showed he was a stallion in bed but would also make a doting father. She was standing so close he could make out the downy hair on her upper lip.

The smell of seaweed, come on. Mom's turban, for chrissake.

Not for a moment did Nikolic doubt Sandrine was the one. None of the usual calculations mattered. Not kindness, humor, even her proportions which were unknowable, due to the sexless chef's coat. The draw was animalistic. It was beyond his control.

And suddenly she whispered. She leaned toward Niko smelling of freesia and onions and whispered, "Could anything be more boring?" She took off her glasses, wiping them with a small blue cloth. Her front teeth were gapped. Nikolic was filled with panic. A flawless reply was required. How to transmit wit, confidence, intrigue? This is what he heard himself say:

"Chickens are dangerous."

Sandrine raised her eyebrows and stepped back. This alarmed Nikolic enough that he stepped forward, stubbing his toe against her shoe. He wanted no space between them. And she, incredulous, whispered back, "*Chickens are dangerous?*" and looked at Nikolic fully, as if she were faced with an exotic creature, one she had up to this moment never encountered, really looked at him, searching his face with those grey eyes so full of light and hope.

5:10 a.m.

Clive was only home for a few minutes before he went to the bin and took out the torn-up paper. He pieced it together on the countertop, found his phone and made the call. Then he stripped the bed and threw a load of towels in the wash. He's never used the machine that came with the apartment, always drops his laundry at the place on the corner. But he needed to keep busy. He went through the cabinets, chucking old capers, truffle mustard, never opened, a gift from someone. He swiped at surfaces, dusting motions. Moved a side table from one end of the sofa to the other and back. The water rings Lucy left on his credenza Clive never bothered to buff out. She was lazy and careless, broke things he cared about. Checking the time, he saw it was late morning in Germany. Lucy would be pedaling along a canal, jet-lagged, her bike basket full of sausages. Finally the buzzer went.

On his way back from the bathroom Clive stops in the doorway to his bedroom. Leans against the jamb. The Murray Hill mammoth lies flat on his back, bedsheet coiled around one leg. Austin. He was quite cheerful about being woken at three in the morning. Arrived wearing another disgraceful shirt, carrying an objectively small but fatally presumptuous overnight bag.

In the years before Jane was old enough to take over the basic household chores there were many months during which Dad tried to spackle the holes left behind by his wife's sudden death. On birthdays Clive would arrive home to a strained presentation: buckets of fried chicken takeaway, a sloping Victoria sponge, one or two gifts fumblingly wrapped and strangled by Sellotape. These sorts of memories Clive pushed away when he moved to America. There was always a special sort of pain in identifying love as love when it came from his father. It upset him to recall that slipshod cake or the cheap plastic toys Dad bought at the corner shop after Clive fucked up at football. It was much less complicated to see his father as emotionless, inept, a robot.

Moving quietly, Clive goes to the bed and gets under the covers, squashing the pillow under his neck. Austin stirs. Still asleep, he flings an arm across Clive's chest and Clive has to fight the impulse to immediately fling it back. He closes his eyes. Joshua always thrashed around in the night. Treated the bed as a fucking mosh pit. Clive used to wake up kicked to death. But Joshua is gone. Without him, it's still life.

Outside, a mourning dove coos.

Lucy will be working out the U-Bahn map. Memorizing infinitives. To do, to be, to go. To leave your friend behind.

Clive gives it another few minutes, then picks up Austin's arm and rolls out from under it. Trips over one of the man's mistreated clogs. Creeps down the hall to the kitchen.

The remains of his dinner lie on the countertop: a sawed-at loaf of rye, orange peelings, a piece of cheese. A fly walks slowly across the rind. Scattered next to the plate are the contents of his pockets. Metrocard, coins, a small hex key and the matchbox from Walter Wolfe advertising Deebley's power tools. Dad always kept a yellow box of Swan Vestas on the arm of the sofa. If Newcastle was down a goal, he'd meticulously line up the corners of the matchbox with his pack of Woodbines, over and over again, never taking his eyes off the screen.

Clive slides open the Deebley's box. Six or eight matches jumbled in different directions. He got to Clive, damn him, old man Wolfe, in his too-tight skin and stripey pajamas, rhapsodizing about Diane Schwebe's underarms.

Enough.

Clive takes out his laptop. Before he can change his mind, and at eye-popping expense, he books the next flight to London. It won't leave until this evening.

In the bedroom Austin sleeps face down, the green duvet pulled around his waist. A golden beam spills from the bathroom, transforming his body into a landscape of valleys and hills. One tan leg has freed itself and lies against the duvet like a shadowed brook. Among the greens and browns, the pillowcase is a bright patch of yellow.

Gently moving Austin's arm to one side, Clive gets back in bed.

5:19 a.m.

Diane rolls down the window and unclips her hair, letting the wind fling it across her face. Already she can smell the ocean. She's allowed her relationship with nature to lapse, spent too much time indoors lately, even on weekends. Months have passed without a deep breath of winter's spiky air or a face warmed by early summer sun. Over the last year she's spent so many unbroken stretches battered by the city's hard angles that when she does escape, even to New Jersey, the sight of green trees, curves, and rippling grass feels soft on her eyes. What a loss it's been for so long, of light and color.

You let me love you in the country, Dom said. What has she been fighting? Restriction. Control. The prison of accountability. None of it engendered by Dominic. Dread can be its own tyrant.

Over the bridge and the briny smell grows stronger. The dark morning is still, no wind to speak of. Faintly, in the distance, she can hear the gentle lapping of waves. The last time she came to the Rockaways was one Saturday in July, more than a year ago. Dominic had read an article about surfers. They ate tacos, held hands, waded but did not swim. Sharks were rumored. Briefly, it rained. They stayed where they were sitting, the surfers kept surfing. The marriage was unfractured. It was before she succumbed to fear.

The taxi stops at the last corner before the beach. The cabbie seems out of breath, as if all this hectic driving has taken a physical toll. Diane swipes her credit card and tosses it loose into her purse. She pulls her coat around her, gets out of the car and heads toward the water, stopping obediently when told DO NOT WALK. The taxi takes a hard right and burns through the intersection. She can see the driver silhouetted inside the car, shaking his head. Yes, it's all unwise. In the distance, a baby cries.

Crossing to the beach, wearing her coat like a cape, Diane stops at a trash can. She yanks at the sash binding her waist, pulls it free and drops it in the garbage. Streetlamps light her path across the boardwalk. A sign warns that the beach won't open for another half hour but there's no one to stop her. Diane rushes down the sandy ramp, ripping off her shoes and digging her feet in the sand.

She had guessed it would be dark. But a surprising amount of ambient light spills onto the beach from streetlamps and apartment towers, cottage porchlights across the boardwalk and high-rise rooftops lined with red bulbs to warn approaching planes. Diane sinks to her knees, the sand is so cold it feels wet.

What lies in the direction she's looking, southeast of here, out in the black sea? Bermuda? English pioneers shipwrecked on their way to Jamestown. From the wreckage they built a new boat, eager to join their compatriots in the new world, men slowly starving to death. Like Diane, they set about fashioning their fate.

On an empty city beach, she is surprisingly unafraid. The day has exhausted her reserves of sensible behavior. Jetliners leaving JFK wink and flash in the sky. The tide is low, a trail of litter marks the distance between where she sits and the water's edge. Beer cans, potato chip packages, candy wrappers, what appears to be half a towel. The remains of a picnic. Diane closes her eyes to better hear the sound of waves.

Last night, sitting in the kitchen, trying to tell Dominic about the day she stood on First Avenue, unable to find her way home. She was in her forties, without a map, useless at landmarks, confused by a compass. Mistaking satellites for stars. And instead of discerning what lay before her, Diane conjured something else entirely, the story of her past. How do people survive their own imaginations.

She opens her eyes, struck by the feeling of being watched. Ten yards away stands a skinny dog with patchy fur, long legs and a triangular head. Coyote. They consider each other. She sifts cold sand through her fingers. Without taking his eyes off Diane, the coyote noses around the leftover picnic. Stares at her for another long minute and then, as if to demonstrate his lack of concern, the coyote yawns. One last snuffle at the candy wrappers, and he goes, trotting leisurely down the beach.

A wave of exhaustion hits her. And Dominic, will he sleep? Insomnia comes on Dom hard in times of stress. But this is no longer her concern. As a child Diane always had a difficult time falling asleep. She hated for the day to end. Her mother used to come upstairs and sit on Diane's bed holding her highball, ice cubes clinking in the dark. Quietly, she would sing, and on occasion let Diane have a sip.

Let me be by myself in the evening breeze

Closing her eyes again, the sound of waves breaks her heart.

Listen to the murmur of the cottonwood trees

Stars and the faint suggestion of sunrise. A throat clearing of sorts. The beginning of astronomical dawn, it's called. Or maybe it's civil dawn. In any case, it's still dark. A measure of calm floods Diane from ankle to sternum. A freedom, a lifting.

The waves break in foamy splashes.

Send me off forever

But I ask you please

Don't fence me in